Praise for the novels of Christopher Golden

THE SHADOW SAGA

OF SAINTS AND SHADOWS
ANGEL SOULS AND DEVIL HEARTS
OF MASQUES AND MARTYRS

"Harrowing, humorous, overflowing with plot contortions . . . abundantly entertaining. A portent of great things to come . . . a writer who cares passionately about the stuff of horror." —Douglas E. Winter, author of *Run*

"You can damn near chase me a mile these days with a vampire novel. Talk about your boring genre . . . then along comes Christopher Golden . . . and reminds me there is no such thing as a boring genre, just boring writers. A crew to which Mr. Golden does not belong. His work is fast and furious, funny and original." —Joe R. Lansdale, Edgar Award–winning author of *The Bottoms*

"Golden combines quiet, dark, subtle mood with Super-Giant monster action. Sort of M. R. James meets Godzilla!" —Mike Mignola, creator of *Hellboy*

"One of the best horror novels of the year. Filled with tension, breathtaking action, dire plots and a convincing depiction of worlds existing unseen within our own. One of the most promising debuts in some time." —*Science Fiction Chronicle*

"Passionate . . . Excellent . . . Golden has written one of the best . . . a deep probe into the inner workings of the church and a surprise explanation for vampires. [A] brilliant vampire novel in a blizzard of bloody tooth bites this year." —*LitNews* (published on Compuserve) and *Dark Channel*

"Golden stands many time-honored concepts about vampirism on their heads." —*The Overlook Connection*

continued . . .

THE FERRYMAN

"With his customary style and economy, Christopher Golden has penned a powerful and haunting tale."
—Clive Barker

"Kept me reading long into the evening on more than one night. Golden delivers . . . good, old-fashioned story-telling . . . and he doesn't back away from the consequences of the darkness he has set upon his characters. I liked his deft touch with his characters, his crisp prose, and how he lets the story unfold. And I especially liked the relationship Golden built between his characters . . . We should all be so lucky as to have such friends."
—Charles de Lint

"Christopher Golden offers an intelligent, compelling ghost story in the classic horror tradition. Superior characterization, an exquisitely detailed setting and superbly orchestrated suspense."
—*Publishers Weekly*

"Once in a very long while, a horror novel will come along that is so believable and frightening that it will live on in the reader's mind forevermore. *The Stand* and *The Exorcist* were such books and so too is *The Ferryman*. Christopher Golden is a talented writer who makes the audience give credence to events in his novel as if they occurred in the real world."
—*Midwest Book Review*

STRAIGHT ON 'TIL MORNING

"A dramatic and funny coming-of-age story . . . A horrific and ultimately sorrowful thriller. A bizarre combination of *The Wonder Years* TV series and *The Lost Boys* film, this fantastic tale entertains." —*Publishers Weekly*

"The *Stand By Me*-cum-*The Outsiders* feel of the first half of the novel is real, and honest, and a great read in and of itself; add the twisted fantasy element . . . and this book becomes perfectly unique. A grown-up, odd, compelling journey through adolescence, and hearthache—and of course Neverland . . . a fascinating and completely engrossing book. One that makes you read and read . . . straight on 'til morning." —*The 11th Hour*

"I defy anyone to read a few of these scenes and not be swept up. Golden's imagination was working overtime when he crafted a way to blend this coming-of-age story with not just a bona fide childhood classic, but Gaelic mythology as well, as the novel progresses from the mundane to the weird to full-blown high fantasy. Golden keeps those pages flying by, without forgetting to bring it full circle and give your heart a tweak or two in the very end." —Brian Hodge

continued . . .

Strangewood

"Christopher Golden gradually brings into being a world of haunted and perilous fantasy which, while moving into greater solidity, never loses touch with its painful, sweet embattled human context. [*Strangewood*] is a notable achievement—Christopher Golden has written a beautiful and wildly inventive hymn to the most salvific human capacity, Imagination."
—Peter Straub

"I read *Strangewood* in one sitting . . . a daring and thoroughly engrossing blend of wonder and adventure, terror and tenderness. *Strangewood* is what Oz might have been if L. Frank Baum had grown up on a steady diet of Stephen King."
—F. Paul Wilson

". . . a tour de force that examines the themes of love and faith, revenge and retribution. Truly frightening, and inspiring."
—Nancy Holder, Bram Stoker Award–winning author of *Dead in the Water*

". . . enthralling . . . The imagination that it took to create this world—well, I am in awe of Christopher Golden."
—*Midwest Book Review*

". . . will lead readers to wonder if Christopher Golden is actually a pseudonym for a collaboration between Dean Koontz and Peter Straub . . . Do not read just before going to bed unless you want to journey to *Strangewood* while you sleep."
—*BookBrowser*

"Original, suspenseful, and often genuinely creepy."
—*Science Fiction Chronicle*

"Excellent dark fantasy."
—*Locus*

THE
GATHERING
DARK

CHRISTOPHER GOLDEN

2003
50TH
ANNIVERSARY

ACE BOOKS, NEW YORK

THE GATHERING DARK

An Ace Book / published by arrangement with
the author

PRINTING HISTORY
Ace mass-market edition / July 2003

ISBN: 0-441-01081-4

ACE®
Ace Books are published by The Berkley Publishing Group,
a division of Penguin Group (USA) Inc.,
375 Hudson Street, New York, New York 10014.
ACE and the "A" design
are trademarks belonging to Penguin Group (USA) Inc.

PRINTED IN THE UNITED STATES OF AMERICA

10 9 8 7 6 5 4 3 2 1

For Lily Grace Golden.
Everything I ever dreamed.

ACKNOWLEDGMENTS

First and foremost, profound gratitude to Ginjer Buchanan, for never losing interest in Octavian and his world. There are still many journeys ahead.

Thanks are also due to all of the folks who wrote or e-mailed or badgered me at conventions to return to The Shadow Saga. I hope you're as pleased as I am.

Special thanks, as always, to my wife Connie and our children, with whom all things are possible. And a grateful nod to all of you who've lent an ear or an eye or the force of your telepathic encouragement . . . especially Tom Sniegoski, Megan Bibeau, Jose Nieto, Lisa Delissio, Amber Benson, Rick Hautala, Bob Tomko, Jeff Mariotte, Allie Costa, Hank Wagner, Nancy Carlson, and the inde-fatiguable Peter Donaldson. To my family, each and everyone, with love.

PROLOGUE

NO matter how much the city did to clean up the underground, the subway always stank like piss. New York Transit cops hustled a homeless woman in a rank, stained parka older than its owner up the stairs toward the street. The rattle and roar of a train came up from deep within the crosstown tunnel, followed almost immediately by the hissing hydraulic scream of brakes. Newspapers blew across the tile floor.

In the morning it would be spotless. The night crews would have done their work. The electronic news tickers that ran along the walls and the small screens that carried images from the highest-paying content provider would be sparkling, without a smear or smudge.

Depressing as hell.

Peter Octavian had seen many faces of this city over the years, seen it rise and fall, breathe new life into the world, grow cruel and corrupt and yet somehow also vibrant and joyous. To his mind, the fascistic effort to clean up Manhattan drained the city of its character.

Nights like this, though, he could pretend he was back in another age, a time when he understood more about people. For it was raining up above, the storm clouds heavy and low, the puddles growing, the streets slick. Taxis pretended not to see you in the rain, which meant the subways were flooded not with rain but with people who wished they were safe in the back of a private cab.

Grime from the streets was tracked all through the station. The tile walls dripped with accumulated moisture. The air itself was damp and cold.

A rare smile on his handsome, stubbled features, Octavian pushed through the turnstile, turning up the collar of the heavy canvas jacket he wore. It hung past his knees and seemed to rasp as he walked. All around him, city people rushed home from working late, or out to meet a date, and never once did any of them meet his gaze. But he watched them. His attention would have been barely noticeable even if someone happened to glance at him, but still he was wary, always on guard.

Some people were not what they appeared to be. It was a dark truth he knew perhaps better than anyone else on Earth.

Sometimes shadows were just shadows and the monsters were right in front of you.

He took the steps two at a time. Even before he emerged from the station, the cold rain sliced down into the shelter of the underground, tiny pinpricks like ice needles jabbing at his face. Defiant, he stepped out onto the sidewalk and lifted his face to the roiling storm above, the night sky dark with layers of black. The winds blew the rain nearly sideways, and his hair, already damp from walking to the station downtown, quickly began to drip streams of water down his face. He paused to orient himself, then turned north and strode quickly across the street.

A cabbie blared his horn. There came the shush of tires through a puddle and the sprinkle of water onto the pavement. The rain itself, each individual drop, seemed to reflect the neon glitter of the city's electric life. People hurried by in ones and twos, huddled under black umbrellas like mourners.

Half a block later, he heard the music. A Caribbean rhythm, an old Bob Marley tune, though Marley himself was decades dead. This was a new millennium leeching from the last, filled with a dread of the unknown future.

Octavian thought it wise, that dread. As the twenty-first century grew from infant to toddler, humanity could reach higher, touch the sky, open doors perhaps better left closed. Already the human race had learned a great deal that it might have wished never to know. The past brought comfort, memories of safety. Or the illusion of safety. Yet that was enough for most.

The chant of Marley and the Wailers rang sweetly from the open door of a dive bar called The Voodoo Lounge, whose neon sign was only half lit. Just inside the door stood an enormous man with ebony skin and a bald pate that gleamed with reflected neon red. His left eyebrow had two thick rings through it, and a long, rough scar curved from above his right eye, through the brow, and across the bridge of the nose to his left cheek.

When he smiled, a miracle happened. The giant became handsome. His name was Agamemnon. Though Octavian could not imagine a child with such a name today, the man insisted it had been given him at birth by his mother, and he would accept no substitutes, no nicknames nor terms of endearment.

"Peter!" he rasped, voice like distant thunder. "What brings you?"

They shook hands.

"Agamemnon. Good to see you. Had a call from Bradenton."

"He's on the bar tonight," Agamemnon said. "Listen, you don't have a cigarette, do you?"

"Sorry."

"Nah, it's a shitty habit. Just gives my hands something to do."

Octavian nodded as though he understood, and perhaps he did. Why else did he paint if not to give his hands something to do? He stepped through the open door of The Voodoo Lounge and the music pounded against his eardrums. Despite laws to the contrary, smoke wafted across the air. It had the distinct scent of hashish.

"Hey!" Agamemnon called. "Buy an umbrella!"

A small, uncommon smile creased Octavian's features. Once upon a time, it would not have been so rare.

The place was packed with people, and now he understood why the door was open. Though it was cold outside, the body heat within was almost infernal. Men and women of every race pushed up to the bar, jostled with one another for position or simply to cop a feel. On the dance floor, bodies gyrated, beads of sweat glimmered on foreheads wrinkled with intensity. Laughter bubbled in the air and the pheremonal musk of sex sought and promised hung heavy as the rain's own moisture on the room.

Bradenton was at the bar, grinning broadly as a woman removed her top. Her breasts were dark and perfect and she leaned back so that all those around her could get a look.

"That's worth a double shot!" Bradenton crowed, then poured her three fingers of tequila.

Though he was tall, the bartender was thin and bony, his face edged like granite. He had an inch or so of bristly hair on his head and a well-groomed goatee that made him look almost severe. A Chinese dragon was tattooed on his throat, its tail wrapped around his neck before ending at the base of his skull.

As though he had sensed the attention on him, Bradenton glanced at Octavian. His expression became grim and he excused himself from the press of flesh. Another bartender filled the void almost instantly. The bare-breasted woman never bothered to put her top back on.

"Peter," Bradenton said when they met up at the far end of the bar.

"You know I don't do this sort of thing anymore," Octavian said gravely, eyeing the other man carefully.

"It's serious, amigo, and I don't need this crap in my bar."

Several seconds ticked by as the men stared at one another. At length, Octavian dipped his head and then nodded once.

"Great! Oh, man, thanks so much."

Bradenton stepped back a bit, grabbed a bottle of Crown Royal, and poured a shot. He slid it across the counter to Octavian, who tossed it back without a word. The glass clinked on the mahogany bar as he set it down.

"Anyway," the bartender went on, "the stuff in the papers about this magician guy? Calls himself Mr. Nowhere?"

"I've read the coverage." Already, Octavian began to scan the bar for some sign of malevolence, something out of place.

"He's here," Bradenton said, voice low.

Octavian gave him a hard look. "So?"

Uncertain, Bradenton poured him another shot. "You've read about him. He's made people disappear in five different bars in the city. Makes a big deal about it, like he's some old-time stage magician. Makes them disappear in front of crowds of people, and they never come back."

The man scratched at the dragon's tail tattooed on the back of his neck. "I've seen him do it, Peter. Twice in here in the last week."

"Why don't you call the cops?" Octavian asked dismissively.

He left the shot on the table and took a step back, out of the immediate range of the lights above the bar. Something was in here, he felt that now. Something that shouldn't be. Better to be in the shadows, to watch from the dark.

"You haven't seen him do it, man. This shit is real. Nothing the cops can do. But you—"

"I helped you once, Bradenton. Doesn't mean I make a habit of it."

The bartender stared at him. There was something in his expression, more than disappointment, almost disgust, that made Octavian bristle with both anger and humiliation. Once he would have killed the man for the look in his eyes.

"You know all this shit," Bradenton said. "Magick."

Octavian sighed tiredly and turned away from the bar. As an afterthought he turned and tossed back the second shot of Crown Royal after all. Then he closed his eyes and let his senses focus on the dark presence in the room.

After a moment he opened his eyes and strode across The Voodoo Lounge to a far corner. At a round table, a gallant-looking old man with silver hair and a black cane sat encircled by a dozen people or more.

"Indeed," the man said. "It is among the highest forms of magick. Physical translocation. Most magicians never achieve it. To me, well, not to brag, but it's little more than a parlor trick. I've been at this game for quite some time."

A chill ran through Octavian; fear like an itch at the back

of his brain. Dread swept over him in a crash, then receded like a wave upon the shore. Mr. Nowhere, the media called him. Typical, to give such an unsettling figure a show business name. Yet here he was, bedecked in the image of show business, albeit an image stolen from bygone days, the elegant stage magicians and prestidigitators of nearly a century earlier.

Beneath the magician's voice was a rasping, angry sound, a swarm of bees, the revving of a racer's engine.

Octavian hated to be afraid.

He stepped forward, insinuated himself among the small throng around the magician. They gazed in adoration at the charming old man, as though they could possibly not have heard the stories in the media. But this was a modern age, and nothing on television could be perceived as truly real. Everything seemed somehow contrived, even the worst tragedies, the most heinous crimes. Fiction and reality were almost indistinguishable to these people. They sensed no danger.

Fools.

"Where do you put them?" he asked, voice clipped, cold.

The magician glanced up. His eyes twinkled merrily. "They're all quite safe, I assure you. All part of the show."

"That's not what the authorities think. How long do you think you'll be able to pretend they're coming back?"

The smile slipped from the magician's face as if it had never been there, an illusion no less stunning than levitation or sleight of hand. People began to back away, and Octavian had to revise his opinion of them. Fools they might be, but they could feel the danger now, could sense that a battle had begun.

"Perhaps I ought to show you how the trick works," the magician suggested.

He had a thin white mustache so fine that Octavian had not noticed it at first, and as he spoke, he stroked his fingers across it like the villain from an old Hollywood serial.

Octavian scraped the back of his hand across the stubble on his chin. He stood like a gunfighter, legs slightly parted, long canvas duster draped across his body.

"Try me."

With a laugh, the magician glanced at his audience, who had backed away even further. They were anxious, even scared, but they wouldn't stray so far that they would not be able to witness the outcome. The music in The Voodoo Lounge had changed from reggae to old blues. B. B. King sang "The Thrill Is Gone" on the sound system. Other customers began to move closer, trying to figure out what was going on.

"Excellent," the old man said. "Pay attention, my young friends. You'll never see magick like this again in your lives."

With a flourish of his hand, the old man sketched a symbol in the air. Like the neon in the windows, the symbol took form, began to glow, and to flow like mercury.

"Now you see him," the magician said, and the sound of angry bees that buzzed beneath his voice increased.

A flick of his wrist, and the symbol hanging in the air flowed toward Octavian. With a single motion, he sidestepped the burning energy, duster flapping as he moved. His fingers steepled together, both hands shot out and he captured that energy between his palms.

He gave the magician a hard look, then crushed its glow between his hands. With a pop, it was snuffed out. The stench of brimstone rose from his fingers.

The magician gaped at him a moment, and it was almost comical. Then terror swept the old man's features, his face etched with it.

"I'm still here," Octavian told him. "Now, bring them back."

The buzzing grew louder and the old man's face began to change, to grow ugly. "Fuck off, mage. So you've got your own little parlor tricks. You don't have the power to challenge me. They're mine now. All of them. And more where they came from."

A sad smile blossomed on the face of Peter Octavian. He glanced at the fascinated crowd. "Pay attention," he said. "Now you see him . . ."

All that time, his hands had been held before him as if in prayer. Now he opened them, fingers contorted in a gesture of ancient power. A flash of bright blue light burst from his hands.

The old man was gone.

In his place was a hideous creature whose flesh seemed hard as rock, edges sharp as diamonds, skin so red it was almost black. Jagged ridges ran in two identical strips up its face and across its leathery skull. Its belly was enormous as though it were grotesquely pregnant.

Screams drowned out the music.

People ran.

"*Now* you see him," Octavian repeated softly.

Blue light arced from his hands again and this time he seemed to dance with it, a series of steps and hand motions that were almost balletic. He spun around, the energy trailing off his fingers in ribbons.

With it, he sliced open the creature's vast stomach.

A wet, hollow sound echoed in the room and the demon screamed. For a moment its innards seemed endless, an entire world contained in the recesses of its gut. Then, one by one, five people spilled out, covered in a rancid sort of afterbirth. They choked and wept, and one of them vomited, but they were alive.

What remained of the demon burst into flames, but it was already dead.

Someone shouted for a fire extinguisher.

Octavian turned and strode toward the door. The place was silent now, save for the music. The patrons of The Voodoo Lounge had gathered round in horror and awe, but now, as he headed for the door, they parted to let him pass. Out of the corner of his eye, he saw the topless woman again. Suddenly uncomfortable with her nakedness, she covered her breasts with her arms and looked at the floor.

Afraid of him.

It was the thing he hated most, for people to be afraid of him. He would not be able to come in here anymore.

Bradenton and Agamemnon met him at the door.

"Peter, that was . . . holy shit, man, that was amazing."

Octavian ignored him. Instead, he glanced regretfully at Agamemnon, of whom he was quite fond.

"You won't see me here again."

Agamemnon nodded silently.

The mage turned up his collar and stepped out into the icy, driving rain.

CHAPTER 1

A light spring breeze whispered down off the mountains and gently swayed the hand-carved chimes that hung outside the propped-open door of Sweet Somethings. The music the wind drew from those crafty wooden flutes was far subtler than what might have come from any of the metals often used to forge such elegant creations. It lingered in the air and suggested to the mind images of faraway places, of hot afternoons in some remote village in southeast Asia, of pipe music played by Pan or Pip.

Or, at least, that was what the chimes suggested to Keomany Shaw, the woman who had hung them there in the first place.

This early in the morning it was almost too cold to have the door of her confectionary shoppe wide open, but Keomany did not mind the goosebumps that rose on her arms or the chill that crept tendril fingers up beneath her sweater and light cotton jersey. As a fresh breeze blew through the shoppe, she gave a delicious shiver and a smile teased the edges of her mouth.

She stood in the middle of the shoppe with a clump of paper toweling in one hand and a bottle of Windex in the other. Showcases filled with homemade fudge and hand-dipped chocolates gleamed. Displays of penny candies and jellybeans were tidied—errant mixtures repaired before closing the night before and steel scoops ready in each plastic dispenser. Candles and chimes and the little gift items she carried were free of dust, as were the shelves upon which they sat.

The air was laden with the deep, rich aroma of chocolate, a fragrance almost as delicious to her as that of the earth itself on a fine spring day. A day like this one.

May Day.

Keomany did a little pirouette, as if the wooden chimes outside the open door were her musical accompaniment, and then flushed slightly as she glanced out through the display window to be sure she had not been seen. A twinkle in her eye, she went out to the sidewalk to clean the front window and the glass door. When she stepped outside Sweet Somethings, though, Keomany could not help but pause and glance around her.

How could I ever have left here? she thought.

The village of Wickham was nestled snugly among the mountains of northern Vermont, just over an hour south of the Canadian border and even farther from the nearest thing that could legitimately be considered a city. After high school Keomany had returned to Wickham as infrequently as possible, despite her parents' pleas, and after college she had managed to ensconce herself in the publicity department of Phoenix Records for three full years without setting foot on Currier Street. The little half-English, half-Cambodian girl might have drawn strange looks and whispers in northern New England, but New York City had barely noticed her.

For the longest time Keomany had thought she wanted it that way. Yet what a revelation to discover that it made her feel lost, without identity.

She stood now on the curb of Currier Street and her gaze slid along the storefronts—the ski shops and mom-and-pops and restaurants, The Lionheart Pub, Harrison's Video, The Bookmark Café, and the Currier Street Theatre—and she felt more at home than she had felt since becoming a teenager. In the six months since she had moved back to Wickham, Keomany had felt this way more and more each day. Sweet

Somethings was her place. Wickham was her town.

Her old life had somehow become her new life. It was a revelation. Though there were still cell phones in evidence and the whole town was wired for the Net, and in spite of the tourists that spilled into town for the skiing in the winter and for the kayaking and hiking in the summer, for the most part, Wickham still felt the way she imagined it had when her grandparents had been children here.

Her gaze went to the mountains then and for a long moment Keomany could not look away. The first of May, and the world was in bloom. Every breeze was redolent with the rich scents of the green coming back to the trees and the fields, the blossoming of flowers, and the heavy, pungent smell of coffee beans roasting at the Bookmark three doors down.

"Mmm," she whispered to herself. "Hazelnut."

Might have to get myself a cup, she thought. And then she took one last deep breath, inhaling coffee and vanilla from the café and lilacs in bloom somewhere near.

At last, Keomany turned to work. She sprayed Windex on the broad plate glass window, sunlight refracting microscopic rainbows in every drop, glistening in the instant before she wiped it all away. She began to whistle but stopped when she realized how her own music clashed with that of the chimes above her, the wind's melody.

It was just after nine o'clock and Keomany worked in silence save for the chimes and the rumble of cars passing by on Currier Street and the hellos from friends and acquaintances—and this time of year that was most of the town—who happened by. The store did not officially open until ten, but when Walt Bissette came by for a pound of peanut butter fudge and then Jacqui Lester stopped in to sneak a few diet-breaking caramel cluster turtles, Keomany did not turn them away.

After the place was clean to her satisfaction, Keomany arranged a bunch of fresh lilies she had bought in a vase on the front counter by the register and then sat and read from a romantic fantasy novel that had pulled her in the night before. When the mountain breeze carried Paul Leroux into the store at half past ten, she barely noticed.

"Sorry I'm late," he offered.

Keomany glanced up at Paul, then at the clock, and then her gaze settled once more upon the young man she had impulsively made her assistant manager.

"Paul," she said, nothing else but his name, but it carried all her feelings on his tardiness, how she had come to expect it, how she indulged him most of the time, how it was becoming tiresome.

"I know," he said, blue eyes so earnest. He pushed his fingers through his straw blond hair, which fell too long over his forehead in something approximating style . . . or what might have approximated style somewhere other than northern Vermont.

"Keomany, seriously, I know. I'm gonna buy a new alarm clock this afternoon. Swear to God. As soon as Jillian comes in, I'm gonna run over to Franklin's and buy one."

She stared at him a long moment, trying desperately to be stern, though it was hard to be angry with Paul. He was a good kid and a hard worker, smart and charming and as gentle a soul as she'd ever met. The kid had graduated from the regional high school the year before and managed to convince just about everyone, himself included, that he was just taking a couple of semesters off before starting college. But Paul wasn't going to college next year. Keomany had known that the day he had applied for the job. He didn't have the fire in his eyes that it took to leave Wickham. It was sad in a way; if he never left, he might never really be able to appreciate the town.

Meanwhile, though, despite his frequent lateness he was an otherwise responsible and reliable assistant manager who seemed genuinely enthusiastic about the shoppe and who was well loved by the clientele.

Keomany closed her book and set it on top of the counter. "This can't happen while I'm away, Paul. Even if there are no customers this early in the morning, the sign says we open at ten. That means we open at ten. It's only two mornings you have to actually be here on time."

"I know," he said with a sheepish smile. "I promise." He actually held his hand up as though he were taking some kind of oath, and Keomany chuckled softly and shook her head.

"All right, Boy Scout. At ease."

Paul laughed and unzipped his light jacket as he strode deeper into the store. He hung it up in back, and by the time he returned, Keomany had gathered up her book and her car keys. She snuck a nonpareil out of the display case—always a good idea to sample her own wares as long as she didn't get fat doing it—and moved around to the other side of the register.

"You're in a rush to get out of here," Paul said.

The taste of chocolate on her tongue, Keomany licked her lips and nodded. "Just looking forward to a couple of days off. I've never been to a Bealtienne festival up here but it's so beautiful this time of year that I can't wait."

"Yeah, what's up with that, anyway?" Paul asked, his curiosity apparently genuine. "It's like a wiccan thing or something?"

"Or something," Keomany replied, jangling her keys. "It's a Druidic celebration of the earth at the peak of its fertility. Maybe if you're good, I'll tell you all about when I get back."

"Yes, O Earth Goddess."

"Bet your ass."

He smiled, this handsome kid who was only five or six years younger than she was and in the space of an eyeblink she had considered and discarded the idea of sleeping with him sometime. Whatever the age difference, there were so many ways in which Paul was really just a kid.

Keomany was about to go out the door when she turned and shot Paul one last admonishing glance. "Oh, and if you're going to be seducing Jillian while I'm gone, please don't do it during work hours."

The kid actually blushed. Jillian was a year younger than him, still a high school senior, and Paul had been sweet-talking her since Keomany had hired her. Whether it had gone further than that, she had no idea.

"Hey," Paul protested.

"Call 'em like I see 'em," she said, and then she was out the door and the music of the wooden wind chimes followed her all the way across the street to where her car was parked.

As she pulled out, Keomany saw Paul standing in the open door of her shoppe, the handpainted sign for Sweet Somethings just above his head swaying slightly in the breeze. She waved but by then Jane and Ed Herron, an older couple who were regulars, were walking up toward the shoppe and Paul's attention was on them.

Keomany gave the place one last glance and then turned her attention to the road and the trip ahead of her. The steering wheel clutched in one hand, she reached down and clicked on the radio, coming in just a few lines into a blues-rock tune that the local pop station had taken to playing every hour or so in the last few days. She still had no idea what it was called or who sang it, but the woman's raspy voice reminded her of Joan Osborne, and maybe a little bit of Sheryl Crow.

For a moment she was tempted to change the channel, but as it always did, the song cut a groove down inside her, and despite how often she heard it, Keomany left it on.

As she drove south out of Wickham, she glanced around at her hometown. The village was small enough that she at least recognized more than half the people she saw on the sidewalk or driving past. Many she knew by name. She actually slowed down to wave and call hello to Annie Mulvehill, with whom she'd gone to high school, and who was now a police officer in town. Probably the first female ever to have the job in Wickham.

Keomany's apartment was behind her, on the northern end of town, just far enough away from her parents, who still lived in the house over on Little Tree Lane where she had grown up. As she drove by the turnoff that would have taken her there, she felt a twinge of guilt that she had not been able to go by and see them the night before as she'd promised. But she'd make it up to them when she returned.

A frown creased her forehead. Despite the sunshine and the blue sky and the inescapable rhythm on the radio, a chill shuddered through her and Keomany actually slowed the car to glance back at the turnoff. Something made her want to go there now, made her worry about her parents. It was foolish, of course. She'd called them on the phone that morning and they were fine.

Relax, she told herself as she eased her foot back down on the accelerator. Whatever earth magick she had dabbled in since college, she had never had a premonition before and doubted she was starting to have them now. But there were goosebumps on her arms and a cold feeling still at the base of her neck. So just the same, premonition or not, she would give her folks another call just as soon as she reached Brattleboro. It was only a couple of hours. Not a lot was going to happen in that time.

Still, some of the good feeling of the day had gone out of her now and Keomany was no longer smiling as she passed the fire station that marked the town line.

On the radio the song ended and she was surprised when the deejay's voice cut in.

"That was Nikki Wydra with 'Shock My World.' And we'll have more of the hits of today coming up on WXTC, right after this."

Keomany laughed out loud and glanced down at the radio. "No shit!" she said, as though it might actually respond. She shook her head and turned her attention back to the road.

"No shit," she said again.

It had been a long time since she had heard the name *Nikki Wydra*. Somehow, though, she had always known that one day she would hear it on the radio.

Her unease now quickly forgotten, Keomany left Wickham behind, dwindling to a dark point of nothingness in her rearview mirror.

———

"OH my God, I'm gonna puke."

Nikki Wydra sat on the edge of a metal folding chair with her head in her hands, her breath coming in quick, short gasps. Her face was flushed, she could feel the heat in her cheeks, and her eyes were wide with a kind of panic she hadn't felt since playing Dorothy in the seventh-grade production of *The Wizard of Oz* at the Haley Middle School.

"You're not gonna puke."

That comforting voice, and the equally comforting hand

that gently rubbed her back between her shoulder blades, belonged to Kyle Shotsky, the drummer with her band. Though she could not see his face, not with the way she was bent over, breathing fast and trying not to throw up, Nikki still took some solace in Kyle's presence. She knew that face intimately, the warm brown eyes and perfect hair, the small dimple on his chin. He reminded her of Billy Campbell, the actor who had played the dad on *Once and Again* years ago. Most people didn't even remember that show, but Nikki wasn't going to forget Billy Campbell.

The fact that Kyle looked a lot like Billy Campbell probably had a lot to do with why she had slept with him in the first place. Though she liked to tell herself it had nothing to do with why she'd hired him to play with her band.

Nikki's breathing had slowed. Her stomach hurt, but suddenly she did not feel quite as nauseous.

"You're not gonna puke," Kyle told her again, his firm hand gripping her shoulder now.

"Maybe you're right," she replied, amused by the surprise in her own voice. Nikki glanced up at him, saw the concern there and that all-encompassing warmth. "Thanks."

His strong fingers caressed her face. "Hey. It's what I'm here for."

"No. You're here to play the fucking drums. Just like I'm supposed to be here to sing."

Frustrated, Nikki carefully stood up and began to slowly pace the length of the green room at El Dorado. The room was little more than a converted storage area with a couple of small tables, a shitty little old TV set, a bunch of folding chairs, and a curtain in case someone wanted to get changed without the other members of the band seeing them. There was a ratty sofa against the far wall but it stank like cat and was stained with what might have been coffee in the best-case scenario, and blood in the worst.

Nikki had seen enough blood in her lifetime, thanks.

The only things about the El Dorado's green room that didn't suck were the bowls of peanut M&M's, the fresh-cut flowers, and the beer and spring water in the fridge. It might have been the most popular club on the scene in Philadelphia, but it was just like a hundred other clubs she'd played in her life.

"I don't get it," Kyle said, voice probing but still gentle. "Why's tonight different? I've done dozens of live gigs with you and I've never seen you freak like this."

"I fucking hate Philly!" Nikki shouted, shaking her head in a little tantrum so that her blond hair lashed across her face.

Kyle grinned at her. "It's the City of Brotherly Love."

She glared at him. "I hate it."

"It's your hometown, Nikki. That's why we're opening the tour here, remember?"

"I remember, all right? That's why I feel like I'm gonna puke."

The furious gaze she was inflicting upon him lasted only seconds longer before Nikki let out a long shuddering breath and let a ripple of nervous laughter escape her lips. She rolled her eyes, turned, and paced halfway across the room again. When she lifted her gaze, it fell upon her guitar, a fat-bellied electric-acoustic, all tuned and ready to play. It sat upon a stand near the refrigerator.

Suddenly she felt very stupid.

If her mother Etta were still alive, she would have given her daughter a stern talking-to and then a loving hug and pointed her toward the door. It was all her mother's damn fault in the first place, she thought. Nikki had grown up in a constant haze of blues music while her mother spent her nights in a constant haze of inebriation. All her life Nikki had played that same music, from Elmore James and Robert Johnson to Bonnie Raitt and the Allman Brothers Band.

In front of people. Audiences. And she never failed to get applause. It might have been the smoky rasp in her voice, the only thing of value other than a love of music that she had inherited from her mother. But secretly she always believed it was the emotion that backed up every word. The love and the pain and the fear. Some songs called for that, though most people would never understand. Blues songs, sure, but even love songs; to really pull them off you had to know what it was like to truly be afraid.

Nikki knew.

Kyle moved to her and slipped his arms around her from behind. "They're waiting."

And they were. The rest of the band was already out in the wings of the stage, ready to go on. The roadies were done setting up and tuning, the sound guy was set. It was all on her now. The show couldn't start without her.

Nikki closed her eyes, heart fluttering in her chest, and leaned back into him, letting Kyle take all the weight of her in his arms. "What if they don't like it?" she asked, voice small.

She felt him stiffen.

"What are you talking about, darlin'? I'm sorry, Nik, I'm not trying to be difficult, but I don't—"

Swallowing hard, trying to keep the nausea from coming back, she turned to face him. "I want to change the order. Let's start with 'Son of a Preacher Man' instead."

Now the smile was gone from Kyle's face. He stared at her as though he thought she was a lunatic, and Nikki had to allow that maybe she was. Kyle cocked his head to one side and studied her a moment. She cared for him. He was a good man and a talented drummer. But he had never been that bright. When understanding dawned upon him, she could see it in his eyes and that sudden realization made her look away, staring at the floor, at the flowers, at her guitar. At anything but that moment when he *got it*.

"I'm an idiot," Kyle whispered. Then she heard him chuckle softly. "You've never played your new songs in public."

Without meeting his gaze, she nodded. "Actually, I've pretty much never played an original song in public. Not ever."

"Not ever?"

A knock at the door interrupted them. The club's manager, Rich something, stuck his head in. "Everything all right?"

"Fine," Nikki said, too harshly, too quickly. "We'll be right there."

"Great," Rich replied, choosing to ignore the tone in her voice, the tension in the room. He pulled the door shut behind him.

While it was open, however, Nikki had heard them. The audience. They weren't chanting her name or stomping their feet or any of that crap that happened at major venues, but er thjthere was a buzz out there, a hum of conversation and anticipation that made the place tremble.

Or maybe it was just her trembling.

"Nikki?" Kyle ventured.

Swiftly she crossed to the fridge and pulled out a bottle of spring water. She spun the top off and took a long drink before at last looking him in the face again.

"I've always played covers. I know those songs inside and out, they're a part of me. I understand how they're gonna make the audience feel because I know how they make me feel. If I grind out something sexy, I know it's going to go over because I've got every note inside me."

Kyle shook his head. "But these new songs, they came from inside you. The CD is really great, Nik, and I'm not just saying that because I'm part of the band or because I'm head over heels for you. It's music that gets under your skin in the best possible way. The single is tearing up radio. Trust me, this is no different. People will feel what you feel when you sing the new stuff, just like when we do covers. Don't be so terrified."

The words made her wince. Her eyes narrowed and Nikki glanced sharply at him. "I'm not terrified. Not of this. If you'd seen half the shit I've seen, you'd know what a joke it is to use that word about something like this. I mean, there's fear and then there's *terror*."

"So what are we still doing in here when the audience is out there?" Kyle hooked a thumb toward the door and raised one eyebrow.

Nikki took another long draught of water, then put the cover back on and set the bottle down next to the flowers. They were fresh and the scent filled the room, mixing rather unpleasantly with the cat piss odor from the stained sofa. But they were pretty, at least.

"You're head over heels, huh?" she asked idly.

"Pretty much."

"Good."

With a deep breath she shook back her hair and walked

to her guitar. It was a beautifully crafted instrument with mother-of-pearl inlaid on the neck, and she picked it up and slid the strap over her head. The same strap she had been using for six years, since long before the horrors she had seen in New Orleans, when she had learned the difference between fear and terror.

Without another glance at Kyle, Nikki strode to the door and flung it open. The buzz of the crowd washed over her, embracing her and lifting her up the way nothing else ever could. Rich was waiting in the corridor and gave her a look of utter relief.

"So we still opening with 'Son of a Preacher Man'?" Kyle asked as he followed her down the corridor that led through the back of the club and into the wings behind the stage curtains.

Nikki cast him a quick glance over her shoulder. "Fuck that. We start with 'Shock My World.' We're gonna show Philly how to groove."

The rest of the band stood up quickly as she swept into the wings. The curtains were open on a darkened stage, all their equipment and instruments up there already except for Nikki's guitar. She did not wait for them, did not hesitate a moment longer.

Nikki Wydra marched onto her hometown stage with her guitar strapped across her back and the crowd began to roar. Her nausea and her hesitation were forgotten. The band rocked right into "Shock My World" and the audience thundered their approval. When Nikki began to sing, she felt the ache in every word. It was more of herself than she had ever given to anyone, only she was giving it to hundreds of people at once. Her song. Her music. Her heart.

This right here was what she lived for. This was home. Not this club. Not Philadelphia. Just the stage.

This was home.

———

ON a shelf above the desk of Father Jack Devlin was a little jar with a perforated lid, the kind of thing a child might have kept a captive spider in. There was a tiny demon in the jar and it had been there so long that Father Jack hardly even noticed it anymore.

It noticed him, however.

In fact, during all the long hours Father Jack spent poring over dusty, decrepit, leather-bound books and tapping at his computer keyboard as he searched the Net, the demon never took its burning orange eyes off the priest. Father Jack knew this, of course. The little fucker stared hateful daggers at him day and night and had done so for nearly two years. He just couldn't bring himself to care.

The demon in the jar on the shelf above his desk was a problem Father Jack had solved a long time ago. There were so many others to be dealt with . . . and most of those, unsettlingly enough, were a hell of a lot bigger than the hideous, contorted, glaring thing in the jar.

Currently the priest was bent over a sheaf of loose, yellowed pages that had come from a thirteenth-century French manuscript that some fool had tried to burn once upon a time. The other volumes used in his research had been set aside, and though the computer screen threw its dim glow upon the desk, it also sat dormant and ignored. The scorched lower corners of the pages had left certain phrases forever obliterated, and some only partially blackened and obscured. But without those words . . .

"Shit!" Father Jack snapped.

He sighed and sat back in his chair with a heartfelt sigh, sliding down so as to almost disappear beneath his desk. His eyes itched and he reached up to remove his wire-rimmed glasses, rubbed at the corners of his eyes, and massaged the bridge of his nose. There was a two-day growth of reddish-gold stubble on his chin that matched the color of his hair. He needed a shower, and a shave, and some rest. But first he needed to solve the problem that was before him.

So much for intuition. Had he actually thought he was going to be able to figure out what those missing phrases would have been just by context? *Arrogant jackass*, he thought miserably.

Father Jack slid his glasses back on, and when he glanced up, he was eye to eye with the little Cythraul. Its hideous, desiccated face was pressed up against the glass of the jar, three-fingered hands planted on either side of it, grinning at him, relishing his frustration. He had never seen it so active, so aware.

An involuntary shudder went through him, and Father Jack cursed inwardly that he had allowed the thing to get to him. Abruptly he stood, the legs of his chair squeaking on the wood floor, and he snatched the jar from the shelf and slapped his palm over the top, covering the air holes.

"Don't mess with me today," Father Jack muttered.

The Cythraul snarled, thin lips peeling impossibly far back to reveal tiny little needle teeth that filled its mouth. Its orange eyes went wide and it hurled itself upward at the lid of the jar, gnashing its fangs at the metal, hoping to get just a taste of his flesh. It would slow in a moment and then fall into a kind of coma. But it would not suffocate; it would not die.

As the little demon began to falter, all the anger went out of the priest and he shook his head and put the jar back on the shelf, sighing once more, knowing it was overly dramatic but not caring. A little drama always made him feel better.

When he looked up, Bishop Gagnon was standing in the open doorway of the office with his arms crossed, face as pale as always, one pure white eyebrow raised in inquiry.

"Roommate problems?" the aged Bishop asked.

Father Jack chuckled and it occurred to him that there was an edge of madness to it. He looked up sharply, wanting to make sure the Bishop did not think so as well. He was far from insane, though a little more of this might well turn him into a lunatic eventually.

"I couldn't kill him if I wanted to," Father Jack said. He leaned against his desk and slid his hands into the pockets of his black pants. Black everything, after all. It was the uniform. "And I want to. That's the thing, Michel. I want to."

"As well you should," the old man said, his words still accented with his native French. "But that is the difficulty of the job we have set out for us, Jack. With all of the shadows loosed upon the world, all the darkness returning, we must attempt to recreate the knowledge that once kept them under our control."

"Not *our* control. Theirs. Careful the way you phrase things, Michel."

"Of course," said the Bishop, one hand fluttering upward in dismissal. "Of course."

It was a constant struggle between them. Fully a decade had passed since the Roman Catholic Church had splintered and collapsed. Revelations of sorcery and a sect of dark magicians in her ranks had brought the church down. While it had been only in the last few years that Rome had begun to reorganize with new leaders and a new focus, things had happened much more quickly in America. The Church of the Resurrection—the Americans had very quickly abandoned the use of the word *Catholic*—had branched off almost immediately when Rome collapsed.

It had suffered its own tribulations in the meantime, perhaps the greatest of which had been the witch hunt for pedophiles among the priesthood. But without the archaic secrecy Rome had always insisted upon, the Church of the Resurrection had flushed that element from its ranks in a style nearly as brutal and unrelenting as the notorious Inquisition had been. The net result, however, was that the United States now had a far larger and more organized Catholic Church than anywhere else in the world.

Yet here they were, this very moment, repeating the sins of their fathers. For nearly two thousand years the Roman Church had held the reins on demons and other supernatural creatures—or most of them at least—with the sorcery found in a book called *The Gospel of Shadows*. A sect within the church had been trained in the book's secrets. But now every member of the sect was dead, and the book had disappeared during the horrific vampire jihad that had exposed the truth to the world ten years earlier. They had been tainted by power and dark magick, the men and women of that sect. They had been evil.

But without them, without the secrets of that book, the shadows were rising again. The demons and the beasts of the darkness, the shades of the dead, all were returning to the world, testing the boundaries and finding them shattered.

In order to stop them, the Church of the Resurrection was now forced to attempt to recreate *The Gospel of Shadows*, or at least to build a new one, spell by spell, secret by secret, curse by curse.

But Father Jack couldn't figure out a spell to kill vermin like the Cythraul. How was he supposed to recreate the accumulated occult knowledge of thousands of years of infernal combat? And meanwhile he had to worry about the politics of present-day religion, and a former Roman Catholic priest who had become a Bishop in the Church of the Resurrection sometimes forgot that it was dangerous to forget the difference between the two.

"Jack?" the Bishop prodded.

The priest looked up at him and for a moment he saw himself as he knew Bishop Gagnon must see him: rumpled clothes, white collar hanging loose, in need of a shave, eyes red behind his glasses from poring over the scorched manuscript pages.

"I guess I just need a break," Father Jack said. "Maybe I'll take a walk."

The reed-thin old man glared at him suddenly, a glint in his eyes that felt to Father Jack like the wrath of God.

"You'll do no such thing," Bishop Gagnon commanded sharply. "You can stroll around Greenwich Village another night, Father. Right now, every hour that passes costs us more souls in Hidalgo."

Father Jack stared at him, mouth open slightly in astonishment. The Bishop had never spoken to him like this before. Granted, they were both under incredible stress. Hidalgo was a tiny town in Texas a stone's throw from the Mexican border. In the previous seventy-two hours it had been the site of a demonic manifestation, creatures called Okulam that had blown in with a particularly fierce spring thunderstorm. The church just called them soul-leeches, for the disgusting things fastened themselves to the backs of their victims' necks and infiltrated the minds and spirits of human beings. They took control, these vicious demons, and left only when they had cored the soul right out of their host.

God help him, Father Jack didn't know what to do about it. The manuscript he was studying had been written by early French settlers in North America, what would become the American Colonies, and it referred very specifically to a past manifestation of the Okulam. Without *The Gospel of Shadows*, it was all they had to go on.

Bishop Gagnon crossed the room and laid a hand on Father Jack's shoulder. There was no strength in the old man's grasp and barely any weight to his touch. It was as though the Bishop were little more than a ghost, haunting Father Jack.

"Not to put any pressure on you, my friend," the old man said, and now the wrathful glare was replaced by a kind, tired smile.

"Of course not," Father Jack replied with a nervous chuckle. Then he collected himself, took a deep breath, and met the Bishop's gaze again. "All right, Michel. Time to get back to work, I suppose."

"I trust your intuition, Jack. Your mind. You'll work it out."

"What if I don't?"

"Then the President will have to firebomb the whole town to keep the Okulam from spreading."

"But no pressure," Father Jack whispered.

Bishop Gagnon gazed at him a moment longer and then turned to walk from the office. Father Jack slid into his chair, eyes going once more to the charred manuscript, but abruptly he turned and called after the Bishop.

The old man paused at the door and turned to face him.

"I'll get to the bottom of this, Michel. I *will* work it out. But I want you to think very carefully about your stance on my request to speak to the mage. If you'd let me speak to him before . . ."

Bishop Gagnon scowled. Father Jack had not finished his last sentence, but the old man knew what he had been about to say.

"My policy regarding the man you call the mage is costing lives, is that what you're telling me, Father?"

The priest stared at him. "Yes. It is."

The Bishop faltered, dropped his gaze, and Father Jack could see the old man's throat moving as he swallowed. At length the Bishop glanced up at him again.

"You know who he is, this man? What he is? What he's responsible for?"

Father Jack would not look away. "I know he may well be the only reason the darkness has not already swallowed the world."

A kind of bark issued from the old man's throat that might have been laughter. "If the darkness does 'swallow the world,' as you put it, he'll be the man to blame."

The priest took off his glasses once more and rubbed at his tired eyes. "With all due respect—"

"To hell with your respect," the Bishop snapped, hatred and revulsion in his voice. Not for the priest, Father Jack knew that, but for the mage, and for the truth the old man was being forced to face. His stubbornness had already cost so many lives.

"Fine," Bishop Gagnon said. "You make sense of those pages, Jack. When the situation in Hidalgo is dealt with, you have my permission to approach the mage. For all the good it will do you. Perhaps meeting him in person will help you realize that this 'man' is not the noble warrior you think him to be.

"Peter Octavian is a monster."

CHAPTER 2

BLOOD red roses.

Peter Octavian took a step back from his canvas and narrowed his eyes as he studied the painting upon which he had toiled for the past three days; a single tree in the gardens of Constantinople, nightingales roosting in its branches. And beneath it, a tangle of wild rose bushes that seemed set to strangle the trunk of that lone tree.

He frowned deeply as he stared at those roses. Blood red, yes, but that was wrong. The color was all wrong but at first he could not decide how to fix it. Peter closed his eyes, his mind skipping back across centuries to another springtime, to a city under siege, and he could still see those roses as clearly as if he had walked among them yesterday. He could hear the nightingales sing and feel the breeze, and beneath the overriding odor of ox dung, he could still catch the lingering scent of those roses.

His eyes opened and Octavian stared at the painting again. With a slow nod, he moved toward the easel, palette in his left hand. He dipped his brush into a small glob of black paint. The roses had bloomed early that spring of 1453 in the weeks before Constantinople fell to the Turks, but they had been dark roses whose petals were a lush crimson. Blood red roses, yes, but blood that had begun to dry; blood that stained.

Peter daubed black paint onto the red, mixing the two, and then used the very tip of the brush to detail the edges of each petal, as though every one of the roses was slowly opening to reveal a darker heart within.

"Yes," he whispered to himself as he stepped back to regard the painting once more.

At last satisfied, he set down the palette and brush and stretched, muscles in his neck and shoulders and back popping loudly in the silence of his apartment. It was the second day of May, and though he could still taste the memory of winter in the air, it was warm enough today that the windows all along the front of the apartment were wide open.

Peter lived on the basement floor of a row house on West Fourth Street in Greenwich Village, half a block from a lesbian bar called the Fat Cat and just around the corner from the legendary White Horse Tavern. It was not much to speak of—a single bedroom, a living room, a narrow galley kitchen, and a bathroom—but it was perfect for his needs, particularly since the living room was rather large and doubled as his studio.

He also liked the neighborhood a great deal. West Fourth Street was comparatively quiet and the locals tended either to be friendly or to keep to themselves. The row house belonged to Jarrod and Suze Balent, both of whom were musicians who made their living playing in the orchestra for various Broadway shows, he the cello and she the violin. They were good for a cup of coffee and a chat now and again, but weren't around enough to become a nuisance. Best of all, they seemed to sense when he wanted company and when he did not.

Peter took a last look at his newly completed painting and he smiled again. His heart was light, as it always was when he finished a new canvas, when he had successfully prised from his mind a bit of the past that haunted him. Barefoot, he padded across the wooden floor in jeans that were slightly too long, the edge of the denim fraying in the back beneath his heel. Not that he was overly concerned, given that both the jeans and the button-down shirt he wore were spattered and smeared with a dark rainbow of color.

Time for a little celebration, he thought as he went to the bathroom and began to wash up, scrubbing the paint from his fingers under hot water from the tap. He would phone Carter Strom and let him know that the final piece for the new show had been completed, and unless he had some other pressing plans, Carter would do as he always did—pick up his wife Kymberly and meet Peter at the White Horse. In the years since Peter had first begun to express himself with paint, discovering both a talent and an untapped source of income, that had become a ritual for the three of them: the artist, his agent, and the agent's wife.

Among Peter's few friends, fewer still were in New York City. Carter and Kymberly were primary among them.

Peter stepped back into the living room and glanced at the clock, pleased to discover that it was early yet, not even two o'clock in the afternoon. He had been so focused the past few days that he had barely seen the sky. Immersed as he was in the painting, he had stepped outside only to pick up the newspaper and breakfast at the deli on Twelfth Street, and even then he'd barely noticed the world around him. It was like that when he was working.

Now that he was through with the painting, the world was flooding back in, his awareness of things other than that canvas suddenly returning. Some time away from the apartment would do him good.

Peter had just begun to unbutton his shirt when the doorbell rang. The Balents always knocked and Carter never would drop by without calling first. Aside from the rare messenger or courier, nobody rang his doorbell. One of the things he had liked the best about this apartment when he bought it was that it had its own entrance, not even a shared foyer with the house above it. A trio of brick steps led down from the street to his sunken residence. Nobody came down those steps by accident, but at first there had been those who had come looking for him. He had used simple magick to install a ward around his door, to keep the curious away.

Now, though, he was curious himself. His bare feet made

almost no noise on the floor as he crossed the room and opened the door.

Upon the landing at the bottom of those brick steps stood a lanky, thirtyish, redheaded man in wire-rimmed glasses whose only remarkable quality was that he wore the clothing of a Catholic priest. They might not call themselves Catholics anymore, but the uniform had not changed.

The priest seemed taken aback, almost surprised that the door had been answered at all.

"You look lost," Peter told the man.

His visitor actually took a step back when he spoke, and Peter was about to shut the door when the priest laughed softly, self-deprecatingly, and clapped one hand to his face in embarrassment. It was such an unself-conscious gesture, and there was such warmth in that laugh, that Peter found himself lingering longer in the open door than he otherwise would have.

"I'm sorry," the priest said, still a bit embarrassed, but smiling in spite of it. "I guess you're just not what I was expecting."

"I get that a lot. What can I do for you, Father?"

The priest raised an eyebrow. "Father? I'm surprised to hear you use the term."

Peter's good humor was fading. He could feel himself preparing to step back, to close the door on the man. "Don't they call you people that still?"

"The faithful do, yes."

"Then you shouldn't be surprised. I may not believe in you, sir, or your church, but there are a great many things I do believe in. Now is there something I can do for you, or did you just drop by to have a look?"

For a long moment the priest was speechless. He shifted awkwardly there on the doorstep, scratched at the back of his neck, and then that grin returned.

"Guess we're getting off on the wrong foot, here. That wasn't my intention. Mind if I take it from the top?"

Peter didn't know why, but there was something about the guy that made him nod his head. "Give it a shot."

The priest thrust out his hand. "Mr. Octavian, my name's Jack Devlin. Technically I'm not supposed to be here, but there are some things going on that . . . well, I could use your help."

"Why aren't you supposed to be here, Father Devlin?" He did not shake the priest's proffered hand.

"Jack," the man replied, lowering it. "Or Father Jack."

"All right, Jack. Why aren't you supposed to be here?"

The priest's expression had become deadly serious. "My boss, Bishop Michel Gagnon, says that you're a monster. That you'd be unwilling to help us. But he authorized my paying you a visit if I could at first restructure a spell from a partially destroyed French text that we need to stop the spread of a demon infestation in a small town on the Tex-Mex border. I was unable to do that, but I think that you can. Or that you may know how to stop them without even having to figure out the text."

Peter narrowed his eyes. His right hand strayed to his cheek and he idly scraped dried paint from his skin. Sunny as it was, his bare feet were still a little cold with the door open and the breeze that swirled down into the apartment.

"Tex-Mex?" he asked doubtfully. "Isn't that a style of cooking?"

"It's shorthand for—"

"I know what it's shorthand for," Peter replied, at last rewarding Father Jack with a smile of his own. "It just seems a bit slangy for a priest."

"Maybe I'm not the sort of priest you're used to," Father Jack suggested.

Peter nodded slowly. "Maybe you're not at that." He stepped back and held the door wide to allow the man into his home. "Come in, then. But no promises, Jack. I don't know if I can help, or even if I'll want to. But I'll listen."

"Good enough," said the priest as he crossed the threshold.

Peter closed the door behind him and gestured toward the sofa set beneath the high windows. "Have a seat while I put on a pot of tea. You drink tea?"

Father Jack was glancing around the room, taking in every canvas, every splatter of paint, every overgrown plant. "I've been known to," he replied as he set himself down on the sofa. "Thank you."

"No trouble at all."

In the little galley kitchen Peter filled a battered tea kettle with tap water, set it on the burner, and turned on the stove. His day had taken an unanticipated turn, but in his long, long life he had learned that any day, any hour, any minute might turn out to be laden with the unexpected. And as such things went, the bespectacled, redheaded priest seemed harmless enough.

Leaving the kettle to boil, he returned to the living room to find that Father Jack had risen from the sofa and was standing with his arms crossed, gravely studying the half-dozen paintings Peter had done for the new show.

"See anything you like?"

The priest glanced over at him and then back at the paintings. "I like them all. You're quite an artist, Mr. Octavian. I'd no idea. There isn't anything about you being a painter in—"

Father Jack paused and blinked several times, obviously uncertain how to continue.

"In the file the Church of the Resurrection has on me?" Peter suggested helpfully. "Honestly, Jack, do you think it surprises me? Even if your people weren't keeping tabs, there have been enough books written about my past and the Venice Jihad, not to mention Salzburg and then New Orleans, that you wouldn't even need to do your own homework."

The priest pursed his lips tightly, almost prissily for a moment as though Peter had offended him. "Actually, I *prefer* to do my own homework."

"An admirable trait," Peter replied carefully. "But when I opened the door, you said I wasn't what you expected. So something tells me you weren't as prepared for this conversation as you'd like to have been."

"True."

"Why?"

Father Jack's gaze ticked toward the paintings again and then back to Peter. A truck went by out on the street and its rumble shook the walls of the apartment, the squeal of its brakes rattling the windows.

"I didn't expect an ordinary man."

Peter laughed. He strode to an antique high-backed chair

he had picked up the year before off the sidewalk two blocks away and slid into it. The chair was set strategically among several of the potted plants that needed little sun. Nearby there was a ziggurat-shaped water fountain that plugged into the wall and provided an undercurrent of noise, the bubbling of a tiny brook over stones. In the midst of his living space, it was a place of manufactured peace for Peter, among things that lived and breathed and spoke of the earth.

Now, though, on the edge of that chair, he shot a hard look at his visitor, and when he spoke, his tone was decidedly different from that which he had used throughout their limited conversation thus far.

"You mistake me, then, sir. For I am far from an ordinary man."

Father Jack glanced around as though wishing he had never left the presumed safety of the sofa, that soft and forgiving island amid what now appeared to be dangerous waters.

"I hardly meant—"

"I know what you meant," Octavian said curtly. "You've read about me in books and your Bishop calls me a monster and you know I have a certain facility with magick and so you expect some kind of smoke and mirrors for your entertainment and a man who is perhaps more imposing physically than the unwashed painter in grimy clothes in a Spartan little basement apartment. Do I have that much right?"

Father Jack slipped his glasses off and clutched them in his hand, then raised his head high, as though a man without spectacles was somehow gifted with greater dignity than one who wore them.

"Are you aware that your speech becomes more formal when you're angry?" the priest asked.

Peter smiled, not now the friendly, lopsided grin he had worn before but something far colder.

"Oh, I'm not angry, Father. You haven't seen me angry." He held his hands out, palms upward, and sketched slightly at the air with his fingers. "And you haven't seen a single bit of magick. Not even a card trick. But that doesn't mean it isn't real."

The priest took a deep breath but kept his gaze locked

with Peter's. "You're not telling me anything I don't know, Mr. Octavian. I'm sorry if I've offended you. If you'd like, I'll go now."

Peter slid back in his chair and crossed his hands on his lap. "Sit down, Jack."

After only a moment's hesitation, the priest complied.

"You know, I'm not the only one whose speech gets a little uptight when tempers flare."

Father Jack's hand was shaking when he raised it and slid his fingers through his neatly trimmed hair. Slowly, carefully, he put his glasses on once again and regarded Peter with an admirable display of calm.

"So tell me what I don't know about you. That is, if you'd care to."

Peter considered that a moment. Then he sat forward again, fingers steepled under his chin, the bubbling of his little ziggurat waterfall whispering in his ears, calming him.

"First, why don't I tell you what you do know. Or what you think you know. And you can tell me where I'm wrong."

"That really isn't—"

"No. I insist."

Father Jack nodded, sitting stiffly on the edge of the sofa cushion. When the tea kettle began to whistle, he actually flinched, then huffed out a short, embarrassed breath.

Peter rose. "Let me get that."

In the galley kitchen he took a pair of brittle old China teacups and poured hot water from the kettle into each. He knew they were more appropriate for aged English women, but he was fond of them just as he was of the antique chair in the living room. There was texture to old things, impermanent things, that he appreciated now in a way he had not always.

Moments later he returned with a tray upon which sat the teacups, a variety of tea bags, milk, and sugar. He set the tray down on the end table beside the sofa and stood while he dipped a bag of Earl Grey into his own cup and then stirred sugar into it.

"Allison Vigeant's book about the Venice Jihad says I was born in 1424," Peter began, not looking at the priest as

he poured just a drop of milk into his tea. "She made that
up, Allison. Or someone did."

Now he did glance up and he saw that he had Father
Jack's undivided attention. The man did not seem even to be
breathing. Peter raised his cup toward the priest.

"Drink your tea."

Father Jack laughed but it was a hollow sound, for effect
only. He did, however, reach over and pick up a tea bag and
begin preparing his own tea. Peter turned and went back to
his antique chair among the plants and the mist of the ziggurat waterfall. He sipped the tea and found it exactly right.
Over the rim of the cup he regarded the priest.

"I don't know what year I was born, but that's near
enough I suppose. My father was Constantine the Eleventh
Palaeologus, the last emperor of Byzantium, but I was ille-
gitimate, a bastard, and therefore not exactly royalty myself."

"You . . . you were a soldier," Father Jack said, tea held
halfway to his lips.

Peter frowned at him. Out on the street someone honked
a car horn and the priest started, spilling several drops of tea
on his lap. He barely noticed.

"We were all soldiers in those days." He closed his eyes.
"I can see it all still, you understand. The blood and the rain
storms and the men digging in the mud that spring when the
Turks hammered at the walls of the city harder than ever
before and tried to tunnel beneath them. That was our job
for a time . . ."

Our job. Faces flashed across his mind, images of friends
who had been dead many hundreds of years and yet for
whom his heart still ached.

"We were supposed to keep the Turks out," he said, a
rasp in his voice that he did not like.

His eyes opened and he glanced over at one of the canvases propped against the wall. It showed the ships in the
water of the Golden Horn, feeding the assault on Constantinople, their bone-white sails pregnant with the wind, as
though God himself were spurring them on to the city's destruction.

Peter shook his head. "They did the impossible, you
know. The Turks, I mean. They could not pass the barrier

the Emperor had placed to guard the entrance to the Golden Horn and so the Sultan ordered his armies to transport their ships across the land." He stared at the priest. "Across the land, Jack. Do you have any idea of the enormity of that?"

"I can only imagine."

The mage laughed then, a long, hearty sound that surprised him as it came out. He gazed longingly at his paintings again and then back at the priest.

"No. You know, you really can't. It was 1453, Jack. You don't have a clue. Another world, not just another time. And so to your suggestion that I was a soldier I say, yes, I suppose in your terms I was a soldier. But we were a city at war and I was an able-bodied man in service to my Emperor, my father. I was a warrior, Father Devlin."

"A warrior."

Peter hung his head a moment and took a long breath. Then he took another and looked up again.

"Look, you came here for a reason. I don't want to waste your time."

"You're not," the priest said quickly, and apparently with great sincerity given the expression on his face. "Please go on."

He sipped thoughtfully at his tea. "I wanted to kill Turks. As many Turks as I could. They were destroying the empire, destroying my home and my friends and the women I had loved or had wanted to love, and they were tearing apart my world. I wanted to kill them with a passion that is yet another thing I'm afraid you cannot possibly imagine.

"But the city was falling, you see. It was only a matter of time. I don't mean weeks, I mean hours." Peter pointed to the easel, to the painting he had just completed. "That is the night, right there. Those trees and the roses in early bloom and nightingales singing and a man came to me who was not a man and he offered me a chance to become a far greater warrior, an invincible warrior who might slaughter Turks by the hundreds."

Peter leaned forward and set his teacup on the floor. He had lost his desire for it entirely. He gazed steadily at the priest.

"What else was I to say? He took my blood and gave me

his, and in all the ways that really mattered, I died. My name then was not what it is now, as I'm sure you know. He gave it to me, the one who made me a vampire."

Though he had been unable to stop Constantinople from falling, Octavian had spent years killing as many Turks as he was able, a new family around him. He remembered how it had changed him, had brought him to the point where killing seemed all he knew how to do, where it had seemed like a good idea.

"I allowed myself to be lulled into the belief that I was not a warrior, but a hunter," he said.

"A vampire," Father Jack whispered. "You were a vampire."

"Yes," Peter replied. "And back in the day, that meant all the things we thought it meant. All the rules, all the bullshit, all the . . . all the cruelty and bloodshed . . ."

He waved his hand as if brushing it all away. "Bullshit," he said again. "There's no such thing as vampires, Jack. Not the figures painted by the legends of myth and pop culture. You know that or you wouldn't be here. But call them that if you want, for lack of a better word. I was one of them, but I became tired of killing. It wasn't what I wanted, not what I signed up for."

A bitter laugh escaped him.

"I changed my life, left the others who had become like a family to me but now hated me for pointing out what they already knew. It was evil, what we were doing. We didn't have to live like that. And so I didn't. Then I found out the truth."

On that last word his gaze fell upon the priest again, and though he knew this man was not of the same church, not one of the men who had wrought so much evil in the past, still he could not help but feel fury boiling within him.

Peter could see Father Jack's Adam's apple bob as the priest swallowed nervously. The man knew what Peter was speaking of, but it was a dangerous subject. For almost by chance, some years past, Peter had been the one to discover that vampires were not evil, but only supernatural. That of all supernatural creatures they were the only ones whose nature was a combination of human, demonic, and divine. That

from the earliest days of the Roman Catholic Church, its
hierarchy had conspired to use magick to control all supernatural creatures and that vampires were the only creatures
they had not managed to bend to their will.

He had learned the truth. That the limitations upon their
ability to shapeshift, to alter their bodies on a molecular level,
and most of the traditional weaknesses—to the sun and to
garlic and to the cross—had been implanted in the minds of
a few of his kind and then spread like an infection, the church
fathers knowing that creatures with total control over their
molecular structure would burn in the sunlight if they believed that they would, and would be scattered to dust by a
stake through the heart if they believed that they would.

But Peter had created of the truth a kind of antivirus, and
it spread just as quickly.

"You discovered that the Church was about to make a
final purge to try to wipe your kind from the earth forever,"
Father Jack said.

The room fell silent then save for the sound of the priest
trying to catch his breath and the burbling of the little fountain, and the distant noises of the city beyond the little basement apartment on West fourth Street.

"All of this is documented," Peter reminded him.

And it had been. Exhaustively. What Peter had learned
set off a series of battles between humans and vampires, and
among the vampire clans themselves, that laid waste to Venice and Salzburg and part of New Orleans. Vampires had
learned the truth, that they did not have to be monsters, did
not have to be predators, that they had a choice in the matter.
But some had wanted to stay in the shadows. Some embraced
that new truth, but others ignored it.

"I lost a lot of friends and a woman I loved very much.
I spent the better part of a thousand years in Hell, learning
sorcery and losing my sanity. When it was all over and done
with, nearly every vampire in the world was dead."

Father Jack stared at him. "And you were human."

For the first time, Peter glanced away, unsettled. He
looked at his hands, pictured his own mirror image, the one
he saw every morning, the one with the graying hair and the
lines around the eyes and mouth.

"Yes. I lived. I found a way to exorcise the demonic and the divine from my body. I could have had one of the survivors change me back, make me a vampire again. But I chose to stay like this. To live."

The priest set aside his own tea and gazed at Peter as though they were in the intimacy of a confessional. "And it haunts you."

Peter did not like the sound of that. He narrowed his eyes, ran his long fingers over the paint-spattered legs of his jeans. "Let me tell you now what you don't know."

"Please."

The mage turned his hands over, and when he did, there was a tiny ball of green fire burning in the center of each palm, a pair of glaring, verdant suns that cast their glow upon the entire room and threw sickly shadows across the face of Father Jack Devlin, across his suddenly wide eyes. Peter could see the magick reflected in the man's glasses.

"It's for effect," Peter said, voice low. "But it's a good one, isn't it? I mean, there's a promise in it. Not an empty threat, this power. This is what I learned in Hell, while demons were picking at my mind like carrion birds on a dead dog."

He snapped one hand closed, snuffing out the light in it, but the other flared more brightly and Peter held his hand up higher, twisted it around so that the burning orb became a flame that played along his fingers.

"I'll never be just an ordinary man," Peter said. "But I feel like one. When I was young, I was angry. At my father, at the Turks, at the world for not coming to save my city in time. My memories of my time in Hell and my life as a vampire are dim. There's something I'll bet you didn't know. I remember my human life, my youth, very well, and the last few years of course. But the time between . . . it's as though it happened to someone else. I remember the people I cared for and why, of course. Some of those who are still alive are still part of my life. But in many ways it's as though I was a young man then, and now my life has begun again.

"Do you want to know why I did not take the gift of immortality from one of my friends again?"

The priest nodded.

Peter waved his hand and the magick was gone.

"Because when you live forever, nothing matters as much as it does when every heartbeat is a tick of the clock closer to the end. Life is vital. It has texture and preciousness that you lose track of very quickly if you do not have to worry about things as mundane as wrinkles and cholesterol and cemetery plots. When I was a Shadow . . . shadows of humanity, that's what vampires are . . . when I was a Shadow, I always felt that no matter who stood beside me in battle or lay beside me in bed, I was somehow still alone."

He smiled wistfully. "It wasn't until I was human again that I remembered that the living feel that way too. Living is a journey we all end alone. The difference, then, my dear Father, is this: when you cannot die, it no longer matters how you live. Mortality gives meaning to the journey.

"So I'm human. And I'm alone. And yes, I'm haunted. I have always loved art and now I paint to escape some of my ghosts."

Peter opened his hands and clapped them together like a gleeful child. "Now you know all there is to know about me. And can I just say, who needs therapy more than I do?"

But there was no humor in it, and Father Jack clearly understood that, for there was not even the flicker of a smile on his features.

"Your tea is getting cold," he told the priest.

Father Jack regarded him carefully. "I don't really like tea."

Peter laughed incredulously. "You lied?"

"It seemed rude to do otherwise."

"Until now?"

"Oddly enough."

The mage let that sink in and then nodded once. "All right. I'll stop toying with you, Jack. I just wanted to make sure you really understood what was going on here. If I'm a monster as the Bishop says I am, then so be it. But I figure that's for you to decide. It sure isn't up to me."

"I didn't come here with villagers bearing torches to try to burn you out, Mr. Octavian."

"You couldn't," Peter replied. "That's why I let you in. There are wards on this place. If you meant me harm, or even if you were searching for me for your own purposes, like some of the obsessive lunatics who showed up when I first moved in, you would never even have found the place. You would have been unable to see it at all."

"You have stalkers?" the priest asked, eyebrows raised.

"Used to. But humanity does its best to forget what upsets it, doesn't it, Father? People still have to be reminded that the Holocaust happened, and that was barely three quarters of a century ago. The world is trying to forget about vampires, and there are so few of us—excuse me, of them—remaining that its easy for conspiracy theorists to start talking about mass hallucinations and genetic experimentation and supersoldiers and all that sort of crap. Kind of amusing, actually. The point is, if you meant me any harm, you wouldn't be sitting on my sofa drinking tea."

"You'd be dead."

Father Jack gave an uncertain chuckle. "And pleasant a prospect as that is—"

"It brings us to why you're here."

The priest nodded.

"You're here because you want me to help you with a spell to do some demonic pest control in Hidalgo, Texas."

The man had been reaching up to push his sliding glasses higher on the bridge of his nose and now he paused as if frozen and stared at Peter, his cheeks the color of his hair.

"I didn't tell you it was Hidalgo."

"No, you didn't. You also didn't tell me that as a priest in service to Bishop Gagnon, your primary responsibility is to attempt to recreate the contents of *The Gospel of Shadows* to try to rein in the demons and other supernatural creatures that have been running around without their leashes on ever since the Roman Church lost its war with the vampires and could no longer control them."

The priest's mouth dropped open. "How . . . how can you know this?"

Peter stood up, careful not to kick over his teacup. He walked over to the door and pulled it open, then glanced back at Father Jack. "I'm a mage, my friend. At a guess, I'd say as powerful a sorcerer as ever walked the earth. Well, save one.

"You can go now. Thanks for dropping by."

Obviously confused, the priest stood up and slowly strode toward Peter, shaking his head, mouth working but without words coming out of it, as each response he considered was analyzed and then jettisoned.

"You're welcome. For the tea, I mean."

That stopped the priest. He had been about to step through the door but now he stopped, only feet away from Peter, and glared at him with real anger shining in his eyes for the first time.

"You're really just going to let all those people in Hidalgo die? Those demons will keep spreading if they're left unchecked. It could be an epidemic unlike anything we've seen."

"Nuke the town," Peter replied.

"You're joking."

A ripple of guilt went through him, and at last Peter relented. "Maybe a little," he confessed. "I'm sorry, Father. But I cannot help you. Not in good conscience. You see, I was once part of a group of beings who numbered a great many monsters among them. So was your Bishop Gagnon, so he should understand. I just reminded you what happened the last time a religious organization came into the kind of sorcerous power *The Gospel of Shadows* represented. You really think I'm going to help you start that all over again?"

Again Father Jack opened his mouth, and again no words came out. The priest had no response to that. He turned and walked out of the apartment and started up the brick steps toward the street.

On the second step he paused and turned.

Peter stood inside the door watching him. He had waited, for he sensed that the priest was not quite through with him yet.

"I suppose I understand. At least partially," Father Jack allowed.

"That's all I ask," Peter replied. "Did you bring that French manuscript?"

The priest's face brightened and he reached inside his black jacket and withdrew a sheaf of faded parchment from an inner pocket. At the bottom it was scorched, portions of it burned away.

Peter nodded once and whispered words in a Hellish language. The air around the parchment seemed to shudder and warp like heat rising over blacktop on a hot summer day, and when it subsided, the pages of that arcane French manuscript were whole again.

Father Jack stared at the pages in his hand and a slow smile crept across his face. He looked up at Peter gratefully.

"Tell the Bishop you figured it out for yourself," the mage told him. "I wouldn't want to spoil my reputation."

CHAPTER 3

ON the drive back up to Wickham, Keomany kept her window down and the radio turned up loud, her silken black hair blowing across her face almost constantly. At times it obscured her vision but she only laughed and plucked it away from her eyes, and whenever she heard Nikki Wydra's song on the radio, she cranked it up even louder. It was played so often that she figured by the time she got home she'd know all the words.

The road hummed beneath her tires and the little Kia seemed almost to float along without her help. Keomany was tired, but it was the sweet blissful sort of tired that was so wonderfully rare. The Bealtienne festival had been all she had hoped for, and more. Two nights and one full day of harmony and partying, of practical idealism, of dedication to the everyday magick in nature and in humanity. Keomany had run into a handful of people she had known from similar festivals in New York, but she had also met a lot of new faces, made new friends. She'd gotten on particularly well with Ellen Cortes, a crafts shop owner from Connecticut.

Then there was Zach. Tall, broad-shouldered, well-muscled Zach with the sparkling blue eyes who had given a fascinating lecture on the significance of Great Trees, Standing Stones, and Stone Circles the previous morning and then talked his way into Keomany's room that night.

Now, with the wind blowing across her face and the sun shining warm upon her through the windshield, she shivered with the delicious thrill of remembering the feel of his hands on her, the things he had done with his tongue, and the good-bye kiss they had shared this morning. She did not even remember if she had gotten his last name, but she had his phone number. Keomany wasn't sure if she would call Zach or not, but even if she never did, she knew she would get a shiver every time she thought of him and of the Bealtienne festival.

A tiny smile played at the edges of her lips that she had not summoned but neither could she banish it, a fact that only made her smile more broadly and chuckle to herself.

With a sigh she settled more deeply into the driver's seat of the Kia, the sun and her memories of the night before making her warm and tired in that satisfied, sleepy way. The wind whipping across her face and the loud radio were meant to keep her from closing her eyes behind the wheel, but it still took a lot of self-control for her to shake off that contented feeling and stay awake.

Just get home in one piece, she thought.

Home. The word echoed in her mind along with the thrum of her tires on the highway. Once upon a time it would have ruined her mood to be headed back to Wickham, but things had changed. Much as she wished there could be a Bealtienne festival every weekend instead of once a year, she looked forward to tending the flowers at her place, and to getting back to work at her shoppe. Keomany had every confidence in Paul and Jillian, but opening Sweet Somethings had been her dream, and it meant the world to her to take care of the shoppe, to stand behind the counter and serve her customers. The beautiful thing about her business was that her customers were always happy. It was unlike almost any other job in that way. Homemade fudge and hand-dipped chocolates were magical products to sell. There might be those who wished the prices were lower, but nobody ever complained about what they had bought.

An ancient Madonna song recorded the year Keomany

was born came on the radio. She began to sing along but her voice dropped off. A blue Dodge pickup was just to her left and she could hear the same song coming through its open window. A battered BMW sailed past her going much too fast.

Her eyelids grew heavier, her whole body warm.

Madonna sang along to the sound of her tires humming against pavement and then the music was gone as Keomany's eyes closed and her chin began to dip and finally her head canted forward. It was the sensation of falling that snapped her eyes open, rocked her back in the seat. There was an instant of *knowing*, where she understood that she had fallen asleep at the wheel, and her hands gripped the steering wheel so hard they hurt. Her entire body was rigid in that slice of time.

Then she saw the Dodge pickup looming too large in her peripheral vision. Her rearview mirror was a whisper away from the Dodge and the driver laid on the horn. It seemed too loud through her open window, blaring like an air raid siren, and she cut the wheel hard to the right.

Too hard.

All on instinct.

The little Kia had drifted from the middle into the fast lane, and now it darted back across the highway too far, sailing all the way to the breakdown lane. If there had been another car in the slow lane—or a lunatic like the one in that battered BMW . . .

Keomany couldn't think about it. She hit the brakes and let the Kia roll onto the soft shoulder, tires kicking up gravel. Her legs were weak and they hurt from the sudden rictus of her muscles and her hands were shaking as she put the car in park. Her chest rose in ragged gasps as she laid her forehead upon the steering wheel.

A tractor-trailer thundered by and the Kia shuddered as though it might be tugged along in the truck's backwash.

"Oh my God," Keomany whispered as she glanced up over the top of the steering wheel and out the windshield. Just ahead of her on the soft shoulder was a green sign showing the distance to Montpelier and Montreal. Another half-dozen feet and she would have torn right through the steel struts that held up the sign.

"Holy shit."

She got out of the car and stood back to stare at it. Blinking in amazement, she walked a circuit of the Kia and marveled at the little car as though it were the most extraordinary vehicle ever built. Not a scratch on it. Or on her.

"Holy shit," she said again, out loud this time, and it occurred to her how sadly ineloquent trauma had made her.

The thought made her laugh. It was a little crazy, that sound, but she shook her head and then slid back behind the wheel of the car and continued to let the strained giggle roll out of her because she needed to.

Just for fun she said "Holy shit" a third time and then laughed some more. Keomany sighed and ratcheted around to look backward along the highway and she waited several minutes until there wasn't a car in sight before she pulled out.

She kept to the slow lane for almost twenty minutes, and when she at last moved back into the middle, she shuddered. Her skin was tingling all over the way it had when she was a little girl and had done something naughty and then gotten away with it.

This was like that. It made her feel lucky and somehow brand new.

A short time later Nikki Wydra's song came on for the third time and Keomany laughed and sat up straight and sang along at the top of her lungs.

But she kept her eyes on the road.

And she didn't feel tired anymore. Not at all.

＊＊＊

DESPITE the giddiness she'd felt after nearly dying, by the time Keomany drove past the fire station and into Wickham late that afternoon, all the benevolent energy she had built up at the Bealtienne festival—and in bed with No Last Name Zach—had completely dissipated. She was relieved to be home but there was a kind of bitterness in it as well, for she felt very keenly that something had been robbed from her, that the exuberance she had been feeling had not merely been tainted, but stolen.

It had soured her disposition, and she had never liked to feel sour.

Still, as she drove through town, she tried to force herself to cheer up at least a little. She was fine, after all. Pissed at herself more than anything. It was foolish to let the incident ruin what had been an otherwise perfectly pleasant break.

So intent was she upon her mood that though she noticed how deserted the sidewalks were on the normally busy Currier Street, it failed to register as anything particularly remarkable.

Keomany parked the Kia across the street from Sweet Somethings and climbed out of the car. She paused and took a deep breath to center herself, to touch the earth with her mind and speak to nature with her heart.

And she recoiled.

"What the hell?" she muttered and she stared around as though she had just woken up. Something had seemed off ever since she had fallen asleep behind the wheel, but that was just her nerves. This . . . this was something else.

Eyes narrowed, she glanced back at her car. The window was open. If it was just a smell, she ought to have caught the odor before she got out. But it was more than that, much more, and it had simply not affected her until she had left the car and exposed herself to Currier Street.

With a shudder of dread, she started toward her shoppe. But everything seemed off kilter, soiled in some way, as though the air itself had grown thick and damp with rot. Halfway across the street she froze, with no thought at all given to the possibility of being struck by a car.

What did she have to fear? There were no cars moving on Currier Street.

Damp with rot? What had made her think that?

Yet whatever had formed the image in her mind, she could not shake the thought now. The air did indeed have an unpleasant taint to it, not merely when she inhaled it, but when she *touched* it in the way that those of her faith could. Paul Leroux might tease her about being an earth goddess— and that was fine because goddess she most certainly was not—but she did have a connection to the magick in nature.

"What the hell is going on around here?" she asked aloud.

This was not simply the bad feeling left over from her near-collision. The town seemed deserted, the air had a strange texture to it, like the sky pregnant with moisture just before a storm, and yet this was different still from that. There was a copper tang in the air that she scented in her nostrils and tasted upon her tongue and a wild thought cantered across her mind, that at any moment the sky would begin to bleed.

The late afternoon light had changed just in the few minutes since she had driven into Wickham. Now it was not golden but coarse orange, the color of rotten pumpkins.

Keomany began to shake her head. Somebody else might have chalked it up as simply odd and brushed it off. A person who could not feel what she felt in the earth and in the air might have tried to go about their business. But this was not right.

Keomany Shaw was an earthwitch, and no fucking way was she spending another minute on this street.

Earthwitch, she thought with a laugh. *You're not even that strong in it.* There had been dozens at the Bealtienne festival with more sensitivity to the earth than she had, with real ability to read ley lines and to call upon their power, to influence the weather, to uncover the secrets of the world.

But if she could feel what had happened here this strongly, she had a feeling those others might have been crippled by it.

Her throat was dry and it hurt when she swallowed as though she was already getting sick from whatever dark poison filled the air. She turned to walk back toward her car.

Something moved.

Just out of the corner of her eye.

A chill raced through her and her skin prickled with gooseflesh as she turned to try to pursue it, the only thing she had seen moving since she drove into town. Down along the street between two parked cars. It might have been a dog running low but she knew that was not it. Her single glimpse of it was burned on her retina, a flash of blackness darker than shadow. She could feel the malice emanating from it.

But it was gone.

"Get in the goddamn car, Keomany," she muttered to herself.

An anger rose in her, doing combat with her fear. Nobody had ever benefited from backing Keomany Shaw into a corner. It made her cunning and hard and stubborn. This was her town. Her parents were here somewhere. Her friends. It was her place. Her shoppe . . .

Keomany had reached the car. Whatever strength her anger had given her was not enough to overcome her fear. She'd leave, go back to the edge of town, and find a pay phone. Hell, chances were it wasn't the whole town anyway, just here. But the sky . . . the dirty orange color of the overcast sky was growing darker. She could drive to the police station. They'd think she was nuts for claiming to have had some kind of premonition, but *something* was going on down on Currier Street.

The shoppe . . .

Keomany glanced just once at Sweet Somethings. The shoppe was dark but she could see Paul Leroux behind the plate glass, staring out at her with wide eyes as though the sight of her terrified him, as though she were the thing that had tainted the world of Currier Street.

She saw him mouth her name.

Then Paul withdrew into the darkness of the shoppe and the rotten-pumpkin light that filtered from the sky—though not from any sun she'd ever seen—could not penetrate those shadows.

"Fuck," she whispered.

Keomany glanced around at the other stores and restaurants, looked at the empty, parked cars, and stared carefully at the place where she had thought she had seen that slinking, jagged shadow thing. *It has teeth*. The words skittered across her mind. *I don't think I saw them, but I felt them*.

The Kia beckoned to her from behind but she could not retreat into it. Not if Paul was inside the shoppe. He might have answers, and she wanted that, but the uglier half of that thought was that she might be the only chance he had of ever leaving Currier Street—or this infected version of it—again.

Holding her breath, she ran toward the shoppe.

The street was solid beneath her feet but everything else seemed completely surreal. A sound had begun to rasp across the sky as though the town of Wickham itself were breathing—like the distant rolling thunder of jet engines and yet somehow all around her head, whispering in her ears.

As Keomany reached the sidewalk, there came another fluid slice of darkness in the edges of her vision. She spun, heart thudding in her chest, to stare a moment at the entrance to the Currier Street Theatre, where she thought she could see a kind of pus-yellow streak in the air as though the thing that had just ducked out of sight beneath the theatre's marquee had left a trail in its wake.

Damp rot, she thought again. The whole street smelled of it, and it felt that way too, as though the world were becoming nothing more than the desiccated remains of reality.

The door of the shoppe was open perhaps two inches. As she reached for the knob, a putrid wind blew and it swung further inward as though it were an invitation. The hand-carved wooden chimes struck one another with a sound more like brittle, hollowed bones. Keomany hesitated only a second, staring at her outstretched fingers, and then she shoved the door open the rest of the way.

It's my place, she thought. *This is my place.* And the thoughts made her mind skip like a stone across stagnant water to her own apartment, and then to her parents' home. Images of their faces swam up into her head like ghosts—an analogy that made her stomach churn so badly she nearly threw up. But she saw them so clearly in her mind right then, her broad-shouldered dad with his hair prematurely white and the map of Ireland on his face and her tiny wisp of a mother with her perfect Cambodian features and silk black hair that made her look more like Keomany's sister.

In the foyer of the shoppe, she could feel the Kia parked back on the street tugging at her as though the little car had its own brand of magick. The safety of her parents was more important than whatever might happen to Sweet Somethings, or even to Paul . . . but Paul worked for her. He was her responsibility in a way. And after she'd seen his face, she couldn't just leave.

There was no sign of him as she entered the shoppe and

rushed across the floor to peer behind the counter.

Her breathing was heavy and sounded too loud. The smell of chocolate that always hung in the air remained, yet it made her even more nauseous somehow. Keomany had remained silent save for small utterings of fear and astonishment. There had been dark things in motion out on the street, and in the back of her mind she had feared drawing their attention.

Now, though, she could remain silent no longer. She could see that everything was as she had left it, the shoppe clean and orderly, despite that its interior was only barely lit by the rotten pumpkin orange sunlight leeching through the display windows. But it was wrong. All wrong.

Her place had been marked by something just as surely as if a pack of wolves had broken in and pissed all over the floor to tag their territory.

"Paul!"

Her gaze swung toward the door that led into the back room. She ran to it, her footfalls too loud now, echoing like her voice. A certainty grew in her that every step, every shout was a beacon to those jagged shadows flitting about outside but she called his name again as she ran to the door to the back. Beside it there was a double switch plate. Keomany switched on the lights for the front and the back room with one slip of her hand.

There was a spark and the sound of something sizzling for a second, then nothing. It surprised her not at all. Her throat was dry and yet her lips were salty and only as she ran her tongue over them did she realize that she was crying. One hand fluttered to her face and she smeared her tears across her cheeks.

"Oh my God," she whispered.

The taste of her own tears, that salt on her tongue, made it all real. She had known it was, of course, but the queer texture of the world had insinuated that it might all be some hallucination, some hyperreal dream. Hell, it had occurred to her that she might have fallen asleep at the wheel and died.

But no, this was not death. Not yet.

Then Keomany laughed, a lunatic chuckle that she had called upon God, now and back when she thought she was going to crash her car. There might be a God, she was willing to allow that. But she had dedicated her life since the age of sixteen to another worship entirely, to earth magick, to the goddess all around her.

But not here, Keomany thought with a chill. *She's not here now, not in this place. Because it isn't natural at all.*

"Paul!" she cried a third time and she stepped through the door to the back room and peered into the shifting darkness and again she froze. Any one of those shadows, black upon black, might have been one of the furtive shadow things she had seen out on the street.

She narrowed her gaze and bit her lip hard enough that she could taste the copper tang of her own blood. Like her tears, though, it crystallized the truth of her surroundings for her. Keomany took three more steps into the pitch black room but would go no further.

"Paul?" she asked, hesitant now.

His face loomed out of the darkness, pale as the moon.

"Keomany? Tell me it's you. Are you real?" he rasped in the tiniest little-boy voice.

Her tears. Her blood. Keomany felt the truth of it inside her just as she felt the filthiness of her surroundings on her skin, breathed it in through her nose with utter revulsion.

"Yes, Paul." *What happened here? What's going on? Did I see . . . things out there?* She wanted to ask all of those questions but that was for later, in the car, after they'd picked up her parents and gotten to the police.

Not the Wickham police, she decided, but elsewhere. The next town. Or the one after that. Maybe even all the way to Montpelier.

"Come with me," Keomany told him, and she began to turn.

"No," Paul said curtly, little-boy voice turning shrill. "You stay."

It seemed as though the very air trapped her then, becoming like taffy, tugging at her arms and her hips and her legs. She was moving through something with substance that slowed her as she turned to look at him again, to see what the change in his voice had wrought in his expression. His face, however, was the same.

But it was only his face.

Keomany had moved to one side and let the light seep in from the front of the shoppe and that tainted illumination showed her what had become of Paul. His face was suspended in the air in the midst of the room upon the tip of a rancid, pitted thing like a tentacle the color of oxidized copper. How it spoke she did not know. It extended, this limb, back into the store room among shelves of hand-dipped chocolates and shipping materials, and now she could hear something thick and fat and wet sliding along the concrete floor and in her mind she recalled the image of a manatee she had seen at the New England Aquarium when she was a girl. Yet she knew that this thing, if she saw all of it, would be nothing like that. It would be worse than what she had already seen, the face and the putrescent limb and . . .

"Oh, you poor bastard," Keomany whispered to Paul.

She had taken in all of this in the tiniest fraction of a heartbeat and in the very next she saw the shadows deeper inside the room begin to unfold. They were sharp, those shadows, and they were coming for her.

Keomany screamed and stumbled, turned and fled back into the shoppe. Something hissed from behind the counter and she glimpsed other dark things rising back there. The smell inside Sweet Somethings had changed once more, the air now heavy with an acrid stench like burning rubber. With another small shriek she launched herself toward the front door and collided with a floor display unit of glass and metal candlesticks. Now she did not even have the luxury of screaming as she fell, the display crashing to the floor beside her with a clanging of metal and a spray of shattering glass.

Tiny pinpricks of fear ran across her flesh like the legs of a thousand spiders. Keomany felt as though her throat was closing up and tears began to sting her eyes. Her hands lashed out to either side in an attempt to leverage herself up and shards of broken glass cut her. She looked back toward the store room and now she saw them far more clearly than she had before, as if they had gathered the darkness of the room to carve their own bodies out of those shadows.

The creatures were not black but the indigo of the midnight sky. Their near-skeletal bodies were covered in a strange armor plating like some insectoid carapace, their heads sheathed by the same chitinous material save for the long, whipping tendril that dangled from beneath each of those plated heads like some obscene and deadly rapier tongue. If they had faces under there, Keomany could not see them, and it was that more than anything else that snapped her from the paralysis of her terror and sent her scuttling backward, slicing her palms to ribbons on broken glass, toward the door.

"What the hell are you?" Keomany cried as she finally spun onto her knees and launched herself to her feet.

The shadow things hissed in unison and her back felt exposed, a target simply waiting for the attack. In the space between eyeblinks she imagined in excruciating detail the long, slender, blue-black talons of the things raking her back, slicing her throat, and ripping her chest open. She could feel the hunger in them, could sense their malign intentions, as though she was receiving those savage images of her own mutilation directly from their minds.

They came after her, then, scrambling and capering like monkeys, those hideous rapier tongues darting about as though they might reach for her, thrust their foul points into her flesh.

Keomany raced for the door.

It was closed.

She did not even slow down. When she reached the door, she thrust herself forward, pulling her legs up beneath her and crashing through the plate glass of the door, her mind consumed wholly with her terror and the thundering of her heart in her chest and the knowledge that if she did not escape these things she might end up like Paul.

In a tangle of limbs and shattered window she tumbled across the sidewalk and a sliver of a thought plunged into her brain, how the tinkle of broken glass upon the walk sounded like wind chimes. Then the display window of the store exploded outward and the shadow things began to leap out after her, crouching and dancing madly in a way that drove home her thought that they reminded her of monkeys.

But she was out of the shoppe now. Sweet Somethings was behind her. Paul was worse than dead and there was no way to know what had happened to anyone else. All she knew was that she had to get off Currier Street and she had not torn herself up crashing through that glass door to die here on the sidewalk or to have herself hollowed out and leave some demon behind wearing her face.

The shadow things came at her and Keomany was already in motion. She felt herself simply flow off the ground as though the sidewalk were helping her up. *I am not going to die,* she thought.

She ran for her car. The sky had darkened, that rotten pumpkin orange seeming to thicken the air, and she understood that whatever was going on here in Wickham, it had been a mistake for her to think that it had happened while she was away. It was happening right now, this moment, still going on, and whatever it was, she had drifted right into the middle of it.

Blood trickling from her hands and slipping like tears down her face where she had cut herself rolling in glass on the sidewalk, she reached into her pocket and grabbed her keys and raced for the little Kia. It seemed to call out to her, to beckon, to urge her on.

I'm not going to die, she told herself again.

Which was when strong indigo talons clamped on her shoulder from behind and others slashed at her legs and then one of them barreled into her from behind, clinging to her back and driving her down to the pavement again. Still no traffic on the street. Nothing moved except the shadow things and her . . . their victim. And she felt it then, the thing she had feared most of all, the thing that made hot, disgusting bile rage up the back of her throat.

Something sharp pushed into the flesh of her back, injecting itself beneath her skin, probing, and she thought of mosquitoes.

"No!" Keomany screamed, her face mashed against pavement. Then, more definitively: "No!"

All of this was unnatural. These things, demons, whatever they were . . . they were an abomination against nature, an atrocity perpetrated against the earth itself. All of this, the putrid orange sky, the fetid air, and the surreal texture of the world of Currier Street . . . it was all wrong, and yet beneath it she could feel the earth, the natural world she worshipped, bucking against it, fighting this cancer that was growing on its flesh.

She felt the thing's filthy proboscis under her skin and the weight of them on her, talons holding her down, cutting her, and a rage blossomed inside Keomany unlike anything she had ever felt before.

Her teeth bit down on her lower lip.

"Get . . . the fuck . . . off of me!" she shouted.

Then Keomany *pushed*.

The pavement all around her shattered as tree roots thrust up from the earth and impaled the shadow things that were on top of her. Other roots twined around their legs and necks and hauled them down to the buckled road. Keomany heard their carapaces crack, saw the living roots slithering through wounds in their bodies like serpents in the bones of the dead, and she knew that it was her doing.

The natural world was striking back at these parasites upon its flesh, and yet it was more than that. It was her. She had summonded them. Even now she felt in the core of her, not in her heart but in her gut, that she was controlling each root as though they were her own fingers, extensions of her self.

Earthwitch, she thought giddily as she staggered to her feet, watching the roots tear the faceless, armored things apart.

"I'm an earthwitch!" she screamed at them, as though it meant anything at all to them.

Keomany had seen power in others who worshipped as she did, but she had never imagined this sort of power within herself. It was too much for her to make sense of all at once, not when she still had to get away from Currier Street alive, not when she had to make sense of what was happening here, of the evil that had infected her hometown, pervasive evil that was spreading like disease.

Bloody and exhausted as she came down from the adrenaline rush of what had just happened, the earth magick that had just surged through her, she stumbled to the little Kia, her keys miraculously still clutched in her hand. Other shadow things were crawling out from beneath nearby cars and several were crouched in the doorway of the Lionheart

Pub glaring at her, but they were slow to approach.

Behind her, seven or eight of the things lay dead or broken beneath the writhing roots that had erupted from the street. These things were evil and savage, but they were not irrational. This was a new thing, what she had just done, and they were hesitant to test its power.

Keomany snatched at the door of the Kia, and a tiny shard of glass still stuck in her flesh sent a fresh jolt of pain through her. She practically fell into the driver's seat, thrust the key into the ignition, and turned it. In the moment before it caught, she was sure the engine would not start, but then it roared to life somehow louder than before, as if it felt the fear and rage and panic in her.

Then she was driving, tearing off down the street with the accelerator pinned, heart hammering in her chest. She could taste her own blood on her lips along with the horrid, syrupy air that blew through the window. She had to slow slightly to turn and her tires shrieked as she rounded the corner onto Briarwood Road. She sped up again and the sky began to change color, the rotten orange bleeding out of the air and sifting back to bright, perfect blue with just a few wisps of cloud. Her chest rose and fell rapidly and she realized for the first time that she was moaning to herself in a soft, keening wail with every breath.

Keomany looked in the rearview mirror and the sky was blue there as well. The intersection with Market Street was ahead and she could see cars going back and forth. Up ahead she saw a couple walking their dog. Quiet Al Pratt and his funny, quirky wife whose name Keomany could never remember. The dog was Brandy, though, she knew that.

The Kia coasted to a stop and then she pressed her foot down on the brake and kept it there as she bent over the steering wheel and let the tears come. Huge, wracking sobs that shook her entire body.

A rap at the passenger's side window made her cry out and jump in her seat. She looked up to find Al Pratt staring at her with deep furrows of concern wrinkling his brow.

"Keomany," the man said, his voice muffled by the closed window. "What's the matter? What's—" He faltered when he saw the cuts on her face, the blood on her clothes and on the steering wheel where her ravaged hands had smeared it. "Jesus God!"

But then Al Pratt's concern and his shock were drowned out by the abrupt intrusion of a police siren. Wickham was a small enough town that the sound was rare and both Keomany and Al—not to mention the man's wife and Brandy the dog—looked quickly up to see a police car tearing around the corner up at the intersection with Market Street. It roared down Briarwood Road toward Currier, and Keomany leaned out the window, craning her neck to see where it was going, frightened for whichever officer was inside that car.

The police car disappeared.

The air shimmered like the surface of a lake and the police car was swallowed up by it just as though it had crashed in the water. Reality wavered around the vehicle as it sped into nothingness, and in the folds and whorls of that fluctuation in the air she saw the putrid orange sky again. Just hints of it. But it was there.

"Holy shit! Did you see that?" Al Pratt's wife shouted. "Al—Jesus, Al, did you see that?"

But Keomany was barely listening. She was staring, mouth open, heart hammering again. Her tears and her blood were drying on her face. *I just came from there*, she thought. *That's where I was. So everything in that direction, everything around Currier Street . . .*

"Oh, no," she whispered, reaching for her glove compartment, snatching her cellular phone from it and punching in numbers. "No, no, no."

The sky was blue again. She had thought it was going to be okay. Something awful had touched Wickham, some evil she could not begin to understand, but she had for just a moment imagined that it could be fixed. There had been evil in the world before and there were ways to deal with it, and if none of those ways were effective, she would just take her parents and leave it all behind.

Keomany clapped the cell phone to her ear and closed her eyes and whispered prayers as it began to ring on the other end.

"Goddess, please," she said. "Dad, pick it up. Pick up the—"

There was a click. A rasp of breath. Keomany felt relief wash through her body with such strength that it almost hurt. Her father was a lifelong smoker and you could always hear it in his voice, in his breathing, even in his sleep.

"Dad? Listen, Daddy, this is important. You've got to get out of town. Leave the house now but don't go through the center of—"

"*Hello, Miss Shaw.*"

A rasp of a voice, like distant thunder.

"*It was nice to see you,*" said that voice that did not belong to her father. "*Come back soon.*"

CHAPTER 4

THE morning of May seventh was lovely in Paris, and yet cooler than those unfamiliar with the city might imagine. It would warm up later in the afternoon, but particularly in the long shadows of the narrow streets around Montmarte, the night's chill held on all through the early part of the day. Still, it was lovely in Paris in the spring. The city had a vigor and joy to it that was palpable, and all the trees and gardens were in bloom.

Kuromaku lived in Bordeaux in the south and had taken a train to Paris. He loved to travel by train so that he could watch the extraordinary French countryside pass outside the window, reminding him with every mile why he had chosen to settle here of all the places in the world a lonely wanderer might have come to rest.

He had arrived the previous day and spent the afternoon along the Seine as always, exploring yet another wing of the Louvre and then visiting the Notre Dame Cathedral to gaze up into the eyes of the gargoyles, searching for some trace of the dread they had once inspired. In the evening he had met with Sophie Duvic, an attractive young woman who had become his attorney when her father had passed away the year before. Lawyer and client had dined in a tiny corner

restaurant in the Latin Quarter and then strolled among the
vibrant night life of the City of Lights.

This morning it was all business, and Kuromaku was
bored.

The office of David Truchaud was situated in a spectacular location on one of the tiny streets that criss-crossed
Montmarte, within sight of the white steeple of Sacré-Coeur
that jutted like a beacon of faith from the top of that hill with
all of Paris unfolding below it. Among the women's boutiques and fine French and Italian restaurants, tucked into
buildings that had seen the ghosts of centuries pass through
their doors, there were some of the most respectable businesses in all of France. Truchaud's office was entered by
walking through a tall, Medieval doorway into a courtyard
filled with colorful flowers in bloom. The silence in that
courtyard was extraordinary. Several doors led off the courtyard, but Truchaud's offices were accessible from the one
farthest to the right, and up the stairs to the second floor.

The architecture was admirable but the décor was depressing as Hell. Kuromaku had managed to gather quite a col-
lection of antiquities over the years. He bought and sold them
as a business and a pleasure and had amassed a significant
fortune in doing so. But in rooms as staid as these—all dark
wood and very little light—the paintings and antique furniture Truchaud had decorated his headquarters with solicited
only gloom from those who came through the door. Kuromaku's own estate in Bordeaux was sprawling and open,
every room planned so that it was awash with light on days
when the sky was graced with the sun.

It seemed to him a horrible shame that they could be so
close to such tranquil beauty as was to be found upon Montmarte, and yet exist in such dreary surroundings.

And so he sat in an uncomfortable yet extremely valuable
wooden chair in Truchaud's office and did his level best not
to fall asleep. The room was so dark and the voices of Truchaud and his attorney so monotone that it was quite a feat
to keep his eyes from fluttering closed. As it was, he had lost
the thread of the conversation and perked up only when Sophie spoke.

Now, for instance.

"Kuromaku," she said, voice somewhat urgent.

He lifted his chin, hoping he appeared to have been deep in thought rather than excruciatingly bored. With the slender fingers of his right hand he reached out and adjusted the crease of his pants at the knee.

"Yes? I'm sorry, what was that?"

His attorney did not smile as many would have done. Kuromaku was Japanese, though he lived in France, and Truchaud was of a grimly serious breed of Parisian businessmen. The proceedings were to unfold with a sobriety and dignity that left no room for amusement at Kuromaku's lack of attention. He knew he ought to be embarrassed, but could not find it in himself to worry overmuch about any unintended insult. He was bored, pure and simple. The rest, as his American friends would say, was all bullshit.

"I asked if you had any more questions before the deal is concluded," Sophie explained.

Kuromaku let his gaze tick from her face to Truchaud's ruddy features and wispy white hair, then to his young, bespectacled attorney. "None at all. I am very pleased that Monsieur Truchaud has agreed to sell his vineyards to me and I look forward to caring for them for quite some time."

"I am confident you will be a splendid caretaker," Truchaud replied, nodding his head politely toward Kuromaku. "I am pleased to have found a buyer for my Bordeaux property who actually lives in Bordeaux."

There was an ironic undercurrent to these words that Kuromaku sensed immediately. The man genuinely had wanted to find a local owner for his winery, but was not entirely comfortable with the fact that though he had lived in Bordeaux for decades, Kuromaku was still—to Truchaud's mind at least—a foreigner.

Kuromaku only nodded in return. "You are very gracious," he told the white-haired man.

They had arrived at that moment when all of them realized the meeting was over and their business concluded. Kuromaku and Sophie rose and offered their gratitude to Truchaud and his attorney, then took their leave. There was something wistful in the old Frenchman's eyes and Kuromaku wondered if he already regretted having sold the vineyards, or if he was simply sad no longer to have an excuse to visit Bordeaux.

But then they were walking down the stairs and out into the courtyard and the bright sunshine, and Monsieur Truchaud was forgotten. It was like that for Kuromaku, and always had been. Some people made an impression upon him so that he could never forget them, not in a thousand years. Others drifted across the path of his life like windblown autumn leaves.

Sophie, for instance. He had known the girl—now twenty-six, he believed—since her birth, and had always been fond of her. She had been a bright, happy child and seemed to be at least as competent an attorney as her father had been. Unlike others who crossed his path, Sophie had made an impression.

Now, as the two of them emerged from the courtyard into the narrow street that slashed across the steep hill leading to Sacré-Coeur, Sophie slipped her arm into his and smiled brightly.

"Congratulations, Kuromaku. I hope that you will let me visit the vineyards from time to time. The photographs are quite beautiful."

He paused and turned to gaze quizzically at her, this sensual, lithe slip of a girl, with her golden blond hair and her eyes so bright and blue. *No*, he thought, *not a girl*. Sophie was a woman now. The understanding came as a revelation to him and he felt foolish because of it. How could he not have noticed this before? He had thought of her for too long as the little girl he had once taken on a boat ride along the Seine. And yet now there was a new spark in her voice, a flirtation that shocked him.

Yet as he looked at her, he realized that it also delighted him. When centuries passed one by the way decades did for others, it became impossible not to see that some mortal beings shone more brightly than others. Sophie had ever been one of those and he had always relished her company.

Now Kuromaku saw her with new eyes.

"I thank you for your help," he said, nodding his head respectfully. "And of course I would welcome you as my guest anytime you desire to visit."

Unlike the courtyard inside the building, the narrow street was mostly shadowed by the buildings on either side. Somehow even in those shadows her eyes sparkled more brightly.

"I'll take you up on that soon," she told him, reaching out a hand and placing it flat on his chest, at the place where his crimson tie disappeared inside the buttoned jacket of his suit.

"And I shall be most pleased when you do," he replied. "For the moment, however, let me show my gratitude by taking you to lunch. There is a tiny restaurant atop the Montmarte where we can sit and watch the artists and the street performers."

A moment of silence passed between them during which Sophie left her palm upon his chest and a curiosity crept into the smile she wore. It seemed to Kuromaku that she was examining him closely, wondering if her interest had been properly communicated, and then deciding that indeed it had.

"Lead the way," she told him at length.

And so he did, slipping an arm through hers and escorting her with a formality that was somehow joyous along the narrow street to the nearest intersection, where they turned to climb up toward the peak of Montmarte. The street was so steep that there were stairs in the sidewalk. Vendors stood beside their carts and tried to sell T-shirts and souvenirs to spring tourists.

As they climbed closer to the top, Kuromaku could see not merely the main dome of the bone white structure of the Sacré-Coeur, but the two smaller domes on either side. Here there were a great many people on the street, mostly tourists by the look of them but also some locals. Brightly colored umbrellas jutted above stands that sold the works of the various artists who made their encampment here, but also crêpes and glaces and various other foods one might conceivably eat while strolling.

For all the horrors and advancements that the world had seen in the past decade, certain things were timeless. This was one of them.

As they walked, Sophie glanced happily up at Kuromaku from time to time. Something was being revealed between them here. He felt it just as well as she seemed to. It was not blossoming, precisely; rather it was more that it was an artifact they had unearthed and were carefully brushing away the soil to reveal.

The top of the hill, Montmarte itself, was lined with trees and splashed with warm sunshine. With the white geometry and exquisite architecture of Sacré-Coeur silhouetted against it, the sky was impossibly blue. The air seemed to shimmer with the tapestry of conversations in half a hundred languages. There was a magick to this place that Kuromaku relished. With Sophie at his side he navigated toward the restaurant, hoping it would still be there eleven years after he had last sat upon its patio and watched life upon Montmarte unfold.

"Perhaps," he said without looking down at Sophie, "you will be able to steal a little time from your clients soon, even if only a weekend, and walk the vineyards with me. There is a kind of ancientness to them that you can taste in the grapes, in the wine. A sip of it, with your eyes closed, is almost enough to transport you back in time."

Just as he had not looked at her, neither did Sophie glance up at him as she responded. Rather she let her gaze drift across the faces of those around her and the canvases of the painters at work on the street as she slipped her arm out of his and let her hand drop so that their fingers touched as they walked.

"I'd come as soon as you'll have me," she said, voice barely audible over the hum of the crowd. Her fingers now twined with his as they walked.

Kuromaku smiled.

The tranquility of Montmarte was shattered by the high-pitched, keening whine of a police siren. All at once people scattered, pulling small children by the hand and glancing anxiously over their shoulders as they moved aside to let the police car travel through the horribly clogged street. Yet somehow in the midst of that sea of flesh, an avenue opened for the police car with its flashing lights, as though Moses were behind the wheel.

Kuromaku held Sophie's hand as they stood aside. As the police car passed, the human sea began to roll back in behind it, filling the gap. In that moment he gazed along the vehicle's intended path and his fingers tightened involuntarily upon Sophie's, hard enough so that she cried out, more in surprise than hurt.

Farther along, upon the very steps of the Sacré-Coeur, the crowd was still scattering and not because of the approaching police car or its siren. There in the brilliant sunshine of a perfect spring day, a hole had been rent in the fabric of the world and it gaped, shimmering like liquid silver where it hung in the air.

"My God, what is it?" Sophie whispered.

Kuromaku did not reply. He knew precisely what it was, for he had seen its like several times before. And even as that thought entered his mind, something erupted from the vertical tear in the face of the world, a thing glistening greenish-black with eight or ten legs that clacked upon the cobblestones as it crossed dimensions, its long tail bobbing and darting about behind it. Its body was narrow and it had no discernible face, only a round circle of eyes that glowed a putrescent yellow. To the humans who shrieked in terror and began to flee, shoving one another, trampling the less fortunate beneath the heels of their fear, it might have appeared some hideous combination of spider and scorpion. But those were natural creatures, things of this world. It was not.

It was a demon.

Sophie screamed along with the others and she tried to tug Kuromaku away with her. There were words to her panic, frenzied questions and pleas for him to come on, to run with her. But Kuromaku was not listening. As he watched, the doors of the Sacré-Coeur opened and a middle-aged couple whose olive skin might have made them Italian or Greek poked their heads outside, obviously curious about the commotion.

The demon was upon them instantly. It scrambled up the steps of the cathedral and that scorpion tail whipped around and jabbed at the exotic features of the woman. Its sharp point punched through her head, obliterating it in an explosion of blood and brain and bone shards that splashed an obscene pattern against the whitewashed face of the Sacre Coeur, the latest masterpiece painted at Montmarte. Her husband cried out in grief and horror and for a moment, just a moment, he stared at the headless corpse of his wife as it tumbled wetly down the steps. Then he realized his own peril and turned to flee.

Too late.

The demon slashed its tail in an arc that tore the man in two, his bisected remains falling not far from where his wife lay dead. The sky echoed back the screams of those who fled. Vendors' carts were toppled, people stumbled over them, artists left their easels and works-in-progress to be crushed beneath the retreating wave.

The police car halted and the doors popped open. Two officers appeared with their guns drawn, faces pale with panic. Nothing they had been taught had prepared them for this—not that such abominations were unheard of in the world in these times, but such things happened in other cities, not here. Not in Paris.

"Kuromaku, please!" Sophie cried, pulling at his arm. "Run!"

He narrowed his dark eyes and turned to her. "Find cover. This will be over momentarily."

"What?" She clutched his arm more tightly. "What are you talking about?"

Kuromaku smiled gently and reached down to remove her hand. The crowd was flowing around them still but thinning, and he walked her several steps toward the café that had been their original destination.

"Get inside. Wait. I'll return."

With that, he spun toward Sacré-Coeur once more, leaving Sophie behind as he began to run. Kuromaku weaved a serpentine path amid the stragglers the mass exodus had left behind. Dozens of people were on their knees or sprawled on the ground, injured, several possibly dead. But there would be time to help them later. For now he sprinted toward where the police car was parked. Behind the imagined safety of their opened doors, the officers shot at the arachnoid demon but the thing ignored them.

It was the cathedral that held its interest.

The demon scrabbled up the steps on its spider legs and froze before the doors of the Sacré-Coeur, scorpion tail poised above it. An ear-piercing chittering noise began to rise from the monstrosity, as though it were screaming at whatever lay within the cathedral. Its tail twitched, daggerlike tip drawing back, and then it stung forward at the open door-way.

As though the air above the threshold of Sacré-Coeur were solid concrete, the demon's stinging tail sent up orange sparks of eldritch energy and the beast staggered backward two steps. It shrieked even more loudly and then began to attack with such fury and speed that its tail was blurred as it sparked again and again off whatever power impeded the demon's access to the cathedral. It raged and screamed and tried to push itself bodily through the door but it could not enter.

Sacré-Coeur was holy ground. The demon was filth and would not be allowed to enter. But soon it would turn its rage to the surrounding area and then more people would die.

Kuromaku ran at the police car, pausing when he was only a few feet behind the officer who had been driving. He and his partner were shouting to one another, wide-eyed with fear. In the distance more sirens could be heard but there was no time to wait. If an army of Paris police arrived on the scene, there was simply a greater chance of more carnage, not to mention the probability that stray bullets would kill those cowering in terror within the cathedral.

"Stop!" Kuromaku shouted to the officers in French.

They spun, weapons aimed now at him rather than the demon. But only for a moment. They saw this Japanese man in a business suit and dismissed him as a threat.

"You must get back, sir," the older of the officers instructed him, barely restraining his panic. "Find somewhere to—"

Kuromaku reached down to his side, slipped his hand into *nothing,* and withdrew as if from nowhere a *katana,* the long curved sword he had carried into hundreds of battles since that day in 1194 when it had been presented to him by his master, the shogun Yoritomo. The katana shimmered into existence now as though he had crafted it from the air itself. He knew well that was how it would seem to those terrified onlookers who now watched the horror unfold from the safety of some shelter or other.

Kuromaku leaped onto the hood of the police car, drawing the attention of the police officers. He smiled at them each in turn as they stared up at him in astonishment and saw the sword held lightly in his right hand.

"Gentlemen, I hope you will do me the favor of not shooting me, either accidentally or otherwise," Kuromaku said.

Then he jumped down to the cobblestones and raced across the space that separated him from the demon. It continued its attack, thrusting its deadly tail again and again at the cathedral as though by sheer evil intent it might tear a hole in the fabric of the wards that protected the place. Its chittering wail had grown even louder and higher pitched and Kuromaku wondered for a moment if the demon was smarter than it seemed, if indeed that scream was not its voice but some effort to find a frequency that might destroy the barrier that kept it from ravaging that holy place.

The katana felt warm in his hand as though the metal were alive. His legs pumped and he sprinted toward the demon from behind. It had barely noticed the bullets that had torn into its flesh, had punctured at least two of its eyes, viscous yellow pus now seeping from those wounds. All of its malign attention was focused on the cathedral.

But now, abruptly, it stiffened and fell silent for an instant before whipping around to face him.

"Damn," Kuromaku whispered.

The police and their guns presented no danger to the thing, but it had sensed him coming. It could feel what he was, or perhaps merely what he meant to do. Somewhere nearby the sirens of approaching police cars grew louder and there were screams from hidden onlookers, and yet there was a kind of desolation to the Montmarte now, as though some hideous apocalypse had already occurred. The place had become a battlefield.

Kuromaku felt right at home.

A war cry tore from his throat as he raised the katana with both hands and leaped into the air, legs tucked beneath him. The demon's stinger tail flashed in the sunlight as it punched toward him, too fast. Kuromaku brought his blade down and it clanged as the metal scraped along the demon's tail. He had parried it, but nothing more.

Now he landed on the ground in a crouch, only feet in front of the monster. Close enough to smell the putrid stench emanating from its punctured eyes and to see the intelligence and bilious hatred in those that remained. Its pincer-like maw opened and clacked shut several times as though it were yearning to tear into him, perhaps to consume him. If he tried to retreat, it would impale him with that tail.

Kuromaku rolled forward and rose again in a single smooth motion that ended with the katana whickering around in a sidelong arc that severed the demon's foremost pair of legs. Black, fetid ichor spilled from its wounds and it rocked backward to compensate for the loss of those appendages. He snapped into a combat stance with the sword above his head, pointed directly at the demon's face, then thrust it forward, plunging it into another of the thing's glowing yellow eyes.

He had seen it all in his mind—he would bury the katana in one of the demon's eyes and the beast would rear back. Kuromaku would ride it forward and then cut, slicing the blade across and down, blinding the demon completely.

But the demon did not rear back. When his blade entered its eye, the abomination pushed forward, pincer-mouth snapping loudly as it tried to reach him. The katana sank too deep into its mass, and when he tried to tug it out or cut a wider wound, the blade grated against bone. The demon drew back, scorpion tail suspended just above it.

The sword was trapped. Kuromaku struggled to free it even as he glanced up and saw the gleaming black dagger of its tail descending. In an eyeblink it would split his chest, shattering bone and tearing flesh.

Kuromaku evaporated. His body, clothing, even his sword turning to mist. The demon's tail cracked cobblestones and it shrieked in fury at his disappearance. But Kuromaku had not disappeared. As nothing more than mist and awareness he slipped along the ground beneath the demon. Its tail was dangerous, but that was not its most vulnerable point.

Underneath that horror his body took form again, molecules reknitting themselves into flesh in an instant, and he lay upon the rough cobblestone in a pool of foul gore from its severed legs. Before the demon was even aware of his presence, Kuromaku thrust the katana up into its soft underbelly and sliced the blade through thick muscle, cutting a wound three feet long. A shower of stinking viscera rained down upon him, soaking through his clothes and drenching his hair. He could even taste it on his lips, and though Kuromaku relished the flavor of blood and the feel of it in his mouth, running down his throat, this was different. This was not human, but demon blood, dripping from its entrails, and it was all he could do not to vomit.

As the demon collapsed upon him, Kuromaku became mist once more and his essence slipped from beneath the grotesque cadaver even as it twitched several times where it now lay upon the cobblestones. Then, at last, it was still. As mist he drifted for several seconds back across Montmarte, sunlight glinting upon the moisture in the small cloud he had become. The mist began to spin, whipping up small bits of litter and grains of sand, a dust devil that abruptly took on human form once more. His suit was clean as if newly pressed and his katana had disappeared back into the nowhere void from which he had drawn it. This was not precisely magick unless it could be said to be some form of molecular sorcery, but he knew onlookers would view it as such.

Kuromaku stood in the midst of Montmarte surrounded by overturned chairs and carts and shattered easels. Several of those wounded or killed in the exodus still lay where they had fallen but he did not need to go to them. Police and medical emergency personnel were even now rushing to their aid. The two officers whom he had urged to stay back stood and stared at him only a dozen feet away but they did not approach. He had likely saved their lives but their terror was plain in the dull gleam of their eyes.

On the patio of the café where he had hoped to share a pleasant celebratory lunch with his attorney, he saw Sophie standing beside a table with her hand upon it as though she might at any moment topple over. Her mouth was agape and there was a sadness in her eyes. No fear, though, and he was relieved to see that.

Kuromaku ran his hands across his lapels to smooth them and tugged at his jacket to make certain it sat right on his shoulders. Then he strode over to her. Sophie watched him come with almost no expression at all. Her face seemed absolutely still now, right up until the moment he stood in front of her and reached out to touch her shoulder.

She flinched.

Pained, Kuromaku glanced away from her. "I see. Perhaps lunch must wait until another day."

"No, I . . . that was incredible," Sophie said, voice almost hoarse.

Kuromaku met her gaze once more, saw her searching his own eyes for answers, for explanations.

"You're one of them," she said.

He frowned. "You must have known, Sophie. I have been a client of your father's since before you were born. Have I aged even a day in that time?"

A girlish smile twitched at the corners of her mouth. "I know. I mean . . . I suppose I knew. But you always seemed so civilized. Sophisticated."

From within the café several waiters and waitresses now emerged along with some of their patrons, all of whom crossed the patio tentatively to gaze over at the stinking mass of quickly rotting demon flesh that lay in front of the doors of Sacré-Coeur. Some of them gave Kuromaku a wide berth but others barely noticed him; apparently they had not been looking out at the conflict as it had occurred. Probably hiding under a table, he would have wagered.

"I did, eh?" he asked gravely. "And what do I seem now?"

Sophie licked her lips anxiously and glanced around at the growing number of people who had joined them on the patio. When she spoke again, she stepped nearer to him and her voice dropped.

"You're a vampire," she said, as if the word were foreign to her lips. And perhaps it was.

"Such a broad and vulgar term," Kuromaku told her. "I'm no more a vampire than you are a chimpanzee. They still hide in the shadows and tombs, fancying themselves creatures of darkness right out of Stoker's fevered imagination.

I'm a businessman. Once upon a time, I was a warrior. Nothing more."

Those last two words rang hollow, even to Kuromaku himself, but Sophie did not challenged his assertion. For a long moment she only stared at him, shifting nervously from foot to foot. The media coverage of the Venice Jihad and subsequent melees had revealed to the world the existence of vampires and demons, and the difference between traditional vampires and beings like Kuromaku himself, who had once called themselves shadows. Books had been written, films made, thousands of hours of news coverage devoted to the revelation that the supernatural was fact rather than fiction, that evil existed. While the Roman Church crumbled for its part in the Venice debacle, faith in general thrived around the world.

For if demons existed, why not something else? Why not divinity?

Kuromaku smiled as he thought of it, glanced back across the Montmartre at the dead demon, this revolting, savage, filthy beast whose very existence proved to millions the existence of God. To millions of others, however, it would be perceived as just another hoax. No matter how much video was shot of it, no matter how many images ended up on the Net, there would be those who refused to acknowledge its existence for the very same reason; because if this thing was real, chances were there were more benevolent powers in the universe as well, and that just fucked up their worldview completely.

"If that smile is meant to be comforting—" Sophie began.

He raised an eyebrow and his grin widened. "It wasn't. I'm sorry. And there's nothing amusing about what just happened here. I was just thinking that no matter how many times the darkness bleeds over into the light, some people refuse to believe there's anything to be afraid of."

Sophie's bright blue eyes were no longer sparkling. She glanced past him at the blood and brain that was painted in a fanned arc across the front wall of Sacré-Coeur and she shuddered.

"But there is."

Kuromaku placed a hand gently on her shoulder. Startled,

she let out a tiny gasp and looked up at him. He nodded, kneading her shoulder just a bit.

"Yes. There is," he said. "But not everything in the shadows is something you need to fear."

For a long moment she stared at him. Then, at last, she gave an uncertain nod. Sophie licked her lips to moisten them, her body shuddering as her breathing quickened, and she stepped closer and laid her head upon his chest.

"Thank you," she whispered.

He frowned. "For what?"

"For being a light in the darkness."

Sophie withdrew from him and glanced around. Kuromaku followed her gaze and suddenly he saw their surroundings with clarity for the first time. The hundreds of spectators, the dead and the wounded, the blood-splashed cathedral, the remains of the demon, the police and EMTs. He had seen all of it before but this was the first time he had truly taken in the entire scene.

All of Montmarte was silent save for the barked orders of the police and the low whispers that rippled through the crowd. Some of them were staring at the blood or the demon, but the majority of the crowd was focused instead upon Kuromaku himself. Several official-looking police officers were muttering among themselves, casting furtive glances in his direction as though they were preparing to question him. This was bothersome only in that he knew there was nothing he could tell them that they did not already know.

"It's going to take me a while to . . . figure out what to make of all this," Sophie said. "But to begin with, do you mind if we go somewhere else for lunch?"

Kuromaku smiled. "By all means."

Yet even as he slipped his hand into hers once more and they walked away from Sacré-Coeur—her fingers trembling, wrapped in his own—Kuromaku felt a cold, numbing dread snaking through him. This was far from the first instance of demonic intrusion upon this reality in recent months. The frequency of such terrifying events was increasing at an alarming rate. There were so many others who dealt with such things that Kuromaku had been content to remain at his estate in Bordeaux and continue to conduct business as usual.

The blood that now stained the pure white of Sacre-Coeur
had wrought a change in him, though. It had acted as a cat-
alyst.

All of this demonic activity was a sign of something
larger. There was no doubt in his mind about that now. The
darkness was spreading across the world and honor demanded that Kuromaku, ronin and vampire, stand against it.

THE MORGAI SANG

The leaved and spotted gray mass of heavy sky
lay serene as Hadley mist thought I had seen it one
again.

So we all had wondered what he was to say these
years. I often was to support to more day than any
darkness we wondered, despite the world and it may
partial that it would know and the other and others.

CHAPTER 5

THE sky was pregnant with the promise of rain. Black thunder clouds hung heavy over the rolling fields of Suzdal, a rural, Medieval town outside of Moscow. The wind gusted and the clouds moved swiftly across the sky. The air was thick with humidity and yet somehow the rain held off, as if choosing its moment, perhaps taunting the farmers in Suzdal, who needed the precipitation for their crops.

Allison Vigeant crouched in the high branches of a tree atop a hill and surveyed the town that unfolded below, the colorful wooden homes and the green-gray dome that jutted up from among them, identifying the church at the center of town. She wore blue jeans, black shoes, and a ribbed green cotton shirt. Her hair was dyed a blazing red. These weren't the clothes for a stakeout, nor was she dressed to be inconspicuous in a rural Russian village.

Fuck inconspicuous.

In her years as a CNN reporter, Allison had visited Russia several times and enjoyed it immensely. The history and grandeur of the place had a storybook quality not even England could match, and a catalog of tragic tales in its past that lent even the most picturesque cities an air of melancholy that had always appealed to her.

But she had spent the past three weeks scouring Moscow and Saint Petersburg and the bloom was off the rose. She was tired of Russia, sick of the food, and demoralized by the squalor she had encountered in the neighborhoods where here search had taken her. But what had soured her mood perhaps more than anything else was simply that all of that time in those two prominent cities had been wasted. Allison had been certain that her quarry would have found some abandoned structure in Moscow or Saint Petersburg to set up their sanctuary.

It was their pattern. They gathered for strength in numbers—not that it ever did any good—and always in the largest cities so they might still hunt the fringes of human society and somehow pass unnoticed. They fed on children and the poor and homeless, and they did everything they could to keep the location of their nests a secret.

But she always found them.

It had been this way for five years. But with every victory Allison and her team achieved, the more desperate the predators became, the deeper underground they went. They had become quite good at hiding, but that instinct to band together, to seek solace in solidarity, was always their undoing. Eventually, she and her team would find them.

Eventually.

Crouched in the tree, she leaned her head against its trunk and laughed softly to herself.

"Fucking Suzdal," she whispered. "Christ."

All those days and nights prowling Russia's most prominent cities, and here they were, camped out on an abandoned farm in a quaint little town a short ride from Moscow. Allison sighed and repositioned herself in the tree. Time to get rolling. From her position she could see the seventeenth-century farmhouse with its crumbling chimneys and green-gray roof that matched the church dome. Beyond that was the barn. They would have to hit both buildings.

A mobile communications unit was tucked inside her ear, and its microphone piece sewn into the turtleneck of her sweater. She knew her words had been picked up by the entire team but did not care, and given their silence, apparently neither did they. The original commander of the squad,

Roberto Jimenez, had died of a heart attack fourteen months ago and he had been the only one who had ever treated Allison like a person. To the others, she was a tool. Often enough they did as she instructed, not because she had the authority to command them but because they knew she would keep them alive. But Allison Vigeant was not officially a member of the United Nations Task Force Victor.

She worked for them. Received a check. Was sanctioned by the U.N. and therefore protected from those who might take it upon themselves to view her as part of the problem instead of part of the solution. Allison was a tracker for TFV, a scout. Her lover Will Cody, who had died in New Orleans five years before, would have appreciated the irony in that. She was their scout, just as he had been for another military operation such a very long time before.

At first she had relished the job, wanting to eradicate them from the earth just as much as her U.N. associates. She had done most of the killing herself, when she could. But with Jimenez dead, the playing field had changed. Even the new name, Task Force Victor, was a joke, Victor being the military representation of the letter *V* used in communication. *V* for vampire. They didn't even want to use the word.

None of them trusted her now. And because of that, Allison did not trust them either.

In the dark skies above, lightning flickered up inside the clouds and thunder boomed in the distance, echoing across the hills and fields.

"Vigeant here," she said into her comm unit. "Ready to go, Ray?"

"Whenever you are," a gruff voice said in her ear.

Ray Henning was the new commander of the Task Force. An American, which had put a great many noses out of joint at the U.N., Henning was a good man and a good leader, but that did not mean he felt any differently about her than the rest of his team did. His team. She had to remind herself of that sometimes. Often she thought of them as *her* team as well, but they were not. Not at all.

"Allison?" Commander Henning prodded.

"Green light," she replied. "It's a go."

The roar of engines filled the air, a sound to drown the

distant thunder. Trucks painted the same dark gray as the sky
appeared from hidden places beyond the treeline and burst
up from irrigation ditches, racing across the fields of the old
farm. She could see only five from her vantage point but she
knew that there were eight trucks. Ray Henning would be in
one of them, but she was not certain which. None of the
trucks were marked, nor was there any indication on the uni-
forms worn by the Task Force that would indicate rank. Henning was sure the vampires would try to kill him if they
identified him as the commander. Allison didn't have the
heart to tell him that the vampires would try to kill every last
one of them, not caring who was in charge.

Her, on the other hand . . . they'd do whatever they could
to kill her. She was the Bloodhound, after all, or at least
that's what the vamps called her.

The trucks rumbled across the fields, surrounding the
house and barn. She could imagine the chaos inside—if any
of the vampires holed up on the farm was awake to notice
the attack. Shouts of fear and anger as they tried to figure
out how to escape. Chances were they had dug hideaways in
the basement where they might hope to avoid detection. Task
Force Victor would find them.

"Keep an eye out," Commander Henning said over the
comm. "It's overcast today. I don't want any of them getting
brave."

"That's why I'm here," she replied coolly, choosing not
to add *asshole*, though the temptation was strong.

"Move!" came the order on the comm.

Across the field the doors to all of the trucks opened at
once and the members of Task Force Victor poured out. All
of them wore body armor that covered them from throat to
toe. Choosing her own wardrobe was one of the perks of just
being a scout. Every member of the team was armed with
an UltraLite semiautomatic assault rifle loaded with specially
devised ammunition. Every bullet carried a payload of a
toxin that prevented the vampires from altering their molecular structure—the first wound would make sure they could
not escape by becoming mist or a bat, and the rest would
tear them apart. Several members of the team were armed
with liquid napalm throwers. Once all the vamps were down

for the count, the place would be razed to the ground.

They'd done this a hundred times in a hundred towns.
Every time, Allison was pissed off that it wasn't the last time.
The vampire population had dwindled to almost nothing, but
almost was never going to be enough.

Gunfire ripped across the sky, echoed off the thunderclouds. Task Force Victor had split into two teams, surrounding the farmhouse and the barn, and now they moved in.
Armored soldiers shot at the doors and windows in short,
quick bursts, then tossed tiny, pear-shaped hand grenades
over the thresholds. The small explosives thundered, creating
a chorus of concussive blasts that tore holes in the walls of
both structures.

Like clockwork, Allison thought.

Task Force soldiers rushed into the gaping holes torn in
the walls and more gunfire erupted from inside. The vampires
would have begun to die by now. Allison saw several of the
soldiers brandish the liquid napalm throwers and saw the
orange flame that spat from the mouths of those weapons.

I should be down there, she thought. *What if these are
the last ones? What if it really is almost over?* She knew it
was not likely that those who had gathered, hidden away, on
this farm were the last vampires on earth. The idea seemed
almost ridiculous. But it was possible. And after what she
had suffered at their hands, what she had become, she wanted
to be sure that she was there at the end, that it was she who
slaughtered the last one. And not with a bullet, nor with fire,
but with tooth and fang, the way it ought to be.

"Need any help, Ray?" Allison asked, breaking the pro-
tocol of a mission for the first time in years. Something was
getting under her skin. She did not want to sit here anymore.

"Do your job. We'll do ours," the commander replied
curtly.

"Don't ever tell me my job," she snarled.

But she did not move and Henning did not say anything
more. The mission continued to unfold, gunfire echoing
across the town. Russian citizens would be coming out of
their homes any time now. The older ones would remember
times when they expected warfare at any moment, and might
well think the entire town was under attack. There were U.N.

security advisors on site for just such an eventuality. The townspeople were their problem.

The human ones, anyway.

The barn was already on fire. Through a massive hole in the side wall she could see two vampires burning, staggering around, likely wondering why they could not change, why they were dying, these things who had thought themselves immortal.

Burn, you fuckers. Burn.

A sudden movement at an upper window of the house caught her eye. Allison glanced toward it just as two vampires crashed through the window with a shattering of glass that was somehow audible even over the cacophony of the gunfire. The vampires began to fall toward the ground, but both changed in midair, transforming with a fluid warping of flesh into large black bats.

They got brave, she thought, and glanced quickly up at the sky. The thunderclouds were so thick and black that it was nearly dark as night now. The vampires had no reason not to make a run for it. In the past, some of them had even tried when the sun was out. But most of them were too afraid, still trapped by the superstitions that had been inculcated within them for centuries. Their kind had complete control over their molecular structure, but that meant that those who believed the sun would burn them or that a stake through the heart would kill them would die just as quickly as if the myths had been true.

Some had overcome such foolishness, the brainwashing of centuries past. But most of them were either incapable of shaking their fear and their faith in their own limits, or unwilling to stop believing the superstitions, because that would mean giving up so much more. If the sunlight could not destroy them, they weren't truly creatures of the night. That would mean they had a choice, that they were not evil by nature but by inclination.

So they fed upon humans as if they were cattle, relished the taste of blood and the screams of the tortured and dying, and they hid from the sun.

Unless they were forced to be brave. Unless they had no other choice.

Allison leaped from the branches of the tree and spread her arms. Even as she fell, she felt her body change, muscles and bones popping and shifting, and those arms became wings. As a brown-feathered hawk, she flew skyward, beating her wings swiftly and gaining in her pursuit on the fleeing vampires immediately. Her beak opened and she let out a cry and she powered after them, closing the distance even as she rose higher.

The vampires must have heard her, but there was nothing they could do but flee more quickly and speed toward the treeline. If they turned to mist, it would slow them down, and she would be able to track them, simply waiting until they took solid form again. Among the trees at the edge of the rolling fields they might stop and fight her. On the ground, the Task Force soldiers would be too close. In the sky . . .

With another cry she swooped down on the nearest of them. As a hawk, she willed her talons to change, not in shape but in substance. They were not flesh now, but *silver*. It was the one part of the legends that was at least partially true—other than the bloodlust, of course. Silver was poisonous to them, and to Allison as well. It hurt . . . but that did not stop her from using it when necessary.

She attacked the nearest one, dropping on it from above, her wings beating powerfully, bearing her along at incredible speed, and she tore into it with those silver talons. Even with the thunderheads above, the vampire had to focus all its will upon keeping this form and not bursting into flame with the wan daylight bleeding through the storm clouds. When she slashed silver through it, the vampire screamed with the high-pitched cry of the bat it had become.

Then it burst into flame.

In midair it began to transform back to human form. She released it from her talons and saw it burn, orange-red flame stoked up by the oxygen rushing past the vampire's falling body. It exploded in a shower of burning cinder and ash that drifted toward the field below.

Allison flapped her wings and rose higher, keen eyes peering about for the second one. The death of its companion had bought it time and it was nearly to the trees. She sped

after it, beating her wings even harder than before, talons flesh once more so the weight of the silver would not slow her down.

As she gave chase, lightning lit up the sky once more and at last the rain began to fall. Slowly, at first, but then the clouds seemed to open up and a heavy downpour showered the field below and the sky became even grayer than before.

The rain pelted her, but she kept flying.

The surviving vampire reached the trees. She saw the bat descending and then it disappeared among the branches, behind the veil of the rainstorm that now obscured the Allison-hawk's view. Furious, she flew faster, tucked her wings in and sped toward the ground at an angle that brought her to earth only feet from the trees. Inches above the ground she changed again, from hawk to jaguar. She felt the muscles of the big cat rippling beneath her silken coat but she had no time to enjoy the pleasures of this form. On foot the vampire had only three choices—wolf, rat, or man.

Allison lowered her jaguar-muzzle to the ground and sniffed. She caught the scent of the rat instantly.

Fool, she thought. But she understood the vampire's rationale. As a man or a wolf he could not escape her, but as a rat it was just possible it might hide from her, there in the shadows of the trees, under the roots and the brush.

It had no idea what she might become. And there was no way for it to escape a jaguar. She prowled the roots of trees, pinpointing the scent of the rat, and she trotted deeper into the wood, fifteen, perhaps eighteen feet. Then she let her flesh ripple and bone pop once more and she stood up straight, human again, blue jeans and green, ribbed turtleneck and black shoes.

Her hair was perfect.

"You lose," she said to the rat she knew was cowering behind a low bush. "You can keep running, but I've got your scent now. You can't get away."

The vampire transformed, blossoming up from behind the brush like some enormous, hideous flower, growing from rat to man in the space between heartbeats. Male. She hadn't been able to tell the sex before. Both of the escapees had been male. He was handsome in a way that she thought ex-

otic; swarthy and dashing, with a smile that would have been charming if he had not been so damned nervous.

"So you have me, Bloodhound," he said in an accent that was not Russian, but Greek. "What are you going to do with me?"

Allison smiled in return. "What do you think?"

His face went even grayer than the sky. Rain fell in fat drops all around them, pattering the leaves of trees and bushes and beginning to mat the hair of the two predators that now faced one another.

"Why? Why do you do this?"

"Why do you?"

The vampire tilted his head, studying her. "I am what my bloodfather made me."

"You are a creature of uncertain fate and equally uncertain purpose," she replied. "We've got the souls of angels and the hearts of demons, but all that means is that we can choose. When it came time for you to choose, you chose badly. You fucked up."

The vampire shook his head and gazed at her with soulful eyes that did not reveal the malignance in its heart.

"Two schools of thought. You say we may choose, yet I believe we are what we are made. But even if you are correct, why do you waste time with us? We are a handful of mosquitoes left to leech at the flesh of the world. There are things far, far worse than vampires in this world. More of them every day. Hell is coming to earth, one horror at a time, and you're worried about a few pitiful bloodsuckers whose only wish is to survive."

"What the fuck are you talking about? You expect me to excuse what you've done because there are demons on the loose? Are you a moron?"

The vampire winced as though she had slapped him. His upper lip curled in barely controlled anger. "Derby, England. Tracy, California. Groznik, Uzbekistan. Hidalgo, Texas. Whispers travel fast. And they're only beginning."

Allison stared at him, a cold finger of dread tracing along her spine. "What are you talking about?"

The vampire smiled. "You'll see. Better kill me now. I'm such a plague upon humanity, such a danger to the world,"

he sneered. "Go on. Make yourself feel better. It will all be over soon enough."

"What do you know?" she demanded, stepping in close to him, snarling, hands clenched into claws.

He lashed out at her then, clutched her throat in a savage grip that began to crush her windpipe.

"Kill me, you bitch. I know you. Allison Silverhands. Bloodhound. Traitor. Do your job, you fucking—"

Pain shot up her fingers as her claws turned to silver and she lashed out, tearing at his face with one hand and punching the other through his chest. She ripped out the vampire's cold, black heart. Then she tore out his throat and his grip relaxed on her own.

At last, he gave in to the presence of the sun beyond the clouds, and he burned, raindrops hissing, evaporating as they hit the flaming cinders that were left behind.

Whispers travel fast. What the hell was that about?

———

CLUB Jinx was one of the hottest venues in Los Angeles, but almost nobody played there just as another stop on a tour. It was too small for that, too intimate. There were no tables and no chairs, just benches along the walls and a balcony up in back, and the bartenders never filled the glasses to the top to cut down on the amount of alcohol that would slick the floor during any given performance.

The performers who played at Club Jinx were almost always there because the publicity people at their label had set it up as a showcase for L.A. media. According to what Nikki had been told, they would all show up tonight: *L.A. Times, Spin, Rolling Stone, Variety, The Hollywood Reporter,* so many others.

No pressure or anything.

"Nikki?"

She looked up from her guitar, which she had been idly strumming and tuning—something she almost always preferred to do herself instead of leaving it to a roadie—to see Aaron Belson standing a few feet away with his hands in his pockets. Aaron had a hundred-watt smile and an aw-shucks good ol' boy manner that might not be a put-on, but in a

town like L.A., where nobody would believe it anyway, it might as well be.

Across the green room, Nikki saw Kyle perk up. He'd been drinking Gatorade and shooting the breeze with Boyd, the bass player, but now both of them turned their attention to Aaron. The other guys in the band were out working with the roadies, preparing for the show. That was good. It made Nikki less nervous.

"What's wrong, Aaron?" she asked.

That good ol' boy smile made her want to hit him. "Not a thing, darlin'. We're all thrilled about this showcase. You're gonna blow them away. Kickstart this tour with a killer buzz."

Nikki stared at him. "But?"

Aaron chuckled. "But . . . I just heard you're planning to throw in some old songs. Cover songs, Nikki. I thought we'd agreed you'd stick to the music on your disc. If you play somebody else's music, the audience will think you're not confident enough in your own material."

For a moment she just gnawed on her lower lip. Then Nikki scowled and shook her head slowly. "Aaron, my heart's going a mile a minute. I'm used to entertaining people, getting down in a groove and bringing them down there with me. Most people, they come to see me for that. To come along for the ride. But the club out there's filled with people who are here to put me under a fucking microscope. That makes me nervous."

"Understandable," Aaron said.

"Oh, I'm so glad you understand!" she snapped. "Since you're not going to be the one up on the stage. I need to throw in a couple of songs that are going to make me happy and comfortable, because if I'm not, they're gonna know it, and they're gonna be on me like fucking vultures. So if I want to play 'Love Me Like a Man' and 'Son of a Preacher Man,' I'm gonna play them. And you know what?"

The good ol' boy grin was gone, replaced by a look of grave disapproval. "What?"

Nikki smiled. "They're gonna love it. Now, unless you want to cancel the show, why don't you go have a seat.

We're going to be starting soon and I don't want you to miss a minute."

For a long moment, Aaron hesitated, obviously dissatisfied with the turn the conversation had taken. Much as she wished she didn't, Nikki understood. This was the label's money they were playing with here, not just her career. They had invested in her, and she respected that they had to safeguard that investment. But at the end of the day, if she didn't feel good about what they were doing, that was going to come through on stage, and nobody would benefit from that.

"Trust me," she said emphatically.

Aaron nodded. "I do. We do, Nikki. Just promise me you won't open or close with a cover, please?"

She put out her hand. "Deal."

He shook it, then glanced over at Boyd and Kyle. "You guys have a great show. It's an amazing disc and we all believe in you. This is just the start of an incredible ride, so hold on tight. We're just getting started."

Nikki smiled at Aaron and then he left, shutting the door behind him. The second he was out of the room, Boyd laughed softly and Kyle shook his head.

"Was it just me," Kyle asked, "or did he sound almost genuine at the end there?"

"He's not that bad, you guys," Nikki chided them.

Kyle walked over to her and smiled as he reached out to tuck a lock of her hair behind her ear. "Babe, that's one of the things I love about you. You always want to give people the benefit of the doubt. But trust me on this: Belson's your number one fan right now because of the buzz. Maybe he's right, and we're in for a long ride, but if he's not . . . the first time they put out something with your name on it that tanks, he's gonna be telling everyone in hearing distance that he predicted it, knew it all along, and never understood why the label backed you for so long. It's just the way these guys are built."

She punched him lightly in the stomach and he let out a melodramatic little "oof" followed by a bark of protest.

"And maybe you're just a cynic," Nikki said sternly.

"In this business, only the cynics survive."

The words stung her more deeply than she ever would

have expected. Nikki frowned and turned away from him, smoothing the legs of her pants and then checking the fit of the shirt she wore, a burgundy silk thing that buttoned down from the top and then flared open below her breasts to reveal her abdomen. Sexy but not whorish. Of all the things the label people had tried to get her manager to convince her to wear, this was the only one she even considered. Most of the time it really did seem all about the packaging, but Nikki spent a lot of time convincing herself that the label had signed her because of her music, because of her talent. She couldn't become a cynic, would not allow that to happen, but the truth was that she did wonder if Kyle was right . . . and what if he was? What if it was true that only the cynics survived?

"Then I guess I'm as good as dead," she told him, and she shivered.

"Hey, Nik, don't be—" Kyle began.

He was interrupted by a knock on the door, and Nikki was glad. She was really fond of the drummer. Kyle had been very good to her. But she was not going to get into this argument with him, not going to be revealed as naïve or infected with his cynicism. That would be too much like surrendering, when she knew she should feel triumphant that she had even gotten this far.

The door to the green room swung open and Bones, one of the roadies, poked his head in. "Ready when you are, Nikki."

The rumble of the crowd could be heard from the front of the club, but this was more the buzz of conversation than anticipation. The lights had obviously gone down, for Nikki could hear some cheering—probably from the hardcore fans that had heard about the showcase event on her website and bought up the couple of hundred tickets that hadn't been given away by the label—but it wasn't like other shows. It was more subdued. She had never felt more pressure over a gig.

"I'm ready," she lied. Her gaze ticked toward Kyle. "Let's go."

Boyd and Kyle both came up behind her and followed her out of the green room into the dimly lit corridor back-

stage. They stepped over wires and slid past roadies and lighting guys scrambling into position. At the entrance to the stage, Trey and Sara waited for them. She played keyboards, he played guitar. And that was her band. Nikki had spent years on the road pretty much by herself, but it was nice for her in that moment to realize that she really wasn't in this alone. She glanced around the group gathered there, nodding to each of them.

Without a word she led them onto the stage. Nikki and Trey picked up their guitars, Boyd grabbed his bass, Kyle and Sara sat down behind their instruments. The lights were warm, but not as hot as they were at some clubs. Still, when she glanced out at the audience, she smiled at no one in particular, not wanting to meet the eyes of the critics. At the front of the stage a small mob had formed, the diehards, the people who had come out to see her. It was them she would play for. Always them.

Nikki raised her right hand, and when she brought it down, the band slammed into the opening chords of "Shock My World." She loved the song, but would never have started with it if the label hadn't insisted.

By the first chorus she realized it had been the right choice. The fans in attendance erupted with joy and sang along, obviously surprised that she would play the song at the beginning of the set. Surprised, and thrilled. And the critics would see that, would have to feel at least a little of that enthusiasm.

Nikki smiled, and for the first time, she let her gaze drift deeper into the club, feeling relief wash over her. This was going to be fine. It really was. The second tune was her favorite cut off her disk, "Been Down This Road Before," and she followed it with the first of her covers, "Love Me Like a Man." It wasn't her song and they all knew it. Bonnie Raitt had recorded (the best-known version) years ago, but nobody in the audience seemed to mind as Nikki ground against the guitar and put her heart into the suggestive lyrics.

It made her feel good, let her relax into the groove. With a laugh she glanced around at Kyle, who grinned as he hammered the drums. When she turned back to the audience, she looked down at the guys and girls who were right up in front, swaying back and forth with their arms in the air.

All but one.

In the midst of the crowd gathered right in front of the stage there was a woman who looked frozen. She stood completely still, watching Nikki on stage with an expression that seemed somehow both sad and patient, as though someone had dragged her along and she would rather be anywhere else. Nikki sang a few more lines, but she was distracted and her eyes wandered back to the motionless woman, a pretty Asian with black, silken hair, dressed in a baggy, unflattering sweatshirt. There were cuts on her face, healing, but there. She looked as though she had been attacked by a cat.

A shiver went through Nikki. The woman's expression was unnerving.

She started to turn again, looking around to Trey and Sara off to her right to get some moral support, so that she could shake the weird vibe she'd gotten off the woman.

Then a spark of recognition hit her. Nikki had been playing guitar so long, performing since she was a child, that she didn't miss a note with her hands or her voice. But her thoughts were spinning as she looked at the audience again, trying to appear as nonchalant as possible, never forgetting how vital this performance was to her career.

Her gaze locked with the haunted eyes of the unmoving woman in the audience. Nikki knew her now.

Keomany Shaw. Nikki hadn't seen her in years, and if someone had asked her the day before, she'd have said a reunion with her old friend would have thrilled her. But Keomany was just standing there, gazing up at the stage with a face etched with sadness, as though they were the only two in the room and the music did not even exist.

Nikki forced herself to look away, to find a way to settle back into the groove again. Whatever had brought Keomany here, whatever had made her look so forlorn, it would have to wait until she had done the job she had come to do. The music had to come first. The music, and the critics who were scrutinizing her every move.

All through the rest of the set she avoided looking at

Keomany as best she could. Nikki had no idea what had drawn the other woman here, but there was one thing of which she was quite certain.

It wasn't going to be a happy reunion.

CHAPTER 6

AS much as the city of New York had changed in the early years of the twenty-first century, there were things about it that remained remarkably the same. Technology ran rampant, particularly in Times Square and the surrounding blocks, as well as in the subway stations, and yet some of the neighborhoods seemed almost to move backward in time.

Perhaps it was a response to the tech evolution going on elsewhere, but though the Village had remained as eccentric and eclectic as ever, it had also regressed to a more genteel age. Trees were cultivated along the sidewalks more than ever before and a kind of neighborliness had begun to blossom that was almost alien. The businesses in the area also reflected these subtle changes.

Once upon a time The Hovel had been a counterculture restaurant, but more and more over the years counterculture had become simply culture. Vegetarian dishes and world cuisine were the order of the day and no one gave waiters with green hair and multiple piercings a second glance. Ritual scarring and drastic body modification were still common enough, but growing less so, given that the shock value of it had worn off.

Peter Octavian sat at a small table on the sidewalk patio

in front of The Hovel with Carter and Kymberly Strom, enjoying the warm spring day and the view up and down St. Marks Place, watching the world go by.

"So .what do you think of the place, Peter?" Kymberly asked as she snapped her chopsticks at the Ocean Stir Fry Plate on the table before her. Kymberly was an attractive, dark-skinned woman with truly regal African features and an easy grin that had charmed Peter the first day he met her.

"It's . . . interesting," Peter replied with a wary glance at the souvlaki that had been set in front of him.

Carter laughed loud enough to draw the attention of others who were having lunch on the patio, but he either did not notice or did not care. Peter's agent was a big, heavyset bald man with enormous hands and an accent from his native Austria. People at gallery shows were often astonished to learn that this was Carter Strom, a respected figure in the art world. But Carter liked that: challenging people's expectations.

"Kym, haven't you realized yet that Peter doesn't like things to change?" Carter asked his wife with a broad wink at Octavian. "He's upset we didn't go to the White Horse. You should have said something, Peter."

He pronounced "something" as *zumzing*.

Peter gave them a lopsided smile. "If it bothered me, I *would* have said 'zumzing.' "

Kymberly laughed at his teasing, but Carter shot him a stern look.

"You make fun uff the man paying for lunch? Not very wise, I think."

The conversation deteriorated further and then they were all occupied with eating their lunch. Peter was surprised to find that his souvlaki—which he would usually only buy from a sidewalk vendor; they always seemed to have the best—was quite tasty. Throughout their lunch he hid quite well the fact that Carter was right. He was not pleased with the change of plans. Kymberly had been ill when he had finished the last painting for the upcoming show and so they had put off their celebratory lunch until today, when Carter had insisted that Peter try someplace new. The Hovel wasn't very far from his apartment, but ever since he had become

mortal again—ever since he had begun to age once more—
Peter had found comfort in things that were routine.

Once upon a time he had faced in battle a sorcerer named
Liam Mulkerrin. The man had used magick to prolong his
human life, so that as he neared the century mark, he still
looked barely sixty. Peter knew that he could similarly ex-
tend the time remaining to him, but in his heart of hearts he
was afraid of what would come after.

It was strange to him, because he also relished his mortality. After all the years he had spent knowing he could not
die, to be human again made him appreciate every second
that ticked past on the clock, for he knew he would never
get it back again. Anytime he wished, he could ask for the
gift of immortality from Kuromaku or Allison; either of them
would be pleased to give it to him. But he would not.

Peter feared what was after death, but he found a pleasure
in the smallest things in life that he knew he would not have
felt if the specter of his own eventual demise did not loom
ahead of him. He wanted to live a simple, mundane life as
part of the flow and rhythm of humanity, after so many centuries existing outside of it.

But Carter and Kymberly had reminded him today that he
had taken such desires to the extreme.

The Hovel was a fine restaurant, the world that churned
along St. Marks Place vibrantly alive. And the souvlaki was
tasty.

"Thanks for suggesting this place," he said as he finished
his meal.

Carter looked up with one eyebrow raised. Then he
smiled. "You are very welcome, my friend."

"Kymberly, I'm glad you're feeling better," Peter added.
"Now just stay healthy. The show's only a few weeks away
and I won't get through it if you aren't there."

Her expression was soft and kind and Peter reflected that
she did, indeed, remind him of a queen. He had met royalty
several times in his life . . . his father had been an emperor
. . . and Kymberly Strom had the bearing of a monarch.

"I wouldn't miss it, Peter. And it will be wonderful, of
that I'm quite certain."

"I wish I shared your confidence," he told her.

A busboy came and began to clear some of the plates from the table. Carter began to go over some of the details of the upcoming gallery show again, but Peter was never very concerned with such things, preferring to leave them in his agent's hands. He nodded solicitously, but then let his gaze drift across the patio.

A trio of girls whose ankles all bore identical rose tattoos sat chattering happily to one another several tables over. Further along there was a fiftyish couple toasting one another with fluted wineglasses and sharing a glance the intimacy of which was both inspirational and intimidating. On the other side of the table where Peter and the Stroms sat were two young men who spoke softly to one another, ignoring their lunch, their hands clasped across the table. A first or second date, Peter thought. And beyond them, three couples arrayed around two tables that had been pushed together.

And from the street a scream.

Peter snapped his gaze up to find the source of that horrid, guttural, animal sound. When he spotted the woman crossing the street toward the open patio of The Hovel, he stiffened immediately. She looked forty, but given the filth and grime that covered her and the snarled nest of her hair, she might have been considerably younger or even older and he would not have been able to tell. Her clothes were torn but she hugged herself in a way that kept them clinging together.

As she crossed the street, a car locked on its brakes and the driver sounded the horn. The filthy woman's head moved with fits and starts like a nervous bird, and she walked with the same jerky motion. Her eyes were wide, and when the driver of the car shouted out the window at her, she seemed not to notice.

Abruptly, as if at some unseen horror that had appeared in the middle of the street, the woman let loose another ferocious scream. Then this strange creature rushed the rest of the way across the street, paused on the sidewalk just beyond the shrubs that lined the patio, and began to jabber to the large party at the two shoved-together tables, all of whom were studiously avoiding looking at her. One of the men rose and strode purposefully toward the entrance to the restaurant,

likely to bring a hostess or manager to shoo the homeless
lunatic away.

"Poor thing," Kymberly said, the sadness in her voice
palpable.

"Someone like that, it's terrible," Carter added. "Probably
she was a patient at a hospital somewhere, and her insurance
ran out. They do that, you know? Put the crazies out on the
street when they can't pay."

But Peter was not paying any attention to his friends.
Instead, he was *listening* to the woman. This horrid vision
of madness who was speaking to the people on the patio,
insulting them in a language not spoken on Earth in tens of
thousands of years . . . a language Peter had only ever heard
spoken in Hell.

"Excuse me," he said, standing up so quickly that the legs
of his chair scraped loudly upon the patio stones.

"What? Oh, Peter, no. Don't get involved. There's nothing you can do."

He paused and glanced at them, a frown creasing his forehead. These were his friends, certainly. But how well did
they really know him? Not well at all, in fact, for he had
only given them a little of himself. They had seen the artist,
the soft-spoken man who kept his hair too short, did not
shave often enough, and who had begun to go gray at the
temples.

Then he smiled. "Let's see."

Peter moved past the young men on their date, who had
stopped holding hands, their time together now soured by the
madwoman's approach. He strode toward the large group at
the joined tables, some of whom glanced at him curiously as
he approached. At the edge of the patio he simply stepped
over the shrubs.

The nattering, grime-covered woman turned on him, spit-
tle flying from her mouth as she threatened him in that ancient tongue. Then she blinked, as though a bit of awareness
had crept into her mind, and an agonizing scream erupted
from her throat.

"I can help," Peter told her.

But then her eyes narrowed again as the thing inside her
regained control. It spat at him, and where it flecked his

cheek, the saliva burned. Peter quickly wiped it on the leg of his jeans and the denim began to smolder there until he slapped at it a couple of times.

The thing inside the woman was grinning madly.

Peter raised both hands and contorted his fingers as though he were a puppeteer controlling some invisible marionette. Under his breath he muttered several words, and then he whipped his arms back, tugging hard. The woman's mouth opened and she screamed again, only this time, those who heard that scream would have noticed that there were two voices screaming—one the woman's and one a low, guttural, savage snarl that had not been there before.

A yellow fog the approximate shade and stink of urine erupted from her mouth as though she had vomited it up. It began to dissipate but Peter would not allow that. With a wave of his hand and a flick of his wrist he crafted a sphere of energy that enveloped that putrid yellow fog completely. Then he whispered to it and the sphere grew smaller and smaller until at last it disappeared with a tiny pop like a bubble blown by a child. Those who were nearest to him might have heard a muffled, guttural shout of pain in that moment, but it was abruptly cut off.

The woman collapsed and Peter grabbed her, held her until she was steady enough to stand. She stared at him with moist, brown eyes filled with fear and anxiety.

"Where am I?" she asked.

"Greenwich Village. New York City," he told her.

Her mouth dropped open in astonishment and she gazed about her. Tears began to streak her filthy face and she shuddered. Then she turned to him again, almost violently. "When?" she demanded.

When he told her the date and the year, she covered her mouth and could not speak for twenty or thirty seconds. Peter waited patiently, and when a small moan escaped her, he touched her shoulder gently.

"It's over now, though. It's done. Is there someone you can call?"

She bit her lip and then slowly nodded. Peter slipped his phone out of his pocket and handed it to her. For a long moment she only stared at it and then she began to dial. It took three calls before she reached someone, and when she did, there was a great deal of sobbing, during which he turned back toward the restaurant for the first time.

The patio was crowded with patrons and wait staff who stood and stared at the bizarre tableau he and this woman created. They had given up any pretense of not being interested and were openly gawking now. All save Carter and Kymberly, who had apparently paid the bill and were now making their way out of the patio—the proper way, rather than over the shrubs.

His friends hurried toward him. The look on Carter's face was one of great concern, but there was something almost beatific about Kymberly's expression.

"That was extraordinary, Peter," she said.

"Yes. Extraordinary, true," Carter agreed. But then he took Peter by the arm and leaned in toward him. "What did you just do? What happened here? Who is this woman?"

Peter glanced at Kym and then back to her husband. He sighed slowly. "I don't know who she is. She was possessed by a demon. I . . . helped. I get the impression she's been . . . lost . . . for a long time. I'm letting her use my phone to try to find someone to come and get her, to take care of her."

They were staring at him. Then Kymberly shook her head slowly.

"You told us about your past, about the Shadows and your magick. But it's all been so prevalent in the news this last decade that I supposed we never imagined you were telling the truth."

"You thought I was lying?" Peter asked, taken aback.

"Not lying, precisely," Carter replied. He pronounced "precisely" as *pre-zeiss-li*. "We thought perhaps you needed to spin such wild tales as inspiration for your paintings."

Kymberly seemed almost embarrassed. "I suppose it was too much for us to believe that you lived what you were painting. We'd heard of Peter Octavian . . . of you. But it seemed like a perfect marketing tool."

"A tool," Peter repeated.

His gaze ticked back and forth between his friends but he did not know what to say. He supposed he should not have been surprised, and maybe in his heart he was not. Human beings spent a great deal of effort trying to put order upon the chaos of the world in their own minds, to make sense of things. As such, they often refused to believe in anything that did not fit their ordered image of the universe right up until the time when denial was no longer an option.

But he was disappointed in them, and he felt it keenly.

"We . . . we saw that thing that you pulled out of her," Kymberly was saying. "And then the green flame that came from your hands. I never would have believed it if I had not seen it."

Peter smiled sadly. "No. I suppose most people wouldn't."

He had no idea how this was going to change his relationship with the Stroms, but he was in no mood to discuss it with them now. There were people in the world who knew precisely who and what he was, but all of them were so far away. He felt very alone suddenly.

"Excuse me?"

Peter turned to find the grimy woman holding his phone out to him. He reached and took it from her, fighting the urge to clean it before slipping it back into his pocket, not wanting to embarrass her.

"Did you reach someone?" he asked.

She nodded, wiping at her face, her tears leaving swaths of clean white skin. "My brother. He lives up in Katonah. Still, thank God." For a moment she paused to catch her breath, perhaps to prevent another jag of crying. "He's on his way down to get me. Do you think they'll just let me stay right here until he arrives."

Peter's eyes narrowed and he turned to search the crowd on the patio for the manager. "I'll make sure of it," he said.

When he looked back at the woman, there was the flicker of a smile on her face. "I'd kiss you, but I don't want to get you dirty."

"I don't think I'd mind very much," Peter told her.

"Oh, I couldn't!" she said, looking down at her clothes.

"Another time, then."

Despite all the horror she had experienced—all that she was experiencing even in that moment as she tried to put together how much of her life had been torn away, how long she had wandered under the sinister control of some infernal intelligence—the woman grinned broadly. It lasted just a moment, that full-wattage smile, but Peter thought it was a hopeful sign that she would be able to come out of this with most of her self intact.

It took a lot of effort to convince the Stroms to go on about the business of their day and leave him there at The Hovel with the woman—whose name turned out to be Janelle King—but eventually Carter admitted he had another appointment and he and Kymberly reluctantly departed. Peter was relieved when they were gone. He needed some time to himself.

Though he wasn't foolish enough to try to convince management at The Hovel to let Ms. King into the restaurant dressed as she was, they were kind enough to allow the woman to sit there while he made a run to the deli two doors down, just to get some food into her. A short while later, her brother arrived to pick her up. Their reunion was heartbreaking.

Peter started for home without waiting for them to even get into the brother's car. He wanted to be home, to put some Mozart on the sound system and brew a pot of tea and sketch the face of Janelle King. He often sketched in addition to his paintings, but his pencil sketches were not for public display. He often painted moments and places from his past, but for the most part, he avoided depicting people in his paintings.

The faces he saved for his sketches, and the sketches he kept. They were just for him, those faces.

To help him remember.

———

IN the time she had spent sitting on the curb in front of Peter's apartment on West Fourth Street, Nikki had made up her mind half a dozen times to leave. It had been more than an hour and she felt ridiculous just sitting here waiting like some junior high girl hoping for a glimpse of her crush. But every time she opened her mouth to put voice to her desire to depart, words failed her. She couldn't do it to Keomany.

After her showcase the night before last, Nikki had beckoned her old friend backstage. During the time they had known one another—when both of them lived in New

York—the two young women had both felt lost, searching for something they couldn't even name. That kinship had created a bond between them, though they had not really kept in touch.

But as soon as Keomany had begun to tell her story, silent tears slipping down her face, Nikki had reached out to embrace her. Her friend had shaken in her arms, as though something inside her had shattered into a thousand pieces.

Now—thirty-six hours later and all the way on the other side of the continent—they sat side by side on that curb and Nikki reached out and slid her arm around Keomany.

"How are you holding up?" she asked.

Keomany smiled wanly. "I feel like shouting. I wish he'd get back."

"Me too."

Then Keomany winced as a thought struck her. "God, Nik, what if he's not even around? What if he's out of town?"

Nikki had thought of this already. If Peter didn't show up by nightfall, they'd have to rethink their plan.

"I have some other friends we could talk to," Nikki told her.

Keomany nodded. "I know. I know and that's . . . thank God for you. I didn't know who else to come to." Her voice quavered but she kept it together. Whatever had shattered inside Keomany they had managed to put it back together, but she was still fragile.

Nikki didn't blame her. She had been through a lot herself, but she had never had to do it alone. Nikki massaged Keomany's shoulder. "You did the right thing."

But Keomany was looking past her, up along West fourth Street. A hopeful spark shone in her eyes. "Is that him?"

Nikki followed her friend's gaze, and she saw him.

"Peter," she whispered under her breath.

In her mind she had played this scene out a hundred ways, and in each of them she had hung coolly back and remained aloof, let him fumble with his words, making certain he knew that she could live without him. But as she saw him walking down the street in blue jeans and a crisp white button-down shirt, Nikki felt herself rising from the curb almost as though she were being pulled toward him by some outside force.

A laugh escaped her lips as she took several steps toward him. His expression was a million miles away, but that was nothing new for him. She saw that he had gotten a bit gray—prematurely, if you went by his biological age—but otherwise he looked just as she remembered him, that ragged cut hair, that strong chin. Peter had come within twenty feet of her before he at last lifted his gaze. His eyes widened as he saw her.

"Nikki?" he asked, as though he thought her a mirage.

"Hey, stranger," she said, and for a trio of heartbeats, she managed that aloofness she had planned for so long.

Then that familiar, almost goofy grin lit up his face and she could not help herself. She crossed the twenty feet between them in a run and collided with him with such force that Peter had to take two steps back to keep them both from falling. He wrapped his arms around her and she pressed her face against him and they both laughed and just held one another.

Then Nikki pushed away from him and tapped his chest as she narrowed her eyes. "Why didn't you ever try to get in touch with me?"

Peter looked stricken. "You told me not to."

Nikki shook her head. "Fucking men." Emotion welled up inside her but she would not let herself cry. She bit her lip lightly and then glared at him again. "In all the time you've been alive, you haven't learned better than that?"

Stop it, she told herself. *Stop telling him the truth. It's only going to hurt more after.*

But she didn't care. It didn't matter. Neither did Kyle. He was a sweet guy, but she had never stopped being in love with this guy, the man right in front of her.

Peter stared at her, the depth of his melancholy visible in his eyes. "Nikki, I just wanted to respect your wishes. I wasn't very good company and you wanted to get back out in the world, and—"

"And I wanted you to come with me!" she shouted, loud enough that it echoed off the buildings up and down the quiet street. "You can paint anywhere!"

But that last part she had already said to him, many times.

She sighed. "I'm sorry. I didn't come here to rehash old conversations."

Peter looked down at the ground, then past her to where Keomany stood on the sidewalk in front of his apartment. At length his gaze returned to Nikki. And all of a sudden she realized something—deep down in his eyes, she saw a glint of the edge that had drawn her to him in the first place. Hope fluttered inside her.

"You have no idea what it means to me, seeing you today. I needed something . . . I don't know, a sign, I guess. I think maybe you're it," Peter told her. "I was feeling a little lost."

Nikki reached up to touch his face. "We all feel that way sometimes. Sometimes *most* of the time. What's wrong? Can I help?"

Once again he took her in his arms but this time there was more tenderness to it, and a kind of relief. It gave her a comfort she had nearly forgotten, just to be held by him.

"I never tried to find you because I didn't think I was the same person anymore. I was afraid that if I followed you—"

Nikki shushed him and Peter stopped talking. She hugged him more tightly, and when she spoke, she did not look up to meet his eyes.

"How could you be the same?" she asked, searching his eyes. "You went through a lot of changes, Peter. In the course of a couple of years you lost almost everyone you cared about. I'm not even going to talk about what you went through before that."

She pushed him back now and looked up at him, smiling at the absurdity of it all. "You were fucking depressed, you asshole. Anybody would be. Maybe that's why you're such an amazing painter; all great artists are depressed. But I know the old you's in there somewhere, I can see him in your eyes, and I need him now.

"I need *you* now.

"There's something awful happening up north, something terrible and unnatural. Human or shadow, artist or sorcerer, we both know that what you are at heart—what you'll always be—is a warrior. When you tried to give up that part of you . . . that's what got you so lost, Peter.

"Now it's time to change that.

"Time to go to war again."

———

THE train rolled south toward Bordeaux, traversing beautiful French countryside that Kuromaku never tired of admiring, no matter how many times he made the journey over the years. On this particular trip, however, as he gazed out the window of the private, first-class compartment that had been reserved for him, his mind was not on the scenery.

After the horror that had unfolded upon the steps of Sacré-Coeur he had begun to make certain gentle inquiries into similar occurrences—*incursions*, as he thought of them, of demons upon the human world. Kuromaku had been aware that the frequency of such incursions was on the rise, but even the most cursory examination of available data, even a basic search of the Internet, revealed a spike in the number of incursions that was startling.

And deeply troubling.

Once upon a time there had been a force in place to combat such things—a cruel and corrupt organization drunk on its own power—but that force had been eliminated. After years in which the resistance of humanity to their presence had been severely weakened, the evidence suggested that the creatures of shadow, the demons and other monsters, had at last begun to realize that there was no one left with the power to oppose them should they come *en masse*.

Fortunately, the various breeds of hellspawn hated one another and so the likelihood was small that such creatures of chaos would ever manufacture enough order to organize a sizable incursion. Still, the frequency with which shadows were breaching the human world was far too great and Kuromaku knew something had to be done to combat it.

"Where are you?" a soft voice asked.

It took a moment for the words to reach him, lost as he was in his thoughts. Then he turned in his seat and looked at Sophie, who sat opposite him in the private compartment. She wore a sleeveless, pale blue dress that clung wonderfully to her slim form, and her hair was tied back with a ribbon that matched the dress. Her golden hair shone in the sun that streamed in through the train window, but despite her youth there were tiny lines around her eyes as she studied him with a sad sort of curiosity.

"I'm sorry," Kuromaku replied. "There's a crisis brewing. It's getting under my skin. Once we reach Bordeaux, there are people I must notify. After that, I'll be better able to focus."

She leaned forward, her elbows resting on her knees, and the top of her dress gaped open indecently. Kuromaku politely averted his eyes. It was not that he did not want to see what might be seen, only that he did not want to come by such a sight dishonorably.

"I feel like I'm running away," Sophie said, her voice low, and she sat back again.

Kuromaku frowned and searched her eyes for a connection. "You are not running. You are accepting my invitation, that is all."

She smiled softly, nodding slightly. "All right. I suppose I just regret that it isn't under different circumstances. I'm glad to get away, and I am looking forward to spending this time—"

With you, she had been about to say. But Kuromaku understood why she had let the words remain unsaid. They were only just beginning to explore whatever spark this was between them. He knew that she was anxious and wished he could explain to her that it was natural for her to feel that way. She was young and he very, very old. Sophie was human and Kuromaku had not been that for a very, very long time.

A part of him was surprised that she had agreed to his suggestion that she return to Bordeaux with him, after what she had seen him do. After what she had seen him become. Most women, no matter how adventurous they thought themselves, would have locked themselves up in their rooms and changed their telephone numbers. It had happened before.

Now he focused his gaze upon hers and smiled. "You really are a remarkable woman. I'm not sure you realize that. A rare creature."

The sun was still upon her face but he thought the glow from within her then was even more brilliant. "How is it you always know just what to say? And from you it doesn't sound like bullshit, when if another man said it, I might just laugh?"

"Because I would never say it if it wasn't true," he told her, with utter sincerity.

Sophie regarded him carefully a moment, something else going on behind her eyes that Kuromaku could not decipher.

"My father respected you more than any other client he ever had," she said, her voice low. "I've had a crush on you since I was twelve years old."

All thoughts of demons were obliterated from his mind. Kuromaku looked at Sophie, her petite body beneath that light summer dress and her eyes searching his for some vital bit of information, and he could think of nothing else.

"Apparently I don't always know just what to say, because I have no idea how to properly respond to that," he confessed, smiling playfully.

Sophie lowered her chin so that when she gazed at him now, looking up at him, there was an incredible seductiveness about her glance. And yet he did not think it was purposeful.

"You spend too much time thinking about what's proper," she told him, then let her gaze drop to the floor. "I have to ask you something."

"Please do."

Sophie looked up at him and locked her gaze with his. "Do you drink blood?"

Kuromaku raised an eyebrow. For a long moment he simply looked at her and then he leaned back against his seat. "The simple answer is yes."

Her lips must have been dry, for Sophie ran her tongue along them to moisten them. She looked very nervous, and Kuromaku could not blame her. The woman had agreed to accompany him even after discovering that all the rumors about what he was were true, all her suspicions had become reality. If she had indeed been attracted to him since she had been a girl, that helped him to understand her decision. But now she needed to know more about what he was.

"And the complex answer?" Sophie prodded.

Kuromaku regarded her carefully. "I'm surprised you didn't ask this question before we left."

She glanced away. "Maybe I was afraid that I wouldn't have the courage to come with you if I knew the answer."

Kuromaku let his gaze drift for a moment out the window to the French countryside the train sped through. Sophie had been nothing but honest with him and it was only fair that he do the same. Honor demanded it. He turned to face her again.

"Very little of what is thought to be true of those you would consider my kind is accurate. Fundamentally true are two things: silver can be poisonous to us, and we require blood to survive. Perhaps what you're asking is do I kill for blood, or take it forcibly. The answer to that is no. I am not a predator."

Sophie blushed as she glanced down, the silken flesh of her neck gleaming in the sun. "Do you want to drink mine?"

From her tone it was clearly a question, not an invitation. Still, it gave Kuromaku pause. How to answer this honestly without frightening her? At length he nodded once.

"Yes. But not as much as I want to kiss you."

He could hear her sharp intake of breath from across the cabin. Sophie looked up at him, smiling open-mouthed in a way that was incredibly erotic. A stray lock of her hair had hung loose from where the ribbon tied it back and now she reached up and tucked it behind her ear.

"Well, why don't you then?" she asked.

A shiver went through Kuromaku. He was unused to such boldness in himself or in his lovers. Certainly he had enjoyed the attentions of a great variety of women in his long life, but with those he had truly cared for there had always been a bit of ritual and courtship involved, and never such a frank revelation of attraction. Yet there was a vitality to this electric connection he felt with Sophie that could not be denied.

He rose to cross the compartment. There could be no mistaking his intention here, nothing subtle about the process of kissing her. His only purpose in moving those few feet from one side of the compartment to the other was to kiss this beautiful young woman whose blue eyes drew him so magnetically toward her.

Something rocked the train hard and he stumbled, reached out to plant a hand flat upon the broad window to keep his balance. The entire compartment was thrown into a filthy gray gloom. From a perfect, clear day, the sun had abruptly been blotted from the sky.

Sophie swore under her breath.

Kuromaku saw the sudden fear etched upon her face and he turned to look out the window. The landscape had changed. They were passing through the village of Mont de Moreau and he could see buildings on fire. A forest of enormous posts, perhaps torn from a fence, jutted from the lawn of a home they sped past. Humans had been impaled upon those posts.

Winged demons circled like vultures in a sky filled with a thick soot that had cast everything but the fire in a drab gray, as if they had passed from their world into a realm of demons. And perhaps they had.

The train rumbled as if the tracks were no longer smooth. Sophie lurched over to grasp Kuromaku by the waist, and she stood with him, staring out the window. With a scream of brakes and a terrible, stunted shuddering, the train slowed to a halt in the midst of that infernal landscape.

"What's happened?" Sophie whispered. "My God, what is it?"

"I'm not sure," he confessed. "But I fear we will be forced to find out."

CHAPTER 7

KUROMAKU had fought in many wars, had slain enemies both human and otherwise. Yet never had he seen a vision so hellish as that which unfolded beyond the broad window of his train compartment now. The village of Mont de Moreau had been transformed into a tableau of damnation that was positively Boschian. But this was no painting, no portrait dredged up from the fevered imagination of a troubled artist.

"Armageddon," Sophie whispered beside him.

They stood together and stared out at the ravaged village, at the dark, heavy sky, clouds hung low and stained with a hideous orange light. Kuromaku shook his head, mind awhirl as he tried to make sense of it.

"Impossible," he said. "The rest of the world was unaffected."

"As far as we know," Sophie replied, her voice very small.

"True. But look out there. This has not only just happened. Recently, perhaps. Hours ago, no more than a day. But nowhere else that we know of. If this is Armageddon, it is Armageddon writ small."

Screams and shouts of alarm and horror had erupted

within the train and the cacophony continued as passengers reacted to the infernal domain where their journey had come to an unforeseen end. In the filthy sky two large shapes circled the forest of impaled human corpses like vultures. A moment later one of them darted downward, growing larger and larger until it landed among the dead upon their stakes. Kuromaku cursed under his breath. The thing was an abomination, a red-scaled beast with black-feathered wings, a trio of prehensile tails each tipped with a vicious stinger, and a long, thin beak. It reached for the nearest stake, upon which a woman had been impaled through her back, so her arms and legs dangled toward the ground in a macabre, gymnastic bit of puppetry.

It tore her from the stake, and Kuromaku was glad that he could not hear the sound of it through the glass. The winged demon drove its sharp beak into the wound at the dead woman's back and tore free a chunk of flesh, which it gulped down. Then it spread its black wings and took off once more into that dreadful sky. The thing flew above the train, and both Kuromaku and Sophie craned their necks to watch its flight.

Out of the corner of his eye, Kuromaku spotted something else up there. Something moving in the thick, bilious clouds, like a man o' war jellyfish floating there, dyed an infected red, tendrils swaying beneath it like a storm of solid rain. He only caught a glimpse of it before the clouds swallowed it again, but that one glimpse made him think it was larger than any living thing he had ever seen or imagined.

Silently, he prayed that Sophie had not seen it. Already, what she had seen was enough to crush a human spirit.

Sophie gripped his arm at the bicep and Kuromaku glanced down at her crystal blue eyes. She seemed paler than he had ever seen her, her facial expression a mask of calm that must have taken extraordinary effort to maintain. Kuromaku thought that it was a mask brittle as a China teacup, and he feared what might happen to her mind if the mask were to crack.

"What do we do?" she asked in a whisper.

Kuromaku had no time to formulate an answer. And any answer he might have given would have been eclipsed by the impact that struck the car they were in at that moment. It rocked over to one side and they tumbled together in a tangle of limbs and slammed into the wall beside the compartment door. For a moment Kuromaku was certain they would tip over, he felt the train tipping, but then it slammed back to the ground, still upright.

The screech of rending metal and the shattering of glass filled the car along with the cries of the other passengers. Kuromaku leaped to his feet and reached his hand to his side as his sword manifested there at the nearly unconscious summons of his mind. He drew the katana with the ring of steel upon steel and grabbed Sophie's hand, helping her to stand.

His own astonishment had dulled him for several moments, the horror that had enveloped them almost impossible to believe. But now they must believe or die. Adrenaline seethed in him now, and he sublimated all wonder, all fear, and gave himself over to the instinct of the warrior.

"We are not safe here," he told her. "Stay by me."

With a tiny, hollow laugh, Sophie swore in French. "Where else am I going to go?"

Kuromaku rammed open the compartment door and lunged into the passageway, Sophie close behind him. To the left was a crowd of terrified passengers, many of them bleeding or injured in the abrupt stop or the massive impact upon the train. To the right there were others, but rather than crowding into the corridor to escape whatever was outside, this group were stumbling headlong toward Kuromaku and Sophie.

He pressed her back against the wall of the corridor and people streamed past. An enormous bear of a man reached out and grabbed Kuromaku's shoulder, tried to sweep him along.

"Weg rennen, du idiot!" the German man bellowed, eyes frenzied and wide.

Kuromaku shook him off, knocked his arm away. Instead he stood as tall as he was able and tried to see what pursued these people. At the back of the fleeing passengers he saw a man and woman together hustling a small boy along in front of them.

Then he saw what it was they ran from. It was a rich

blue-black, the color of lividity bruises on a dead man. The thing loped after the passengers, its plated body, limbs, and razor talons so thin it seemed like every inch of it was a blade slicing the air. Its head was sheathed in a hard black shell from beneath which a spiked proboscis extended, darting ahead of it, wagging like the sensitive antennae of some nightmarish insect.

The thing was nearly upon the family of three, and the woman screamed. Her husband grabbed at their son and the boy stumbled, began to fall.

"Kuromaku!" Sophie cried.

But he was already moving. He stepped away from the wall, pushing the husband and wife behind him, even as Sophie reached down and caught the falling boy, tugging him up and toward her.

The plated scythe of a creature froze and its head turned up toward Kuromaku, where he stood before it in the passageway. The spike that protruded beneath its face-shell whickered toward him as if taking his measure.

Silent, it leaped at him, fingers like daggers slashing down toward him.

Kuromaku lowered his head and lunged forward, the point of his katana cracked through the demon's armored chest, and he impaled it. The demon's only cry of protest was a bizarre, almost hydraulic hiss. Then it slid off his blade to the floor of the passageway.

More screams came from the next car. Heavy thuds struck the outer skin of the train. Metal tore and more glass broke, and in that passageway, no one spoke. All eyes were upon Kuromaku. He saw them staring at him, wide-eyed, as though quietly praying to him for deliverance.

Then someone at the other end of the car screamed and more of those scything monsters leaped into the corridor from the compartments on either side, apparently having crashed through the windows. Kuromaku hissed air through his teeth and let loose a guttural shout of fury and regret.

He snatched Sophie's hand. "Come," he told her.

But she held back. He stared down at her. "We must find shelter."

Her head shook. "What . . . what about everyone else?"

Kuromaku glanced once more along the corridor to where the monsters had begun to drive human passengers down onto the floor, tearing into them. The wet sound of their talons ripping flesh could be heard in among the screams.

He sensed the one behind him more than he heard it, and spun, decapitating it with a single swipe of his blade. Then he snapped around once more and shouted at Sophie to be heard over the cries of agony and anguish. The sounds were deafening, the horror overwhelming.

"If we stay, we die with them! You are my priority! We must survive to find a way out of this!"

Once more he tugged at her arm, and though she hesitated a moment, it was only a moment. Then they were running down through the train car. At their heels came the family Kuromaku had saved. He hoped that they could keep up.

At the end of the car came a thunderous noise and the door to the train crashed inward, two of the scything demons atop it. Others followed, swarming in after them.

"Here!" Sophie shouted.

Kuromaku turned, saw that she was leading the family into a side compartment, carrying their little boy herself, and he swore. Then he followed them inside and rushed past them to the window. With a single blow he shattered the window and shards of glass rained down around him and blew out onto the blasted, ruined landscape.

In the preternatural darkness outside the train Kuromaku could still see the town and the hideous forest of the dead, and darting silhouettes like night-black cutouts against the putrid orange sky. Screams came to them, there in the compartment, but most were from inside the train. The car rocked with each new impact.

Immediately beyond that window he spied only two of the scythe-limbed demons, as well as a plodding, mammoth creature covered in porcupine quills. It lumbered toward the train on two massive feet like those of an elephant. The enormous creature had twin upturned tusks jutting from its mouth and a flat, bald, apelike pate. Where its eyes ought to have been were only long, wet vertical slits that seemed to pucker and breathe like the gills of a fish.

With one rapid glance over his shoulder to confirm that

they were still alone in the compartment, Kuromaku leaped out through the shattered window, landing in a crouch on the ground below. In his right hand, he gripped his katana, but now in one fluid motion he reached down with his left and withdrew from that same impossible place the wakizashi that was its mate. The grip of the short sword felt good in the palm of his left hand. So often he sparred or did combat with only the katana that sometimes he forgot the beauty of fighting with both blades at once.

The lumbering, quilled behemoth opened its tusked mouth and let out a long bellow. As if in response, the two skeletal, razor-edged demons twitched and turned in Kuromaku's direction. The spikes from their mouths searched for him as though they could use those wavering needles to see with.

They sprang at him, streaking across the ground that separated them. Kuromaku braced to meet their attack, then sidestepped, leaping in with balletic grace into a pirouette in which both swords spun with him in a circle, the blades so swift they blurred almost to nothingness.

Jagged claws gored his back but Kuromaku did not flinch, merely completed the motion he had begun. His swords found plated flesh, one cracking and slicing through the abdomen of a scythe-limbed demon, severing it in two, and the other coming down to cleave the head of the second demon in twain. Skull and natural-shelled helmet fell away like the twin halves of a walnut.

He glanced quickly in both directions along the ravaged, derailed train. There were others, many others, so many that he could never have counted, and they swarmed across the train, leaping through windows and capering up into doorways and tearing through the metal skin of the train.

Twenty feet away, the elephantine beast covered in quills bellowed at him again. The wet slits where its eyes ought to have been now spread open like twin vaginas and Kuromaku saw that tiny, green-black, pinprick flames guttered in their depths. It took one shambling step toward him, and Kuromaku knew then that it was too slow to catch them.

He spun toward the shattered window of the train, knowing any moment could bring more demons over the top of it, or through the interior door of the compartment.

"Come!" he snapped, his voice a low rumble that he prayed would not garner attention. He reached up toward Sophie, but she stepped aside to allow the other woman to jump out ahead of her. The woman's husband passed their son down to her, and then Sophie came out.

The man was last, and he shot a nervous glance over his shoulder before leaping out onto the blasted terrain.

All throughout the horror that unfolded around them, the young boy had remained pale and wide-eyed, yet silent. *Shock*, Kuromaku knew. The boy was too stunned to respond to their surroundings. He had shut down. *Probably for the best.*

A loud bellow came from behind them and Kuromaku spun to see that the enormous quilled demon had come closer, but only just.

"This way," he instructed them quietly, then he turned and led them off toward the village at an angle that would take them around the field of impaled corpses. It was the only thing to do. There was no telling what might lurk on the other side of the train, away from the village. At least in the village itself, there might be shelter of some kind.

Unconsciously he sheathed the wakizashi, the short blade disappearing beside him. He reached out for Sophie's hand. She clasped his, fingers twining. Together with the young couple, the father holding his son in his arms, they ran toward the village.

Another bellow came from behind them, but now when Kuromaku turned, he saw that the quilled beast had turned its back to them. A barrage of quills sprang from its back, fired like arrows from a bow. They sliced the air toward them and Kuromaku stepped in front of the others, let his flesh take those painful spines.

Instantly, a fire raged through him.

Poison, he thought.

It seeped into his blood and Kuromaku doubled over in pain, teeth gnashing.

"Run!" he commanded the others.

Sophie balked, reaching for him, calling his name.

"Get out of range!" he roared. "Go!"

She must have seen something in his eyes, for she did

what he had ordered. Sophie ushered the others on and they kept on toward the village, running across an open expanse of land just beyond the field of corpses.

The poison was agony to him but it did not keep Kuromaku from changing. He willed his body to become mist, nothing but molecules of moisture in the air, and in that way he cleansed himself. He drifted after the others, propelling himself, and transformed once more into a hawk. His wings beat until he was behind them once more, then he glided to the ground and once more took the form of a man. The katana was a part of him and so he had taken it unconsciously into himself. Now it manifested once more in his hand and he surveyed the land around them.

Satisfied that there were no enemies near, he hurried up beside Sophie. They had reached a street. Ahead, on the edge of the village, what had once been a sizable chateau was engulfed in flames that seemed garishly bright in comparison to the sky. Tongues of fire leapt into the air and yet the air was already so hot and dank that there seemed little heat from the blaze.

"What do we do?" Sophie asked, staring at the burning chateau and then at the village beyond. "Where can we hide?"

For the first time Kuromaku really focused on the French family that accompanied them. The man was thin and darkly handsome, his wife also slender but taller than he. The boy had his father's complexion and his mother's hair. The husband and wife were whispering fearfully to one another, he stroking her hair. When the man looked up at Kuromaku, his gaze was defiant.

"What is happening here? How can this be?" the man asked in French.

"I wish I knew," Kuromaku replied. "But somewhere in Mont de Moreau there must be a locked basement, or a windowless storage room in the back of a shop. We must find some refuge. Soon enough those things that attacked the train will tire of it."

"And then we die," the man replied. "Even if there are no windows, there are doors. You saw what they did to the train. Like bees in a hive."

But even as the man spoke, Kuromaku looked past him, through the curtain of flame that leapt from the burning chateau, and on a hill in the midst of the village he saw the spire of a church jutting into the hell-stained sky. Even at this distance the steeple looked white, he could see stained glass windows that were unbroken, and the church called to him like a beacon.

"There," he said, pointing. "Stay close to the faces of the buildings," he snapped off in rapid-fire French, reaching out for Sophie's hand and getting them all moving deeper into the village, toward the church. "Head for the church. Whatever happens, do not stop. I will keep them off us as best I can."

He shot a quick look back at the train. It had come off the tracks, the rails twisted and torn, the skeletal, scythe-limbed demons still tearing at it. Several of the three-tailed carrion beasts circled overhead. They had to move now while the demons were focused on the train. It pained Kuromaku to know it, but the deaths of those remaining on the train had bought them this time to escape. He could not have saved them all—not against those odds, not and still have saved Sophie. She had come at his invitation, and he cared for her. He would not trade her life for that of strangers.

The only wise choice now was to find safety, find time to determine what evil was afoot here, and do everything in his power to stop it from spreading beyond this little village.

For Mont de Moreau, and the people aboard that train, it was already too late.

———

IN the tomblike silence of his basement office, Father Jack Devlin poured two fingers of Crown Royal into a tumbler and tossed it back before he had even set the bottle back down upon his desk. The whiskey burned its way down his throat, a little nugget of warmth that slid down inside him. He cupped his hand around the tumbler and let his gaze drift, seeing nothing. A niggling feeling at the back of his neck made him look up. He snapped his gaze over to the big mason jar on the shelf above the desk, where the hideous little Cythraul demon stared back at him. Its mouth was drawn taut in an obscene grin.

"Fuck you!" he screamed.

With a snarl, his chest rising and falling in heaves, Father Jack stood and snatched the Cythraul off the shelf, opened the bottom drawer of a filing cabinet, and set the jar inside.

"Little shit. See how you like it in there."

A tiny sound came from the jar, and Father Jack thought the Cythraul was laughing at him. He slammed the drawer of the filing cabinet and slumped once more behind his desk. With a pained sigh he leaned far back in his chair and slipped his glasses off. He set them on the desk and ran both hands across his face, through his red hair. For a long moment he held himself there, trying to make sense of what had come to pass in the previous twenty-four hours.

But he could not. Could not make sense of it. Could barely comprehend it. The implications were so vast that each time he turned his mind to it, the priest felt a flutter in his heart that he had never felt before. It was fear. He knew that. For it was accompanied by a chill deep inside him, a cold dread that the whiskey could never warm.

Which did not stop him from trying.

Jack Devlin had never been much of a drinker, but now he poured himself another generous shot of Crown Royal—the fifth or six—and downed it quickly, drawing the back of his hand across his lips. *Why the hell are you even using the glass, Jack?* he thought bitterly.

But he knew the answer. The whiskey was bad enough on its own. Drinking it straight from the bottle would seem far too much like giving up.

"Fuck!" he screamed, and he threw the whiskey glass across the office. It struck the filing cabinet where he had stashed the Cythraul, and shattered there, shards falling upon the carpet.

Father Jack started to laugh, shaking his head. He felt like an idiot. Throwing the glass was a bit of melodrama he had seen in too many movies, and now here he was copping from some film or another because he couldn't find a way to get a handle on his own emotions.

"Idiot," he whispered to himself.

He laughed again, shaking his head, and then fell silent. There was a sheaf of paper on top of his desk, along with his computer, but he had no interest in looking at the reports from Hidalgo again. He knew what they said. His face crumpled and his eyes grew moist.

"Oh, dear Lord," he whispered to himself, not kneeling or clasping his hands, but penitent and reverent just the same. "Where do we go from here?"

The silence in the office deepened. After a moment Father Jack closed his eyes and sighed. Then he rose and crossed the office, grabbing his trash can so that he could begin picking up shards of the broken glass.

When he was on his knees on the carpet, a knock came at the door. Whoever it was did not wait to be invited, and the door swung open before Father Jack could even begin to stand.

The priest stared in amazement.

Peter Octavian stood in the doorway. Behind him were two women Father Jack had never seen before. The mage raised an eyebrow and leaned casually against the door frame.

"I'm sorry, Father. If we're interrupting prayer time, we can come back later."

For a moment Father Jack only stared at him. Octavian was an enigma, one moment an amiable man, a regular guy, and the next waxing nostalgic about ancient battles and fallen cities any historian would kill to have seen with his own eyes. As he leaned there, Octavian's eyes sparkled with humor and benevolence. The priest felt himself a good judge of character, and he liked Octavian, despite the sorcerer's history and the fact that the man made him nervous. Now, though, Octavian must have seen something in his face, for he stood up straighter and frowned as he studied Father Jack.

"What's wrong?" he demanded. "What happened?"

Careful not to set his hands in any broken glass, Father Jack gave up his task and rose. "Come in, please," he said, gesturing to Octavian and his companions, an earthy blonde who looked somehow familiar and a petite Asian woman with long, silken hair.

"What brings *you* here?" the priest asked.

Octavian looked thoughtful. Then he stepped aside to let his companions enter the room. "Father Jack Devlin, meet Keomany Shaw and Nikki Wydra. Nikki, Keomany . . . Father Jack."

The priest's hands fluttered in the air as he waved them toward his desk. "I just broke a glass. There's nowhere to sit. A dungeon down here, actually. So watch your step, but come in."

He turned abruptly to look at Octavian face to face. "I was just getting ready to call you."

Octavian nodded slowly, as if the news did not surprise him. "I don't suppose Bishop Gagnon wanted to invite me for dinner."

Father Jack could not muster a smile. "No. I'm afraid not."

The two men stared at one another for several seconds. It was Nikki who broke the silence.

"Father Devlin—"

"Please," he said reflexively. "Call me Jack. Or Father Jack. My father was Father Devlin."

Nikki blinked and glanced at Keomany before looking back at him.

"Sorry," Father Jack said, chagrined. "Very off-color humor. Sort of ingrained in me. But please do call me Jack."

Nikki smiled and the priest felt warmed by it in a way the whiskey had been unable to accomplish. He realized then where he knew the name from. She had been involved with Octavian during the New Orleans business, some kind of performer now, he thought.

"Jack," Nikki said, "Peter tells me you're an expert on the crazy stuff. Something terrible's happened in a town called Wickham, in Vermont. Keomany's hometown, actually. We could use your input."

Father Jack listened, his gaze ticking toward the anxious-looking Asian woman and then back to Nikki. But Octavian seemed to haunt the office, drifting around, studying the books and the paintings and the plants in a way that unmistakably marked him. He had been a detective once. For years. Father Jack saw now that he still had that eye.

"I'd be happy to help in any—"

Octavian stopped at the filing cabinet. Father Jack stopped speaking, surprised to see the mage bend and open the bottom drawer, removing the jar and holding it up so the light passed through, illuminating the Cythraul. The sorcerer gave the priest a look that Father Jack could not read.

"What was this filed under?" Octavian asked.

"P," Father Jack answered instantly. "For pain in my ass."

The mage smiled. "We'll get to Keomany's story in a moment, Jack. Meanwhile, why don't you tell us what's got you so skittish."

Octavian glanced at the broken glass on the floor, then at the bottle of Crown Royal on the desk, and Father Jack nodded. This was what he had been about to call Octavian about anyway. Bishop Gagnon would not approve, but he was past the point of caring. With a heavy sigh, Father Jack moved to the desk and leaned on it. He had no chairs for his guests and so would not take the single seat in the office.

"Hidalgo," he said.

The mage frowned. "I restored that manuscript for you. The Okulam should have been no problem at all."

"They weren't," Father Jack replied. "I translated the last of that and phoned it in. Our people in Texas scoured the town of Okulam in just under two hours."

Nikki Wydra shook her head as though his words weighed heavily upon her. "Why do I hear a 'but' coming?"

The priest nodded. "But. As of yesterday morning, Hidalgo was gone."

The other woman, Keomany, uttered a tiny gasp and looked stricken by his words. Her elegant features went slack.

"What do you mean gone?" she asked, the first time she had spoken since her arrival.

"Gone," Father Jack replied. "Or possibly not. Something is still there, that much is certain. Father Tratov reported that witnesses claimed the sky changed color, that it went dark, turned—"

"Orange," Keomany whispered. "Orange like rotten pumpkins."

The priest stared at her, his mind racing as he realized the connection between this woman and Hidalgo. Slowly he nodded. "Orange. That's right. But then the sky was blue again and the town seemed to have disappeared. Only at the edge of Hidalgo, there's some kind of . . . membrane. It's invisible, but it can be pierced. Father Tratov sent two of his deacons through it. He reported the orange light seeping out when the membrane was torn."

"And they never came out," Octavian said.

Father Jack looked at him gravely. "Not yet. And then after they'd gone through, it hardened. Maybe it takes a while. Whatever the process, it's impenetrable now."

The mage gazed at him. "And you think the town is still there, on the other side of that membrane?"

"Don't you?" Father Jack asked.

He saw the way Octavian's eyes ticked toward Keomany, as if measuring his response against her needs. At length, the mage nodded slowly.

"Let's hope so."

"It was the same in Wickham," Keomany said.

Father Jack listened as she told her story. It echoed what had happened in Hidalgo, and the dread in him began to grow even larger. This was no longer an isolated incident. It was no longer just a tiny village on the Tex-Mex border. It was a town in Vermont. And who knew how many others.

"What's going on?" Nikki asked aloud, though Father Jack doubted her question was meant for any of them.

Octavian had begun to pace. Father Jack watched him, his own mind working on the problem, trying to find some reason behind it. He and the mage had spoken at their first meeting about the growth in the number of events in which demons had appeared upon the earth plane. The frequency had been increasing radically, particularly in the last year.

Mulling it over, he looked at Keomany, who was watching Octavian even as Nikki laid a comforting hand on her shoulder.

"You didn't say how you escaped," the priest said.

The woman glanced at the ground. "I . . . just lucky, I guess. Timing. I got out right before it was all closed off. I . . ."

And she said no more. Father Jack sensed there was a part of the story Keomany Shaw had not shared with them, but he chose not to push her on it. Not yet. If, at some point, it seemed some missing facet might be the key to what was happening, he would insist. For now, he let it lie.

"Peter? Any thoughts?"

Octavian looked at him. "You've considered that the Oculam had to have slipped onto this plane somehow? That there had to be a crack?"

"A breach, yes, it's only logical," Father Jack agreed. "My guess would be that whatever's happening in Hidalgo came through the same breach, that it leaked somehow."

"But that would mean there had to be some kind of breach like that in Wickham, too," Keomany said, shaking her head. "My family's lived there for decades. I grew up there. I lived away for a few years, but I've been back awhile now. I don't remember anything freakish. No demons."

Silence descended upon the office for a moment as they all glanced at each other. One by one, each of them focused on Keomany. Father Jack gazed at her with deep sympathy. But there was really only one way to know.

"Oh, shit," Keomany said, as her eyes lit up with understanding. "We have to go back, don't we?"

Octavian set the Cythraul jar down on top of the filing cabinet. The thing leered disgustingly at him but the mage ignored it. He walked to Father Jack and held out his hand. The priest did not hesitate. Nothing in his life, nothing in his research, had prepared him for this. With his resources and Octavian's memories and magick, an alliance was the only reasonable course of action.

After they had shaken hands, the mage turned to the two women. He reached out to gently touch Nikki's shoulder, but his gaze was on Keomany. To her credit, she did not look away.

"Not just back," Octavian said firmly, face to face with Keomany. "Back isn't enough. We have to go *in*."

CHAPTER 8

AT dusk in Venice the setting sun cast a reddish-golden hue across the domes and spires and arches of the city and onto the cobblestones of the broad piazzas. Despite the filth of the canal waters and the grime in its back alleys, for those few precious moments each day Venice became a fairy tale kingdom, a wondrous place where anything was possible, if just for a moment. In its narrow alleys, which had long since been cast into darkness by the angle of the sun as it slid west, the shadows only deepened and those things that now seemed possible were far more sinister.

Allison Vigeant feared nothing from those shadows, those darkly ominous alleyways, and yet this night—her first visit to Venice since the Jihad—she remained in the Piazza San Marco, where the laughter of tourists created a kind of veil that separated her from the rest of the city. The Basilica di San Marco stood glorious guard over the piazza at one end, four golden lions crouched like sentinels upon its roof, the last rays of the sun glinting from the ferocious statues.

It was possible a day might come when she would feel comfortable here, in this city once known for its serenity. But Allison could not imagine it. She sat on the patio of a pleasant trattoria that catered to the tourists and served gelato out a window so that people might eat it while wandering the cobblestones. A five-piece band played Italian music and American standards at the edge of the roped-in patio, and people stopped to listen briefly before wandering on.

Allison sat on the uncomfortable metal patio chair and sipped a perfect bianco. Out in the piazza the golden light continued to bleed from the air and a deep blue replaced it, all of these extraordinary colors that slipped by each day almost unnoticed. The pigeons that swarmed the piazza in search of sympathetic humans to feed them—and often perched atop the heads and arms and shoulders of such people—fluttered in formation up from the cobblestones to the eaves and ledges where they had made their nests. There had been children in the piazza with their parents, families, and older couples. Yet now, as nightfall came on, there seemed only young lovers and small troops of traveling students.

Venice changed with the onset of night.

The music from the band seemed to increase in volume, as did the laughter from the patio and the clinking of wineglasses within the restaurant. Across the piazza, even the lapping of waves that spilled onto the cobblestones from the Grand Canal seemed louder as well. And yet everything else grew silent.

Allison shivered and tipped her wineglass to her lips once more. The wine was so dry it left her even more parched than she had been, and she realized she ought to have ordered something else. Her gaze rested upon a gondola all the way on the other side of the piazza. A pair of dark-haired women were holding hands and speaking with one of the gondoliers, perhaps haggling over a price for his services. Seeing the women together made her think of old friends she had lost, and a kind of melancholy swept through her. Still, it was a welcome relief from the anxiety she had been feeling . . . about Venice, about everything.

"You look troubled, babe. I hate to see lines on that pretty face."

The voice seemed to drift to her out of the gathering dark, and yet out of her past as well. A smile spread across Allison's face as she turned and looked up at Carl Melnick. It had been a decade since she had seen the man, and though the years showed on him, Allison thought they had improved his appearance. Carl had always had a rather ordinary face, but now there was a thickness to it, and contemplative lines around his blue eyes, and his hair had gone a salt-and-pepper gray that lent him a certain dignity.

"Hey," she said, voice barely a whisper as she stood to embrace him. Carl had been a news producer for CNN during the time Allison had been a reporter there, and they had been quite friendly as associates, but not really outside the office. Allison was surprised at the intensity of the pleasure she felt at seeing him.

"Allie-cat," Carl said, holding her close. "It's really wonderful to see you. I'm so glad you called me."

The embrace grew suddenly awkward and Allison took a step back from him. For a moment they just looked at each other and then she laughed brightly and motioned for him to have a seat, then slid back into her chair.

"You look great, Carl," she told him.

"Flatterer," he replied. "One of us is getting old, and it isn't you."

Allison winced and looked away from him.

"Sorry," Carl said quickly. "I wasn't . . . I mean, I guess I didn't think that would be a sore point for you."

"I didn't choose to be what I am, Carl. Somebody took that decision away from me. There are benefits, I'm not going to lie. But for the most part, it's a terrible existence. Fucking miserable, if you want the truth."

The news producer laughed, eyes sparkling, and waved the waiter over. "Who says I want the truth?" He ordered a beer and then turned his attention back to Allison, but now all the humor was gone from his face.

"We all thought you were dead, Allie. After New Orleans, that's what the news said. I found out a little over a year ago that you were still alive, but I kept it to myself because, well, it's a secret, isn't it?"

Carl reached across the table and laid his hand over hers. Allison had to force herself not to flinch, not because she wanted to pull away from the warmth and comfort the man was offering her, but because no one had bothered to do such a thing for a very long time. The intimacy of that touch, there on the patio of that trattoria in Piazza San Marco, was almost too much for her.

Grief sharp as needles jabbed her heart. She had thought it would be a pleasure to see Carl, a bit of nostalgia and companionship, and that was partially true. But the pleasure was overshadowed by the pain it brought her to be reminded of the life she had once led, the dreams she had pursued.

"You're alive," Carl said, his eyes so earnest. "I can't tell you how glad I am of that."

Allison held his hand between hers. "Thank you," she said. "I wish I could feel as good about it as you do. It helps, though, seeing you here. For a long time I've felt cut off from the world. It's nice to feel connected again, even just for a couple of hours."

Carl smiled and Allison leaned back, letting go of his hand. What she had said was true, but it was not all of the truth. Her old friend had been kidding her before—*who says I want the truth?*—but she was certain there was some truth to the sentiment as well. Her pain she would try to keep to herself.

With a tiny sigh, she forced herself to smile and found that it did not feel as false as she had expected. Carl wore a green linen suit with beige sneakers and a shirt open at the neck. He looked more like a Florida retiree than one of the best connected newsmen in the world.

When Allison glanced up to meet his gaze again, she found that he had been taking her measure even as she took his.

"You do look amazing," he told her. "I'm not sure I've ever seen you in a dress before."

Allison self-consciously smoothed the wrinkles in the yellow sun dress she had put on that morning. The strappy heels she wore matched the color of the dress exactly. Her sunglasses were propped up on top of her flaming red hair. It was so rare that she had opportunity to dress in a light-hearted, feminine manner, that she relished it.

"I'm not sure I have, either."

Carl laughed. The waitress brought his beer and poured it for him. When she walked away, he took a long draught from it and then wiped his lips politely with a cloth napkin.

Abruptly the pleasantries of their reunion evaporated. Though Allison had no doubt that Carl was genuine in his feelings, that he was as glad to see her as she was to see him, both of them knew that there was business to conduct, news to be shared, a crisis brewing.

He leaned closer to her, over the table, and his blue eyes seemed to have dimmed to a steely gray, as though dusk had fallen over them as surely as it had over Venice.

"What do you know?" he asked.

Allison nodded to confirm that they had moved on. For a moment she was uncertain how to begin. The man had come all the way from London, where he was now working, and she should at least be able to explain herself. She removed her glasses from her forehead and set them on the table, shaking out her hair. Neither of them had bothered to look at the menu, but dinner was forgotten.

"Whispers travel fast," she said.

His eyes narrowed. The band had been playing Italian tunes pretty steadily, but now they kicked into "Fly Me to the Moon." Allison loved that song, but Carl had not seemed even to notice the music or much else about their surroundings from the moment he had sat down. She could smell garlic frying inside the restaurant, the scent wafting out the door.

"What does that mean, exactly?" he asked.

"I was hoping you could tell me. I can't give you details—you don't have the clearance—but I was on an op and a vampire said that to me. 'Whispers travel fast.' Something about them just getting started. And he rattled off the list of locations that I gave you before."

Carl nodded, reached into his jacket, and pulled out a pad of paper. He riffed through a few pages and came to the one he wanted, then read from it.

"Derby, England. Tracy, California. Groznik, Uzbekistan. Hidalgo, Texas."

He glanced up at her from beneath salt-and-pepper eyebrows and Allison nodded.

"And you've got nothing?" Carl asked.

Allison lifted her wineglass and sipped from it. As she set it down, she glanced around her at nearby tables to see if they were being overheard. With the music, it would be difficult for anyone to hear them unless they raised their voices. A quick survey of the piazza did not reveal any suspicious observers. Not that Allison expected anyone. She was simply trained by her profession to be paranoid.

The waitress returned. Allison almost sent her away, but Carl asked very politely if he might order for both of them. He did so, in Italian, asking that they both be served a local fish selection without bothering to check the menu. The waitress nodded and went off.

"I don't trust Henning," she said.

Carl blinked. "He's the CO of Task Force Victor?"

She nodded. "No reason not to trust him, save that he doesn't trust me. I talked to some other people at the U.N., people I've known since Jimenez was still in charge of the Task Force. Something happened in Derby and Groznik, that's certain, but everyone got skittish when I asked about it. Either they knew and weren't telling, or they knew something was up and that it wasn't healthy to be too curious."

Carl smiled. "But you didn't give up," he said, taking another draught of beer.

"No. I didn't. We keep records of all supernatural events worldwide. I did some checking on that list. Got nothing on Hidalgo or Groznik, but Derby and Tracy, California, both got hits. Two years ago, a massive sinkhole opened up on the grounds of a thirteenth-century priory in Derby that had been converted into a hotel. Whatever came out of it had wings and hooves, and witnesses described it as 'like something out of an old Hammer film.' That's the British for you."

Carl had tipped his beer glass back again but now he froze and looked at her. "Pretty much all of the breaches I know of—all the demons that've been recorded as coming through to this plane—don't look a damn thing like pop culture devils."

"This one did. It was also apparently huge, given that it tore down half the priory and ate nearly all of the guests before the local military destroyed it and a U.N. special ops team was called to seal the hole. Thing is, I didn't know a damn thing about it at the time. Guess they figure each team is on a need-to-know basis. Or at least, this particular team member is."

"You said you got a hit on Tracy, too."

Allison nodded. "A bunch of fire-breathing, serpentine demons nested in the body of a thirteen-year-old girl, then burst out of her, turning her body into a portal for something larger and even more grotesque. The descriptions of the thing are downright nasty. Dozens of people were killed. Others were mauled or burned by the demon vermin. At least five of the townspeople went completely nuts and never recovered. Miraculously, the girl survived."

The aging newsman took a deep breath and let it out slow. He sat back slightly in his chair and regarded her thoughtfully, as if turning over what she had said in his mind. Then he gave a small shrug.

"I've got nothing on Groznik still, but the way the Russians are, that's not surprising. Hidalgo, on the other hand, that's new."

"New?"

"Demon infestation just in the last couple of weeks. Church of the Resurrection went in and cleaned it up. End of story, supposedly."

"But?"

Carl raised an eyebrow. "But . . . no one's been able to get in touch with anyone in Hidalgo for a couple of days. I looked a little closer. The government's got the news blacked out on it, but they won't be able to keep a lid on it much longer. No one can get into Hidalgo, either. There's some kind of field around it, and you can't even see it, or so the story goes. Like it's still there, but it's invisible."

Allison stared at him. "Like it's been, what? Shunted somewhere else? Shifted into a parallel plane?"

"Pretty much my thinking," Carl confirmed.

The enormity of it began to sink in and Allison felt her throat go dry. "Nothing like that has ever—"

"No," he agreed. "Never on record, at least."

"Jesus."

"Yep."

Allison looked up at him. "Tracy?"

Carl just nodded. "And Derby. And Groznik, at least from

what my sources tell me. Word's just coming in that a town in northern Vermont's also been . . . erased, or whatever. And on the way here I got a call on my mobile. Mont de Moreau in France. It's spreading."

"Whispers travel fast," Allison muttered to herself.

"If that's what they are . . . the things that are doing this . . . whispers? If that's what they are, they damn sure do. Salzburg's gone too."

Allison froze. Stared at him. All of it finally clicked into place. "Salzburg," she said. It was the site of the biggest breach that had ever been torn between worlds. Tracy. Hidalgo. Derby. "They're all places where there have been breaches before."

Carl nodded. "See why I wanted to meet here?" he asked. And she did.

A decade earlier she had come here to Venice for an investigative report into the world of vampires and the humans who willingly volunteered their throats and their blood. Under an assumed name she had posed as one of those volunteers. It had nearly cost her life, and it had ended with her bearing witness to the tearing of reality and what might have been a devastating demonic invasion into this reality, thanks to powerful magick from a book called *The Gospel of Shadows*, wielded by a sorcerer named Liam Mulkerrin.

Peter Octavian, Will Cody, and their bloodkin had stopped Mulkerrin and the breach had been sealed. But . . .

Night had fully enveloped the Piazza San Marco by now and Allison glanced around the square as through new eyes. All seemed well. Quiet. But the images of that night years ago were still fresh in her mind, the horrors that had unfolded here, the towering, infernal beast that had stepped through a tear in the dimensional fabric onto those very cobblestones. The blood of hundreds had been spilled that night, the acolytes of Mulkerrin had been destroyed along with innumerable vampires—shadows—who had yet to fully understand and embrace the true extent of their gifts. All of that was over now. A handful of vampires remained in the world and Allison was hunting them, one by one.

But that night . . . the breach had been enormous. Buildings had been damaged, roofs had collapsed. It seemed impossible, staring out at the piazza now, but Allison had been there.

As she watched, a twentyish couple paused just beyond the trattoria's patio and twirled into a few seconds of romantic dance, inspired by the band and the wonder of Venice. Allison shuddered and shook her head.

"Nothing's happening here. I don't sense anything out of the ordinary at all." She turned to look closely at Carl.

He shrugged. "Neither do I. Not sure what that means. All I do know is that other than Venice, there's certainly a pattern."

Allison raised her wineglass and was disappointed to find it empty. She set it down and ran a finger idly along the rim. The glass hummed. She was trying to make sense of it all in her head but knew that there was no way she was going to be able to do that just sitting there.

"So what now?" Carl asked.

With a soft chuckle, Allison raised an eyebrow and regarded him evenly. "Now? Now I get into it. Now I do a little traveling, figure out what the hell's going on. The more I think on it, the more I wonder if the way to solve this isn't by visiting Derby and Mont de Moreau, but by trying to figure out where it's going to happen next, and getting there before it does."

"You're going to call Octavian, aren't you?"

Allison frowned, stared at him more closely. "That sounded an awful lot like a newsman's question, not a friend's."

"Sue me," Carl replied. "A leopard can't change its spots. But not to worry. I'm not going anywhere with this story until I know more about it. We'll look for a pattern, organize a map of known dimensional breaches, see if we can't make an educated guess where it's going to happen next. Meantime, let me see what more I can find out about those places already affected. You can reach me by mobile if you need me."

"Thank you. Really." Allison felt warmed by this simple companionship, by the idea that for the first time in a long time, she was not alone. "I remember what it was like to

want the story. To want to be the one to tell it. You report
whatever you want to. It's your job."

"You won't get in dutch with your bosses at the U.N.?"

"Fuck 'em. What're they going to do, send Task Force
Victor after me? I'd love to see them try."

———

THE morning after the meeting with Father Jack, Peter sat
on the bed in the hotel room Nikki and Keomany were sharing and listened to the sound of the shower running. He tried
to fight the image that surged into his mind of Nikki under
the steaming spray of water, rivulets of it running down over
her perfect breasts and the pale expanse of her belly.

How many times had they showered together? Ten?
Twenty? It pained him that something like that, the very
thought of which made his heart skip a beat, could have
registered so little that he could not remember how many
times.

He rose from the bed and walked to the television,
tempted to turn it on but not wanting to seem presumptuous.
Instead he strode to the window and opened the curtains. The
hotel looked down upon Forty-Fourth Street and he watched
the gleaming yellow roofs of cabs as they wove in among
the rest of the traffic. The taxis were so numerous and so
insistent they seemed almost to be the only things moving
down there, the only things alive.

Peter pressed his fingers on the window. There was dust
on the glass.

From the bathroom came the squeak of pipes as Nikki
shut the water off. He had to fight the urge to flee the room,
to go downstairs where Father Jack and Keomany were
having coffee, waiting for them. The rented Lincoln Navigator was already packed up, with the exception of Nikki's
things. Keomany had come downstairs right on time to tell
Peter and Father Jack that Nikki wasn't ready, and that she
had asked if Peter would come up. He could feel the plastic
keycard in the back pocket of his jeans.

The bathroom door swung open and in a cloud of steam
Nikki emerged, wrapped in a towel, her hair very wet. "Peter?" It took a moment for her to spot him by the window.

Something in his chest felt broken. He could not help but smile as he looked at her. Even from here he could smell that familiar aroma she had, the hot water on her, the shampoo in her hair.

"You summoned me?" he offered, his grin broadening.

Nikki laughed and nodded. "Hey, there he is," she said. "I know that guy, that smile."

He stared at her for a long moment. "You know, I don't think there's anything in your wardrobe that you look better in than a white cotton bath towel."

One of her eyebrows shot up suggestively. "There's a face cloth."

Peter laughed. His feelings about Nikki had grown so complicated in the time they had been apart. He loved her, but he had been a different person entirely when they had met and she had fallen in love with him. When she had needed to go out and pursue her music career, he had been in the midst of figuring out what he wanted to do with his own life, now that he wasn't immortal anymore.

And now . . .

"Aren't you supposed to be rehearsing for your tour?" he asked.

Nikki gave him a wistful look. "Actually the tour's already started. Officially, at least. I did a gig in Philly that was supposed to kick it off. But I have a few weeks before the real tour starts. Another couple of days won't make a difference."

Peter gestured around the room. "Sort of surprised you're not at the Drake or the Waldorf. What with the hit single and all."

"Not yet. But hitch your wagon to this star, my friend, and we'll all be staying at the Waldorf in no time."

He gazed at her a long moment before speaking again. "Why did you want me to come up, anyway? Just so I could give you a hard time for taking so long to get ready?"

Her smile was strangely shy; her head tilted to one side and she hid behind the cascade of damp hair that spilled in front of her eyes. "Maybe I just wanted to find out if you'd come."

The tone of her voice as she spoke those words felt like

an electric charge surging through him. Peter stared at Nikki
for several seconds, then he strode over to her and put two
fingers under her chin. He raised her face up to him so their
eyes met.

"Any time. Any place," he said. "You know that."

"Except Los Angeles," she replied, a tiny frown knitting
her brows together.

Peter brushed locks of wet hair away from her face. "That
was then. This is now. I spent a lot of time reminding myself
what it meant to be alive. Now I'm just living for all I'm
worth."

She opened her mouth to reply but he silenced her with
his lips. He was through being hesitant, through worrying
what would happen when she had to go back to Los Angeles.
Their kiss deepened and a small moan escaped Nikki's lips
and she let her body mold itself to his. Her towel came un-
done and began to slip, but was trapped between them.

When their kiss ended, both of them breathless, Peter lay
his forehead against Nikki's and she chuckled softly to herself. "I feel like I never left." Then she pushed him back,
one hand clutching her towel in place. "Can we pretend that,
do you think? That I never left."

Peter shook his head. "No. We can't. What we can do is
not talk about this for a couple of days. When we come back
from Vermont, when it's all done, then we can decide where
to go from there. For the moment, I've only got two things
to say to you."

Nikki blinked, her expression a combination of hurt and
curiosity. "And they are?"

"The first is, hurry up and get ready. I don't have a spell
to help you, and you're already going to miss breakfast.
Every hour that passes is another in which Keomany doesn't
know what happened to her parents and her town."

Her expression became grim and she nodded. It was the
truth, and she knew it. They were being greedy, stealing time
for themselves.

"What's the second thing?"

Peter smiled, ran a hand through his the graying hair at
his left temple. "I can paint anywhere."

ONLY days after she had fled her hometown, Keomany sat in the back seat of the rented Lincoln Navigator and stared out the tinted window at the green hills and valleys that rose and fell on either side of the highway. With every mile they drew closer to Wickham, and with every mile her throat became dryer, her heart sped faster, and the images in her mind became more and more inescapable.

The rotten pumpkin sky. The black, skeletal demons. The unnatural silence on the street, the emptiness of it, as if the whole town had been hollowed.

Keomany closed her eyes and pinched the bridge of her nose.

A gentle hand touched her shoulder. "Are you not feeling all right?"

She opened her eyes again. Father Jack was studying her with genuine concern and she forced herself to smile. "As well as can be expected, I suppose."

The priest nodded as though he understood precisely what she felt. *It must be something they're trained for*, Keomany thought. For though she was sure Father Jack had seen his share of chaos, somehow she doubted he had any idea what she was feeling. The terrible certainty that she would arrive back home and the place would be barren, deserted, nothing but a ghost town. The idea that the hellish possession of the town would have ceased and left only the bones of the town where her life had been. She would go to her parents' home and find that they, too, were now only bones.

The night before, she had dreamed precisely that.

"Keomany, when we get there, you don't have to come into the town," Peter said.

He was behind the wheel, and Nikki in the passenger seat. Keomany had watched him a lot during the hours they had been on the road—watched both of them, in fact. Peter was an enigma to her. Despite what she knew of his past, what she knew he had once been, he seemed on the surface to be a normal, average, thirtysomething guy. But Keomany had always been able to sense the true nature of things. Perhaps that was part of being an earthwitch, or perhaps it was simply that she was a good judge of character. Either way, she saw beneath the surface when it came to Peter.

Underneath the chamois shirt and the blue jeans, under that almost mundanely handsome exterior, Peter Octavian *burned*. It was not just magick that coursed through him, but fierce passion and honor. Keomany found it strange that Octavian kept these things almost hidden, as though the face he wore were a disguise, like Superman receding beneath the persona of an earnest reporter.

Keomany saw him, though, for what he really was and it helped her to understand why they all automatically deferred to him, why Father Jack had handed him the keys to the Navigator, why Nikki so obviously still loved him.

Nikki glanced into the back seat at her and Keomany blinked, realizing she had not responded to what Peter had said.

"You sure you're all right?" Nikki asked.

"No," Keomany admitted. Her gaze ticked toward Peter. She saw him looking at her in the rearview mirror. "But I'm not staying behind, either. That's my family in there. My friends. It's my town."

Peter nodded and said nothing more on the subject. Unlike Father Jack, she had a feeling that his apparently understanding had a depth and truth to it. It helped.

Keomany let her gaze drift out the window again. She saw a little town in a valley off to her right, homes sprawling out from the center of town, where a picturesque white church marked the heart of the community. Another quaint and peaceful New England village, where every day seemed just like the last. And where—as she had learned—anything could happen.

When they passed the sign that announced that Wickham was five miles away, she flinched. As those last few miles rolled past, Keomany fished into her pocket book and took out a rubber band, then tied her raven hair back in a tight ponytail.

"Take a right here," she told Peter.

He followed her directions as she guided them toward Wickham. Since she had left, Keomany had felt only a glimmer of the connection to nature that had been hers the last time she was here. It was still there—a new awareness of the world around her, of the order of things and the health of the land—but not so much that she could wield it. Not so much that she felt able to reach out and touch the soul of the earth itself, the way she had on that day.

Now, though, as she drew closer to home, Keomany felt it growing in her again. She was an earthwitch, and what happened in Wickham was like a huge wound in the flesh of the world, a scar upon nature. It was as though the wound was hers, and yet at the same time, she felt the earth trying to heal itself, felt that she could tap into that.

It was the most incredible feeling she had ever had, being a part of something. *No, of everything.*

Half a mile outside of town Peter drove the Navigator down a gentle slope from the top of which the village ought to have been visible. There was nothing there but a kind of haze, as though a cloud had dropped to earth and made everything past that point in the road out of focus.

A hundred yards from the barren land that had replaced Wickham—from the bubble of air that shimmered and blurred her vision—Keomany saw a phalanx of police cars and two military Jeeps. The road was blocked. The men and women posted at that roadblock were armed. When the Navigator rumbled toward them, they raised their weapons and trained them on the huge black Lincoln SUV.

"Thank God it's a rental," Father Jack said.

Nobody laughed.

Peter parked the Navigator in the middle of the road and killed the engine. He glanced at Nikki first, then into the back seat.

"Sit tight. I'm going to have a little talk with them."

He opened the door and stepped down from the driver's seat. Keomany leaned forward to get a better view and she noticed that Father Jack had done the same.

Peter had his hands up as he approached the police and the MPs, but there was something different about him now, as if the warrior that he had hidden away was now revealed. It was in everything about him, the way he walked, the way he held his head, the sheer energy that radiated from him. This was what he had come here for.

This was who he was.

When he reached the first police officer, Peter spread his arms wider and his fingers sketched at the air as though he were conducting an orchestra. One of the M.P's shouted in alarm, demanding to know what he was up to. The man barely finished his sentence.

A bright flash of green light burst from Peter's hands, rolling like a wave over those who had been guarding the road. As it struck them, they fell one by one to the ground, unconscious.

"Jesus!" Father Jack hissed.

Nikki glanced back at him, smiling. "Was that a prayer, Father, or were you taking the Lord's name in vain?"

The priest did not respond. He only stared, just as Keomany did, as Peter turned his back on the men and women he had just rendered inert with a gesture and walked back toward the Navigator. Tapped into nature, Keomany felt as though she could sense the power of the earth itself, even access it a little. But she could not imagine the kind of magick that Octavian had at his disposal. A thousand years in hell, and he had brought this back with him.

Peter opened the door and smiled in at them. "It was just going to take too long to explain," he said. "And we're kind of in a rush."

CHAPTER 9

PETER Octavian took a deep breath of sweet Vermont mountain air. His heart sped with anticipation, a kind of adrenaline high filling him. For so long he had been denying himself this rush and now he could not remember why. Something about wanting to live normally now that he was mortal again, wanting to have an ordinary life.

What the hell was I thinking? he asked himself now.

In Venice and Salzburg and New Orleans he had faced horrors unimaginable. He had spent an eternity in Hell and somehow been reborn on the other side. Nearly every person he had ever loved, human or vampire, had been taken from him to that place after death. He had wanted to live, to be bored, to paint and be human and love and cry. But Peter Octavian had seen the destruction of his home and his family and his loved ones before. For hundreds of years, it had been the pattern of his life. It had been foolish of him to think he could escape that, that he could hide away the truest part of him.

There on the outskirts of Wickham, with the sky so blue above and a massive, barren landscape before him, the warrior in him came awake for the first time in a very long while.

"Peter?" Nikki called from inside the Navigator.

He had been standing just inside the open passenger door. Now he grinned up at her. "I'm fine." Peter climbed up into the rented SUV and slammed the door. He glanced over his shoulder at Father Jack and Keomany.

"Jack, the guns?"

The priest turned into his seat and reached into the back of the Navigator for a metal case that he dragged over into his lap. As Nikki and Keomany watched, he opened the case. Peter eyed its contents with satisfaction: a quartet of Heckler and Koch nine-millimeter semiautomatic pistols, gleaming silver, and a dozen replacement clips, already loaded.

"Very nice," Peter said. "The Lord provides, huh?"

Father Jack smiled. "Or the Bishop does. Even if he doesn't know it." Then the priest glanced up at Nikki, who was leaning over the front seat to get a better look. "These things have a hell of a kick. Most demons are vulnerable to traditional weaponry if you hit something vital, or shoot them enough." His gaze went to Keomany. "But all the ammunition is also blessed, just in case."

"Will that make a difference, really?" Nikki asked.

Peter nodded, watching as Father Jack pulled out the first of the HKs, checking the weapon's action and confirming that it was loaded. "It's a kind of magick all its own, isn't it?"

"I don't need a gun," Keomany announced.

"What?" Nikki asked.

She had beat him to it. Peter frowned as he studied the woman who had brought them all here, her gentle Asian features now grave. Her choice of words was curious. Not that she did not want a gun, but that she did not need one. It reminded him that there had been something he had been wanting to ask her about her exodus from Wickham.

"You don't need one?" he asked now. "So how will you protect yourself? Better yet, maybe it's time you tell us how you got out of here alive the last time."

Nikki shot him an admonishing glance as though he were being harsh, but Peter ignored her. They were here together, a unit, and the truth of it was that he was the only real warrior among them. It fell to him to keep them alive, so he needed to know everything about the people he was with. Father

Jack had a modicum of sorcerous ability, knew enough spells to combat certain kinds of enemies and to protect himself and possibly others. But he was also going to have a gun. Nikki was fast and smart, but beyond that she would be armed.

Keomany was staring at the open case with obvious distaste. "They're unnatural. Guns."

"What do you call what's going on out there?" Peter asked, tilting his head toward the windshield, beyond which the distorted air that marked the perimeter of the reality disruption was clearly visible.

The woman nodded. She looked up at Nikki and smiled almost shyly before turning her gaze to Peter.

"I'm an earthwitch."

Father Jack held up the gun in his hand. "Meaning your religion won't allow you to handle one of these?"

"That's not what she means," Peter said.

Keomany glanced at him and a kind of understanding passed between them. For Peter, it was as though he were looking at her for the first time. Her pupils seemed to glow dimly even in the sunlit interior of the Navigator, as though dawn were fast approaching behind her eyes.

"We're not talking about pagan rituals and dancing naked around the fire, are we?" he asked.

Keomany smiled softly. "Well, there's plenty of that too. But no, we're not. I've known a lot of earthwitches with a certain amount of power. Weather influence, mostly. But when I was trapped here . . . something happened. I tapped into Gaea herself. At least I think I did."

There was silence inside the vehicle but Peter was not going to let it last long. Soon enough the cops and MPs outside would be waking up, and he didn't want to have to give them another jolt if he could avoid it. Even if he was careful, there was always the possibility he might seriously hurt one of them.

Nikki reached across the front seat and took his hand, but her attention was on Keomany. "So you're a sorceress?"

"No." Keomany shook her head.

"Magick has many sources," Peter said. "Or so I believe, given everything I've learned about it. It's possible it all comes from one place, different kinds of energy, manipulating molecules. What is today's science but yesterday's magick? Father Jack and the Bishop would tell you it comes from God. Maybe it does. But I've met an earthwitch or two before—though they called themselves other names. Gaea is a real source of power. It's the heart of this world."

"The heart?" Father Jack asked. "Or the soul?"

Keomany looked to him and her eyes shone more brightly. "That's it exactly. Gaea's the spirit of this world."

"Mother nature," Nikki said, pushing her blond hair away from her face. "Well, I'm sure this kind of shit really pisses her off."

"You could say that," Keomany replied.

Peter nodded, wanting to move on. "Jack, take two of the guns for yourself. Give Nikki the other two." He gazed at Nikki, reached over, and put his hand on her upper arm, the contact meant to reassure himself as much as her. "You remember how to fire a gun?"

She grinned as the breeze picked up, blowing through the window and rustling her hair. "Something tells me a demon gets up in my face, it'll refresh my memory."

"It might not come to that," Peter replied, but the words sounded hollow, even to him.

He faced forward again, gripped the steering wheel with one hand, and turned the key in the ignition. The Navigator roared to life, the engine like some caged beast. In his peripheral vision he saw Nikki accepting the two guns from Father Jack, then he dropped the transmission into gear and accelerated.

The Navigator lurched toward the distortion field, which shimmered and flickered as they drew nearer to it. It was as though the view of a barren wasteland that had replaced the village of Wickham was little more than a blurred, static-filled image broadcast on a ballooning television screen. Peter guided the vehicle around the roadblock and the fallen sentinels who had been guarding it.

The distortion field loomed before them now, stretching out as far as they could see on either side and reaching up toward the sky at an odd, curving angle so that it seemed Wickham had been swallowed up by some warped dome of electricity. As the Navigator rolled closer, Peter could even hear a sort of hum that was being emitted from it.

"What if it's real?" Nikki asked suddenly, a hitch in her voice.

Almost unconsciously, Peter let up on the accelerator. "What?"

"What if it's just blurring our vision but that's really all that's left?"

"Then where did the town go?" Father Jack asked.

"Let's find out," Peter answered, ignoring Nikki's question mainly because he had no satisfactory answer.

Right arm stiff as he gripped the wheel, he thrust his left hand out the window. It was not easy to make his throat and lips form the words, but he spoke in a guttural, demonic language known to no one else on earth. Hell had taught him many things.

A moist ball of pink light blossomed around his left hand, which was closed into a fist. As he opened it, spreading his fingers out, the light turned from pink to crimson. He muttered the words again, grunting deep in his chest.

In the back seat Keomany turned to Father Jack. "Is he all right?"

Peter ignored them.

With a final word, punctuated by the clack of his teeth coming together, he clenched his fist again and the sphere of damp crimson light flashed away from his hand as though a silent explosion had occurred in his palm. The sphere grew enormous in half a heartbeat and, soundless, it struck the distortion field.

"Holy shit," Keomany whispered.

Father Jack grunted. "Was that a prayer or a curse?"

The crimson sphere burned through the distortion field. For a moment it did nothing but create a red-tinted window through which they could see that barren wasteland in focus for the first time. And that was precisely what it was on the other side of that window. No sign of the village of Wickham, or its people.

But Peter's magick burned deeper, seeking beyond appearance, tearing at the distortion field but also seeking out the source of it. A shudder went through him as he kept his foot pressed on the Navigator's brake, waiting for an opening. If the infernal denizens of other dimensions could make breaches into this world, Peter could return the favor.

The crimson sphere glowed brightly, and then it exploded into shards of red-tinged light that were instantly swallowed by the sickly orange glow that erupted from within the distortion field. *Rotten pumpkins*, Peter thought. *That's how Keomany described it.* And he could see the comparison. The orange light was impossibly dark and tainted, and where it streamed out of the hole he had blown in the distortion field, it seemed as though it had been vomited into existence.

Unnatural, he thought. *Keomany's right. This has nothing to do with our world.*

"It isn't just distorting our vision," he said quietly. "It's a dimensional displacement."

"Explain," Nikki demanded.

"You were right. Wickham really is gone. Sort of. It's been shunted out of this plane of existence and into another."

"So what now?"

Peter frowned, took his foot off the brake, and put it down on the accelerator. "Now I drive."

He floored it. Father Jack shouted an objection but Peter barely took note of the words. Out of the corner of his eye he saw Nikki brace herself on the dashboard with one hand, but in the other she held one of the HKs Jack had given her. Keomany said nothing.

The blue sky disappeared above them. Peter took one look in the rearview mirror and spotted several of the cops he had knocked unconscious getting to their feet. One of them had drawn his weapon and was brandishing it, shouting after the Navigator, but one of his fellow officers reached out and grabbed his arm, pushing it down.

Then the Navigator was bathed in that vile orange light. The vehicle shuddered and Peter kept both hands locked on to the wheel. He had torn a portal through realities but it was still not a smooth transition. The Navigator jerked as though they had burst through some invisible membrane and a hairline crack spiderwebbed across the windshield.

The light dimmed and the engine whined as though it struggled against something, and then they were through, driving beneath a filthy orange sky through air thick with heat and a charnel house stink that made Peter begin breathing through his mouth.

"We're through," Father Jack whispered. His words were barely audible over the hum of the engine.

Peter drove slowly. Cars were stalled or parked or crashed at intervals and he had to weave around them. Some were turned over, others merely had the windows shattered. One had been wrapped around a telephone pole at high speed and had collapsed in upon itself like an accordion.

The road was littered with human corpses, or what remained of them. The dead were mostly bones and dry snatches of parchment skin and sun-bleached clothing. He spotted two smaller skeletons with tufts of fur stuck to their bones and thought they were too small to be dogs. Cats, probably. Things that might have been this world's version of carrion birds picked at some of the cadavers, but Peter paid them no mind. The scavengers weren't the real evil here.

"Keomany," he said, "show me the way. Let's check the downtown, where you were before you left. I want to find the things responsible for this. It's the only way to reverse it."

"My parents," she said softly, gazing out the window and studying each of the corpses they passed.

"We'll check on them soon," Peter told her. He glanced in the rearview and she met his gaze. "But you should be prepared."

In her reflection he could see the glow behind her eyes grow brighter, as though each were its own tiny eclipse.

"Drive," Keomany told him.

Peter avoided colliding with the stalled or wrecked cars but he no longer bothered going around the remains of the dead. The wheels of the Navigator crunched bone and bumped over those who had had the misfortune to be caught out here upon the road by the sleek black demons Keomany had described, or by whatever else now infested Wickham.

All four of them were on guard. The windows were rolled down and Father Jack and Nikki held their nine-millimeter semiautomatic weapons in their laps, but there was nothing casual about this. There had been few buildings where they had entered the displaced area, but now as he followed Keomany's direction, Peter drove them into a more closely settled area of Wickham. Many of the homes had been burned out, some still smoldered. Others had been caved in from outside or had picture windows that had been shattered. The dead littered lawns and in one place the skeletal upper torso of a man lay upon a shingled roof with absolutely no evidence as to how it had come to be there. A picket fence had been turned into a thicket of spikes adorned with the impaled bodies of a dozen dead cats.

"Left," Keomany said, a hitch in her voice as though she were trying not to be sick. "That's Currier. It leads into the downtown."

Peter turned, but as he did, a motion off to his left caught his eye. He glanced in that direction, at a house that was seemingly untouched, and saw a heavy curtain fall back to cover an upstairs window, as though someone had been watching their progress and had ducked back so as not to be seen. Dimly he heard the barking of a dog.

Demon or human? he wondered, wishing he had gotten a closer look at the figure behind that curtain. It would have been good to know that there were at least some who had survived this horror.

"Where are they all?" Nikki asked, as though echoing his thoughts.

"The people or the monsters?" Father Jack replied.

Nikki sighed heavily, anxiously. "Either. It's like it's been abandoned."

"No. It's not abandoned. I'm sure we've been noticed," Peter said. "My guess is they're taking our measure."

There was no response to that. He turned onto Currier Street and in the back seat Keomany cursed loudly in astonishment. Peter did not need to ask her what had affected her so deeply. They were rapidly approaching what had clearly once been a lovely shopping district, a classic downtown New England street full of boutiques and restaurants. The entire east side of Currier Street had been put to the torch, leaving nothing but blackened and charred remains smoldering where businesses had been. At the far end of the devastation, a small fire still burned.

"Your shop?" Nikki asked, her pain for her friend's loss evident.

"No. I'm on the other side," Keomany replied.

Peter had known from the moment he had heard her story that Wickham itself might be rescued, lives might be saved, but the village would never be the same again. Despite however well she might have prepared herself, he understood that Keomany was only now beginning to realize the truth of it.

As he drove, Peter glanced from side to side, watching both the ruins and the hollowed faces of the remaining stores for some sign of an enemy. Something he could fight against. He knew he could get them out—tearing another hole in the displacement field was not going to be difficult—and it might be possible to collapse part of it as well, but without figuring out the source of this magick, there was no way he could return Wickham to its rightful place in the world.

A prickling sensation went up the back of his neck and he glanced sharply to the left. In the darkness within a restaurant something shifted, quickly seeking cover in the depths of the ravaged business. Peter said nothing to the others.

"Here," Keomany said.

But he had already seen it. Sweet Somethings. The sign was still hung in front of it, though the windows were gone. Broken glass lay scattered across the sidewalk. Peter pulled the Navigator up in front of it, put it in Park, and glanced over his shoulder.

"Do you need anything from inside? I can go in for you." She shook her head.

Father Jack raised one finger. "Peter? I know you say they're watching us, but it looks like they don't want to be found. Can you track them?"

Peter frowned. "We won't need to. Look around, Jack. It's only a matter of time before they come after us. In the meantime, we're going to keep poking around, kicking the bees' nest, trying to get a reaction. They're here, all right. And now that we're in, they're not going to let us out without a fight. But while they're leaving us alone, let's go look for Keomany's family."

In the back seat, Keomany said something so quietly Peter did not hear her.

"What?" he asked.

In the rearview mirror he saw her staring out the window and looked to see what had drawn her attention. A postal truck had crashed through the front of a bakery and what remained of the postman hung out the door, his chest torn open, ribs split, a gaping cavern where his organs ought to have been.

"Bobby Donovan," Keomany said, staring at the dead postman. "He was two years behind me in school. He asked me out once, when he was a freshman. It must have taken guts. I wish I'd gone."

Once more they all fell silent and Peter turned the Navigator around and drove back the way they had come, more vigilant than ever. Several blocks up Currier, Keomany told him to turn. Instantly the area became more residential and again most of the homes had been burned or ravaged. There were more cars wrecked or overturned or simply abandoned, and there were more bones.

Peter was focused on a house up on the left that was untouched. In the filthy orange light that seemed to envelop every structure, to fill their lungs with its stink, he could not be sure at first what it was that he saw on the lawn. A body, to be sure, but as he drove nearer, he saw that this corpse was not wisps of hair and flesh on a withered, skeletal frame. He put on the brakes and stared at the dead man who sprawled on the lawn, limbs jutting at odd angles, head caved in.

The corpse was fresh.

Somewhere nearby a dog was barking, its anger muffled by windows and doors and walls. He glanced up at the house with the dead man sprawled on the lawn and he knew the sound was coming from within. A dog, alive, barking angrily.

From the garage.

Peter stared at the garage door, which was one of those with a row of square windows along the top. In the gloom within he thought he could see a human face illuminated by that sickly orange light. Possibly more than one.

The dog kept barking.

Dead cats impaled on a picket fence.

But no dead dogs.

On the other side of the street, two houses up, was another home that had been untouched. Peter sped up, came to a sudden stop in front of the house.

"What?" Nikki demanded. "What is it?"

Father Jack began to speak.

Peter shushed them all and listened. There were sounds he had not noticed before, a distant rumble like thunder underground, a small earthquake rolling their way. He put the sound out of his mind and listened more closely, staring at this new house, a beige ranch-style with an ancient, rusted television antenna on the roof that seemed odd in a world of satellite and cable.

And he heard it, coming from inside the house.

Barking.

"Keomany," he asked, speeding up again without looking back at her. "Please tell me your parents have a dog."

"Two," she said quickly, obviously sensing something in his manner. "Muggsy and Bonkers. Why?"

"I think there are people still alive in some of the houses that haven't been attacked. I've heard dogs barking at all of them. It's possible that—"

But he did not need to finish. Keomany understood. Quietly she began to pray, not only to Gaea, but to God as well, a God he guessed she had not put any faith in for a very long time. In a low voice, Father Jack joined his prayers with her own.

"The . . . the second right," she said. "Little Tree Lane. It's number seven."

Peter drove a little faster, no longer paying attention to the houses they passed. His mind was awhirl as he tried to make sense of what had happened in Wickham. The town had been shunted through a breach to some infernal landscape, some parallel hell—that was obvious. Whatever the primary life-forms were here, whatever the demons were, they were afraid of ordinary dogs. It might be a pheromone thing or just the barking, he did not know. But things that were afraid of dogs could not be responsible for an event of this magnitude, stealing an entire village from one plane of existence and displacing it to another. And yet he was sure it had not been mere chance.

Some savage intelligence had done this, some demon of incredible power.

So where was it?

The little green sign marking Little Tree Lane still stood, though the house on the corner had been reduced to rubble. Peter slowed the Navigator to make the turn.

Thunder shook the pavement beneath the vehicle. The ground bucked and rumbled.

"Peter!" Nikki cried, grabbing hold of the dashboard again. "A fucking earthquake now? Come on!"

"Not an earthquake," he said as he slammed on the brakes.

Just ahead of the Navigator a sinkhole appeared in the pavement, no larger than a sewer grate. Then the road cracked as something slammed at it from beneath. Once. Twice. The third impact tore the pavement up, pieces of it struck the front of the Navigator's roof and broke a headlight. Had they struck the already cracked windshield, it would have shattered, but the chunks of pavement thunked down around them.

A huge head poked out of the hole in the street, accompanied by clawed, three-fingered hands that seemed absurdly tiny in comparison. The massive thing that hauled itself up out of the ground resembled a mole, but only in its snout and small claws and rough body shape. The thing was three times the size of the Navigator and its ridged hide reminded him of an armadillo. It sniffed the air and turned toward the Navigator and Peter saw that it had no eyes.

But it knew they were there.

"Slogute," Father Jack said. "I'd no idea they were real."

"Everything was real once," Peter told him.

Nikki leaned out the window, took aim, and fired three times. The bullets cut into the monstrosity and it turned and slithered its fat belly across the street away from them. On the lawn of the ruined house on the corner it paused, then turned to face them again, blind face searching, sniffing. Riv-

ulets of thick white pus slid down its chest where the bullets
had pierced its flesh.

"All right. Let's try that again," Father Jack said. He and
Nikki both pointed their weapons out the window.

"My parents!" Keomany said. "Their house is right up
there! Please just go!"

"Or at least save your ammunition," Peter said.

He spoke the words calmly, yet they must have carried
his conviction with them. Nikki and Father Jack both turned
away from their windows to shoot him a quizzical look. Peter
gestured out the windshield toward the hole the Slogute had
made in the road.

The things that leaped out of that hole, scrambling on top
of one another like a colony of ants, were hideously thin.
The creatures had long arms with talons like black knives,
their skeletal forms covered in something that looked for all
the world like the carapace of some enormous insect. Their
heads were plated as well, dark tongues like rapiers jabbing
from beneath those blank, blue-black skull coverings. An image flashed through Peter's mind of horseshoe crabs, their
shells and tails, and then he saw that this was truly what they
looked like, these things, their faces were like the shells of
horseshoe crabs, tongues like the crabs' tails.

He did not have to ask Keomany if these were the same
demons she had run up against before; their indigo carapaces
gleaming a filthy purple in the rotten pumpkin daylight
matched her description perfectly.

"There are more," Keomany said behind him.

Peter glanced over his left shoulder and saw the things
leaping and almost dancing out from behind the houses they
had just passed. Then, like ants, they were swarming from
everywhere, from among shrubbery and from overturned cars
and from the wreckage that had once been a neighborhood.

The Slogute had begun to burrow into the ground again
as if nothing out of the ordinary were happening. Or perhaps
it was frightened. Not of him and his companions, Peter was
sure.

Of *them*.

"Just drive!" Keomany cried.

"They're not letting us go any further," Nikki said, voice cold.

"So we do it here," Peter said.

He killed the Navigator's engine and opened the door, both of his hands crackling with green energy. The indigo demons were swarming, more coming up from the collapsed street every moment. When the first of them leaped atop the hood of the Navigator, its taloned feet scraping the vehicle with a shriek of metal, Peter raised his right hand and with a gesture he crushed the demon in a circlet of green flame that cracked its shell and snapped it in two.

The magick flooded through him and his entire body was engulfed in brilliant, verdant power that lifted him up off the ground, crackling around him as though he were cradled with a ball of green lightning.

As one, the swarm of demons paused.

A whine like hydraulic engines rose up from the skittering beasts, and then they swept in toward the Navigator.

CHAPTER 10

NANCY Carling and her sister Paula had carefully mapped out their trip to Spain with the travel agent before departure, knew where their hotels were, how many hours it would take to drive their rental car from place to place, and what to expect when they got there. Neither of the sisters had ever been to Spain before, but both of them had long desired to explore this nation where romance and history echoed in every architectural flourish.

Upon their arrival in Seville, Nancy and Paula had been disappointed. Driving from the airport to the hotel had taken them past long rows of enormous apartment buildings that seemed to have been transported from some gritty dystopian future. The mazelike interior of the city had them hopelessly lost until they chanced on a sign pointing to their hotel, which they at last discovered on a narrow street with barely enough room for a single car to pass a pedestrian.

The hotel had been attached to some kind of church—an older building but without the grandeur of the religious edifices they expected to find here—and a U-shaped courtyard in front of the two buildings was all the parking that was available. The inside of the hotel was beautiful, with tiled fresco walls and hanging plants, as well as smaller interior courtyard gardens whose flowers gave the whole place a wonderful, wildly aromatic bouquet.

After they had checked in, they walked deeper into the San Juan area of Seville and discovered the city's heart, a sprawl of alleys lined with restaurants and shops and inconspicuous doorways where men promised live flamenco dancing later that evening. At the center of all of this they had come upon an enormous square that spread out from the most breathtakingly beautiful and massive structure either of them had ever seen.

In touring the Cathedral of Seville they learned that those who had built it had set out to construct a church so immense that anyone beholding it would take its architects for madmen. The Carling sisters had seen photographs before coming to Seville, of course, but they were nothing compared to the awesome reality.

This, then, was Spain.

That night when they sat down for a very late dinner—yet early by the standards of Spaniards, who rarely ate before 10 P.M.—they were already examining their travel plans. They had struck up a conversation with an elderly couple from Scotland who sat at the next table in the otherwise empty restaurant. Only tourists ever ate this early. Stuart and Claire Vandal had done quite a bit of traveling and when the sisters explained their plans subsequent to their departure from Seville—a leisurely drive south to the coastal resort town of Torremelindos—the Vandals grew almost stern.

The aging Scottish couple had insisted that Nancy and Paula would be doing themselves a great disservice by taking the main highway. The Carling sisters must, the Vandals assured them, take the mountain road south out of Seville; a road that wound up into the mountainous region north of the Mediterranean and bring them, about halfway to the coast, to the town of Ronda.

Neither of the women had ever heard of Ronda but the effusive recommendation of the Vandals was too contagious to ignore. By the time they left Seville, they had mapped out their new route.

The dawn light through the curtains had roused them early and the sisters had found themselves excited to be breaking from their carefully laid plans. They were going off the path in a foreign country where they did not speak the language, with a few hundred words of high school Spanish and the fat guidebook to aid them. Nancy knew how silly it was to be so excited, that people did this sort of footloose travel all the time. But she and Paula had only been to Europe once before, and that had been to the U.K., where they spoke English. It was a bit of a thrill to them both.

They set off early after the meager continental breakfast provided by the hotel—snatching a couple of bananas for the road. They had gotten turned around several times just trying to find the secondary highway—the mountain road as the Vandals had called it—that led out of Seville, but eventually they managed and were soon rolling south.

The spring morning was chilly but Nancy had the window rolled down regardless, the wind whipping her strawberry blond hair across her face. In the passenger's seat, Paula tied her chestnut hair back with a rubber band so that she could read from the travel guide without it getting in her way.

"Cool," Paula said several times as Nancy drove. "This place sounds cool."

Nancy had read the entry on Ronda two nights earlier, after they had first met the Vandals. It was brief, but unquestionably interesting. The region where it was located had been home to human beings since Paleolithic times. A broad, rocky plateau loomed high above the Guadalevin River valley. The rushing water had carved the plateau in half thousands of years ago and the city of Ronda sprawled on either side of the dizzyingly high, narrow canyon cut over the ages by the river.

"Did you know the ancient Romans built a castle there?" Paula asked, glancing over at her sister, even as Nancy tried to find a radio station without static.

"I read that," Nancy reminded her.

The Romans had been just the beginning, actually. The height of the plateau and its daunting cliffs made it a perfect natural fortress. When the Moors had taken control of southern Spain, Ronda had become the capital of an independent Moslem sovereign, and remained a Moorish city for several centuries. For a city with such a grand history, Nancy had found it amazing that she had never heard of Ronda before, but she was intrigued.

She drove through the hills amid groves of olive trees and Paula took over trying to find something worth listening to on the radio. They talked about friends new and old, about the odd people at Nancy's office and the new museum job Paula had secured. The sisters had had their share of squabbles growing up, as close siblings always did, but since Paula had moved from their hometown of Baltimore to Los Angeles, they had been planning this very trip as a kind of reunion. It had been a long time in coming. The same dynamic that had always existed between them lingered, however. Paula asserted herself as leader of their expedition by virtue of her status as the elder sister while Nancy tried not to lose her temper.

Right now, however, all of those tensions had slipped away. The winding, leisurely drive through the picturesque hills eased them both into a rare feeling of well-being, so that they did little more than chat and laugh together. When at last they gave up trying to find a radio station, the Carling sisters began to sing, challenging one another to name the television series to which a particular theme was attached, or match a product to its advertising jingle, or name the band responsible for some horrid one-hit wonder.

In this way they soon found themselves at the turnoff that led up a long road into Ronda, past the high ramparts that had been built on the two far ends of the city where the plateau sloped down to the valley floor.

"Here we are," Nancy said as she drove up the steep hill into Ronda.

Paula leaned forward to peer through the windshield. "It doesn't look like much," she sniffed. "The guide made it sound amazing."

Nancy punched her leg. Her sister let out a satisfying cry of protest and she smiled. "Give it a chance. It's an adventure, remember?"

"Okay, but *ow!*" Paula replied, glaring at her.

The moment passed quickly, however. They wove their way through streets lined with offices and hotels, gas stations and apartment buildings, following signs that announced that the *Centro de Ciudad* was ahead. A public parking garage loomed up on the right and they managed to squeeze the rental car down inside of it, though making any of the corners in the underground complex was quite a trick. This sort of thing was exactly why Nancy would not let Paula drive.

Their travel guide had a brief write-up about the city, but no map. Fortunately they were able to buy one very cheaply at the hotel above the garage. With her camera on its strap around her neck, Nancy slid the thick travel guide into the pocket of the light spring jacket she wore. She was a diminutive woman and seemed nearly always to be chilly, and so she found it made sense to always have a jacket along, even if she did not need it. In early May, the temperatures in Spain could vary greatly, particularly when they passed from bright sunshine onto shadowed sidewalks.

The sisters followed the *Centro de Ciudad* signs on foot for several blocks, examining the various structures for age and Moorish influence. The Moors had controlled this part of Spain for ages and built mosques and palaces unrivaled elsewhere in the West. Yet Ronda, despite the travel guide's description of it as a former Moorish stronghold, seemed devoid of such influences.

They had been in the city less than fifteen minutes and passed by dozens of gift shops selling masks and clothes and souvenirs, but Nancy had seen nothing of the marvel that the Vandals had led them to believe they would find.

"Give me the map for a second."

Paula frowned at her. "You're supposed to be taking pictures. I can read the map."

"The guide says there's a new city and an old city. This must be the new city. You have to cross the ravine or whatever to get to the old."

Paula stopped short on the sidewalk outside a restaurant with a bullfighter on the sign. "Hello? I know that. I have the map?" She brandished it like a trophy.

They stared at one another for a long moment and then began to laugh.

"All right, map-lady," Nancy relented. "Where do we go from here?"

"Turn around." Paula raised an eyebrow at her.

Nancy turned and found herself looking at a large circular, whitewashed building surrounded by a high wall and fronted by an arch and black wrought-iron gate.

"The bullring?" she asked.

"The bullring," Paula confirmed.

Their attention had been diverted from reaching the old city for a moment. They paid to enter the empty building, which the guide identified as the oldest bullring in all of Spain, dating back to the late eighteenth century. The inside was impressive, with a two-story gallery supported by Tuscan arches and a stone barrier surrounding the ring itself. The sisters toured the ring, and though Paula lamented that they could not witness an actual bullfight, Nancy was glad there were no events that day. She did not want to watch such a spectacle.

Back on the sidewalk in front of the bullring, she glanced at her sister and smiled. "Where to?"

Paula smiled back, consulted the map, and set off along the street. They had their share of squabbles and always had, but they had promised each other that there was no way they were going to let themselves get mired in silly arguments that would spoil their vacation. Sometimes it wasn't easy to keep that promise, but at the moment, they were a team.

Nancy gazed around her, enjoying the way the sun caught the edges of the whitewashed buildings. The light seemed to have an almost unearthly quality here, and she did not know if it was the elevation of the city or simply her pleasure in viewing it. The smells from the restaurants were enticing but she wanted to make sure they explored more before stopping for lunch. They had left early and still had a couple of hours before they would be nearing starvation.

The breeze was even cooler than she had expected and she zipped her jacket, taking care to leave the camera accessible. She had taken some wonderful pictures of the bullring and only hoped that they communicated half of the structure's majesty. The travel guide jutted from the outside pocket of her jacket, but she needed to make sure it was accessible.

The Carling sisters had walked only a short way when the old city came into sight. Paula gestured to Nancy with the map in triumph, but they were both smiling and began to walk a little faster.

When they reached the bridge, they stopped.

Nancy discovered she was holding her breath but found she could not help it. Across the bridge was the old city of Ronda, parts of which dated from the Moorish occupancy, as far back as the twelfth century. The road on the other side of the bridge rose up to the peak of the plateau and so the buildings seemed stacked one upon the other. To the right they had a perfect view of the craggy cliff face that fell away from the edge of the old city in a breathtakingly steep, sheer drop to the valley floor, which spread out below, dotted with ancient ruins and a village of whitewashed houses.

The bridge itself was one of the most incredible things Nancy had ever seen. With Paula beside her, she walked to the edge of the new city and stared down into the ravine— what she now remembered that the travel guide had referred to as the "Cleft of Ronda."

"It must be a thousand feet," Paula said.

Nancy stared down at the rocky gap, at the walls from which trees and shrubs grew against all odds, at the tiny mouths of caves, at the river far, far below. "I think it's deeper," she said.

The bridge was a series of arches constructed upon other arches. At its center was the highest of them, and in the body of the bridge a tiny barred window. The guidebook had noted that this segment of the bridge had once been used as a prison.

"And this is the new bridge," Paula said, grinning at her sister.

"What do you mean new? What were the dates again?"

"I don't remember exactly, but this one was late seventeen hundreds."

"And that's new?" Nancy asked.

"For this place? Yeah. There are a couple of other bridges across the gap that date back to the Moors."

Nancy smiled and gazed out at the panorama again. This was the reason they had come to Spain, the magical quality of places like this, where you could almost hear the ringing of clashing swords still echoing off the buildings or feel the rumble of passing wagons in the cobblestones beneath your feet. With very few exceptions, America was a land of make-believe, where the only magic kingdom came with a giant mouse that wore pants and talked in a high squeaky voice.

The camera hung around her neck and she raised it now, clicked it on, and snapped a photograph of the Cleft, trying to get some perspective on its height by including part of the valley in the background. She took several more photos of the old city from this side of the bridge. Then, at last, with Paula leading the way, she stepped onto the bridge itself. The sun was warm there in the open above the Cleft of Ronda and the air seemed to sparkle.

Nancy raised the camera again. There was a high barrier on either side of the bridge for the safety of people walking across, but a kind of high ledge ran along the inside of it. She had to get a better view over the side of the bridge. Though she recognized with a kind of sadness the fact that she would never be able to take a photograph that would accurately communicate the majesty of this place, she was determined to try.

"Careful," Paula warned.

"Always," Nancy replied.

With her left hand on the barrier wall and her right hand clutching the camera, she stepped up onto the ledge where the view was dizzying and spectacular. As she did so, her right knee pushed up the bottom of her jacket and the travel guide popped out, slipped over the top of the barrier wall, and fell into the Cleft.

"Oh, shit," Nancy whispered.

Paula stepped up beside her and together they watched it tumble, pages ruffling, end over end, down and down until at last the tiny speck it had become landed soundlessly in the brush beside the river. The fall had seemed to last an eternity.

"Great," Paula sighed. "We're fucked now."

———

KUROMAKU had no idea how many hours had passed since he had led Sophie and the others to the church. The journey through the ravaged city of Mont de Moreau had taken them through abandoned streets, entire blocks on fire, and they had been set upon several times by demons.

The black-armored, scythe-limbed creatures had kept their distance, but their path had led them into skirmishes with two more of the lumbering, poison-quilled monsters they had seen at the site of the train derailment, as well as a small clutch of *J'ai-Pushti*, a race of tiny yet savage demons referred to in the oral histories of Central Africa. *J'ai-Pushti* were much like vicious goblins, no more than nine inches high, yet despite their size they were formidable when traveling in packs. Sophie and the family she had saved from the train were covered with scratches, but Kuromaku had made certain none of them were fatally injured.

In the church they had washed their wounds and made introductions. The couple were Alain and Antoinette Lamontagne. They had been traveling on holiday with their son Henri, planning to visit friends in Nice. Now their son seemed almost catatonic, sleeping for hours and only gazing around wide-eyed while awake, as though trying to convince himself it was only a bad dream.

Kuromaku could not blame him.

The Lamontagnes were handling the situation far better than he would have expected, however. Perhaps it was simply that they could not deny what they had seen and felt; perhaps it was nothing more than instinct and not wanting to die. The five of them, Alain carrying his son, had made it to the church alive.

But where to go from here?

Kuromaku had expected to find the church full of people fleeing the demons and the hellish vista their town had become. Where else would they run? Yet the church had been empty when they arrived, not even a priest here to pray with them, and it troubled Kuromaku deeply. There had been no blood, no evidence of violence, no broken windows—but the front doors of the church had been hanging wide open when they reached it. In the long hours since they had taken sanctuary within that holy edifice, no human had appeared. The only things that had tried to gain admittance were the *J'ai-Pushti*, but the magick inherent in the building's architecture had kept them out, just as it kept out the huge, razor-quilled thing that hammered on the door even now.

It could not enter, but with each thunderous blow on the door, Kuromaku winced. He could hear the thing all the way back in the sacristy, where the priests who presided over this church prepared for each mass and where they kept their holy vestments.

The others remained in the front of the church, among the pews, in the shadow of the cross. Kuromaku retreated twice an hour to the sacristy to peer out the windows—the only panes in the church that were not part of a stained-glass biblical scene—yet the view of Mont de Moreau spread out before him never changed. New fires burned and others dimmed, but the heavy, dark orange sky remained and nothing human moved on the streets. Above the church he saw several of the winged carrion demons they had seen feasting on the dead upon their arrival. The things circled expectantly above, as though certain the death of those in the church was inevitable.

And it is, Kuromaku thought grimly as he gazed out the window. His brow furrowed as he turned their dilemma over in his mind. There was a small refrigerator in the sacristy and there had been a little food inside. They had finished the last of it more than two hours before, forcing the boy, Henri, to eat a bar of chocolate Kuromaku had found on a desk in the sacristy.

A creature of the shadows himself, Kuromaku would survive. But if they did not leave here, Sophie and the others would die of starvation in time.

The vampire swore under his breath and turned from the window. He pushed through a door and strode out onto the altar, a place where once upon a time his kind would never have dared to set foot. The light that glowed outside the stained glass windows cast an eerie, disturbing illumination upon the church. At the bottom of the two steps that led down from the altar, Antoinette Lamontagne had created a bed for her son out of the priestly vestments she had gathered from the sacristy. Her husband sat in the first pew, speaking quietly with Sophie, expression intense.

"What is it?" Kuromaku asked.

Sophie looked up. She had slept very little and her features were drawn and pale. Kuromaku resolved for the hundredth time to find a way to get her free of this.

"A small argument," she told him, her voice echoing in the vast church. "Alain thinks it would be sinful of us to drink the wine of the mass unless it is administered by a priest. He's not sure about the holy water."

Kuromaku stared at Alain grimly. He pointed to the man's unconscious son. "God would deny water to this boy?" he asked in French.

The man's mouth hung open slightly and he turned to stare at his son. His wife gazed up at him and then turned away. Alain covered his eyes as though afraid he might weep in front of them. Then he rose and went to Antoinette and Henri, and he lay down with his son, curling his body behind the boy's, shielding his son with his own flesh.

Sophie slipped out of the pew and walked up to Kuromaku on the altar. She sat down on the top step and patted the place beside her. Troubled, his mind working at the puzzle of their predicament, he sat.

"We can't stay here," Sophie said, voice low, her words heavy with her Parisian accent.

"No," he agreed.

"You've put a lot of thought into this. I wish you would share those thoughts."

Kuromaku turned to face her, aware suddenly of her nearness, of the spare inches that separated them. She seemed so delicate, fragile, though he knew she was hardly that. In that moment he remembered her father, and what a fine man and loyal friend he had been. If Kuromaku could not keep Sophie alive, he would never learn if there might be something more between them, but more than that, his honor would be forever tainted.

She gazed at him and he knew that though she knew what he was, she saw him as a man. Sophie saw his heart. In the time since they had arrived—fifteen hours, perhaps eighteen—he had walked back and forth between altar and sacristy over and over, trying to determine the best course of action. Yet he had shut her out, and he realized now that had been unfair. He owed her honesty, at least.

Kuromaku gazed a moment at one of the stained glass windows, an image of the Nazarene at Golgotha, bearing upon his back the very burden upon which he would soon be crucified. The agony depicted there was plain enough, but with the dark glow behind it, the scene was like something out of Hell itself.

He tore his eyes from it, focusing on Sophie again.

"Do you believe in evil? True evil?"

Her blue eyes shone as she gazed at him, seemingly untouched by the hideous light that filtered through the stained glass, and Kuromaku felt strengthened by them.

Sophie nodded.

"I do not think that I believe," Kuromaku told her. Her eyes widened in surprise and he forged ahead. "I believe in cruelty, in lack of conscience, in pettiness and lust and tyranny. I believe in savagery and the predatory nature of beasts, human and otherwise. But I cannot say that I have ever been convinced of the existence of the sort of epic, operatic evil so many religions have put forward to motivate their subjects to behave.

"If you look into the eyes of a demon, of a monster, and you can see that it wants to kill you, wants to feel your hot blood gushing into its throat, then it is evil, is it not?" Kuromaku asked. He nodded but more to himself than to Sophie. "By that definition, I do not think I have ever seen anything as evil as the things that swarmed our train."

He fell silent for several seconds then. Sophie reached out and took his hands in her own but kept her gaze steady, waiting for him to continue.

"You saw what happened in Paris," he said at length. "The demon that made an incursion there was unable to enter Sacré-Coeur. We should be safe here, but even if we are, we cannot stay. We will starve to death. Our only choice is to escape the Hell that has swallowed this city. Otherwise we will die. The sooner we move, the better."

Sophie took a deep breath and blew it out. "Do you think . . . what I mean is, you do not think that the whole world has become"—she gestured around them—"like this?"

"No. It may be simply that I cannot imagine it, but I do not believe it. Rather than making an incursion into our world, some Hell or another has absorbed Mont de Moreau.

If we can reach the limit of the area that has been affected, we might escape this."

Sophie leaned back in the pew, turned to gaze up at the carved figure of the crucified Christ. "Then we go," she said quietly, her eyes ticking toward the Lamontagnes. "But perhaps a few more hours' sleep first? To rest before we have to endure that again?"

"I do not think that's wise," Kuromaku admitted.

Something in his tone made her flinch. Sophie looked at him with suspicion. "What are you not telling me?"

Kuromaku ran his hand along the smooth wood of the pew. It gleamed as though it had been recently dusted, by cloth or by the palms of hundreds of the faithful, and he had no doubt that it had indeed.

"If you thought that Hell had come to Earth and you lived in the shadow of a church like this one, with its spire beckoning to you, would you not have run here? If you were the priest who had been given this flock to shepherd, would you not remain here to welcome them to a safe haven?"

Sophie frowned. "I might. Or I might wish to go out in order to minister to that flock. Perhaps to lead them here."

Kuromaku nodded, but he was still troubled. He kissed Sophie on the forehead and rose from the pew. Leaving her to explain the terrible truth to the Lamontagnes, he returned to the sacristy only long enough to search for the communion wine. Uncorking the bottle he sniffed at its contents and wrinkled his nostrils. It was terrible stuff, and the last thing he wanted was for any of the humans with him to be even slightly intoxicated. Still, a small sip might give them a kind of strength water would not. Despite Alain's hesitation, Kuromaku hoped that the man would look upon communion wine as a gift of grace.

He returned to the front of the church with the bottle. The moment he stepped out onto the altar, Antoinette Lamontagne rose and approached him, cursing him in French. Kuromaku understood the language but Antoinette's words ran one upon the other with such speed that he could only grasp a fraction of what was said. With a frown he turned to Sophie, who ran both hands through her hair and froze a moment in frustration.

"They won't leave," Sophie told him. "They think it's going to end. Eventually it has to end, they say, and why can't we just wait here, where it is safe, until it is over or until someone else comes to help us? Antoinette refuses to take Henri out of here."

Kuromaku swore under his breath. He kept his chin high, but his nostrils flared in annoyance. "Did you tell them that we cannot be certain it is safe here?"

"They don't agree. It is the house of God, they say. Christ Himself looks down upon us here. They believe we are safest here."

"Then we leave without them," Kuromaku said gravely, his eyes narrowing. In Japanese, he swore again, cursing the Lamontagnes.

Sophie blinked and stared at him. She took several steps closer to Antoinette so that now the two women were facing him together.

"You can't leave without them," she said. "We cannot leave them here to die."

"If they are right," Kuromaku declared, "they will be perfectly safe and we will be the ones at risk." He narrowed his gaze further so that he was staring at Sophie through slitted eyes. "Do not do this. If they will not come, that is their choice. But I will not leave here without you, Sophie. I . . . will not let anything happen to you."

Sophie let her gaze drift toward the ground. "We can't leave them here."

Frustration boiled up inside him and Kuromaku stormed past the women to glare down upon Alain and his sleeping son.

"Fool," he hissed. Kuromaku raised the wine bottle and continued in his imperfect French. "We do not know what has happened. How bad it is. There is no way to know if it will end, or when. We must find the world again," he said, gesturing at the windows.

Alain snapped at him, something unintelligible that Kuromaku interpreted as meaning that God would protect them, given the man's gestures toward the cross.

Kuromaku whipped around to look at Sophie, who shrank back from him as though in fear. He softened, sighed, and shook his head. "God cannot keep you all from starving. There will be no manna from heaven in this place."

Antoinette and Alain were silent. Kuromaku stared at them and then at Sophie, who seemed implacable. He would not leave here without her, but she would not leave without the damnably stubborn parents of a catatonic child. The idea of simply sitting here and waiting drove him wild and he considered forcing Sophie to accompany him. But only for a moment. It was impractical. She would struggle, make them more of a target, and they would never survive it.

And afterward she would hate him for abandoning these people.

"Damn it!" Kuromaku cried, and he hurled the bottle of communion wine at the altar, where it shattered and spilled the blessed blood of grapes across white marble.

At the sound of the breaking glass, little Henri Lamontagne opened his eyes and began to scream. The boy shrieked as though he had woken from the most terrifying of nightmares, rather than *into* one. It was a piercing wail that rose in pitch and volume, so that his father, who was closest to him, clapped his hands over his ears and shouted at the boy to be silent.

Henri kept screaming. Two words, over and over.

"Les Chuchotements!"

The whispers.

In his bizarre catatonia, the boy must have heard their voices, Kuromaku reasoned. He glanced at Antoinette, who stared at her son, eyes wide with despair. Sophie reached for her, but Antoinette was already rushing past her, going to Henri. Kuromaku expected her to hold the boy, to comfort him. Instead she slapped his face with an impact that echoed all through the vast interior of the church.

Silence fell upon them, save that ringing echo.

A flutter of wings came from the shadowed rafters above them, pigeons or other birds that had roosted in among the high beams of the church and had been roused by the boy's screaming. Kuromaku glanced up and saw a pigeon fly down out of the rafters and across the church, to come to rest atop a pew near the main doors.

But something else caught Kuromaku's eye.

Something else lurked in the shadows among the rafters, dark and furtive. *Les Chuchotements*, he thought, and he realized that the boy was not screaming about things he had heard, but rather what he had seen, up in those rafters. Something that he had somehow found a name for.

The Whispers.

Henri was trapped inside his own mind, but for the first time Kuromaku wondered if he was alone in there, or if something had made its way inside with him.

There was more motion in the shadows above.

"Sophie," Kuromaku whispered. "Tell them to take the boy, now. We must go."

Sophie blinked in confusion. "What? They've already said—"

Any words she spoke thereafter were drowned out as Henri Lamontagne began to scream again. This time, however, his eyes were not bleary and unfocused as they had been upon his waking. No, now he was staring directly up into the rafters of the church at the faceless, skeletal demons that emerged from the darkness, pronglike tongues tasting the air before them.

The first of them dropped from the rafters to the pews below.

The boy continued to scream.

"Les Chuchotements!"

CHAPTER 11

NIKKI froze with astonishment as she watched Peter rise up off the ground, completely enveloped in a sphere of magickal energy. Her skin prickled with the static electricity in the air and her face felt warm as if she were sitting too close to a fire. She had seen him use magick before, seen him orchestrate the sorcery that had become a part of him, but nothing like this. In the years since he had become human again, Peter had developed a far greater control over magick. Or it had grown in him, matured somehow.

Whatever its explanation, it was breathtaking to see.

Peter raised his hands as though conducting a symphony and a scythe of energy arced outward from his fingers. The ground that separated him from the demons shook and the pavement cracked and then his magick struck the first wave of the onslaught. Seven of the darkly hideous creatures were blown apart, limbs and burning shells raining down upon the others that bounded in behind them.

"Nikki!"

For an instant she had no idea who was calling to her, so entranced was she by watching her former lover, the sorcerer, at work. Then it was as though a switch had been thrown in her head.

The voice belonged to Father Jack.

"Watch out!" the priest shouted.

A gunshot punched the air too close to her head and the impact on her right eardrum made her cry out. Even as she did, she spun in that direction and saw what Father Jack was shooting at. Not the Slogute . . . the enormous beast seemed to have disappeared into the ground once more. No, the priest had shot one of these swift, cruel-looking demons, the bullet punching through the blue-black shell that covered its chest.

The demon let out a piercing shriek that Nikki thought would have shattered glass.

It went down.

And the others swarmed right over it.

Peter was on the other side of the Navigator, dealing with the huge crowd of the hideous things that had come up out of the ground after the Slogute. Nikki had no idea what Keomany was up to and didn't dare look. For on her side of the SUV, the things were rushing from the rubble of the devastated house on the corner.

Against the filthy orange sky they seemed little more than savage silhouettes, almost surreal.

But real enough.

"Shoot them!" Father Jack snapped at her, even as he fired his own weapon twice more, stepping farther away from the SUV and balancing his aim with both hands.

Nikki did not need to be told twice. She had faced the impossible before, horrors that could not exist in a sane world. But that was back when she had been under the false assumption that the world was sane. She knew better now. She did not even flinch as she brought the weapon to bear. Two of the thin demons rushed from the grass, crossing the pavement as they scrabbled spiderlike toward her. Nikki felt her finger twitch upon the trigger. The gun had a kick and the first bullet went wide.

The demons hissed, a sound like the static between radio stations. Her heart thundered in her chest and she bit her lip, her throat going dry. Too close. They were too close. Faster than she had thought. The first bullet had been her last.

Her finger pulled the trigger and this time she kept the barrel of the gun straight and kept the trigger down. Bullets tore from the weapon and shards of demon shell and stinking black blood shot out the backs of the creatures closest to her.

"Good!" Father Jack yelled as he fired again. Once. Twice. Slowly. "But save your ammunition if you can!"

Save your ammunition, my ass! she thought. The first time she had fired she had not remembered that the gun had the capacity for rapid fire. The weapon felt warm in her hand now as she took aim again at several more of the demons as they rushed at her. Bullets tore them apart.

Others were coming from behind houses and from the new hole the Slogute had made in the rubble, but they were more cautious now, creeping slowly toward them, looking for an opening.

"We have no idea how many there are!" Nikki told the priest. "We need to clear a path, not play 'Remember the Alamo.'"

Father Jack nodded. "Agreed."

He glanced over his shoulder and Nikki watched the demons a moment, checking to be sure they were keeping their distance, before she did the same.

Within that sphere of magick Peter now floated above the hole in the middle of the road. The pavement was strewn with the remains of the creatures and now the sorcerer drifted to the ground. The sphere dissolved around him with a crackle and Peter knelt and touched his hands to the ground.

The hole caved in upon itself, the ravaged area of the street growing larger as pavement and earth gave way and filled in the passage below.

There would be no more demons from that avenue.

Nikki frowned, panic surging through her. She glanced back into the SUV, raced to the back of the vehicle and around the other side.

"Where's Keomany?" she shouted at Peter.

He frowned. There was such power in him that she had expected his face to be somehow inhuman but she saw the emotion in his eyes and his expression and in that moment she remembered the first time she had met him, the way he had gazed at her from the audience in a little club she was playing in New Orleans. The way he had looked that very night when he had saved her from having her throat torn out.

Gunfire echoed off the houses on either side of the street. Father Jack was firing at the demons that had grown courageous enough to approach anew. Nikki glanced at the priest. Beyond him, she saw Keomany. Her friend had left the Navigator and was walking onto Little Tree Lane. Her parents' house was the third on the left and from here it looked intact, unblemished, but there was no way to tell.

Not that it mattered. Keomany would never reach the house. The demons were flooding toward her. They might be afraid of the guns and of Peter's sorcery, but Keomany was unprotected, alone, walking among them.

"Peter!" Nikki cried, chills running through her.

She raced toward the front of the SUV but Peter was already there. A tiny alarm bell sounded in Nikki's mind as she realized they were leaving the Navigator behind—being separated from their transportation—but it did not matter. The only thing that mattered in that moment was Keomany.

Her black hair gleamed red in the filthy orange light.

Peter raised his hands. Nikki saw that they were glittering with green sparks. The air in front of him seemed to shiver. Nikki knew she would never reach Keomany in time. She stopped, planted her feet, and took aim.

She never squeezed the trigger.

Keomany screamed something unintelligible at the things that swarmed in around her, these slender, vicious demons that seemed more like ants than anything else. The pavement was sundered as thick tree roots shot up through it, impaling three of the demons and snaring two more. The ground split beneath several others and they tumbled into the gaping trench beneath them.

As if nothing at all had happened, Keomany strode on toward her parents' home.

Nikki stared after her. "Wow," she whispered as she ran up beside Peter.

"Earthwitch," he said. "She wasn't kidding."

A loud hiss rose up behind them and Nikki and Peter turned, side by side, to find a new phalanx of the faceless demons rushing them, long tendril tongues darting about below the shells that covered their heads.

"Oh, enough of this," Peter snarled.

Nikki leveled her weapon at them and fired, her bullets splintering the shells of the two closest to her and grazing another.

Then a new sound filled the air, a sound like lightning striking a tree, splintering wood. Peter screamed as though he was in pain and she whipped around to find that his face was contorted in agony, his teeth bared, clenched tight. With a release of breath that seemed to explode from him, he cried out in that ancient tongue she had heard him use before.

A tear appeared in the world in front of them, running like a crack from ground to stratosphere and then peeling back on either side to reveal blue sky and golden sunlight beyond. The fissure between worlds widened and the demons screeched at the infusion of daylight, of this world that was not their own.

They began to retreat.

Nikki nodded in satisfaction. She turned to Father Jack. "Get in and drive!" she snapped. "Follow us."

Peter reached out and took her hand and his grip was strong and confident. Nikki ran with him, following Keomany. She saw another pair of demons attack her friend but Keomany would not be stopped. Tree roots tore at the demons and dragged them back into the earth. It occurred to Nikki then that what Peter had just done on a huge scale, Keomany was somehow doing as well: tapping into the real world, the dimension they had come from.

"Why didn't you just do that at first?" Nikki asked him as they sprinted after Keomany.

A demon sprang at her from broken pavement. Nikki spun and shot it through the head, shattering the shell over its skull. They kept running.

"I wasn't sure I could. All I did was return that part of the town to our world, where it belongs."

They raced up Little Tree Lane. Keomany was already walking up her parents' front lawn toward the door. It should have made her breathe a sigh of relief but Nikki was even more unnerved as she went up the steps. With that sickly orange sky and the unnatural feel of the air, with demons lurking in every shadow, it only felt more wrong. This picture-perfect little town that had been Keomany's home had been twisted into something horrid and unrecognizable. A sudden urge to cry welled up in her but Nikki pushed it away.

"Can you do that to the whole village?" she asked Peter as they reached the front door.

"I'm not sure."

She wanted to tell him he had to try, even if the town would never be the same again. But then Keomany was pounding on the door and screaming for her parents. She tried the knob several times and cried out for them again. Then she turned and gazed back at Nikki and Peter.

"The dogs," she said, eyes wide with shock and dawning horror. "I don't hear the dogs."

Peter took her gently by the arm and moved her aside. He waved at the door and it unlocked. As he stepped inside, Nikki heard the roar of an engine and he saw Father Jack pull into the driveway. The demons had begun to form a large circle, creating a perimeter around them at a distance and their numbers were increasing.

In the sky, Nikki thought she saw something huge and dark on the horizon, wings outspread, but then it disappeared among the treetops in a vast wooded area to the east. With all these indigo monsters with their gleaming shells, she had almost forgotten the Slogute. These demons weren't the only things here, and now she wondered what else was in Wickham, what other evils lingered in this otherworld.

Father Jack jumped out of the Navigator, glancing over his shoulder to make sure there was nothing rushing at him, and he ran up toward the front of the house.

Peter went inside and Keomany followed. Nikki glanced again at the priest and then went in after them. It was a split-level home and the door opened onto the landing between levels. The lower portion of the house was dark but upstairs it opened onto a large room with bay windows and the interior was illuminated by that grotesque orange light.

They went up.

At the top of the steps Peter glanced to his right, into what Nikki imagined was the living room. Keomany was right behind him, but Peter stopped and turned to her, held a hand up to stop her where she was, to keep her from going farther. He shook his head, grim compassion etched into his features. Nikki felt all the air go out of her lungs.

"Oh, Keomany," she whispered.

But Keomany would not stop. She pushed past Peter now and he did not stop her. She went to the top of the stairs and looked into the living room. Nikki knew she should stay where she was. She did not want to see what had happened up there. And yet somehow she could not stop her feet from going up the steps.

"They're getting closer," she heard Father Jack say from the front door.

Nikki did not even glance at him. She walked past Peter on the stairs and stood beside Keomany. Over the top of a half-wall that separated the stairs from the living room she saw her friend's parents. Among delicate furniture and shelves filled with antiques, their bodies were sprawled on either side of the splintered coffee table. Their torsos were torn open and completely eviscerated, hollowed out until all that remained of them were shriveled husks that reminded her of melon rinds.

The carpet was stained with blood and the demons had tracked their prints all over it in scarlet, but of Mr. and Mrs. Shaw's viscera there was no sign. Whatever the things had torn out of these people they had either eaten or taken with them.

Keomany whimpered and turned to Nikki, who embraced her tightly. The women held one another and Nikki felt Keomany's breath hot on her throat, felt her friend's warm tears drip on her neck. Cold anger burned in her, as resolute as guilt or grief, but so much more powerful.

"I'm so sorry," Nikki whispered, jaw clenched in fury and shared pain.

"The dogs," Keomany whispered. "Where are the fucking . . ."

She let her words trail off mid-sentence and turned to go into the kitchen. Nikki followed her. The linoleum floor was covered with the bloody demon tracks. Keomany ignored them as she went to the sink and looked out the window above it—a window that gave a view of the back yard. Over her shoulder Nikki could see the broad expanse of lawn and the trees back there, as well as the twin cables that ran from the house to the woods. Dog runs.

And tied to each of the runs, a pair of yellow Labrador retrievers, who even now hid in among the trees as though waiting in ambush for the demons that would come no closer to them than they could reach. Their masters had been slaughtered and the dogs had been unable to help. Nikki could only imagine the baying and growling and barking that had ensued.

"Muggsy," Keomany said. "Bonkers. You poor boys."

From the bottom of the stairs, Father Jack called up to them. "They're coming!"

—

PETER had followed Nikki and Keomany only as far as the top of the steps. He stood and stared at the blood-soaked living room, at the corpses of Mr. and Mrs. Shaw. When he heard Father Jack shout to them that the demons were attacking once more, he snapped his head around and glared down at the priest.

"No they're not."

He marched down the stairs. Father Jack was even paler than he had been before. His eyes were haunted but he did not look away under the weight of Peter's scrutiny. The priest nodded and stepped aside, then followed Peter out the door. He sensed Nikki and Keomany coming down the stairs behind them but did not turn.

The chain of demons that was stretched out in a circle around the property were moving slowly, inexorably forward. They were nine and ten deep in places, hundreds of them, and yet they moved nervously, all of them with their faceless heads tilted toward Peter, waiting for him to attack.

But he had no intention of fighting them. Their number seemed infinite. It was a battle he might not be capable of winning, no matter how much sorcerous power he was able to wield. But defeating these monsters was not the battle he had come to fight. Not at all. There was another victory to be had here, a far more important one. Keomany's parents were dead, but Peter felt certain there were others still alive in Wickham. He wanted to make sure they stayed that way.

Father Jack raised his gun and leveled it at the approaching hordes. Peter glanced over at him.

"Don't bother," he said.

Then he turned and spotted Nikki and Keomany hanging back near the brick steps at the front of the house. "Keomany. Come here, please."

It was as though his voice had awoken her from some horrible fugue state, a trance of grief and impossibility. He suspected the power she wielded was just as much a part of that as were the demons and the infernal landscape around them. More than likely she had already distanced herself from all of this psychologically, just to deal with it.

Nikki took Keomany's hand and together they rushed across the lawn to Peter. Father Jack looked on anxiously, his gun still wavering between the ground and the slowly advancing army of chittering demons that slunk forward, orange light gleaming off their black carapaces.

"We've got to get back into the Navigator," Nikki said. "We've gotta get out of here, Peter."

He shook his head. "No. That's not why we came." He reached out and touched Keomany lightly on the shoulder and her gaze lifted, their eyes met.

"This is real, Keomany," he told her. "You understand that? All of what you see. All of what you feel. It's real."

Her delicate Asian features seemed to break then, and she bit her lower lip as she nodded. Her eyes pinched shut, squeezing tears that slid down her cheeks. Quickly she raised a hand to wipe them away and then stared at him again, almost defiantly.

"Good," Peter said, and though his heart was grim and cold, he offered her a smile. "Then show me what you've got, Earthwitch. Give me one of those roots. Right here."

He pointed to the lawn.

"Peter," Father Jack warned.

"I know. They're getting closer," Peter replied, without even glancing at the demons. "Don't shoot unless they rush us. I think they're waiting for something."

"For what?" Nikki asked.

Peter kept his gaze on Keomany. "I don't think we want to know. Do we?"

Keomany took a deep breath. There was the faintest scent of perfume on her, like lilacs. She backed away from Peter and her brows knitted together as she stretched a hand toward the ground, her fingers curled as she beckoned something forth.

Peter shivered as he felt the power surge up from the earth. It came not from Keomany, as it would with true sorcery, but from the ground—from the very spirit of their world. The village of Wickham was from that other place, from their world, and so perhaps *it* was still connected as well, though it had been displaced. Perhaps Keomany would not have been able to touch the world of her birth if Wickham itself had not been stolen from there. But she did.

Somehow, though she had traveled into this terrible alternate dimension, Keomany was still connected to the world that they had left behind. With every fiber of her being, she called out to it now and it responded by striking out for her, bursting through into this horrid place like lightning arcing up into the sky.

The thick, gnarled root of a tree burst up through the soil and grass of the lawn, growing before their eyes, lengthening and tearing up more of the grass as it reached up. It rose from the ground like a serpent summoned from a wicker basket by some Egyptian snake charmer.

Keomany glanced at Peter for further instructions but he only nodded and thanked her.

His skin felt filthy, coated with a putrescent film that had collected upon all of them like pollen. It was the atmosphere of this strange realm, this place between worlds where some power had secreted the village of Wickham away and changed it forever, baptized the town in blood and cruelty. They were all tainted with it now, but the filth would wash off, might even burn off if exposed to the pure sunlight of their own world.

For all of them save Keomany. It had taken something from her and left a stain on her soul that might never be cleansed.

Peter knew he had to find the being behind this horror, but first there was Wickham to be dealt with. He glanced over at Nikki and took strength from the faith in her eyes.

As if that were some silent cue, the indigo demons began to swarm toward them again.

The things were deadly and swift as they crossed the pavement and danced across the lawn, constricting the perimeter circle they had created. Their talons gleamed hideously in the hellish orange light. Father Jack and Nikki turned on them immediately and began to shoot, gunfire ripping through the first wave of attackers. They would be out of ammunition in seconds. There were too many of the creatures. Keomany had not plumbed the depths of her newfound power yet, but Peter did not think she would need to.

The magick that surged through him was much like electrocution. His muscles went taut, his limbs rigid, and pain lanced through him, deep as the bone. Peter summoned all the magick within him, all that he had learned and that was now a part of him, and he reached out his left hand and gripped the top of the tree root that jutted from the earth in front of him.

Connection.

It was instantaneous. Purely on instinct—as all of his most powerful sorcery had become—he muttered words last heard on the banks of the River Tigris many millennia before. Keomany had drawn that root forth from their world, from the earth they all knew. It had punched a hole into this realm and now Peter used that root as an anchor. He could *feel* the world of his birth. With his mind, with his magick, he reached his power down along that root and felt the edges of that puncture wound between worlds.

With his eyes tightly closed, he tore it wide open.

He had done this earlier, ripped a hole in this dimension that allowed portions of Wickham to spill back into its rightful place. The effort had driven a wedge of pain through his skull. This was completely different. Then he had sensed their own dimension lurking just beyond the veil that enclosed this realm. Now, with Keomany's earthcraft aiding him, he could feel it. Touch it.

Peter could hear ripples of gunfire but it all seemed distant from him now. Nikki and Keomany and Father Jack, they were all so far away. He smelled freshly mown grass and felt the warmth of the sun on his face. He opened his eyes and looked up.

The dreadful pumpkin sky had been wounded. A circular hole gaped in that bilious ceiling; a hole through which the sky was pure blue with white wisps of cloud, and through which the life-giving spring sunlight burned down upon the small patch of lawn where Peter now stood. The grass seemed to yearn for it, the tree root in his hand trembled as the circle of sunlight on the Shaws' yard began to grow. Visually, it was deceiving, for he was not pushing the hellish landscape away. Rather, he had grabbed hold of his own world and was *pulling* them back into it.

Peter took a deep breath, focusing his energy. He propelled it out of him, into that jutting root, and he felt the barrier tear, felt more of Wickham pulled back into alignment with its proper place. White sparks leaped from the blades of grass in the lawn as the area he had affected grew wider and the sunlight spread and the circle of blue sky above blossomed and spread until all of the property that had belonged to Keomany's parents had been reclaimed.

An island of peace in the midst of Hell.

The gunfire died.

Peter looked up to see Keomany staring at him. The demons were shrieking and retreating, scrambling over one another, trampling each other as they fled away from this otherworldly light to the safety of the disgusting realm they knew. The difference was tangible. It terrified them. This time they ran not only beyond the veil that now separated the two worlds, but farther, slipping into the black-orange shadows, into the broken windows of houses across the street or the woods beyond them, into the hole just down the block where the Slogute had burrowed.

One of the monsters, mewling like an injured kitten, turned the featureless, horseshoe-crab shell that served as its face up toward the blue sky, tendril tongue darting out to taste the air, then dropped to the ground and begin to dig insanely. It had given up hope of fleeing beyond the reach of the light of the earth-dimension's sun and now tried to excavate itself a hole in which to hide.

Father Jack took four quick strides toward it, aimed, and

blew the carapace over its skull to pieces. The priest blessed himself and looked around as if searching for other targets, but all of them had gone. Peter had no doubt they were watching from their hiding places, but for now he knew they would not attack again.

Nikki held her gun by her side as she walked to where Peter and Keomany stood on either side of the jutting root. Peter still clutched it in his hand and Nikki glanced at his grip before she met his gaze.

"That's a start." She grinned. "What do you do for an encore?"

Keomany could not seem to summon a smile; her grief was too great. "Can you do this for all of Wickham?"

"It wasn't just me," Peter assured her. "But with your help, I think I can, yes. I think *we* can."

Father Jack muttered something, his voice barely above a whisper. Peter ignored him, focused on Keomany. The earth-witch nodded and laid her hand over his upon that living root. Peter wondered if it were just any tree, of if there was something more to it, if Keomany had touched on the roots of nature itself, the earth spirit those of her faith believed in. In ancient Norse myth it had been called Yggdrasil, the world tree.

Perhaps, he thought, *all trees are part of Yggdrasil*.

"Octavian!" Father Jack snapped, but the intensity in his voice was born of fear rather than anger.

Nikki grabbed Peter's free hand but she was staring back the way they had come. Peter followed the line of her gaze and saw what had entranced her and terrified Father Jack. He felt Keomany's hand slip from his own and then, barely conscious of having done it, he let go of the root himself. The Shaws' property remained bathed in the warm sunlight of their world, but Peter felt cold in spite of the sun.

In the distance, above the tops of houses and trees, where mountains rose over Wickham, the orange sky had darkened and thickened. Ominous storm clouds had formed and even now dipped toward the ground as though they might at any moment touch down and become tornadoes. The air—even there in the place where the world had returned to normal—felt heavy and damp.

Tendrils of storm hung from the horrid sky and their color deepened from orange to bloody red. They drifted toward one another until they began to fuse—two, then four, then six prongs of furious, raging storm that from a distance looked very like antlers, perhaps horns, or the prongs of a crown.

In the massive wall of raging winds and debris that was whipped up from the ground beneath that crown, Peter Octavian was certain that he saw a face. The scarlet storm had black eyes and a slit for a nose and a gaping maw for a mouth.

And the storm came on.

At first it had seemed only to drive in upon itself, a war between ground and sky. Now that massive twist of furious winds, of deadly tornadoes, began to move in their direction. Even over the tops of houses they could see cars and chunks of buildings torn up from the ground and sent to whirl inside that massive storm.

The face in the storm leered at them.

Nikki clung suddenly to Peter's side. "What is it?" she whispered.

Keomany spoke up before he could respond.

"It's the thing that did this," she said. "The thing that took Wickham."

Father Jack had not moved. He simply stared at the oncoming storm, weapon hanging useless at his side. "You've got to be fucking kidding me," he said, voice barely audible over the rising howl of the wind as the blood red storm thundered toward them. "How do you kill that?"

"Let's solve that one from outside Wickham," Nikki said. She grabbed Keomany by the hand and the two women started toward the driveway, where the rented Navigator sat waiting.

Peter did not move. He stared at the face in the storm, at the black eyes like sinkholes in the midst of that crimson hurricane, tendrils of tornado stretching up into the stratosphere forming the crown of this power.

"We can't outrun it," Peter said flatly. "It's all around us."

He felt it, knew it. Though he had pulled a small portion of Wickham back to their dimension, the rest of the village was filled with the power of this thing they now faced.

Father Jack stared at him. "So we just wait for it to reach us?"

"It's already here."

The priest frowned but then he paused and shivered as though he felt it too. Nikki and Keomany stopped on the grass just short of the driveway. They all turned to look at the figure that appeared from the woods behind one of the houses across the street.

This was not like the other things they had encountered, not a skittering, hissing, indigo-armored demon. It was shaped like a human being, though impossibly tall and thin, and it was clad in rags and strips of cloth that clung to it as though pasted on, a papier-mâché effigy of a man. Strips of cloth covered its face as well, or as much as they could see of it, for its features were shaded by the hood of a ragged cloak that swirled around it with a wind churned up by the approaching storm.

Peter Octavian stared at this nomadic figure, this strange tatterdemalion, and he felt afraid.

It strode beneath the structure of an enormous family swing set, and though it did not touch them, the swings seemed to sway aside for it to pass. In its path was a sandbox shaped like a green-and-orange dragon lying on its back, its belly full of sand, a too-cute character out of children's storybooks. The thing walked over it, feet treading sand and then grass again, in a straight line toward them. A white picket fence cordoned off the back yard and the wooden struts shattered as it passed.

Nikki shouted something to Peter but he could not hear her. The roar of the incoming storm had grown much louder, drowning her words.

The Tatterdemalion reached the street, its eerily slender form silhouetted against the house and the woods and the roaring, blood red storm that massed above the trees—the sinister face of the storm glaring down upon them. The creature was close enough that Peter could see that some of it was covered with not rags but actual pieces of clothing—a little girl's sundress, a pair of denim jeans, a green silk blouse.

At the place where the horrid orange light ended and golden sunlight began, at the crossroads between worlds, it stopped. Tendrils of cloth flapped in the high winds. It did not seem even to notice Nikki and Keomany, and though its hooded eyes might have seen Father Jack, Peter was certain it was staring at him.

"Sorcerer," the Tatterdemalion said, and despite the howling winds and the rumble of the storm, he could hear its high, wheedling voice perfectly, as though it had spoken in his ear.

Peter raised his hands, clenched into fists, and magickal fire blazed up around them. He held his breath. His friends were nearby and he could feel their closeness as well as their vulnerability. Whatever this thing was, he would not allow it to lay its hands on Nikki.

"Give back what you've taken!" Peter shouted into the wind, barely able to hear his own words.

The cruel storm had paused, lingering just beyond Little Tree Lane, but it filled up the sky. Beneath it, the Tatterdemalion tilted its head to one side as if studying him.

"You are powerful," it said, voice echoing in his head. *"The Whispers fear you. Yet know this. Your magicks, no matter how ancient, cannot defeat me. They were forged to combat the energies that govern your own realm and many others. But your world is new to me, and I am new to it. The power I bring is like nothing that has ever been here before."*

At that place where the two dimensions clashed, the Tatterdemalion inclined its head.

"I leave you now. Of all my holdings, I have found this land to be least interesting. Therefore I will grant your request and return it to you. I warn you now, though, sorcerer. I will do as I wish in this plane, as I have in all others I have encountered. If you interfere further with my Whispers or my will, you shall be destroyed."

As the words lingered in his mind and Peter tried to make sense of them, tried to formulate some kind of response, the wind whipping around the Tatterdemalion increased. Nikki and Keomany ran the last few feet to the Navigator, afraid the storm was going to strike them in full. Father Jack leaned into the wind, but was so thin that Peter wondered how he managed to keep his footing.

The magick burned around his hands and surged through him and he felt he should strike, should attack the thing, but did not know how much power it truly had. Whatever horror lived in that storm it was as terrible as any of the ancient demons he had confronted during his time in Hell.

The wind whipping around it became a cyclone and for a moment the Tatterdemalion simply stood there. Then the green silk blouse was torn away from it, followed by the blue jeans and dozens, perhaps hundreds, of ragged strips of cloth.

The cloak was twisted around by the wind and funneled into a small tornado of cloth.

And the Tatterdemalion was gone.

In an instant, the space between two heartbeats, the sky above Wickham returned to normal, as though the sun were a spotlight turned on to dispel the filthy orange clouds. The blood red storm became pink mist and showered to the ground, leaving no trace.

The village of Wickham was in ruins, most of its citizens dead, but the sky was blue again and somewhere nearby birds sang and a dog barked furiously.

Nikki stomped across the lawn toward Peter, stood before him, and pointed at the place where the Tatterdemalion had stood.

"Excuse me, but what the *fuck* was that?"

Slowly, he shook his head, gazing at that same spot.

"I honestly have no idea."

CHAPTER 12

THE Cleft of Ronda was breathtakingly beautiful from the vantage point offered by the New Bridge. The Carling sisters remained on the bridge for nearly fifteen minutes as Nancy took photographs of the vistas offered on both sides. From the western view she could see the remains of centuries-old battlements in the foothills below the cliffs of the plateau, and to the east the Guadalevin River flowed through a sprawl of whitewashed houses surrounded by lush trees and other greenery.

Perhaps most startling—and it was a sight Paula insisted Nancy take several photos of—was the view available to them when they had reached the other end of the bridge. Looking back from the Old City to the comparatively new, they could see the back of the government-owned luxury hotel that loomed at the edge of the plateau, and the craggy drop below. They could, in fact, see all around the western part of the plateau, the outcroppings of rock and the striations in its composition, the ledges where dense shrubbery grew, the steep cliff face that made Nancy think that a leap from that height would feel like falling forever.

Not that she had any plans in that regard.

"So," she began, glancing at her sister. "You've got the map. Where to first?"

Paula smiled. "Sure you don't want to toss the map over the bridge?"

Nancy held out her hand. "Try me."

"I don't think so."

While her sister perused the map of Ronda and the descriptions of the various sights in the Old City, Nancy watched the cars and mopeds rumble past. People walked across the bridge as well and she struggled to hear their voices. She heard Spanish, of course, as well as Italian and German, but only one fortyish couple speaking English, and them with British accents, not American. Ronda seemed out of the way, the sort of place that people here knew about but that was not a destination the way other Spanish cities were. Americans had not really discovered it yet, it seemed. She liked that.

"Let's start up this way," Paula said.

Together they set off to the east along a road that ran parallel to the Cleft on one side and what the map identified as the family home of the Counts of Santa Pola. The street ran steeply upward and it narrowed the farther they went, their path taking them on a jag to the right, between two rows of beautifully restored buildings that appeared to have been renovated into apartments. At the northeastern edge of the Old City, not far from the protective ramparts, they found a beautiful archway and an ancient Moorish bridge whose actual age, according to the map, could only be guessed at.

Only a stone's throw away the sisters came upon a strange structure, an array of stone upheavals in the ground with small rounded windows built into them.

"Moorish baths," Paula informed her sister after consulting the map. "The best preserved in the country, according to the write-up. Built at the end of the . . . holy shit . . . built at the end of the thirteenth century. That's like twelve hundred and something."

Nancy pursed her lips. "Thanks. I can do the math."

They descended along a short set of stairs and entered the Moorish baths. Nancy felt herself holding her breath. The place was like an underground church constructed of stone, bare floors punctuated only by enormous stone pillars that supported the ceiling. Beams of sunlight shone down through the circular holes in the roof.

It was not the first time she had been filled with wonder in Ronda, and it would not be the last. The beauty and age of the place entranced her, and as they moved on, she even forgot to keep up the usual back-and-forth jabs with her sister.

They wandered south along streets lined with shops. Elegant old row houses on either side were adorned with second- and third-story iron-railed balconies, some of which had beautiful wood and glass enclosures that were unique in Nancy's experience. These masterworks of carved wood and paned glass hung out above the sidewalk and she yearned to go inside one of the homes, to look out at Ronda from the other side of that glass.

Everywhere they walked there were architectural pleasures, from the churches and their towers on the tallest portion of the plateau to the meticulously laid tiles of blue and green and white that finished the appearance of signs and the corners of buildings with the perfect flourish. A trio of bells, one larger between two of equal size, topped the façade of a convent whose upper windows mirrored the position of the bells, one large round window between two smaller.

They explored museums and gardens that overlooked the plains below, torn between the beauty of the view and the tile work and history within. During lunch at a little restaurant Paula studied the map and pointed out that they had not yet visited the Mondragon Palace, the description of which sounded beautiful, though Nancy suspected Paula was most intrigued by its name. It was the sort of thing that would appeal to her, dragons and moons and such.

"It was built in 1491 when the Moors had been driven out," Paula said. "It sounds like something we shouldn't miss."

After lunch they set off to discover the Mondragon. Even with the map they found themselves turned around more than once, in the shadow of the Church of Santa Maria la Mayor. Paula became frustrated, propping her sunglasses up on top of her head and twining one finger in her hair before assuring

Nancy that, at last, she had figured out the maze of narrow, zigzagging streets on the western edge of the Old City.

The *calle* they strode down now was more of a cobblestoned alley, the buildings laid out in jagged angles to what passed for a road. Unlike the other areas of the Old City, this street seemed in the midst of a renovation that had reached the rest of Ronda years before. Lanterns jutted from high up on the walls. Shops were vacant and for rent or lease and buildings half a millennium old were dilapidated and in need of not merely paint but structural buttressing as well. Some of them had broken and boarded windows, and graffiti on the boards, though most—the ones that were occupied, Nancy guessed—had iron grates over the windows.

"Are you sure this is the way?" Nancy asked.

They approached a three-way junction consisting of a trio of alleys and Paula consulted a sign on the wall, then the map.

"It's just down here," Paula assured her, and they continued in the direction they had been walking.

Despite the faded paint and the grime on the cobblestones, the architecture along this *calle* was still lovely. Some of the buildings had high doors not unlike those the sisters had seen in Seville, and there were one or two enclosed second-floor balconies. On the left, Nancy noticed a wooden door perhaps twelve feet high, lined with iron studs and capped with a beautiful piece of woodwork. A stone arch surrounded the door. It seemed almost too well preserved for this particular area of the Old City.

"Weird," Paula whispered.

Nancy frowned and drew her attention away from the arched door, glancing at her sister. Paula was staring across the alley, at a door almost precisely opposite the one that had drawn Nancy's attention. Yet this other door seemed its complete opposite, and was set into a building that was so ravaged as to appear almost ready to be condemned.

The windows were not merely shattered, but torn out completely, frame and all. Inside there was crumbled masonry and other debris scattered all over the floor. A balcony that hung above the door was rusted and partially separated from the wall. It was not quite precarious, but Nancy would not have wanted to stand beneath it.

The door, however, was the most disturbing thing about this crumbling edifice. Elsewhere along the street, where buildings were in the midst of renovation or boarded up to await its eventuality, there was at least still evidence that efforts had been made to preserve their general appearance. Here, no such artifice had been employed. At some point the entire threshold of the wooden door frame had been filled with brick, which had then been smoothed over with a layer of concrete. Spanish graffiti had been scrawled all over the concrete when it was still wet.

That would have been unpleasant enough, yet a portion of the concrete and brick obstruction had been removed, knocked out and hauled away, to reveal a much smaller door set into the original frame. This door was steel, painted white and without a single mark of graffiti. A padlock held it tightly closed.

Nancy felt the skin prickle across the back of her neck and a shiver of dread run through her. It made no sense to her that this sight should unnerve her so, but she could not help herself.

Paula stepped closer to her, also staring at the door. She reached out to take Nancy by the elbow, gaze never leaving the hole broken through the concrete and that small steel door.

"Let's go," Paula said.

Another moment and Nancy would have followed her, but the furious roar of a small engine interrupted and the sisters stepped aside to let a moped pass. The driver was a handsome teenager with mirrored sunglasses on his face and his beautiful, raven-haired girlfriend clutching tightly to his waist. Both of them wore wild grins that spoke of the exhilaration of speeding along this alleyway.

Nancy found she had been holding her breath. She exhaled and shook her head. Another shiver ran through her but she ignored it, raising the camera that was still slung around her neck.

"Come on, Nance, let's go," Paula urged, taking a step

away, down toward the Mondragon Palace, if that was indeed where the alley led.

"I just want a couple of pictures. This is freaky. I mean, what were they keeping in that they needed a steel door and a padlock, never mind the concrete?"

"That's stupid," Paula snapped. "If you cement up the door, anything inside isn't going to live very long."

With a frown Nancy turned to her. The camera was in her hands and she had opened the lens cover but something in her sister's voice had forced her to look over at Paula.

"You said yourself it was weird," Nancy reminded her. "And you're the one in such a rush to get out of here."

"Well," Paula protested, rolling her eyes to hide her obvious embarrassment, "it is creepy."

Nancy sighed as though she were above such feelings, when in truth she agreed wholeheartedly. Just one picture, she decided. It really was a strange sight. She raised the camera and looked through the lens.

A thump like the clap of thunder echoed off the alley walls and the door shook in its frame, showering loose fragments of cement to the cobblestones and cracking the concrete around it. A crimp had appeared in the steel.

Not a crimp. A *dent*. That had been made from the inside.

Her fingers mindlessly clutched the camera as her mind tried to process what she had just seen and heard. It was as though the dread within her, the fantastical, horrifying image of what the door's true purpose might be, had been summoned into being by her thoughts alone. That sort of thing only happened in dreams, of course.

It was nothing more than a single moment of hesitation, a second, no more, in which she considered the possibility that what she was seeing was not really there. Then Nancy began to turn her head toward her sister even as Paula grabbed her more firmly by the arm.

"Paul, what was—"

"I don't know I don't know I don't know, let's go!" Paula muttered under her breath.

There came another crunch of metal, a new dent in the steel door. Part of the concrete and brick fell away and crashed to the street.

Real, Nancy thought. *Whatever it is, it's real.*

Before the sisters had taken another step, a third impact snapped the padlock and threw the steel door wide, tumbling more brick and concrete onto the cobblestones. The thing that emerged from the dark recesses of that door was unthinkably horrid, a monstrous beast that scuttled sideways like a crab, its flesh a mottled, bruise-dark substance pitted with holes across its body, inside of which wet, slippery tubes could be seen slithering.

In the darkness behind the creature there were other things, black, skeletal figures that flitted there, Reaper-like, but would not come out into the sun.

Nancy's mind could not contain the terror that overcame her then. "No," she said, shaking her head. "No, no, no." This thing could not be real. Nothing like this could exist in the world she knew.

Paula was screaming her name, screaming at her to run, but it sounded distant and tinny like a radio in another room. Then Nancy saw motion in the corner of her eye, felt her sister's fingers twine in her hair the way they had when the two women had fought as children. The skittering crab-thing had paused on its spindly legs as if noticing them for the first time and now there came a sound like regurgitation from inside the holes in its skin. The moist green-black tubes erupted from those holes and shot toward the Carling sisters.

In that same instant Paula had grabbed Nancy's hair, the slick tentacles lashed out at them, there in that grimy, cobblestoned alley. Nancy screamed as her sister yanked her out of the way. Another scream joined her own in terrible harmony and Nancy fell to the ground, skinned her knee, and kept rolling with the momentum of her fall. She stopped herself and looked up quickly, just in time to see those tentacles flay the skin and muscle from her sister's bones.

Paula's screams echoed off the faded walls.

When the thing came for her, its pulsing appendages circling her neck in a fatal embrace, her mind was already gone.

———

HENRI Lamontagne kept screaming. The little boy had awoken from a strange catatonia as if from a nightmare, only to be thrust into a scene of genuine terror. His mother Antoinette clutched him tightly to her breast and his father Alain stood to defend them both.

The ronin warrior Kuromaku, once a samurai, now an immortal thing of shadows, watched it unfold with mounting fury. The skeletal, hardshelled demons whose long slender limbs ended in razor talons, dropped one by one from the rafters of the church. They landed upon the pews and in the aisles—seven of them by Kuromaku's count—and they slipped silently toward the Lamontagnes and toward Sophie, whom Kuromaku had vowed to protect.

But Kuromaku's rage was not at the demons, these things the little boy Henri had called Whispers. Rather, he was furious with himself. How long had the creatures been up there in the rafters, lurking, waiting for the proper moment? Despite the absence of anyone in the church, he had still relied upon the religious magick inherent in the structure to keep them safe. Instinct had told him otherwise, but he had not acted soon enough.

He uttered a curse that was already ancient when he was a boy in Japan and reached down to his hip. The katana solidified in his hand, materializing from nothing, and he drew it from its scabbard in a single deft motion even as he leaped into the air. A spinning somersault that spanned nearly twenty feet landed him in front of the Lamontagne family in the instant before a pair of the black-shelled demons would have torn them apart.

"You will not have them!" Kuromaku snarled, his teeth changing unbidden, his rage causing them to elongate into fangs.

The Whispers hissed at him, pointed tongues darting from beneath their skull carapaces. His hands were raised at shoulder level, the katana held sideways, and now Kuromaku spun in a whirlwind circle, each twist taking him closer to the creatures, his blade cracking their shells and cleanly slicing both of them in half.

Behind him, Sophie screamed.

Kuromaku mentally logged the location of the other five demons. Two nearer the rear of the church, still among the pews, crawling across the tops of the wooden benches toward him and the Lamontagnes. One nine feet away in the main aisle, where the priest would have stood to give communion.

Two others pursuing Sophie as she ran up onto the altar, the demons slashing at the air she disturbed in her wake. She grabbed hold of a five-foot iron candle stand and with all her strength swung it in a solid arc. It connected with the closest demon, striking the eerily featureless black shell where its face ought to have been. A crack appeared there and the Whisper staggered back, hissing. The other hesitated, probing the air in front of it with the sharp tendril that protruded from beneath its facial shell.

Kuromaku leaped into the air again even as the demon closest to him turned, its movements no more than a whisper, as were his own. The blade of the katana swept down and the demon fell under the onslaught, carapace shattered. The ronin moved on without hesitation, as though floating over the dead thing.

"Get back, you bastards!" Sophie screamed in French at the two menacing her. She whipped the iron candle stand around again but the demons dodged backward.

There were a thousand thousand ways Kuromaku could have killed them, an endless number of beasts he might have transformed himself into in order to tear them apart, to pry the shells from them like stripping a lobster to reach the flesh. But that sort of indulgence held no interest for him. Samurai trained all their lives to be swift and decisive and efficient; there was no room for theatrics.

He killed them, punching the tip of the katana through the backs of the demons' skulls, first one and then the other. The Whispers fell dead at his feet there on the altar and Kuromaku froze, staring into Sophie's sky blue eyes. Her breathing was heavy, the fear and exhilaration emanating off her in waves.

Henri Lamontagne had stopped screaming.

"Damn it!" Kuromaku snapped, turning in time to see the last two of the creatures lunge from the final pew toward Alain Lamontagne, who had only his bare hands to protect his wife and child where they huddled behind him in terror.

Kuromaku bounded off the altar, racing for the Lamontagnes, knowing even as he did so that he was too late. The bare instant that had ticked by as he looked into Sophie's eyes had cost him a vital moment. Even as he raised his katanan, he saw one of the Whispers strike, its right arm scything down, long talons sharp as blades slitting Alain Lamontagne open from throat to pelvis.

The other lunged at Antoinette, who curled herself around her son as though her flesh and bone could act as armor for the child. The demon's talons punctured her back like daggers and Antoinette screamed in soul-deep agony, knowing that they would tear through her to reach her son.

Rigid with bitter anger that made bile rise in the back of his throat, Kuromaku cut the last two Whispers down, then hacked at the pieces where they lay on the floor, the katana cutting through wood and carpeting. The clack, clack of the blade on wood was the only sound in the church then, echoing back from those same rafters.

The rafters.

The ronin ignored the wounded woman and her son, turned his back on Sophie as she ran to see to them. He gazed up into the rafters, eyes peering into the depths of every shadow, ears attuned to the slightest creak of the wind. The quill-covered behemoth outside had stopped pounding on the door and the winged, carrion creatures that circled above had not even attempted to enter the church, but these things had.

"Watch the shadows," Kuromaku instructed Sophie, who nodded mutely, her expression revealing a kind of surprise, not at the events that had just unfolded here, but that she had survived them at all.

With that caution, and moving more swiftly than any human could have conceived, Kuromaku raced through the church, searched every darkened nook, and assured himself that each door and window was tightly shut. He investigated the sacristy and the basement and each armoire and closet that he came to.

Only minutes after he had departed, he returned to Sophie's side. She was sitting with the boy, Henri, who seemed to have fallen again into that strange catatonia. His mother barely acknowledged his presence. Instead, Antoinette Lamontagne knelt by her husband's corpse, blood spattered on her clothing, whispering to him in angry French. From time to time her voice would rise higher, become shrill, and she would strike the dead body as though it might elicit some response. All her recriminations were for nothing, however. Alain was dead.

Sophie stared at the woman and her dead husband while she stroked the boy's hair. Kuromaku did not like the hollowness of her eyes. Antoinette was already mad; he could not afford to have Sophie become unhinged now.

"I wish she would stop," Sophie whispered.

"I wish it also," Kuromaku replied gently.

He reached out to touch her shoulder. The connection seemed to spark something in her eyes and she glanced at him, blinking, as though her vision had been blurred but was now clearing.

"Now what do we do?" Sophie asked, searching his eyes for answers, for some truths that she must have feared his lips would not reveal.

"We find another sanctuary."

She shook her head, glanced up into the shadowy rafters, and shivered. "If we aren't safe here—"

"Somewhere without windows, with a single door. A bank vault, perhaps. Somewhere I can keep the three of you safe while I explore this place and find a way out, a way *back*."

Sophie's eyes widened. "You're going to leave us alone?"

Kuromaku gazed grimly at her. "There is no other choice. To do what must be done, to be free to fight and move, I must be unhindered by the need to protect you. Only for a short while. And not until I have moved you somewhere safe."

She looked for a moment as though she might argue, then she only sighed and nodded, her eyes downcast. Antoinette Lamontagne was still muttering to her dead husband, the boy lay motionless, eyelids fluttering as though he was disturbed by his dreams—though Kuromaku was certain his nightmares could not be more terrifying than the reality he refused to wake to. Sophie did not want to be left alone with a raving madwoman and a mentally paralyzed child, but she had made the choice to protect them on her own behalf and on Kuromaku's. At the beginning, Kuromaku would simply have left them behind. But when the train was attacked, that was war. Now, they were all survivors, and he intended to see that no more of those under his protection lost their lives in this infernal place.

"I don't understand," Sophie said, glancing up. "How could they come inside? All the things you said before about the magick of the church—"

Kuromaku nodded, his brow furrowed. "I have been thinking about that," he revealed, feeling his suspicions co-alescing into grim certainty. He let his gaze drift a moment before returning his focus to Sophie.

"There are many Hells," Kuromaku began, voice just above a whisper. Even so it seemed to slink furtively through the pews and up into the rafters. "Thousands of years ago it was . . . common is such a strange word to use, but yes . . . it was common to find creatures from these Hells in this world. Reality is layer upon layer. Or perhaps all is one vast universe and what we think of as portals between dimensions are merely folds in space, spanning galaxies and diminishing them so that they are separated by inches rather than eter-nities."

He reached up to massage his temples and took a breath he did not need.

"I am complicating things," he said grimly. "Where did I begin? Oh, yes. There are many Hells. That is what we have always called them. Whatever they are, many of these places have monstrous creatures, savage things, some of which are merely animals, but others are sentient. Aware." He paused and studied Sophie closely.

"As demons from these many Hells found or forced their way into this world, sorcerers and mages wove new magicks to combat them. Eventually all of that knowledge was col-lected in a volume called *The Gospel of Shadows*. The book is lost to us now but a new effort is under way to gather that knowledge again. Meanwhile only one man in the world knows all of the magick that book once contained."

Sophie frowned. "Who is this man?"

"His name is Peter Octavian and he is my brother," Ku-romaku said reverently. He saw the confusion in Sophie's eyes and shook his head. "Not my brother by birth, nor even by the blood of Shadows, but my comrade in arms, my fellow warrior, a brother of my own choosing."

He paused, frowned. "Yet I wonder how even Peter would fare against these demons. If they can enter the church, it seems clear to me that these wraiths are from a dimension unknown to the ancient mages. All known demon races are magickally barred from holy ground. If we are not safe in this church, it is because whatever they are, these things are unknown, from a Hellish dimension not even the greatest sorcerers of history ever knew existed."

Sophie stared at him, expression blank. After a moment her face changed, as though a wave of awareness seemed to come upon her and she was awaking, for the first time, to the reality of their situation. She reached out and touched Henri's face but the little boy did not stir. With a glance at Antoinette madly mumbling over the corpse of her husband, Sophie stood and faced Kuromaku eye to eye.

There was a fire in her gaze that he was heartened to see. Sophie Duvic had decided that she was going to make it out of this alive. It gave Kuromaku hope.

"You really believe that Mont de Moreau has just been . . . captured somehow? That if we reach the edge of the city, we may be able to break back through into our world?"

Kuromaku nodded solemnly. "I do."

Sophie glanced around the church again. "All right. I will get them to the basement and block the door. But the demons—the wraiths as you called them—will not be held off for long. There was no blood here. I believe that the priests and the faithful, if they made it here at all, were driven out and then killed outside. The ones you killed were here all along. Others may find this place, but I think it would be by accident, I do not think they *know* that we are here. Otherwise they would swarm the church as they did the train."

Kuromaku nodded at her logic. "All right. I will go and find a safer place for you to hide. Once you have been moved there, I will go to the edge of the city and see if escape is possible."

He turned from her, intent upon his mission. Sophie grabbed his arm and pulled him back. When she kissed him, Kuromaku felt as though she were giving over to him a little bit of her spirit, her soul, and it nourished the vampire far more than stolen blood ever had. When the kiss ended, they gazed at one another for a moment.

"Before you go," she said, pointing upward. "Fly up there and make sure there are no more of them."

Kuromaku let his lips brush gently across hers again, committing to memory their softness and the smell of her. Sophie's blue eyes caught and held him a moment.

Without pause he transformed, his body flowing and twisting, much of his physical mass going to that same place where his katana stayed until he needed it. Kuromaku shifted from human to crow, black feathers gleaming in the church. Sophie gasped and stared in amazement.

"I will never get used to that," she said.

He cawed and spread his wings, flew up into the rafters of the church, searched every shadow there and made certain there were no more demons lurking above the pews or the altar. Then he circled once above Sophie and what remained of the Lamontagne family, cawing vows of fealty and protection in the tongue of crows, until at last he flew toward a side door. Sophie ran to let him out, opening it just a crack for him to fly through and then barring it again behind him after he had passed.

Then Kuromaku was out of the church, back into the hellish landscape of Mont de Moreau. The horror of the city's fate struck him deeply once more but he steeled himself against the visions of fire and destruction that met his eyes. He was a warrior. He had seen such devastation before, and then at the hands of men.

The crow soared high above the tall white steeple. Below he saw the wraith demons that had been hunting them, that had swarmed the train and hidden in the church. He saw more of the enormous quill-backed demons and other horror that slunk and crept through the smoldering streets beneath that hideous orange light. Winged carrion eaters flew above and Kuromaku was careful not to soar too high.

But he was high enough.

High enough to see something that made his mind spin, made even one who had learned so many of the world's secrets gaze in incredulous awe. For as he looked to the northern edge of the city, he saw not the barrier he had expected to see, nor the French countryside that would have been there had this atrocity not taken place.

At the northern perimeter of Mont de Moreau there was another city, a sprawling desert village of small, dusty homes and cantinas. This place was not in France, that much was certain. It might have been Mexico, or somewhere in the southwestern United States.

The crow dipped one wing and glided eastward. On that side it could see another city, with sprawling green hills surrounding a busy shopping district downtown, the architecture and the signs upon the stores and pubs revealing it as an English town.

To the south, Kuromaku saw Salzburg, Austria, recognizing it immediately by the view of the ramparts of the massive Hohensalzburg fortress, overlooking down not only the streets of Salzburg, but of Mont de Moreau as well.

Cities from all around the world, impossibly drawn together beneath that dreadful orange sky. All so different and yet all now identical in the horrors that had befallen them, the ravaged streets, the burning buildings, the monstrous beings that prowled in search of human survivors.

A tear appeared at the corner of the eye of that crow, moistening its feathers. Kuromaku did not understand how this had happened but he knew that there had never been such an abomination, such a terrible slaughter, in the history of the modern world.

And to the west . . . at last Kuromaku saw the barrier he had sought, a shimmering field of energy that stretched from the ground all the way up into the heavens. Whatever unimaginable demon or god had the power to drag cities from the real world into this dimension as though building a kingdom of the damned one puzzle piece at a time, the western edge of Mont de Moreau was still the outer perimeter of this hideous montage.

There was no time to find a new sanctuary. If whatever power was behind this continued, they might never find the outer barrier again. Kuromaku had to get Sophie, Antoinette, and Henri out of this damnable place before they were trapped here forever.

Once outside, he would have to discover what was doing this, how many cities had been taken, and what could be done to stop it. But first, they had to escape Mont de Moreau, had to reach the western perimeter before another city was dragged into Hell to block them in, and then another, and another, until the whole world burned and bled beneath that filthy orange sky.

CHAPTER 13

THE moon was high and bright and limned with a halo of shimmering gold that turned the night sky blue around it. The woods were dark, but moonlight illuminated the canopy of branches that sketched at the sky above Nikki's head as she walked side by side with Peter along a path worn over years by other feet.

It was the second time she had lived through something incredible with him, something terrible. Afterward there was a kind of high, an adrenaline rush that nothing in the world compared to, not even performing with her guitar on stage in front of hundreds of people, not even on those nights when she just knew that every heart in the audience was beating with hers and she had them, just had them, right with her.

But that high did not last. In the aftermath, when the surreal tingle in her skin and the heat of her blood rushing through her and the almost sexual flush to her cheeks were over, there was only silence left in her. A quiet unlike anything else in the world.

Images from that first time, in New Orleans, still lingered in her mind, still visited her dreams on long, difficult nights. The blood and death, the sheer cruelty of those who tried to kill her and Peter and all those who believed in what he stood for—it had left a scar upon her soul. Nikki had carried on, and always would, but to have seen that and felt it all was something that would stay with her forever. And when she sang, she knew that some of that dark knowledge was communicated to her audience with every note.

Today had been worse.

In New Orleans, Peter and his friends had been able to put a name to their enemies. The threat had been horrifying, but identifiable. Whatever that thing was—*in the storm*, she could still picture it in the storm, the winds tugging at the rags of the creature and simply carrying them away after it had delivered its warning—whatever it was, the sorcery Peter wielded was not powerful enough to destroy it.

This was an enemy with no name, with power even Peter did not understand. After Wickham had been saved—if that was a word she could use to describe what had happened there—they had slipped away, avoiding the military and emergency crews that moved in as soon as the village had been restored to its rightful place.

More than seventy miles west and higher in the mountains, they had found a small motel that would let them rest and figure out what their next move was going to be. But as soon as Nikki and Keomany checked into their room, Keomany had turned on the television, and they had discovered that Wickham had been just the beginning.

Nikki shivered.

"Hey," Peter whispered as they strolled, hand in hand, along that mountain path, the lights of the motel behind and below them.

She glanced up at him and forced a smile.

"You're cold," he said. "Do you want to go back?"

"Not just yet." Nikki paused on the path and looked again back at the hotel. In her mind's eye she saw those creatures again—Whispers, the demon had called them—and she saw the thing itself, the thing Peter had called "the Tatterdemalion" in the SUV on the way out of Wickham.

But it wasn't the cold that made her shiver.

Didn't Peter understand that she would never be warm again?

"I wish we had been able to share a room," she said as

they picked up walking again, following the trail that would have been used for cross-country skiing in the winter.

Peter laughed softly. "Somehow I think that would've been awkward for Keomany and Father Jack."

They had strolled another twenty feet but Nikki stopped again. She turned to him, reached up to touch his face, forcing him to meet her gaze, to see in her eyes all that was in her heart.

"Tomorrow morning, we're going to figure out our next move, right?" she asked.

"Yes," he agreed, staring back at her curiously. "We all need some sleep. The news is terrible, I agree, but we've got to retrench a little bit, get some rest before we can try to stop this."

"Fine," she agreed, brushing her hair out of her eyes. Nikki gazed at him intently. "I never want to spend another night away from you."

A smile played at the edges of his lips, but he also looked surprised. "Shouldn't you be getting back to L.A.?"

"Do you want me to go back?" Nikki's chest hurt. She would not be able to breathe until he answered.

Peter stared at her. The moonlight glinted in his eyes. "No," he said, his voice a firm, quiet rasp.

"You saw the news," she said. "I don't even know if L.A. would still be there when I got back. I'm not going on tour, not going anywhere, until this is over. I was starting to think, hey, maybe our days are numbered, maybe this is all the time we have. And then I realized that even if I live to be a hundred, there are still only so many days in a life, and I want to spend mine with you."

Peter reached out to touch her as if she might be a mirage, as if she might disappear at any moment. Nikki smiled as his fingers touched her arm and something passed between them, a silent covenant, a promise to each other. She stood on her toes and kissed him, and he held her close against him as though she would fall off the Earth if he let go.

When the kiss ended, Nikki lay her head on his chest, and they just stood there on that mountain trail, warm against the chill night air. She could hear his heart beat.

They stayed that way, there in the dark of the night, for

a very long time. Yet as safe as Peter made her feel, as glad as she was that they had learned this terrible lesson and been given a second chance, she knew that morning was going to come too soon.

———

ALLISON flew above the streets of London. The sun was high and the sky uncharacteristically blue and clear for springtime. With falcon's eyes she gazed upon the city below, laid out in patterns that described its history, from the most ancient foundations of London—the portion of the city that had once been walled in—to the neighborhoods at her edges that had been built to house the less fortunate and were now the trendiest spots in the city.

Exultant, she soared higher, glided on warm air currents above the River Thames, admired the sprawl of the Parliament building.

This was what she was made for. Allison despised what she was, mostly because she had not chosen to become this thing. Her kind had painted its history across the ages in the blood of innocents, thriving on terror. But not all of them. Though she would never be able to shake off the loathing she felt completely, she had at last come to terms with another emotion inside her, rare and often hidden.

It was glee. She hated what she was, but she loved the gifts it gave her. Others had shown her that pleasure could be taken from her immortality, from the malleability of her flesh, but for a very long time, she did not believe it. That had changed.

Allison Vigeant soared, powerful wings outstretched, feathers flat and smooth, over the city of London, and she relished every moment of it.

But her moments were not her own. Once more she circled Westminster Abbey and then she struck off toward an engagement she wished she did not have to keep. It was not long before she found herself flying above the Kingsway, wings fluttering as she alighted upon the roof of the nine-story structure where she was due for a meeting called by her superiors.

It surprised her that there were no guards on the roof. To

the innocent passerby, the faithful subject of the Queen, it was just another office building along the Kingsway. But the British government owned that structure; it housed various ministry offices the sort of which they did not discuss in the papers. From time to time, the Prime Minister also offered certain rooms in the building to the Secretary General of the United Nations for use in the international crusade to erase the last of the shadows, the last of the vampires, from the face of the earth.

Allison had been thinking of late that this crusade was destined to failure. They could bluster as much as they liked, but she had no doubt that there were shadows hidden away in the darkest and most secret places of the earth whom they would never find, not even with her aid. It had also occurred to her that perhaps it was best they were never allowed to think they had succeeded . . . because that would make her the last vampire in the world, and it would be simple logic for them to want to remove her as well.

Still, no guards on the roof. That was something, at least. There would be sensors and alarms, but that was to be expected.

With a strangled bit of birdsong that evolved into a human groan, she transformed from falcon to woman once more. Her wings unfolded as she stood, becoming a long brown duster jacket. She was clad in denim and leather boots and a beige turtleneck sweater beneath the duster. It was still chilly this early London spring day.

Allison stretched and glanced around at the other rooftops and into the windows of the buildings that stood taller than this one. She inhaled the scents of this world capital, the heart of an island in motion. London was an old place, and though she herself was young, it always made her feel like a conspirator, as though she had been a part of this city for ages.

It was a shame she could not enjoy it more, a shame she had to come here to deal with these people. But it was either that, or have them begin to hunt her instead of employing her to hunt others on their behalf.

Enjoying the warmth of the sun on her, she strode across the rooftop to the structure that jutted upward, housing the door and stairwell that led down into the building. The door was a heavy metal thing, wired with alarms and certainly barred on the inside. She could have torn it off its hinges and tossed it aside as though it were made of cardboard, but they would only have billed her for it, deducted the cost from her paycheck.

Allison let her molecules drift, became a fine white mist, and she slid around the edges of the door, finding the thinnest of entries despite the weather-proofing meant to keep the chill wind outside. With a thought, she effortlessly coalesced once more on the top step outside the door, then walked down the narrow staircase to the top floor of the building.

No guards up here, but there were cameras mounted all long the hallway. She smiled at the first one she passed and waved amicably. The urge to brandish her middle finger was powerful but she managed to contain it.

She was meant to be here. Security would have been told to expect her and prepared to witness the reality of what she was. The Brits wouldn't have put anyone in the job who couldn't handle that.

Halfway down the corridor, she found the office she was looking for. It had no name on the door, only a number: 913. Allison rapped lightly on the door to Room 913 and from inside she heard a familiar voice calling for her to enter.

She pushed the door open. There were only two men inside. One of them was Ray Henning, the Commander of Task Force Victor. The other was Rafael Nieto, a lanky, serious man whose hair had thinned and gone silver in the years since she had first met him, but otherwise looked much the same. Nieto was a good man, dedicated to his job. Which was a positive trait to find in one of the most powerful men in the world. Nieto was the Secretary General of the U.N., a job that had, in recent years, nearly outstripped that of the American President in its importance to the peace and security of the planet.

"Allison," the Secretary General said. He smiled and waved her in. "Have a seat. It appears we have a lot to talk about."

"Mister Secretary," she said, nodding a greeting as she closed the door behind her. "Commander," she added, ac-

knowledging Henning, who neither smiled nor greeted her
with more than a grunt.

They waited while she moved the chair beside Henning,
sliding it away from him in a subtle indication that she considered herself apart from him. This would hardly hurt the
commander's feelings, for Allison knew that he disliked and
perhaps even feared her. It accomplished something else,
however. Rather than the two of them facing the Secretary
General across the large desk in the room, it was now the
three of them set in a sort of triangle, changing the dynamic
in the office. Henning stared at her with pale blue eyes. He
was fifty-two but very fit, balding and yet his features were
striking. A handsome man.

But not her friend. Not even close.

The silence ticked on a few seconds too long, into awk-
wardness. Allison shot a glance at the Secretary General, one
eyebrow raised. Nieto sat up straighter and smoothed his
jacket, which hung oddly on him as though he were a department store mannequin.

Outside the window, the unusually beautiful London day
was wasting.

"Are we waiting for someone else?" Allison asked.

"No," the Secretary General replied. "I'm sorry. I was
thinking for a moment. On to business, then. Do you know
why you're here?"

A smiled teased the edges of Allison's mouth. "I don't
want to jump to conclusions."

Commander Henning cleared his throat and the balance
of power in the room tilted in his direction. "What did you
and Carl Melnick talk about in Venice?"

Allison stiffened, her gaze ticked from Henning to the
Secretary General and back again. "Come on, Ray. We both
know you're not in the business of asking questions you
don't already know the answer to."

Commander Henning stared at her but said nothing. Allison turned to Nieto again.

"Mister Secretary, given that we've now got thirteen
towns and cities worldwide that have apparently been erased
from the map, I'd think the United Nations would have better
things to do than spy on its employees. It hasn't been lost

on me that my position as a scout for Task Force Victor is
not unlike the position Will Cody once held for the U.S.
Army. If he was alive, he'd be horrified."

Henning sniffed. "If he were alive, we'd be hunting him."

Cold fury spread though Allison and she turned slowly to
regard Henning again. The two men must have felt her anger,
for in that moment the balance of power in the room shifted
to her. Allison could taste it. Perhaps they remembered, in
that moment, that she was not merely a scout, that she could
have killed every living creature in that building and walked
out unscathed if she were so inclined.

Nieto gazed at her, clearly taking her measure. "Twelve."

"I'm sorry?" Allison asked.

"Twelve. There are twelve cities and towns that we know
of that have been affected by this . . . crisis. The town in Vermont, Wickham, is . . . back."

All the rage left her and Allison sank into her chair, staring first at Nieto then at Henning. "Back? What do you mean,
the town is back?"

"Just as I said," Nieto replied. "Our troops report that one
moment the energy field that seemed to have enveloped the
town was there and the next it was gone and the town was
visible again. Entire blocks had been destroyed by fire. Most
of the townspeople were dead or missing. The survivors are
talking about demons."

"What sort of demons?" Allison asked.

Once more the two men were silent. After a moment the
Secretary General rose and went to the large window that
overlooked the Kingsway below. He spoke without turning.

"Allison, Roberto Jimenez was a good man. A good soldier. I had the utmost respect for him and he, in turn, trusted
you. But Roberto is dead and Ray Henning is your commander now. He asked you a question. I would like you to
answer it."

Slowly, she nodded, but in understanding rather than
agreement. Allison did not like what was going on here, but
it did not surprise her. She lowered her chin slightly, staring
up at the Secretary General from beneath heavily knitted
brows.

" 'Berto trusted me. That's right. Commander Henning

doesn't. Not for a second. In fact, I'm fairly certain if he had his chance, he'd be more than happy to burn me right along with one of our targets. So you'll forgive me if I'm wary of the recent changes in the chain of command."

Nieto turned to face her. He was silhouetted by the blue sky beyond the window. On the opposite side of the street, atop a centuries-old hotel, Allison saw two snipers side by side.

A surge of adrenaline went through her and she tensed, about to dive at the Secretary General, to drive him to the ground and to safety, out of sight of the snipers. But then she noticed Henning glancing out the window as well and she at last translated the tense undercurrent in the room, realizing that they were not assassins here to remove the head of the United Nations.

The snipers were for her.

She smiled. It was not a kind smile.

"What did you and Carl Melnick talk about in Venice?" Nieto asked, repeating Henning's earlier question.

Allison glared at him, studiously refusing to look at Henning. "Old times."

The Secretary General shifted his position, stepping a bit closer to the desk, giving the snipers a clearer shot. Allison wondered if they were to kill her, or simply incapacitate her. Years earlier, a toxin had been developed that would arrest the molecular process that allowed vampires to shapeshift, making them killable. Or simply controllable.

Allison was nearly indestructible. But take away her control over her molecular structure and it would be possible to do her enough physical damage to kill her.

She leaned slightly forward in her chair as if the conversation had suddenly become fascinating, using the Secretary General himself as a shield.

"Why don't you ask Melnick what we talked about?"

"We tried," Commander Henning said. "Nobody can find him."

Allison laughed. "Not if he doesn't want to be found."

Henning angrily slapped the arm of his chair. "Damn it, Vigeant, what kind of game are you playing here? Melnick gave you information about this crisis and I think you gave some in return. I want to know exactly what was said and I want to know now. That's a direct order."

Her lips curled up in a sneer and she lowered her head to look at him, her red hair falling across her eyes like a veil. "An order, is it? All right. I had the conversation with Carl Melnick that I ought to have had with you, Commander. But given that you don't see fit to share any information about this crisis with me and in the interest of world security, I had to go elsewhere."

"World security, my ass!" Henning roared, standing up. "You know more than you're telling!"

"Careful," Allison said, gesturing toward the window. "You might catch a bullet."

Startled, Henning glanced past the Secretary General at the snipers across the street. In the same instant, Allison turned to mist, sliding impossibly fast along the floor and coalescing once more on the other side of the room, just to the right of the large window.

Out of sight of the snipers.

Henning reached for his sidearm. Nieto snapped at him, glaring at the weapon, and the commander put it away. At last the Secretary General sighed deeply and regarded her, and Allison thought he looked, very, very tired.

"Allison, please—"

"If I was your enemy, or the monster Henning thinks I am, you'd both be dead now. I could tear the heads off both those snipers before they realized I had left this room and be back before their bodies hit the street below."

The Secretary General gaped at her.

"If that's a threat—" Henning began.

"Ray," Nieto said, voice cold. "Shut up."

Commander Henning stared at him, eyes ticking back and forth between his boss and his scout.

"Did you hear what she just said? Allison doesn't need threats," the Secretary General said. "Do you?" He glanced at her.

At length she relaxed her guard, leaning against the wall with her arms crossed, ignoring Henning.

"What's this all about, Rafael?"

Nieto slid into the large black leather chair behind a desk that wasn't his. "Peter Octavian."

Allison stared at the Secretary General. "What about him?"

"He was in Vermont when the town of Wickham . . . re-materialized. We have firsthand reports."

Allison nodded. Things were starting to click into place. It seemed inevitable that Octavian would have gotten involved at some point, given his power.

"He's the most powerful mage in the world," Allison said. She frowned. "You don't need me to tell you that. You've read his file. Hell, you've done business with him in the past. If Wickham has returned from wherever it had been taken and Peter was there, you've probably got him to thank for it."

Commander Henning glared at her, still standing, and a ripple of revulsion went across his face. "Or him to blame."

Allison rolled her eyes.

"You said yourself he has power," the Secretary General said, trying to sound reasonable. "It's possible he could be responsible for this."

"No," she said, shaking her head in disgust. "No, it's not. Not a chance."

"Fine," Nieto said, walking to the window again.

He pressed a hand to the glass and for a moment she had to wonder if that was a signal of some kind. But no, it seemed he was only thinking. Commander Henning was on edge, his jaw set angrily. This had been a confrontation long in coming. He had obviously been saving up his ire for just this occasion and she wondered if he was disappointed that nobody had shot her yet. Come to think of it, she was sure Henning was fuming over it. That was good.

The Secretary General turned from the window. "I'm going to give you a chance to prove you're right about Octavian."

"What?" Henning snapped. The Secretary General shot him a withering look and Henning stood a little straighter, suddenly reminded to whom he was speaking. "Sir, this is not the course of action we had agreed upon."

"No," Nieto agreed. "No, it isn't." He loosened the thin

red tie that slashed down his white shirt like a wound. "Allison, I have been in constant contact since the beginning of this conflict with officials from the Church of the Resurrection. They're far more familiar with the workings of the supernatural than we are. Task Force Victor has been assigned to work with representatives from the church to find a way to breach the barrier surrounding Derby, here in England."

"Task Force Victor is a bunch of vampire hunters, sir," Allison said. "What do they know about this situation?"

The Secretary General smiled, his charm returning now that the tension of the moment had passed. "Very little. The church representatives do, however. And the men and women of Task Force Victor are not afraid of anything. Demons have now been added to their target list."

"But I'm not going with them, am I?" Allison asked.

"No," Nieto said. "I want you to find Octavian. He's probably still in Vermont but refused to stop for our forces there. If you're wrong, and he's involved in this, you're to terminate him. But if you're right, and he has the power to break through these barriers, even to tear them down, then I want him working with us and immediately. Every day we lose another city. Every hour more people die."

Allison eyed him a moment then walked right past the Secretary General to the window the man had been staring at moments before. Across the street on the roof of the ancient hotel she saw the two men with rifles, side by side, sighting carefully through their scopes, watching her.

With a bright smile, Allison waved and blew them a kiss.

"I have a condition," she said without turning.

"This is the Secretary General!" Henning sputtered, and she could picture his face reddening. "You can't—"

"What is it?" Nieto asked.

Allison raised her hands to either side of her face, pressed her thumbs to her temples, and waggled her fingers at the snipers, sticking out her tongue. Then she turned to the Secretary General, ignoring Henning, and her smile was gone.

"I'm off Task Force Victor. I'll still scout for the U.N. I'll find the nests, track the shadows who've gone underground, but I answer directly to you. Not just for this, but from now on."

Commander Henning had grown wiser in the past few seconds, for though his face reddened even further, he remained silent, teeth clenched. The Secretary General studied her.

"Can I trust you, Allison?" he asked.

"For as long as I can trust you, Mister Secretary."

"Good enough."

Nieto thrust out his hand and Allison shook it. Then she turned to Ray Henning, her eyes narrowed to slits, her nostrils flaring. When she opened her mouth to speak, her teeth elongated into razor-sharp fangs. Allison stood eye to eye with him, their faces five inches apart.

"If you ever try to draw a weapon on me again, Commander," she said, not attempting to hide her words in a whisper, "I'll slit your throat and let you bleed where you fall."

Before either man could respond, she turned to mist, slid swirling beneath the office door, and was gone.

———

THE restaurant was just called Ellie's, no "Tavern" or "Grill" or "Pub" after the name. It was situated in a ramshackle sprawl of a building that was too large for what was presumably a very low volume of business, and so one entire side of the place had been transformed into an antique shop whose display window was punctuated by a pair of beautiful carousel horses. A huge carved wooden bull, the tip of one horn snapped off, stood by the door.

Father Jack Devlin stood in front of the antique shop, which had not yet opened for the day. Ellie's was serving breakfast already, but apparently the proprietor of the Golden Age did not think people out and about for their early morning meal were likely to want to buy antiques at that hour.

The priest leaned against the Lincoln Navigator, the rented vehicle much the worse for wear, and hit the first speed dial programmed into his cell phone. He had left Peter, Keomany, and Nikki in the restaurant because it was unconscionably rude to speak on the phone in the midst of people having breakfast—or any other meal—but more importantly because he simply did not wish to be overheard.

He laid the phone against his ear and listened to the electric buzz that substituted for a ring. A police car went by and he kept his head down, casting only a surreptitious glance in that direction. He wore charcoal gray pants and a dark green shirt. Nothing to catch anyone's attention. That was good.

A pickup truck rolled into Ellie's parking lot, kicking up dust from the ground. On the other end of the phone line, just as Jack became convinced he was going to get voice mail again, there was an answer.

"Hello?"

"It's Jack Devlin."

"Where in God's name are you, Jack?" Bishop Michael Gagnon asked, his voice an officious snarl. "I've been calling you since I got word yesterday about Wickham."

Father Jack knew that the Bishop's voice on the phone could not be heard by a couple stepping out of the pickup, but he held the phone a little closer to his ear regardless.

"If you got word, then you know where I am," he said.

Bishop Gagnon paused, the line hissing with static. Despite advances in mobile technology, the system was not perfect.

"You're not still there. I had a call from Tivosti in Homeland Security and he said you and Octavian had disappeared from Wickham after . . ."

"Not in Wickham," Jack replied. He glanced around the parking lot, stared at the sprawl of Ellie's and the carousel horses in the window of the Golden Age. "No idea what town we're in at the moment. We are still in Vermont, though. We found a motel yesterday and now we're just trying to figure out what to do next."

"We?" the Bishop asked, disapproval apparent in that single syllable. "You and Octavian? You are partners now, are you? Father Jack Devlin and his pet monster."

He isn't a monster, Jack wanted to say. But he knew the argument would be ignored. The Bishop was deaf to any opinion but his own.

"Octavian's magick is the only reason I'm still alive," he said instead. "He saved Wickham."

The Bishop actually laughed. "Saved Wickham? Wickham is not saved, Father. The town is destroyed, its people slaughtered."

Jack sighed. He leaned back against the Navigator and ran his free hand through his spiky orange hair.

"With all due respect, Your Eminence, there wouldn't be a town or any survivors at all without Octavian's involvement. You have not seen what I have seen, what was inside that village. Evil of such magnitude—"

"That's enough, Jack," Bishop Gagnon interrupted. "You're not going to give me your report over a mobile phone. I will expect you back in Manhattan by nightfall. You can tell me about it then. In the morning, we leave for England."

The priest had been about to argue that he had no car of his own but he knew that he could rent one. It was the last bit of the Bishop's instructions that threw him.

"What's in England?" he asked.

"That is what we shall discover."

There was a click and the line went dead, only a hollow sound in his ear now, like the infinite nothing inside a conch shell. Jack had always contended that it was not the ocean children heard when their parents had them put a shell to their ear, but some other world, some vast, dark nothing. He had been a morbid child with a wild imagination, but it was unsettling to him now as an adult that what his odd thoughts had conjured as a boy had turned out to be possible. With all he had learned about magick and parallel worlds, his theory was not as fantastic as it had once seemed.

He shut the phone off completely just as he had done the night before, not wanting to hear the Bishop's voice again until he had to. Sliding it into his pocket, he strode across the lot and through the front door of Ellie's, wondering if his breakfast had arrived yet. Inside, he was disappointed to discover it had not, but he slid into his chair beside Keomany, the two of them sitting opposite Peter and Nikki, and sipped at his black coffee. It was still hot enough to drink.

His return had interrupted a conversation about Peter's work as an artist and a gallery showing of his paintings that was apparently imminent. In the midst of asking Keomany a question, Peter paused and looked at Jack. Peter had not shaved that morning, and the stubble was dark on his face. It only made him look more handsome, which Jack envied, since he himself looked like a twelve-year-old with a bit of peach fuzz if he did not shave.

"Did you get through?" Peter asked.

Father Jack glanced at Keomany beside him, his heart breaking for the woman, those haunted eyes gazing out from her delicate features. He felt inexplicably as though he was letting her down.

"I have to go back to New York. Immediately." The priest looked at Peter. "The Bishop and I are apparently off to England tomorrow, but he didn't tell me anything more about it."

The truth was that the Bishop had not had to tell him why they were going. The previous night in the hotel they had turned on the news and been horrified by what they had seen. Despite what must have been a huge effort, the United Nations and world governments had not really had a chance of keeping something so massive quiet for very long.

Wickham had been only one village among many afflicted cities and towns.

"He's taking you to Derby," Nikki said quietly.

Father Jack nodded. "That's my guess."

She nodded, her blond hair slipping across her face. "They'll try to break through like Peter did."

Beside the priest Keomany shuddered. He felt her tremble.

"I don't think it will be that easy again. I think we have to find out what the next city will be, and get there before it's completely cut off from the world."

Father Jack frowned. "How do we do that?"

"Keomany knows a whole community of earthwitches ninety minutes from here on the highway. She thinks they can help."

The priest nodded slowly and sipped his coffee. "I wish I could come with you."

Octavian smiled. "I guess the Bishop's not very happy with you at the moment. You or me, for that matter. Is he trying to find a way to blame me for all this?"

Father Jack started to deny it, but there was a glint in

Peter's eye that told him there was no benefit in lying. The mage had a long and nasty history with the church. No matter how much Jack himself knew things had changed—the Church of the Resurrection was hardly the secretive, self-serving institution that the Roman Catholic original had been—men like Bishop Gagnon made it hard to convince anyone of the difference. Particularly someone like Peter.

"It's all right, Jack," the mage said, dragging a hand across his stubbled chin, then reaching for his glass of orange juice. "You do what you have to do. It could be that you'll learn what's really going on, what that thing was in Wickham. I don't think I have the power to take these places back one by one, but maybe with the earthwitches' help, we can find the source. Let's keep in touch."

"Bishop Gagnon won't like that," Father Jack muttered.

Peter's features narrowed, brows knitting together, and his nostrils flared. "I don't think I care what he likes. Tell him he can take all the credit if I stop this thing, whatever it is, from spreading. And if it eats the world, well, he can just blame it on me. Not that there'll be anyone left alive to listen."

The priest smiled. He would have to rent a second car, but that was simple enough. He held out a hand and Peter shook it.

"We'll save the world in spite of itself," he said, half in jest.

But only half.

CHAPTER 14

NIKKI lay sprawled sideways on the passenger seat of the Navigator. The big SUV's engine rumbled and she could feel it all through her. Behind the wheel, Peter seemed to have retreated inward, lost in contemplation, but she had seen him like this before. The weight of the world. No one could expect him to bear the burden, to be responsible for stopping the cataclysm that was facing the Earth now, and yet Peter willingly took it onto himself.

She wanted to reach out to him, but she knew it was best to let him alone until he surfaced from wherever his mind had taken him.

Music played low on the radio and the sun was warm on her face. Her window was open partway, and despite the sun a light rain fell, a spring shower that sprinkled the windshield and sprayed a few drops in through the window. Nikki kept it down. The shower would be over in a moment and she never minded a little rain.

Keomany sat in the back, her fine features very drawn, her perfect black hair a curtain veiling her face. Nikki had seen horrors before, but she had never had to witness the ravaged corpses of her own parents. With what Keomany had seen and experienced, what had happened to her hometown, Nikki thought it was a wonder she was still speaking in complete sentences.

I'd be a basket case, she thought as she peered over the back of her seat at her friend. What a strange turn of events, that this woman she had not seen in years would turn up at one of her performances to draw her back into the terrible, secret shadows of the world.

Only they aren't shadows anymore, are they? Everyone can see them. Just turn on fucking CNN.

And that was the truth. Anyone in the world could turn on the television and watch the apocalypse in progress. The thought made Nikki shiver, but neither her lover nor her friend noticed.

"Not too far now," Keomany said, craning forward slightly to peer at a sign above the highway. "It's north of Brattleboro, this exit or the next. I'll know it when I see it."

"You're sure we shouldn't have called first?" Nikki asked.

Keomany shook her head. "Cat and Tori will be there. In a situation like this, I can't imagine them being anywhere else."

Nikki sat up a little and looked at her, feeling a sadness sweep through her. This ought to have been a blissful moment, with Peter and Keomany around her and the sun and the breeze and the sprinkle of spring rain. Much as she wished, she could not sink down into the moment and pretend that beyond the confines of that vehicle, beyond the reaches of that highway, the world was not falling apart.

It was.

But at least she was facing the unknown with people she cared for, and who cared for her.

"So, Kem," she began, peering into the back at her friend, "tell me about this whole earthwitch thing. I remember you had an interest in wicca way back when, but how did you get into this?"

Keomany sat back against the seat, pushing her hair away from her face. Her eyes were wide, as though she had just woken from a dream, and yet Nikki felt that what she had been pulled away from was the echo of the previous day's horrors. She had not begun the conversation as some honorable effort to distract Keomany from sinking deeper into her grief, but if that was the result, so much the better.

"Wicca wasn't for me," Keomany said, glancing out the window at the forest to the east of the highway. "There's a purity to it, sure, but there are also people who are just in it for the magick. Magick for magick's sake is just bullshit."

She blinked and glanced at the rearview mirror. "No offense, Peter."

"None taken," he said, surprising Nikki, who had thought he would have tuned them out. Peter glanced once into the rearview mirror. "The desire to know magick without a purpose—a benevolent purpose—always leads to dark places."

"Exactly," Keomany agreed, focusing on Nikki again. A sad smile teased the edges of her lips. "Wicca is benevolent, no doubt. But it had become popular, almost faddish, and that meant it drew too many people who weren't benevolent. It was never about magick for me. It was about respecting this world that supports us, gives us life. We take it so for granted, and I didn't want to live like that. The real power is in the earth and in the air. Nature is the soul of the earth. Gaea's the mother of us all."

With a small chuckle, she stopped and shook her head. "I'm preaching."

"No," Nikki protested. "I'm interested. Notice the lack of mocking?"

Keomany nodded. "All right. Anyway, when I learned about earthcraft—"

"Earthcraft?"

"That's what it's called. Simple and to the point, I think. It's based on a lot of old Celtic rituals, ancient druidry, that sort of thing, and it's meant to allow people to tap into nature, to honor Gaea and celebrate all that she provides us. It isn't exactly an original concept, but it *is* benevolent. And the truth is, it works."

Nikki nodded. *Obviously* it worked. They had all seen the proof of that in Wickham. "What I don't understand is where the power comes from. And is it accessible to everyone? I mean, could anyone tap into the forces of nature like that? Sort of scary to contemplate."

For a long moment Keomany just stared out the window, frowning. "I guess I never thought of it like that," she said

at length. "One of the tenets of earthcraft is that anyone can
commune with Gaea like that, honor her, celebrate the festivals and all. The impression it gives is that anyone can tap
into the power, but in practice I don't think that's true.
Maybe two or three out of every hundred at the Bealtienne
festival showed any actual power. Mostly to influence the
weather, actually, and that's an easy one for skeptics to brush
off. Though it's real enough. I was convinced pretty much
immediately.

"Cat can create an earth tremor. She can make plants and
trees grow. Tori can bring rain or snow or disperse clouds.
They're the major practitioners of earthcraft in the northeastern U.S."

Nikki tried to wrap her mind around that. This network
of people—mostly women—across the country, across the
world, who had developed a new way of looking at the world
and discovered magick in the midst of it. If they got together,
they might have the power to change weather patterns in
certain areas, to help crops grow, to feed people who were
starving. If earthcraft grew, it could change the world.

If there was a world left to change.

"That's amazing," Nikki said. "Really. Are they as strong
as you are?"

Keomany shrugged. "Up until what happened in Wickham, the day I came back from the festival, I'd enjoyed the
ritual of it, the joy it brought me, but I'd never so much as
summoned a raindrop, never mind made anything grow. I
don't understand it. Really I don't.

"You asked where the power comes from. Well, it
doesn't. It's here. It's all around us. Earthwitches believe that
we live in symbiosis with Gaea and that we can influence
nature, turn it to our own ends as long as they're pure. Some
people are more adept at it than others. Maybe some people
are just born with a greater . . . I don't know, affinity, or
whatever. I was happy to be one of the majority, someone
who just wanted to be there. It felt right to me. I guess I had
more of Gaea's spirit in me than I knew."

Nikki reached into the back seat and took Keomany's
hand. The two women gazed at each other for a moment and
Nikki found herself regretting that she had let this friendship

slip away and never once tried to resurrect it. Despite all that
had happened, she was grateful for this chance to know Keomany again.

"I guess you do," she said. "We were always in turmoil,
weren't we? Back when we met. But you've got a kind of
peace inside you now, and I have to wonder if that comes
from having connected with Gaea, or if there's something in
nature that sensed that peace, and found you."

Keomany smiled so sweetly it nearly broke Nikki's heart.
Catastrophic tragedy had torn through her life in recent days,
but somehow Keomany could still summon that smile.

"Let's just hope that the coven will be able to—" Keomany began, but then her eyes narrowed and she cocked her
head slightly, listening carefully to something.

A small laugh escaped her lips.

"What's funny?" Nikki asked.

Keomany raised an eyebrow. "The radio. Listen to the
radio."

It was turned down low, a static buzz in the background,
and Nikki had not been paying any attention to the music
while they were talking. Now that Keomany had drawn attention to it, she mentally tuned into the music. Even Peter
smiled, roused from his contemplation by the rhythm, and he
reached out to turn up the volume.

It was her song. Nikki's song. "Shock My World."

"Oh, God," she whispered.

The mood in the Navigator seemed to have been lightened
by the music on the radio, at least for Peter and Keomany.
For Nikki, it was another story entirely. Images flashed
through her mind, memories of being in the studio recording
the song, of singing it onstage at the showcase where Keomany had appeared out of nowhere, of Kyle, whom she had
left behind with little by way of goodbyes and given scarcely
a thought to since.

Auditoriums, bright lights, music charts. All the things she
had hoped for, there at her fingertips.

Right now it all seemed so far away, and hearing that
song on the radio, her own voice and guitar weaving in
through the rhythm, made her feel as though she had been

stolen away into some other world right along with Wickham and Hidalgo and Salzburg and the others.

Nikki through the Looking Glass.

She had chosen to stay. Given the current situation in the world and the quest that Peter and Keomany were on, she could not imagine any other option. The world beyond the Looking Glass would have to wait. Nikki only wished there was some way to know if she would ever get back to the other side.

━━━

THOUGH he had remained silent throughout, Peter had listened very carefully to the conversation between Nikki and Keomany. He was fascinated by this thing Keomany called *earthcraft*, the magick it yielded being so completely different from sorcery. Whatever power Keomany was able to harness—or access—the fundamental concept was attuning oneself with nature, with the world. Sorcery was the renegade bastard of such thought. When Peter did magick, he forced the natural world to submit itself to him, subjugating to his will the very thing that earthwitches worshipped.

It made him uneasy to think about, but now wasn't the time for a conversation on the subject. He figured the best thing for him to do at the moment was keep his mouth shut. They needed the help of Keomany's coven, and his insights into the complex nature of magick weren't going to help at all.

With Keomany directing him, Peter pulled off at an exit north of Brattleboro and they rolled west along a scenic, tree-lined street, passing a farm stand on the side of the road and a shop that sold homemade ice cream. There were a few antique stores and a gas station that looked as though it had been transported to the present day from somewhere around 1950. It was nice to see. Despite all that was happening in the world, this place, at least for the moment, was untouched.

A left on Orchard Hill Road took them on a winding, narrow drive through even more beautiful surroundings, low stone walls on either side of the street. When Keomany had said that the Bealtienne festival had been in Brattleboro, Peter had images in his mind of the thriving Vermont city he had

visited once a decade and a half before. While it was hardly
a metropolis, he had a difficult time imagining this huge gathering of worshippers—Witchstock, in a sense—in the middle
of downtown Brattleboro.

But this was more like it. There were houses here and
there, nice older homes set into the trees or far back on
stretches of farmland. Another turn and they came in sight
of a hill that rose up on their left, covered with row upon
row of apple trees. The field on the right was filled with
young cornstalks that swayed in the wind.

"It's beautiful," Peter said.

"It is," Keomany agreed.

Nikki reached across the gulf between the front seats and
put her hand on Peter's thigh. He glanced at her and smiled.
She made a game attempt at smiling in return, but she was
obviously troubled. Not that he blamed her. Not at all.

A hand-painted sign ahead identified the property on both
sides of the road as Summerfields Orchard and almost immediately they came to a huge red barn building on the left
with a parking lot around it. Peter pulled the Navigator into
the lot, kicking up dust and gravel that shrouded the damaged
Lincoln for a moment before floating away in the air. There
were a handful of other cars in the lot but Peter had seen
another twenty or so in the other lot across the street at the
base of the orchard.

"Nice place," Nikki observed, peering out the window.
"They do pumpkins in the fall? Halloween hay rides and all
that?"

"All that stuff," Keomany confirmed. "Plus they sell crafts
in the shop and they have a bakery in there too. The best
cider donuts you'll ever have. Corn, apples, beans, blueber-
ries, strawberries . . . all kinds of stuff grown right here."

"Gaea's been good," Nikki said.

Keomany might have responded but Peter wasn't listening. He put the Navigator into park and glanced around the
vehicle. Cars, yes, but the barn was locked up tight. The shop
Keomany was talking about was closed. Behind the big red
barn was a rambling farmhouse painted a faded white with
black shutters. It would have been unremarkable, even depressing, if not for the jungle of flowers, a riot of brilliant

colors, that spread out in front of the house and along a path that led toward the barn.

"It's quiet," Peter said.

Keomany and Nikki fell silent, glancing around as if to confirm what he'd said.

"Maybe they're closed today," Keomany suggested.

"Then why all the cars?" Peter asked.

"Oh, God, no," Keomany whispered, opening the Navigator's door and stepping quickly out. The wind seemed to pick up around the SUV, particularly near Keomany, and a dust devil formed, whipping at her legs. "If anything's happened—"

Peter and Nikki stepped out of the Navigator simultaneously. Disturbing scenarios ticked across Peter's mind as he tried to make sense of what was going on at Summerfields Orchard. The air around him shimmered like July heat off pavement and he felt the static crackle of magick between his fingers and along the back of his neck. But just as the wind around Keomany belonged to her, this was his magick, his own sorcery, instinct drawing it from him to make certain he was ready for anything.

He glanced at Keomany, who glared back a moment and then nodded. Together they started across the dusty lot toward the rear of the barn, toward the path that led up to the farmhouse.

Nikki called after them. "Hold up."

Peter and Keomany both paused to glance back at her. Nikki was gesturing at the cars parked near the Navigator.

"Look at the license plates."

With a concerned glance up at the house, Peter strode back toward Nikki. Keomany hesitated only a moment before doing the same. Nikki pointed to a blue Toyota with a Wisconsin license plate. From there Peter quickly scanned the others. Ohio. Virginia. Quebec. Only a couple of the cars were from Vermont and he reasoned at least one of them had to belong to Cat and Tori.

"These aren't just customers," he said, glancing at Keomany.

"No," she agreed. "No, I don't think they are."

"The coven?" Nikki asked.

The wind rustled across the young corn crop but otherwise there was not a sound to be heard. The road had been largely deserted as well. The radio had reported that millions of people had stayed home from work that day, watching the news, riveted to the television as reports continued to come in of the cities that had gone missing.

Quiet.

"Not just the coven. They're mostly New England."

Peter nodded, then started again for the farmhouse. They skirted the barn but he glanced at it from time to time, watching the windows of the shop and the locked doors to make certain nothing was lurking there in the shadows inside the building. Despite the assumption that the cars in the lot belonged to people who had been invited rather than customers, he was not ready to presume that meant all was well here.

He whispered to himself in an arcane language whose words were summoned from deep inside his mind, from an ancient place. He barely understood them himself but he felt their power. A vibrant blue light began to shimmer around his hands.

"Is that necessary, do you think?" Nikki whispered.

Peter glanced over at her, saw the fear in her eyes, and yet he also marked the courage it must have taken for her to feel such fear and continue onward. In New Orleans, years ago. In Wickham, just yesterday. And now today.

"I'm not taking any chances," he told her.

Nikki moved a little closer to him and they moved onto the walk side by side. Keomany was right behind them, and when Peter glanced back at her, he saw that as she passed among the wild splashes of color that made up the garden, the flowers seemed to grow slightly taller before his eyes, and to lean toward Keomany as she passed. Her hair blew around her head in a wind he could not feel.

A cry of agony came from the open windows of the house, the pain in that voice such that birds took flight from the trees beside the barn. Peter began to run. He was only a few yards from the front door when it was thrown open from inside by a tall, slender woman with skin so dark it seemed to absorb the afternoon sunlight. Peter thought that if not for the pain in her expression, she might have been beautiful.

The woman on the front steps of the house did not even look at him, or at Nikki, her eyes were focused only on one spot.

"Keomany," she said, and then she rushed down the steps, pushed past Peter, wrapped her arms around Keomany, and began to cry. "You're okay. We saw . . . on the TV . . . about Wickham and we thought . . ."

"*Ssh,* it's okay, Tori," Keomany said. "It's okay. I'm all right."

Peter studied the two women, trying to interpret their friendship, their intimacy. Keomany had explained that Tori Osborne and Cat Hein were partners and that the two women owned Summerfields together, but he had not realized that Keomany was as close to them as it now appeared.

Tori sobbed quietly as she tried to regain her composure. The tears glistened like diamonds on her extraordinary ebony skin. Her hair was shoulder length, tied into tight rows, tendrils weighted with beads that clacked together whenever she moved her head.

"What's going on, Tori?" Keomany asked. "Why are you closed?"

The woman took a deep breath and let it out slowly, calming herself. "You think anyone's going to shop when shit like this is happening in the world? Gaea's in pain, Keomany. A lot of us felt it. They've been showing up for the last few days, some of 'em witches we didn't even know."

As though someone had whispered a hint of paranoia in her ear, Tori stopped suddenly and glanced at Peter and Nikki, eyes narrowed in suspicion.

"They're friends," Keomany said quickly, running a comforting hand along Tori's bicep. "They're friends, honey. Nikki Wydra, Peter Octavian, this is Tori Osborne. Tori. Meet Peter and Nikki."

The woman looked curious when she heard Nikki's name and visibly flinched when Keomany mentioned Peter's. Tori stared at him.

"The mage," she said. "You're the mage."

Peter inclined his head, the briefest of nods. It was unnerving any time he met someone who knew who he was, and there were many of them. He was famous in his way;

or rather, notorious. Many of his exploits had been documented in the media, much as he had tried to downplay them
in recent years. Given that he had no idea what the average
earthwitch would think of his kind of magick, he hoped to
avoid further conversation on the subject. Fortunately, his
wasn't the only name Tori was familiar with. The woman's
attention turned back to Nikki and she smiled tentatively.

"Nikki Wydra. You're not the singer, are you? The girl
on the radio?"

A sad sort of smile drifted across Nikki's face. Peter
imagined this was the last place she had expected to run into
that question.

"I am, actually," she confessed.

Tori nodded toward her. "Love that song."

"Thank you."

But Tori had already moved on. Introductions made, she
had turned her focus back on matters that were truly important and away from such trifling bits of business as celebrity
and notoriety. As quickly as Peter and Nikki had been drawn
into the circle of their conversation, Tori and Keomany now
shut them out again. The two women spoke as though they
were alone.

"Come in," Tori told her. "We're trying to get a sense of
what's happening, what's really doing this, to see if we can
help."

"We're doing the same," Keomany replied. "We . . . we
met the thing in Wickham. Peter drove it out of there, but
this thing is so much bigger than just one town."

"So much bigger," Tori agreed. "Cat's . . . Cat's in a bad
way, Keomany."

With that, Tori led them up the front steps and through
the door. The interior of the farmhouse was decorated in
antiques, and punctuated with candles and potted plants. In
a side parlor, Peter saw several women sitting together on
the rug, eschewing chairs and sofa for the floor, and speaking
softly to one another over mugs of coffee. In the corner of
the room, two large, powerful-looking men ceased conversation to stare openly at them as they passed.

The hallway took them into the large kitchen at the back
of the house. Here cups and glasses and dishes had been

abandoned, many with half-eaten bits of cake or the remains of fruit salad left behind. Tori turned right and led them through the kitchen. On the other side of that room was a doorway and it was from here that a commotion issued. More than just the noise of anxious women convening, an atmosphere of grievous urgency emanated from that open door that was tangible.

As if born of the intensity therein, a short, gray-haired, matronly woman poked her head into the kitchen and beckoned for them—or rather for Tori—to hasten their pace.

"It's getting worse," the woman said, sympathy choking her words.

Tori's mouth became a thin line, lips pressed tightly together. She pressed on into that other room as if she had forgotten the presence of her guests. Keomany did not hesitate to follow her, and so Peter and Nikki entered as well. Nikki held Peter's hand as they stepped into what must in quieter times have been a vast living room. Now the couches had been shoved against the walls, coffee tables and knickknacks stacked on the far side, blocking a large entertainment center whose doors were closed, cutting off any music or television screen that might have lurked there, offering potential solace.

But there was no solace to be had. Sixteen, perhaps twenty women varying in size, age, and race sat cross-legged in a haphazard circle amid an array of burning candles just as varied as the women themselves. Their clothing differentiated them as well, separating them by style and by class, as well as taste. Heavy curtains had been drawn across the windows off of that room and the candlelight threw ghostly flickers on the walls, the contorted shadows of witches. Several men were in the room as well, dark-eyed and grim-faced like their counterparts in the parlor, though they did not bother to even glance at the new arrivals Tori had brought with her.

None of them looked up, in fact.

The attention of every single person in the room was focused on a single location, the center of the gathering, where a woman of near Amazonian stature lay nude on the floor, sprawled on one side as though she had fallen there, and whimpering.

"I'm here, baby," Tori said, slipping easily through the circle, which parted for her and closed up again. The beads in her hair clacked together and the candlelight gleamed upon her skin as she knelt beside her lover.

"Cat," Keomany whispered. Then she spoke again, and now it was as though she were speaking to no one, or perhaps directly to the earth goddess whom they all worshipped. "What the hell's happening?"

Nikki swore softly.

Peter could only stare. Catherine Hein was just as Keomany had described her. Over six feet tall and powerfully built, even with her pretty blond hair she must have been imposing under normal circumstances, when she was healthy. When she was conscious.

For now the only reaction evoked by the sight of the nude woman was the need to call an ambulance. But it would have been clear even to one with no knowledge of magick—magick of any kind—that no doctor could help Cat Hein.

Her entire body was covered with nearly bloodless cuts, as though a fine, tiny blade had carved upon her a map of the earth. Oceans and islands, continents, all had been engraved in the taut white flesh of the coven's leader in minute detail. From where Peter stood, he could see what appeared to be North America. There were no lines to indicate divisions between nations—to Gaea, the natural soul of the world, nations did not exist—but in a place where he imagined Texas and Mexico kissed, on Cat's left thigh, there was an open wound. The flesh had been gouged out as if with a trowel, and yet once more there was almost no blood. Only the pulsing, raw red flesh inside that wound.

As Tori reached for her lover, Cat moaned and turned slightly, and Peter could see several other such wounds, including one on her belly that might have been northern California. Farther up her thigh, where Vermont would be, a thick scab had formed over a wound that was healing.

Wickham, Peter thought. *That's Wickham.*

A ripple of anticipation spider-walked across the back of his neck. Keomany was a powerful earthwitch, but she herself had said that all of them revealed their connection to nature in different ways. Catherine Hein was so completely in tune with Gaea that it was tearing her apart.

"Turn her over!" Peter snapped.

Heads turned, eyes glared at him. Three of the women in the circle began to rise as if to protect Cat from this stranger in their midst, and the men across the room started to move toward him.

"Who the hell is he?" hissed a Latina girl who looked barely old enough to drive.

Nikki instinctively moved closer to Peter and Keomany stepped between him and the circle.

"Tori," Peter said firmly.

The woman looked up, her carved ebony features hard with fear.

"I might be able to help her, at least for a little while," he told her, raising his hands so they all could see the glow of blue fire that crackled from his palms. "And together we might all be able to fight this. But it has to be together."

Tori sneered at him, lips curling back from strangely sharp teeth. "With your dirty magick, you're going to heal Gaea?"

Keomany held up a hand in front of a woman who tried to move closer to Peter, stopping her there.

"No," Peter said. "But I will find the power that's causing this. I'll find it, and I'll stand, and I'll fight. The healing will be up to all of you. I'm not your enemy."

His words echoed in the otherwise silent room, the only motion that of the flickering candle-shadows on the walls.

"Turn her over," he instructed again.

A fresh tear slipped down Tori's face as she stroked her unconscious lover. At length she turned and slid her hands delicately beneath Cat, careful to avoid the carved map of her flesh. Keomany slipped through the circle to help her and together they gently turned Cat onto her belly, her hair covering her face. Her left breast, partially crushed beneath her body, bulged out from beneath her splayed arm. On that soft whiteness, the shores of Iceland had been delineated in slit skin. As her body was turned, Peter saw more wounds, deep and numerous. Some of them were places the news had already reported as afflicted, others were a surprise to him.

Only one mark upon Cat Hein's body interested him, however.

On her back was a bright red welt smaller than a dime. Peter studied the macabre map of her skin and knew it was somewhere in Europe. He snapped his gaze up to glare at the men watching him cautiously from across the room.

"One of you get me a world map, right now!"

"What are you doing?" Tori demanded. "I thought you said you could help her."

This last was a grief-stricken plea. Peter ignored her, glaring at the men until one of them moved to a bookcase and began to scan through titles, looking for an atlas or an encyclopedia, anything that would have what Peter required.

"That's a new one," Keomany told Tori softly, pointing at the welt on Cat's back.

Nikki was speaking to all of them, however. She glanced around defiantly. "Wherever that is, it's where the darkness is going to fall next. Your friend is in terrible pain and we want to help her. But don't you think Gaea's touched her like this for a reason? Your goddess is in agony and she's connected to Cat the only way she knows how right now. She's showing us where she hurts, showing us where she's been blooded, so we can help her."

Tori softly sobbed and lay down beside Cat, brushing the hair from the unconscious woman's face, whispering soft intimacies to her that everyone tried not to hear.

"Got it," said one of the men, a bearded man who looked more like a biker than some earth magician. He strode over to Peter with a thick book and handed it over. "It's a history book, but it's got world maps. Maybe not exactly up to date, but—"

"Fine," Peter said quickly, snatching the book up and leafing it open. He could have told the man that he had spent centuries walking this world and had no problem at all comparing age-old geography with that of the present day. He remembered. But what would be the point. The man would not have understood.

In the back of the book was a foldout map of Europe, circa 1881. With the book open, Peter stepped through the circle. The women parted reluctantly for him. Whatever chanting or praying they had been doing around Cat before he and his friends had arrived, it was long forgotten now. Several candles guttered out, disturbed by his passing.

Peter held the book out and compared it to the grotesque topography on Cat Hein's bare flesh.

"Spain," he said aloud. He had thought it was Spain but now confirmed it. Carefully he held his finger above the map, then tapped the name of a city written there in boldface black.

"There," he said, his voice a rasp. "The Tatterdemalion's creatures are going there next."

He dropped the book, let it thump to the floor, and held out his hands above Cat's body. Blue fire spread from his fingers and expanded. Two of the men swore and threw themselves backward. The other raced toward Peter with a cry of alarm but Nikki grabbed the man and pushed him backward. He tried to fight her, but Nikki could hold her own. She tripped him and sent him sprawling to the ground.

Most of the earthwitches scattered. Several began to call upon Gaea and a frigid wind lashed at Peter, coming up from nowhere, impossibly, and creating an icy bluster around him.

"Please!" Tori cried, but Peter did not know if she was appealing to him to stop, or to continue.

The spell he had cast was a ward of sorts, and his sorcery lifted Cat from the ground, her arms and hair dangling beneath her. A cocoon of blue light swirled around her, holding her there aloft.

Her wounds began to disappear.

"What'd you do to her?" Nikki asked.

But it was Tori to whom Peter explained. "I've cut her off for now. Put a barrier between Cat and her goddess. Gaea can't touch her and Cat won't have any access to earthcraft for now. Just for a while. Just until this is over."

"It's going to kill her, to be cut off from nature," Tori said sadly. "When she wakes up—"

Peter stared at her. "Cutting her off was the only way to keep her alive. When this is done, I can restore her. But for now we have to take the gift that Gaea gave her and stop this before there's nothing left of this world to save."

Tori nodded. She glanced once more at the strange spectacle of her lover bathed in blue light, hovering above the ground, and then she rose. Slowly, she embraced Keomany and then walked over to Peter and Nikki.

"Where is it?" she asked. "That new wound. Where the darkness is attacking now. Where are you going?"

"It's in Spain," Peter said. "A small town there called Ronda. I only wish I knew how quickly the darkness claims these places, how fast the Whispers take over."

The prone, levitating form of Catherine Hein shuddered. Cat moaned, there in that blue, sorcerous light. She spoke three words that, though muttered softly, as though talking in her sleep, everyone in the room heard with utter clarity.

"Whispers travel fast."

———

ONLY the gleam of the moon illuminated the interior of the Mondragon Palace. Night had fallen in Ronda and the building was closed now to tourists, who would be left to wander the streets or return to their hotels to await the traditional late Spanish dinner hour. The courtyards and gardens were empty, though the fountains still burbled and the wind swept up off the valley floor to rustle the leaves in the trees. Pears bobbed at the ends of branches on the lone fruit tree in the garden.

Just inside, in the moon-glazed dark, a droplet of light appeared seven feet above the ground. It glistened and grew heavy and then it slipped slowly toward the tile floor, a tear drop on the face of reality. As it slid downward, it left a streak of silver behind, a gleaming slit that began to pout open and quickly blossomed until it grew to the shape of an enormous rose petal. Its surface was like a liquid mirror, absorbing and reflecting back the moonlight within the palace.

The tear drop touched the tiles.

A black, razor-taloned hand emerged from within the silver portal, sending ripples to its edges. It was a tentative hand, reaching and searching, as though cautious of what it might find.

Then the first of the Whispers slipped through into Ronda.

Others followed. Safe in the moonlight, they skittered through the city in the night black shadows, investigating each cellar and enclosure so that they might wreak dark havoc upon Ronda and still be able to secret themselves before dawn's light, hiding until the second night, when their master would come to claim them, and this new city, for his own.

CHAPTER 15

JACK Devlin hated to fly under normal circumstances. To-day's flight was anything but. Most of the world's major airlines had severely curtailed departures as the news had broken of the crisis that had now affected much of the globe. Flights that went anywhere near affected areas had to be rerouted due to fear of what might happen if a plane flew into affected airspace. Then the cancellations had begun. Pilots called in sick, passengers gave up their travel plans and went home. Bad enough to wonder what might happen to your own hometown, but on board a plane flying overhead, one had to think about the consequences if a city below suddenly went the way of Salzburg or Mont de Moreau.

Toronto was gone now too.

Now Jack found himself on a private plane high over the Atlantic Ocean with only a dozen other Church of the Resurrection clerics for company and not a glass of whiskey in sight. And damn it if he couldn't have used that whiskey now.

He glanced out the window, doing his best to ignore the imposing presence of Bishop Gagnon beside him. Jack had been summoned to that seat beside His Eminence not as a place of honor, but as a kind of punishment, not unlike a student being called to the principal's office.

"You're awfully quiet, Father Devlin," the Bishop said.

"Just tired, I guess," Jack replied immediately, an automatic response.

Without looking, somehow he could still see in his mind's eye the way the Bishop must have pursed his lips then, as though disdainfully tasting those words.

"At some point, Jack, you're going to stop sulking and realize that Peter Octavian is not your friend. Once upon a time, he was one of *them*. Even those few that remain are still a blight on this world. An infection. If Octavian had not destroyed the Catholic sect of sorcerers that kept demon manifestations in check, it's likely none of this would be happening at all. Perhaps he isn't a vampire anymore, but whatever he is, it isn't *human*."

The engines of the small jet purred, making the seat hum beneath him. Jack felt it in his gritted teeth, in the taut muscles at the back of his neck and across his shoulders. *Sulking*, he thought. *Asshole*.

Slowly, Jack turned to face the Bishop. Solely to keep his hands too busy to wring the old man's neck, he reached up and removed his glasses.

"If you studied your history, Michel," he said, all traces of friendship gone from his voice, "you might discover that it was the mishandling of the species in the first place that led to the clusterfuck that brought the church down. The same ignorant bullshit you're preaching now, *Your Eminence*. Octavian has already proven more capable of confronting this crisis than we are and it's pissing you off. Why not admit it?

"You want to blame him? Why? Because he and others like him performed sorcery over the ages that perforated our reality with badly repaired breaches into other dimensions? Fine. Blame him. But if you do that, you'll have to share the blame, Michel. Unlike you, I've done my research. I know, for instance, that the original breach in Derby was caused in large part by a spell cast by a small group of Roman priests, and that you were among them. The sect you're talking about probably punched more holes in the barrier between worlds than the fucking ancient Egyptians, and we know how experimental they were.

"So don't go pointing fingers, Michel. You need all the help you can get."

Fuming, he glared at the Bishop, challenging the man to contradict him. It might have been career suicide, but Jack found that he no longer cared. The moment he had left Octavian and the others behind in Vermont, he had known it was a mistake, and from the second he had boarded this private jet, he had regretted it, wishing to be back among the people who wanted to destroy this gathering darkness, this insidious threat, solely because it had to be done and not out of any self-aggrandizing motive.

"Are you through?" Bishop Gagnon asked. His voice was light but anyone who knew him well would have heard the threat in it, seen the danger glinting in his eyes.

"If only I were." Father Jack casually slipped his glasses back on, as though whatever the Bishop said now would not matter in the least. He could feel the eyes of some of the other priests on the jet upon him but cared not at all. There were only a few of them he knew, and not one among them with whom he had developed any kind of kinship.

The Bishop paused a moment, lips pressed together in an expression of distaste, nostrils flaring. At length he narrowed his eyes, almost forcing Jack with his will alone to look up and meet his gaze.

"We have a sacred charge, Father Devlin," the Bishop said. "Sacred. We hold in our hands the faith of millions, and we may use it as our greatest weapon even as we safeguard it with our lives. This thing, this great evil that Octavian called the Tatterdemalion, is far more powerful than such a dismissive description could ever imply. Whatever this cruel sentience is, its power seems barely affected by our own magicks. For some reason its attention was drawn to our world. Our seers believe that it sensed the many breaches of the past, found the scars they had left behind, and has been forcing them open again.

"You and Octavian proved that some of these cities taken by the Tatterdemalion may not be gone forever. You, Father Devlin, are going to work with the rest of us to be sure the

U.N. forces assigned to this are able to cross over into the Tatterdemalion's dimension, its stolen empire. There we will determine if the other cities can be recalled into this world. If they cannot, then the breaches the demon has made into this reality will be resealed, this time with magicks of far greater power. Sealed forever."

For a moment Jack felt as though the plane had hit an air pocket and begun to drop, like the world was falling out from under him. But the flight was smooth, the engines still humming nicely. It wasn't the jet.

It was him.

The priest stared at his superior, his chest aching, breath catching in his throat. "You're . . . you're not serious. You can't just leave those cities in there. Even in Wickham there were thousands still alive. You'd be leaving millions behind . . . if it was even possible to seal them off completely."

At last Bishop Gagnon smiled, his pleasure at Jack's dismay obvious and harrowing. "Oh, we believe we can. We may well be able to seal this dimension off from others totally and eternally."

"You can't do this," Jack hissed, beginning to stand up from his seat to look around for support from the other priests on board. "People won't stand for it. Every single person in those cities has loved ones somewhere else, family and friends who will burn you at the stake if you just abandon them, if you—"

Faster than could be expected of a man his age, the Bishop shot out a hand and grabbed Jack by the shoulder. His grip was painful and he shoved Jack down into his seat, holding him there. When he spoke, he leaned in close and Jack could smell garlic and wine from lunch on the Bishop's breath.

"You should keep your seat belt on, Father Devlin," the Bishop suggested.

Jack made no move to comply but the man's hand lifted from his shoulder.

"You are right, of course. I cannot do any of those things. But we, my son, *we* can. We are the Holy Church, you little shit. We are the shepherds of this world and we will tend to our flock whether they like it or not. If the wolf snatches away some of our sheep during the night, we do not stake the others out as a sacrifice to its predations. We protect them, and we learn never to let the wolf near again.

"If it weren't for your heroics in Wickham with that damned monster, we wouldn't even be going in there in the first place. But now that every news channel has reported that Wickham was rescued—and you could hardly call it a rescue, could you?—the U.N. is insisting that an effort be made. So we're going to go in, Father. We're going to do our duty to the faithful, and even to the Philistines. And then we're going to put a fence around the rest of our flock and forget all about the ones lost to the wolves.

"You, Father Devlin, will cooperate because it's the only possibility that some of these cities could be resurrected, and that some of the survivors might be returned to their loved ones. And if you breathe a word of this conversation to anyone who is not on this plane, when this is over you may find yourself locked on the other side of the fence, in the territory of the wolf. Do I make myself clear?"

For several minutes Bishop Gagnon stared at him but Jack did not answer. The question was not posed again and eventually Jack turned away and stared out the window at the blackening sky. Flying east, over the Atlantic, they were chasing the night, hurrying into a darkness that might never lift.

For the remaining duration of the flight, there was utter silence.

━━━

SOPHIE Duvic wanted nothing more than to be able to close her eyes. Everywhere she looked, the streets of Mont de Moreau were alive with menace. Whispers moved inside shattered shop windows and clung to the front of apartment houses. Smoke from distant fires clogged the orange sky and winged carrion demons flew in vulture-circles above as she struggled to propel Antoinette Lamontagne forward.

"Move, damn you," she whispered in French, afraid to raise her voice. Afraid to draw attention.

Antoinette carried her son Henri, deathly still once more, over her shoulder as though he were a rolled carpet or a length of rope. Her eyes were nearly as glazed and her features as gaunt as those of her nearly catatonic son. Antoinette had watched the Whispers slaughter her husband before her eyes and it had leeched all the energy from her.

"Please, please hurry," Sophie urged, reaching out to take the woman by the hand.

Antoinette snatched back her hand as if Sophie's fingers had burned her. Her dull eyes were suddenly alive with madness.

"Go on without me if we are too slow for you," she sneered. But in an instant her anger dissipated and fresh tears sprang to her face.

"Alain would want you to live," Sophie told her. She could hear her own voice, cold and flat, so very matter of fact, and wondered how glassy her own eyes might be if she could see them in a mirror.

The truth was that it had crossed her mind that leaving Antoinette and her son behind might be the only chance for her own survival. She never would do such a thing, would die herself before she betrayed her heart and soul in such horrid fashion. But the thought was there, and it had tainted her so that she could barely stand to look at the Lamontagnes now.

"Let's go," she whispered. "Just . . . let's go."

This time when she reached out for Antoinette's hand, the other woman let her take it. Together they crept along the orange-dark street, keeping close to the buildings. There was a corner ahead where a narrower side street forked off to the right, a centuries-old area of the city that had been restored, its architecture charming once upon a time, and now ravaged by passing beasts. For there were more things abroad here than the Whispers and the carrion fliers and the quilled monsters they had seen before.

The thought of the demons that had swept out of the sewer and nearly dragged Kuromaku down with them made her stomach convulse. Sophie pushed the images from her mind before she threw up again.

At the fork in the road ahead was a building that had once

been a hotel. Empty cars were parked in the street in front of it, some abandoned, some merely forgotten. Corpses picked almost clean lay half-in, half-out of windows. The body of a man had shattered the windshield of a car and Sophie wondered if the man had jumped from the hotel's roof or if his remains had been dropped from high above.

"We cannot make it," Antoinette said aloud. "It's too far. By the time we get there, another city will rise. And another and another. This is Hell, don't you see? It's Hell."

Sophie could not argue. It was Hell, of a sort, but they would make it to the edge of town. They had to make it, before another city was brought into this hellish landscape. Kuromaku had been clear . . . there was only one escape route and it would not stay open forever. She was about to tell Antoinette once again to hurry, but the sound of breaking glass ahead made her pause and crouch low, close to the building. She indicated that Antoinette should do the same but the woman barely twitched, as though she wanted to be discovered.

They had nearly reached the fork, had prepared to round the turn and start up the narrower street that made up the oldest section of Mont de Moreau and cut through the town, directly toward the one area of its perimeter that might provide them a route of escape.

Inside what had been the hotel's restaurant, Whispers moved in the dark. The grimy orange light filtered in only slightly but it glinted off their carapaces. Sophie held her breath as one of them leaped up onto a table inside that restaurant and peered out at the street.

It *saw* them. No eyes, but somehow, it saw them.

Sophie's chest hurt and she found she could not breathe. Seconds ticked past. Antoinette felt Sophie's grip tighten on her and stopped to stare at her, shifting the weight of her son in her arms. Then the other woman must have seen the stark terror on Sophie's face, for she began to turn to see what Sophie was staring at.

The sharp tendril-tongue of the Whisper twitched and darted in the air as if pointing them out.

Antoinette screamed. The Whisper threw itself at the plate glass window of the restaurant, shattering it and landing in a rain of jagged shards upon the sidewalk. For a moment Sophie thought Antoinette was still screaming—that her terrified wail had grown to a strange roar—and then she realized that this was a different sound.

It was an engine.

The Whisper began to lope toward them. Antoinette clutched Henri more tightly. Sophie swore as she saw more of the dagger-thin, black-plated demons rushing out of the restaurant toward them. She started to turn, tugging on Antoinette, knowing they could not outrun the monsters.

The rumble of the engine grew louder. Headlights illuminated the Whisper that had first spotted them and it paused and turned to look up the hill. An aging red Volkswagen tore down the road, colliding with the Whisper, crushing it beneath its tires; the demon's body was snagged on the undercarriage and dragged twenty yards, pieces of it torn off and strewn in the street before the Volkswagen went up onto the sidewalk to swerve around an abandoned truck and the corpse of the demon fell off.

The Whispers on the other side of the street hesitated.

The Volkswagen spun into a turn that made the tires squeal on the road and then shuddered to a halt perhaps fifteen feet from Sophie, Antoinette, and Henri. The driver's door popped open and Kuromaku appeared. He shot a hard look at Sophie.

"Get in!" he snapped. "You drive."

The demons, their scythe-fingers clacking as if in anticipation, rushed across the street toward the vehicle. The engine was still running, the headlights cutting the orange gloom. Kuromaku reached to his waist and from nothing but the air he drew his curved sword. The katana seemed to hiss in a voice not unlike that of the demons as it slashed through the air, slashing downward in a series of arcs and thrusts that cracked the carapaces of the Whispers, hacking their bony figures to pieces.

Sophie was transfixed in those first moments but then, while Kuromaku continued to fight and more Whispers began to appear from beneath abandoned cars and from the rooftops and shattered windows of nearby buildings, she was finally spurred into action. With Antoinette running hard behind her, weighed down by Henri, Sophie rushed to the Volkswagen and threw herself through the open door into the driver's seat. Antoinette had hauled open a back door and now seemed to tumble into the rear of the car in a bundle with her son.

A Whisper scrabbled across the pavement after them. Antoinette just had time to pull the door closed before it reached the car and the demon struck the car with enough force to crack the window and buckle the metal door.

"Drive!" Antoinette shouted in French.

Sophie did not need the prodding. She screamed out the window to Kuromaku, not even certain anymore what language she was speaking. Whether it was French or English, the vampire warrior understood her. He lunged forward, driving the sword through the demon in front of him. A dark spatter of demon blood had splashed his face and she saw his profile in that moment—those handsome, grimly regal features, black hair wild, muscles on the back of his neck clearly visible—and she was terrified of him. In her mind's eye she saw the gentle man upon whom she had placed her childhood affections, a crush that had not disappeared with maturity but only intensified.

Kuromaku turned toward her, wiping filthy ichor from his face, skin glistening with that hideous orange light and torn shirt whipping in the dread wind that had blown up just as they left the church, and she knew that despite—or perhaps because of—her terror, Sophie had never wanted Kuromaku so desperately. Her breath caught in her throat and her chest hurt, just as it had moments before, but now for an entirely different reason.

Survive, she thought. *If you don't live, you'll never get to tell him.*

She threw the Volkswagen into gear. In the back Antoinette cried out as the Whisper who had struck the door now shattered the cracked window and began to reach in after her. Kuromaku snarled something in his native tongue and then the ronin leaped atop the Volkswagen and decapitated the Whisper with a single swift stroke of his blade.

"Go!" he shouted.

Swarms of them were on the streets now, drawn by the fighting. Kuromaku dropped onto the hood of the Volkswagen, his sword at the ready. Sophie gripped the steering wheel in both hands and hit the accelerator. The car lurched and she drove directly at the front of the hotel where the Whispers had first emerged. The road forked and she cut the wheel to the right and the engine whined as she drove up the hill through what had once been a beautifully refurbished district.

At first the Whispers gave chase, capering and loping after them. Several caught up to the car but Kuromaku dispatched them quickly, scrambling over the roof with unnerving agility. One managed to grab hold of the rear bumper and was dragged a ways before it tore itself apart on the pavement.

Three of them leaped from rooftops along the sloping road but reached the street moments too late, as the car was roaring by. Sophie floored it and they gained speed as they surged up the hill. At the top of the grade where the road first flattened slightly and then began to descend, they came to an intersection. She slowed down not at all, mindful of the demons still giving chase.

On a street off to her right, Sophie saw several others, but these weren't Whispers, nor were they the great quilled beasts they had seen earlier. These things were far larger than that, with bodies like that of a rhinoceros, long serpentine necks, and flat heads with massive fanged jaws that reminded her of nothing so much as enormous alligators.

The roar of the engine drew their attention and the demons glanced up, then those long, fanged maws snapped open and closed and they began to give chase.

Kuromaku clung to the hood, ignoring these new abominations. His gaze was intent upon the road ahead and Sophie knew what he was thinking. They had to reach the edge of Mont de Moreau.

She drove faster.

In the back seat, Antoinette Lamontagne began to pray in a voice full of despair and desolation.

———

THE street in the Village where Peter had his apartment was so small that he was forced to bump the Navigator up onto the curb and still the big SUV was going to create a problem if any trucks tried to drive down the road. He was aware of the issue, but could not take the time to care. The clock was ticking. Truth was, the only reason they had come back to Manhattan at all was that the first direct flight from Boston to Seville upon which they could have gotten seats did not depart until quarter to ten that night. Any of the flights with connections—or going to Gibraltar or Malaga, which were also only a couple of hours' drive from Ronda— would have gotten them there even later.

There was a flight out of LaGuardia at 8:25 P.M. That gave them enough time to drive back to Manhattan, pick up a fresh change of clothes for Peter, buy something for Keomany and Nikki to wear, and still get back to LaGuardia with enough time to drop off the rental. They'd arrive in Seville around nine in the morning, rent a car and head south, and be in Ronda before noon.

If Ronda was still there.

The knowledge that it might not be, that all of this rushing around might be for nothing, had Peter on edge. His jaw hurt from grinding his teeth together and his entire body felt electric, alive with a kind of static energy. He wanted to do something, not tomorrow, but now. Tonight.

The lights were on in Jarrod and Suze's row house but the windows of his own apartment—in their basement— were dark. Peter stepped out quickly, saying nothing to Keomany and Nikki. Without being invited they climbed out after him. He slammed the door of the Navigator, not bothering to lock it, and hurried around the front of the vehicle toward the stairs that led down into his apartment. His keys rattled in his hand as he reached for the door. From down the block he could hear loud music—the grind of funky Amanda Marshall songs half a decade old—issuing from the open door of The Fat Cat along with the laughter of women.

Leave it to New York, he thought. *Turn on the news and you can see the world's coming apart at the seams, but this is one city that's not going to hide and hold its breath.*

Nikki and Keomany were carrying their things, including the department store bags from the mall they'd stopped in to buy some fresh clothes while they were passing through Connecticut. Keomany had mentioned that she would have liked to have time to shower again before they got on the plane, but they all knew that was a pipe dream. They'd have just enough time to change and repack their travel bags.

Peter stepped over the copies of *The New York Times* that had accumulated on his doorstep and turned the key in the lock. He pushed the door open and stepped inside. Instantly he felt a prickle of alarm go up the back of his neck. Octavian hissed and gestured for Keomany and Nikki to stay back as he peered into the darkness of his apartment.

Something was there. He sensed it. Something inhuman.

His right hand came up, enveloped in a blue light the color of a robin's egg. The light splashed strange shapes and shadows upon the walls and he hesitated. This apartment and the things inside it—the books and the art he had collected, not to mention the art he himself had made—were all he had of a normal life.

But Nikki was with him, and Keomany as well, and whatever his hesitation about destroying his belongings, he would not risk their lives for simple things.

Blue light flickered around his hand. Something shifted in the shadows at the back of his apartment, in the little corridor that led to the bedroom.

"Show your face," he snarled. "And slowly. You don't want to piss me off right now."

A susurrus of laughter issued from that back hallway, a rolling sound that seemed to curl like mist along the floor. The shadows resolved themselves into a figure. For a moment he could not make out what it was, but then he realized that it was human. Female.

Allison Vigeant stepped into the blue light, chuckling to herself. "Ooh," she said. "Tough guy."

Peter felt a rush of relief go through him. The blue glow around his hand winked out and he reached for the light switch. When he flicked it, floor lamps on either end of his living room blinked into brilliant illumination. Allison stretched a little and yawned.

"Sorry," she said. "I took a nap while I was waiting for you. It's been a while since I've had any decent sleep."

With a lopsided grin Peter went to her and pulled her into his arms. He hugged her for several long seconds, during which their crisis seemed to retreat. Then he stepped back and gazed at her, studying her; the black denim jeans and spaghetti-strap tank top, the scuffed black lace-up boots.

"You look great," he told her, smiling. "Your hair's different." He had been in touch with her since New Orleans—since Cody died and she had gone off with the U.N. to become their hound dog—but had not really seen her in a long time.

"Variety," she replied, pushing a hand through her red hair. "Spice of life. You, on the other hand, have gotten older."

"It happens to the best of us," Peter replied automatically.

Allison's face shut down then, her eyes narrowing and all traces of a smile fading from her lips. "Not to all of us, though," she said.

Regretfully, Peter nodded. He said nothing, however. Anything that needed to be said on that subject had been covered long ago. Allison had never wanted to become a vampire, a shadow. The decision had been taken from her. She had been forced to enter this life and considered it her curse. Allison was haunted by it.

For a long moment he just stared at her. Then he was shaken from his reverie by motion behind him as Nikki and Keomany moved farther into the apartment and closed the door.

Allison's gaze went past Peter and she smiled. "Nikki. Hey."

Peter moved out of the way, and he and Keomany watched as Nikki and Allison met in the middle of the living room. The two women were smiling but they greeted each other awkwardly; a perfunctory embrace and then two steps back to regard one another. Though both had been in New Orleans, they had not had time to grow close, yet they had shared a purpose at one time that had almost killed them both, and so had that much at least in common.

"I didn't realize you two were back together," Allison

said, her hazel eyes widening with curiosity. She put her hands on her slim hips and glanced back and forth between Peter and Nikki. In that moment she looked for all the world like nothing more than a normal woman. Attractive, yes, but still ordinary.

Then she spotted Keomany, who had put down her things and was sifting through the bags of the clothing she had purchased, pulling out clothes to change into.

"Oh, sorry," Nikki said. "Allison Vigeant, my friend Keomany Shaw. Keomany, Allison."

The two women shook hands.

"I read your book," Keomany said. "Remember you from CNN, too. Sometimes I think you're the reason the whole world didn't fall apart when the news about the shadows—vampires and demons and all—first came out."

Allison seemed stunned by this and for a moment said nothing. Then she simply nodded. "Much appreciated. I only wish I really did have the power to change the world."

When Nikki next spoke up, her voice rasped with the ominous weight of her words.

"Well," she said, "someone does."

There were so many things Peter wanted to say to Allison, to ask her, to find out from her what her life was like now. He wanted to be able to tell her about his loneliness, and how he had retreated from the world, and how it had taken seeing Nikki again to make him realize that he had broken his promise to himself that he would make use of his mortal life. There were only two people left in the entire world that he thought would really understand, and Allison was one of them.

But now wasn't the time.

"Allison, it's . . . it's great to see you. Really," he told her, rubbing at his tired eyes with the heels of his hands and then running his fingers through his ragged-cut hair. "But something tells me you didn't come by for coffee, or a nap in my bed."

The vampire's face darkened, her expression grim and no longer beautiful. "No. I didn't. The U.N. knows what you did in Wickham. They sent me to ask if you'd be willing to work with them."

Peter stared at her a moment, an icy chill clutching at his heart. *The U.N.*, he thought. Then he glanced at Nikki and Keomany.

"Get your things together. We can't afford to miss our plane."

They started to do just that, unpacking their dirty clothes from their travel cases and repacking new ones, heading into the bathroom to change their clothes for the plane flight.

"Peter?" Allison asked.

He drew the back of his hand across the several days of beard growth on his chin. Tired, he shook his head.

"The U.N., Allison?" Peter gazed at her, dropping his voice. "There's a presence out there that's strip mining this world, doing more damage than anything since the plague. So the U.N. sent you—probably the most significant weapon they have for something like this—to sit around and wait in an apartment you have no idea if I'm even coming back to. And you go? You do what they tell you, just like that? You sit here and wait while you could be saving lives somewhere?"

Her temple throbbed and Peter saw the spark of real anger in her eyes.

"Don't you talk to me like that," she snapped. "You don't have the first clue what my relationship is with the people I work for. Sure, people are dying out there, but so what if I could save fifteen lives or fifteen hundred? We need you because you're the only person in the world who's got a chance of stopping this thing entirely. Somebody had to come and find you."

Peter sighed, shaking his head sadly. "Don't you think I know what's going on? Did you think I would just be sitting here watching it unfold on TV?"

"So you'll help?" Allison asked, grimly serious.

"Fuck the U.N.," Peter scowled. "That's just what's needed here, a bunch of nations arguing over diplomatic solutions or all-out war. They haven't seen the Tatterdemalion up close, haven't felt the extent of its power. They haven't faced these Whisper demons. An ambassador isn't going to do the job, but neither is straight brute force."

"So what do you suggest? Where are you going now?" Allison asked, searching Peter's eyes.

But it was Keomany who answered. She had repacked her bag and was walking toward the hall so that she might change clothes in the bedroom when she stopped and turned to face Allison and Peter.

"We have it on good authority that the next city the Tatterdemalion will try to take is Ronda, in Spain. We've got a flight soon," Keomany said as she turned and went down the corridor. "Nice to meet you."

Then Peter and Allison were alone. The fan in the bathroom whirred and they could hear the sink running as Nikki washed up in there. Several seconds passed until at last Allison spoke.

"Ronda, huh?"

"You know it?"

"I've been there. You're bringing those two?"

Peter paused, an unfamiliar feeling of nausea beginning to churn in his gut. "They can take care of themselves. Keomany's an earthwitch. They're nature worshippers with an affinity for—"

"I know what they are," Allison interrupted. She was standing only a few inches from him and Peter thought that she had gotten taller since they had last met. Not impossible, given the control shadows had over their molecular structure.

"Then you know she can—"

"What about Nikki?"

Peter blinked, began to respond, and then glanced away. The apartment suddenly seemed too small. He could hear the ticking of the clock on the wall and smell the odors of paint that had been trapped in here since he had gone. This was the life he had built and it felt good to have Nikki here amid it. He dared not leave her behind.

"We've talked about it," he said. "She thinks the safest place for her is with me."

"And what do you think?"

His throat felt dry. Peter did not respond. Allison reached out and ran her right hand across his cheek.

"Have you forgotten what happened to Meaghan?" she asked quietly. Then she turned his chin so that he had to meet her eyes. The pain of the memories reflected in them seemed infinite. "Have you forgotten what happened to me?"

Peter laid his hand over hers on his face and closed his eyes. He did not like to think about what had happened to Allison, did not want to remember how she had been violated, how she had been raped and mutilated and murdered and then brought back to life as a vampire so her torturer could start all over again. He didn't want to think about Meaghan, whom he had loved dearly and who had been an example to them all, and who had sacrificed herself willingly.

It took him several moments to realize that the fan in the bathroom was off.

"Don't let her do this to you," Nikki said.

Peter spun to see her standing in the corridor just outside the bathroom door, dressed now in a light summer dress, her face shining where she had scrubbed it clean, her blond hair swept back from her eyes.

Allison sighed. "Nikki, don't take this wrong. I just don't want to see anything—"

Nikki stormed across the living room until she was face to face with Allison. Her voice cracked when she spoke, and for the first time Peter realized the depth of her fear.

"You don't want what happened to you to happen to me," Nikki snapped. "Fine. You're not alone in that. I'm sorry for what happened to you, Allison, but you can't blame Peter for that."

Allison's eyes widened. "I'm not—"

"You just did," Nikki said. "You as much as blamed him for Meaghan's death and for not being there to help you. What else do you want him to think, implying that every time he takes some fragile human woman along with him, she ends up dead or worse? Well, I'm not fucking fragile, goddamn you! I'm not!"

With a slow sigh, Allison took a step back. "That's not what I'm saying, Nikki."

Peter felt sick. He knew what his heart was telling him, but he also knew that the voice of his heart was wrong. When Nikki turned to speak to him and she saw his eyes, she must have read his feelings there, for she shook her head crossly.

"No," she said.

"Nikki," Peter whispered. "She's right. You'll be safer anywhere except with me. You could stay here. Or go back to L.A. until this is over."

"We talked about this!" Nikki cried, eyes moist, cheeks reddening, as though she were a rebellious teenager lashing out at her mother. "Who's to say what's going to happen? Where the problem will spread next?"

"True," Peter agreed. "But what might happen is different from walking right into the middle of it. This thing . . . this presence is so foreign to me, I have no idea if I can stop it."

Nikki pressed her lips together so hard they went white. Her face seemed carved from granite and she wiped at her eyes, not allowing a single tear to fall, taking a deep breath to control herself.

"I don't want to be alone," she said, choking on the words. "I've spent too much time alone. I can't bear it."

Peter lifted his chin and met her gaze steadily. "Allison's right. If you're there, I won't be able to focus. You're not immortal. You have no magick to protect you except for mine, and I won't be able to do that and fight this thing too. You'd be . . . you'd be in the way."

Nikki seemed about to respond but her jaws clacked shut at Peter's final words. Then her nostrils flared and the pain in her eyes turned to fury. She glared at Allison, lips curled back from her teeth.

"Bitch," she snarled.

Allison flinched.

Then Nikki turned and walked back along the corridor toward Peter's bedroom just as Keomany emerged. Keomany tried to speak to her but Nikki slammed the door, leaving her friend to glance at Peter in bewilderment.

Allison looked at the floor. "I'm sorry."

"So am I," Peter replied. "But you're right. I don't know what I was thinking. Look, I've got to go talk to her, if she'll even speak to me. There's no way to . . . no way to know how this is going to end. I want to say goodbye properly, and then I have a plane to catch."

Keomany had tied her black hair back with a red ribbon and she had put on a fresh change of clothes, brown pants and a white shirt, practical clothing for traveling.

"What was that about?" she asked, obviously upset by Nikki's behavior.

Before Peter could respond, Allison spoke.

"I'm coming with you," she said.

Peter shot her a hard look. "What about the U.N.?"

"Fuck the U.N."

CHAPTER 16

TASK Force Victor had taken over a quaint bed-and-breakfast that had once boasted a stunning pastoral setting. The kind of place that was perfect for romantic getaways, not far at all from Derby and only a bit farther from Nottingham. To Father Jack Delvin, the green hills and copses of trees seemed to have sprung to life from the scenery of some Merchant-Ivory film. His previous knowledge of England had consisted entirely of trips to London, and so he had never realized that there were areas where the country-side was still so pristine.

Now it had been tainted. Soiled forever by what had happened in Derby. The entire town was gone. From the front walk of the Derbyshire Inn the view had been replaced by a shimmering field of energy, a barrier that made what was beyond it appear to be nothing more than ravaged, barren tundra. *So much for romantic weekends away.* Father Jack could still smell all the flowers in bloom, but the promise of spring had been torn away by the horror that had visited Derby . . . and stolen it away.

The priest stood on the lawn in front of the inn with Bishop Gagnon and two of the other priests who had accompanied them. On the street was a single military vehicle. It was dark, long after midnight, and the headlights cut the night, reflected off the moisture in the heavy air. Behind the wheel, the driver of the vehicle sat motionless, waiting for instructions, while a new kind of Hell loomed a quarter of a mile away.

Commander Ray Henning stood beside the vehicle with a cell phone clapped to his ear, conversing in staccato bursts of language that were nearly unintelligible. Jack had taken an instant dislike to Henning. He knew the commander was just there to do his job, and that it was an honorable purpose, but the guy just rubbed him the wrong way. He was an officious prick who clearly had little use for faith or for magick.

Past the commander the road wound toward the outskirts of Derby. There were homes, but only sparsely. All of them had been evacuated long ago. Beyond those homes was the shimmering barrier, the twist in reality that was little more than the wound left behind on the flesh of the world now that Derby had been cut out of it.

It was just like Wickham.

Down the road, Task Force Victor and other U.N. forces under their command were doing their level best to waste ammunition. Huge floodlights had been set up and turned on the barrier, which just seemed to absorb them. Bullets and mortar and explosives and fire had all been implemented by Task Force Victor in an effort to break through into the Hell where Derby had been drawn, all without luck. Even now there were regular bursts of gunfire and explosions as new combinations were tried. From their vantage point, Father Jack and Bishop Gagnon watched two men fire antitank weapons at the barrier.

They exploded harmlessly against it, not appearing to disrupt the energy field at all.

Idiots, Jack thought. How long would it take them to realize nothing so conventional was going to work?

The Bishop did nothing to intervene. From the moment their first brief sharing of information with Commander Henning had ended, Bishop Gagnon had instructed his priests to do nothing. To stand and wait. Their superiors had an agreement with the U.N. Secretary General, but the Bishop assured them it would be best to wait until Henning was prepared to let them do their job.

Under other circumstances Father Jack might have gotten bored. As it was, all he could think about was the town of Derby, and how many of its people were still alive inside there, in that other world, trying to get out but finding no means of escape. How many people were screaming in Derby in that very moment?

"Come on, you son of a bitch," Jack whispered.

Bishop Gagnon shot him a disapproving glance. "Our chance will come, Father. If you are not sure you can do the job, I don't know why you're so eager."

Jack stared at him as though he were insane. "Because what if I can?" he asked. "What if I can help, and we're wasting this time?"

The Bishop did not have a chance to respond. Commander Henning shouted something into his cell phone, then clicked it closed, hanging up on whoever was on the other end. He left his driver in the vehicle and strode up the grass toward them. It all seemed so very wrong, these unnatural things unfolding at the foot of the hill upon which stood the four-hundred-year-old inn.

"All right," Henning said, his blue eyes crystal clear, his white hair combed tight against his scalp. "Time for your boys to have a go, Bishop."

Michel Gagnon nodded his head. "And so we shall."

They both looked expectantly to Father Jack and the priest knew that the time had come for him to explain that despite his studies he was not a very powerful magician. It was possible that he would be able to disrupt the field enough so that he could slip through, maybe with a few others, but it was not likely.

"Look, Commander," Jack began, slipping off his glasses. "Whatever promises Bishop Gagnon made to you, I—"

"Hush," Commander Henning said, waving at the gathered clergymen as he pressed a hand against his left ear. With his right hand he tugged up the collar of his coat. "Repeat that," Henning barked into his collar. "Say again, Sergeant."

For a moment Father Jack was baffled, and then he felt

foolish as he realized that of course the commander had a commlink in the collar of his coat and the audio piece set inside his ear. In the second or two it had taken the priest to make that connection, the commander's pale blue eyes went wide and he stopped demanding information from the sergeant who had contacted him.

"You've gotta be . . ." Henning muttered in amazement as he turned quickly around to look down the road toward Derby, toward the shimmering magickal barrier that stretched from ground to heavens.

The soldier who had been assigned as Henning's driver had stepped out of the car and was staring in the same direction.

Father Jack frowned, not understanding at first what he was seeing. The shooting had stopped, there were no more explosions. In fact, if his eyes did not deceive him, Task Force Victor and the other U.N. troops under their command had packed it in. The trucks and tanks and Jeeps were rolling quickly away from the crackling barrier, away from the hole in the world where Derby should have been. Then the flood lights disappeared behind the barrier, one of them exploding as it did, and Father Jack understood.

"Dear Lord," he said. "It's spreading."

"What's going on?" Bishop Gagnon demanded. "Father Devlin, what has happened? How can this be?"

Jack stared at him. How could the man be so dense? "I don't *know*. For God's sake, all of this is new. How does a city disappear? Just because these spheres of influence from this other dimension have been static so far doesn't mean they're going to stay that way."

The Bishop paled, his face looking grayer, even in the dark. "Hell will overtake us all," the man whispered, and there was a gleam in his eye that might have been madness, or simply the zeal of the faithful.

Henning, on the other hand, had reddened considerably, his features contorted with fury and adrenaline. "Damn it, I didn't give the order to retreat! What's wrong with you people? Task Force Victor, this is Commander Henning. Hold your ground! I repeat, hold your ground."

As Father Jack watched, the vehicles began to slow. Most

of them, tanks included, began to turn to face the expanding barrier as it swallowed everything in its path.

"What are you doing?" Father Jack asked, horrified. "Bullets aren't going to stop that thing! They're going to be swallowed alive."

Commander Henning grinned with satisfaction. "Yes. They are. And so are we. We needed a way in, Father. Well, here it is. Your magick wasn't all that helpful on the outside. Let's hope you can do more from the inside."

A shudder went through Father Jack. He had crossed over into that other world once already, had seen the sort of horror that awaited them, but he had had the world's most powerful sorcerer with him at the time.

"That wasn't part of the deal," Jack told Henning. "I was supposed to help you breach the barrier, that's all."

The Commander rounded on him, reached out to grab Father Jack by the front of his sweater. Jack raised a hand to stop him but Henning slapped it away.

"Get your hands off me!" he protested.

Henning dragged him closer so that they were practically nose to nose. "You listen to me, *Father*." His gaze ticked over to the Bishop and then to the other priests before returning to Father Jack. "We've got a dozen cities now, maybe more, sucked into the devil's mouth. So far there isn't a damn thing anybody can do about it. That leaves only one choice. We go right down the bastard's gullet and try to tear him apart from inside!"

Father Jack felt nausea roiling in his gut. There was a sparkle in Henning's eyes that told him the commander was relishing this moment, that he was thrilled by it. Jack shook his head, unable to find the words to respond. He turned to Bishop Gagnon only to find His Eminence staring toward the ballooning barrier in a kind of rapture that made him shake slightly, his breath coming in thin, reedy gasps.

"Michel? Are you all right?" he asked, afraid the Bishop might be having a heart attack.

Slowly, the Bishop rotated his head sideways, eyes glazed, face slack. When he spoke, his voice was tinged with awe.

"It's the truest test of our faith, Jack. Hell come to claim us. What will you do now, Jack? Now that the devil stares you in the face? Will you blink?"

Father Jack stared at him, then twisted around to glare at Henning. The two men were ignoring him. Beyond them he saw that two of the other priests who had flown to England with the Bishop had turned tail and begun to run. Slowly, Jack finished turning so that he faced the same direction as Henning and the Bishop.

He was just in time to see the shimmering, swelling field of magickal energy sweep across the line of tanks and trucks and Jeeps. Some of the soldiers, like Father Vernon and Father Spencer, turned to run. The officers of Task Force Victor stood their ground and let the blossoming magick envelop them as though they were standing in the ocean and a tall wave were crashing over them.

The sound of static reached Father Jack where he stood in front of the Derbyshire Inn, and a kind of sulfur smell that he could not help thinking of as brimstone.

The dimensional field swept over the troops, even those who had tried to run. Bishop Gagnon and Commander Henning stood their ground. In the car down on the road, Jack saw Henning's driver glancing anxiously back and forth between his commander and the magickal onslaught and there was a squeal of tires and a puff of dust kicked up by the wheels as he did a hard U-turn and took off in the other direction.

"Coward," Henning snarled.

"He won't get far," Bishop Gagnon said dreamily, staring at the wave of magick humming toward them with a kind of breathless adoration.

"Jesus," Father Jack said, lowering his head and closing his eyes. It was not a prayer. "You're both madmen."

But he remained where he was, head down, not wanting to look as the wave rolled toward him. The static grew louder, the smell and sound like the buzz of the bug zapper his aunt Judy'd had in her backyard in Scarsdale when he was growing up. It grew louder still, so loud Father Jack wanted to scream. He could barely contain the urge and at last he threw his head back to bellow his fear.

When Hell swallowed him, he barely felt a thing.

THE airport was jammed with people and Keomany was stunned. She had never imagined so many would have been willing to risk flying with all that was happening. They had talked about it on the drive to LaGuardia, though, and Peter had predicted exactly this kind of madhouse. The modern world had never seen a crisis of this magnitude. People were going to want to be with their loved ones.

The big problem was that airspace over certain cities was restricted, flight plans had to be redrawn, routes changed, and some pilots were likely to have refused to fly at all.

Their flight had been rescheduled for 11:45 P.M.

"Shit," Allison muttered, staring up at the screen amid the crush of people pushing, trying to get to their gates, dragging their wheeled luggage behind them for others to trip over.

Keomany was sweating. It might have been the crush of bodies around her, but she knew it was not that because she wasn't hot, or even warm. She was freezing. So cold that she could barely keep her teeth from chattering. Peter and Allison were so wrapped up in the delay of their flight, trying to figure out what to do, that neither of them had noticed yet. And that was all right. If they knew she was sick, she was afraid they might make her stay behind the way they had done with Nikki.

Damn it, Nikki, Keomany thought. A pain shot through her side and she clutched at it, teeth pressed together in a rictus grin, a poor attempt to hide her discomfort.

The last thing she had wanted to do was leave Nikki behind, but neither could she really argue. As detached as she felt from what had been happening to her, from the deaths of her parents and the extraordinary new connection she felt with Gaea—a connection she believed was providing her with the spirit to go on—she felt it filling her up and knew that she had to go. Earthmagick was driving her on. She had touched the soul of the world and it required her as its instrument.

Keomany had power. Nikki did not. She had wanted to argue that her friend should come along but in her heart she agreed. Gaea was not going to touch Nikki, to keep her safe, and Keomany knew that the being Peter called the Tatterdemalion would look at an ordinary human as little more than an insect.

Another spike of pain went through her. This one in her back. Peter glanced over at her with a raised eyebrow, breaking off his conversation. Keomany forced her smile back on, letting herself be buffeted by the crowd around her, the labyrinth of lines that wound about the airport terminal. Announcements were made on the speaker system but it crackled so badly and the drone of the crowd was so loud that no words could be made out.

She was fooling herself. The Tatterdemalion was not commanding the storm they had seen in that hellish dimension. It was the storm. It was the power. Likely it would think of all of them, even Peter, as insects. But Gaea had touched Keomany's soul and she would not turn away from the purpose that had been given to her.

Listen to me, she thought. *I'm on a crusade. Keomany Shaw, earthwitch, savior of the universe.* The words sounded obnoxiously foolish in her mind, and yet the essence of them felt true and real.

Peter and Allison were still talking heatedly, almost arguing, and Keomany studied them. It was easy to see how Nikki had fallen so quickly for Peter, even back when he had been one of *them*, a vampire. Even now, with all the lines of tension creasing his face, he had an amazing presence, a charm that emanated from him. It didn't hurt that he was handsome. Allison was not beautiful in the supermodel sense, and there was a hardness to her features that ought to have been off-putting. Instead she had the bearing and beauty of a marble sculpture of a Greek goddess. Her auburn hair framed her features and her intense eyes.

It was hard to imagine that she was a monster, that she was a shape-changing, demonic blood-drinker. Keomany shuddered. Not evil, she knew that. Allison was one among the shadows who did not drink blood from humans without invitation. She was not a savage. Not a predator.

Her presence was still chilling.

"Ahhh!" Keomany moaned in pain, clutching at her chest.

The world seemed to swim around her and her legs fell out from under her. She was tumbling to the ground then, crashing into a woman strolling by with a huge piece of luggage. Keomany fell over the suitcase and struck the floor, her head thunking hard on the ground. Her vision blurred and her breath caught in her throat. It felt as though someone had slipped the thinnest and sharpest of blades into her breastbone and punched a hole in her.

She cried out.

Blurry figures appeared above her from a nightmarish swirl of activity. Out-of-focus faces swam in and out of her field of vision and then she felt a strong, comforting hand on her left arm. Keomany blinked and her vision cleared slightly.

The ground beneath her back trembled and the airport shook, dust raining down from the ceiling.

Someone shouted about an earthquake and people panicked and began to run. Peter's voice tore through the miasma around her as he ordered people away from her.

Keomany smiled. "Sorry. I . . . I fell, didn't I?" Her tongue felt thick and the words sounded slurred in her ears.

"What's wrong?" Allison asked, stroking her hair gently.

"Keomany?" Peter began, kneeling by her. She could see his features perfectly now. "What is it? Where are you hurt?"

She tasted salt and felt warm tears slip down her cheeks, so hot against her cold skin. Keomany whispered up to him. "We shouldn't have left Nikki behind."

Allison and Peter exchanged confused, grave glances.

"It's okay," Keomany said. "I understand. I just wish . . . I wish she was here."

"What is it?" Peter asked again.

Keomany laughed softly. "It's Gaea. I can feel her inside me. You cut her off from Cat up in Vermont. Now I'm feeling her pain."

Peter's eyes roved across her body—over bare skin and clothed flesh—and it was exactly the way she had seen many men look at her in her life, wishing they could see what she looked like naked. This was the same, and yet so very different.

"I don't think I'm cut," Keomany rasped. She grabbed

hold of Peter's hand and pulled herself into a sitting position. The world spun dizzily around her for a moment, but then her head started to clear. "I'm . . . I'm feeling a little better, actually. I think . . . Gaea was just . . . just screaming. She's been hurt even worse, and I felt it."

Peter swore. He glanced up at the departures screen in the midst of the airport chaos, as if by sheer force of will he could make their flight leave on time instead of more than two hours late.

"We're not going to make it," he said grimly, his silver-gray eyes narrowing.

A shrill ringing sounded close by. They both glanced over to see Allison frown as she reached into the pocket of her leather jacket and withdrew a cell phone. She flipped it open.

"Vigeant," she announced to the caller.

Then she listened. And she swore. And she hung her head just slightly before thanking the caller and snapping the phone shut, then returning it to her pocket.

"What was that?" Peter asked.

Allison raised her chin and stared at him defiantly. "That was an old friend of mine. Carl Melnick. He's a news producer, one of the best-informed guys in the world. We've been keeping in touch on this thing. There's been a development that the U.N. is trying to keep the world media from reporting . . . at least until someone finally leaks it."

Keomany felt an ache deep in her bones, a dull, throbbing pain that she knew was part of her connection to Gaea. This was where her pain had come from . . . something new had happened. It was getting worse.

"What happened?" Peter asked.

Allison glanced at the two of them, then looked around to make certain no one was paying attention to them now that Keomany's fainting episode was over. Allison moved in nearer to them.

"No new cities have been taken," she said, her voice low. "But from every location, everyplace that's been affected, the void is *spreading*. And fast."

Then Allison crouched down beside them and reached out to put a comforting hand on Keomany's arm. She stared at Peter.

"Ronda may not be accessible much longer. But either way, we've run out of time. There's only one way to get there fast enough now."

A flash of something much like anger went across Peter's face then and Keomany thought that she had seen for the first time the warrior he had once been . . . and the monster he had later become. He shook his head slowly, falling to his knees and letting his hands rest on the travel bag he had been carrying over his shoulder.

"Damn it, Allison," he began.

"You know I'm right."

Through gritted teeth he snarled at her. "You're always right. But with all that's going on . . . the Tatterdemalion can feel every crack in our dimension, every breach that's ever been. Or most of them, at least. That's how it's been slipping its creatures in and getting anchored to drag the cities away. What if it *knows*? What if it feels us go?"

"What choice do you have?" Allison asked quietly.

Her strength coming back, Keomany glanced back and forth between them. "One more question. What are you two talking about?"

But Peter just stared at Allison for several long seconds before standing straight up. He stared around the airport, his gaze lingering in one particular angle, a direction that might have been back toward Manhattan. Then he looked down at Allison one last time and he took a deep breath.

"Damn it!" he shouted in frustration.

The curse echoed through the airport, shushing the cacophony of the crowd for a single moment, forcing hundreds of heads to turn toward him. Then Peter Octavian held his hands out in front of him, palms together as though molding clay. Something grew there in his hands, bright and glowing, fluid as mercury and just as silver. It slipped over his fingers and the sphere grew larger and larger.

As though watching some street magician, people began to gather around them, mesmerized by the work of Peter's hands.

"Back off," Allison instructed them.

There was menace in her tone, and she was obeyed.

The silver, pulsing sphere in Peter's hands was no larger

than a melon but he raised it above his head as though he meant to shatter it on the floor. Instead his hands spread apart and the mercury seemed to sweep them up in a whirlpool of silver, blocking Keomany's view of the terminal.

Her stomach lurched as Gaea screamed in her heart again.

Once more Keomany was falling. Impossible, of course, for she had never risen to her feet; yet still she was falling. Silver magick rained down around her, splashing the ground, silencing the world. She landed on her side, hip painfully striking the pavement.

The pavement.

Keomany blinked as she looked around. The airport was gone. The crowds and the lights and the noise, all gone. The silver sphere of magick had dissolved to nothing, leaving the three of them standing in the middle of what a dozen old movies had taught her could only be a bullring. It was empty. A breeze toyed with a few strands of hair that had escaped her ponytail, and even the wind smelled different here. In the night sky above, the constellations had moved, the stars shifting.

"Ronda? Is this Ronda?" she rasped, turning to stare at Peter in awe. He looked pale and exhausted—*and no wonder*, she thought—but he nodded in return.

"Gaea," Keomany whispered.

From the gallery circling the bullring came a rustling that was not roused by the wind. In the shadows, something stirred.

THE stream that wound through the outskirts of Mont de Moreau ran red with the blood of its citizens and the offal of river demons. Kuromaku crouched on the roof of the aged red Volkswagen he had commandeered and clutched tightly to the frame of the open driver's window beneath him. In his right hand, his katana seemed to glow darkly in the perpetual orange light of this hideous dimension.

"Kuromaku!" Sophie called out in alarm from behind the wheel of the car.

He knew what had upset her. All around the French village new cities had appeared, dragged into this realm by whatever terrible power had transported Mont de Moreau here. Only one edge of the village still shimmered with the dark magick that separated this community from the world where it belonged, the barrier between dimensions. They had to reach that one spot if they had any hope of breaking through, of forcing their way back to reality.

But to do that, they had to cross a bridge that spanned the stream. The water was filled with tiny figures the size of human infants, demons with translucent flesh and pointed, outsized heads that made Kuromaku think of squid. Like some freakish human mutation, they had limbs that seemed a nauseating combination of arms and seal flippers, covered in suckers like those on the tentacles of an octopus. They weren't close enough yet to the bridge for Kuromaku to see such detail, but he had been attacked by similar creatures once long ago, on an island in Greece.

"What the hell are they?" Sophie called.

Nektum, Kuromaku thought. *They're called Nektum.*

"Just drive!" he shouted back. "Don't slow down!"

He wanted also to tell her not to look as she crossed the bridge, to avert her eyes from the grotesque panorama that would unfold on the banks of the stream as they passed. Even now Kuromaku tried to block from his memory the images of Nektum attached to the faces of dead village children, using those suckers to tear the skin—just the skin—from their bodies; of their translucent forms burrowing inside people who were not quite dead yet.

But if he told Sophie not to look, it would ensure that she would do just that. Kuromaku could only hope that she was too focused on driving the car to pay much attention to the Nektum, and that Antoinette Lamontagne would be cradling her catatonic boy in the back seat, perhaps crooning to him softly with her eyes closed as she prayed for deliverance.

He did not have the heart to tell the woman that her God could not hear her; not from this place.

The tires screamed as Sophie cut the wheel to the right, speeding toward the bridge. Kuromaku shouted to her again, exhorting her to drive even faster. The Volkswagen bumped over several ruts in the road but he paid no attention, clamping tighter to his handhold, gaze sweeping the banks of the stream and the support beams of the bridge, where Nektum clung like starfish.

The engine roared. Below him, Sophie was silent. Kuromaku watched the horrid little demons, gauging the distance to the bridge. If they were lucky, they could be partway across before the Nektum even noticed them. Fifty yards from the bridge. Thirty.

Beyond it, Kuromaku could see the shimmering barrier that separated them from the world they knew, the wall that locked them into this hellish nightmare.

A dozen yards from the bridge, the engine whined, and at last the Nektum noticed. Like deformed babies they raised their heads. Kuromaku felt their eyes on him and his grip tightened on the pommel of his sword. The car was only a few feet from the bridge when the abhorrent little things attacked. They moved impossibly fast, swimming lightning fast to the supports of the bridge and then crawling up, scrambling on their bizarre appendages with sickening speed.

"Drive!" Kuromaku shouted.

The engine roared louder as the tires hit the bridge and surged forward, Sophie accelerating even further, moving dangerously fast. The Nektum moved in a blur. The car was halfway across the bridge when the creatures began to launch themselves at Kuromaku, webbed appendages spread out to either side, translucent bodies gliding across the air, mouths gnawing at nothing.

In a crouch, Kuromaku sliced his katana through the air, windmilling the blade around him one-handed. The Nektum were gelatinous, and he felt the tug of their gummy flesh as the sword cut through each one. Their corpses thumped to the roof of the car or onto the bridge. Other Nektum slapped against the car, sticking to the windows and the body of the Volkswagen. He knew it would be only seconds before they tore their way into the car.

Sophie laid on the horn, perhaps thinking that it might scare them off. Instead, even more of the demons flew off the structure of the bridge like a flock of birds rising from a tree. They launched themselves at the car.

The Volkswagen's tires bumped hard as they reached the end of the bridge and hit the dusty road again. Kuromaku hacked at the air, dropped to his back on the roof of the car, and whirled the katana around, cutting up the Nektum. Chunks of their bodies fell upon him, sticking to his clothes. A quick glance back revealed that most of them had fallen away or missed the car entirely and now had massed on the bridge staring after the retreating car in eerily silent hunger.

Sophie began to cry out to him. The tone alone told him that one or more of the Nektum had gotten into the car. Of course they had! Her window was open. In order for him to be able to hold on, he had unthinkingly prevented her from closing off the car.

Damn it! he thought, as he spun onto his knees again on the roof. Several Nektum were still clinging to it. Kuromaku raised his sword even as one of the translucent, unnervingly infantile demons launched itself at his face. Its appendages slapped against his skin, suckers digging instantly into the flesh. In his mind's eye he saw again the awful carnage he had witnessed in Greece centuries before.

His face tore.

Kuromaku screamed.

By the sheer force of his will, of his rage, he transmuted the skin of his face into living fire, burning the Nektum off. The demon squealed as it melted, its viscera boiling and spilling onto the Volkswagen's windshield. The car swerved, Sophie either unable to see or trying to keep away from whatever demons had slipped into the vehicle.

The Volkswagen shuddered to a halt. Kuromaku released his grip and rolled off the roof, even as he willed flame to become flesh once again. He landed on his feet, surveying the car. One of the Nektum shattered the glass of the rear window and it showered down upon a screaming Antoinette Lamontagne, who was trying to shield her boy even as she grabbed at the latch for her door. Another was in the front seat with Sophie, who had shot out one foot and pinned it to the passenger door, and still managed to drive the car a little ways before being forced to stop. The thing shrieked and tore at her boot.

Kuromaku snarled, almost unaware that he had bared his fangs. He sheathed the katana back into nothingness and this time it was his hands that erupted into devastating fire. With fingers of flame he tore Nektum off the car and threw them burning onto the side of the road. He melted the one that had snuck into the back seat and then went around to the passenger window. With his blazing fist he smashed the window, reached down, and grabbed the flailing thing from where it was trapped beneath Sophie's boot. He tore it apart with fiery hands.

Antoinette sobbed in the back seat, covered in shards of glass, bent over her son. Sophie stepped out of the Volkswagen, stared at Kuromaku with eyes wide with shock, and then ran to him. His hands became flesh once more and he embraced her as he glared back toward the bridge. All but a few of the surviving Nektum had gone back to the river, swimming in the blood of their victims and the stink of their own waste. A small group, perhaps four or five, remained on top of the bridge, watching the escapees.

"Come on," Kuromaku whispered to Sophie. "We cannot stop now. We're so close."

"We're not close," she said, her voice muffled against his chest. "We're here."

Surprised, Kuromaku glanced up and saw that she was right. They were less than a hundred yards from the barrier. Now that he saw it, he realized he could hear a low hum coming from the field of magickal energy. The barrier shimmered and sparked and looked to him like static on an old television screen.

"All right. Now we will see what we can do," Kuromaku said.

He had thought, all along, that the unique nature of his species, the command of his molecular structure, might allow him to somehow slip through or even force a tear in the fabric of the thing. Barring that, it had occurred to him that they might try to ram the Volkswagen through it. Anything. They would try anything.

Yet even as he thought this, Sophie began to scream.

"No! No, damn you, no!" The words were French, but the agony in her voice would have come through in any language. Her anguish was a language all its own.

At first Kuromaku had no idea what was wrong with her. He grabbed her by the shoulders, tried to talk to her, to get her to look at him, but then he realized that she was staring at the barrier, at the manifestation of magick that had torn them away from their world.

There were shapes beyond the barrier. Strange geometry. The static was resolving itself into something else. It took the ancient vampire warrior a moment to confirm his worst fear.

A road was appearing in front of them. A road that led up a steep hill to the top of a plateau, where a city of white-washed buildings and church steeples overlooked the dusty plains. The architecture was Spanish. Another piece of the old world patched together in the hellish puzzle being built in this one.

"No, no, no!" Sophie roared, screaming at the city that resolved itself in their path. "What do we do now?" she cried, turning to Kuromaku, pale and quivering. "What do we do?"

He grabbed her elbow and propelled her back toward the Volkswagen, where Antoinette sat staring out the window at the Spanish city on the plateau.

"We hurry," Kuromaku told Sophie as he got her into the car and then climbed in after her. "We move as fast as we can and we get to the other side of this town."

"What if it doesn't end there? What if we can never reach the edge in time?" she asked as she started the engine, her voice a frightened rasp.

Kuromaku did not turn toward her and he did not respond. The words he had in mind would not have comforted her. For there was only one answer, really. If they could never manage to reach the end before another city appeared, then eventually there would be no world to go back home to.

The tires squealed as they tore off up the winding road toward the city high above. The night sky in this new landscape had only just begun to turn orange and there were people on the streets, panicked faces turned to the sky in terror.

Here, the horror was just beginning.

CHAPTER 17

AGAMEMNON stood at his usual post in front of the door to The Voodoo Lounge. An old tune by Blues Traveler leaked from the club out onto the street, but there was nobody there to hear it, no one to be drawn into the place by the lure of the music. In all the time he had worked the door, deciding who could enter The Voodoo Lounge, and removing those whose time it was to leave, Agamemnon had never seen the street so quiet.

No, he thought. *It isn't just the street. It's the city. The whole damn world, for that matter.*

The enormous man felt a twist of something in his gut, a feeling so unfamiliar he didn't even know if he could call it fear. New York City still gleamed with neon life, the trains still ran underground—he could hear them screaming up at him through gratings in the sidewalk—and there were still cabs and cars out on the street. Yet, though it was a beautiful night, he had seen very few people walking. Many stores and restaurants had shuttered early, their windows dark.

Still, Agamemnon raised his chin and kept his arms crossed. He had a job to do. Despite the quiet of the streets, there were plenty of people jammed into The Voodoo Lounge. Regulars, mostly, looking for company, frightened to face the uncertainty of the world alone. All over the city, Agamemnon figured people were glued to their television sets, glancing warily out their windows from time to time, waiting to see what was going to happen next. Waiting to find out if they needed to run.

Or if there was anywhere left to run to.

The crowd of regulars inside The Voodoo Lounge was uncharacteristically quiet. Even the music was turned down lower than usual, on account of the TV set behind the bar being turned up. It did not matter what channel was on now. It was not just the news channels anymore . . . with the possible exception of the kids' shows, every single station had coverage of the crisis.

In front of the door, out on the sidewalk, Agamemnon tried not to listen, tried to let the noise of the city and the low music from the club drown it out. But the city was too fucking quiet. New York City had fallen into a hush, as if the five boroughs were holding their collective breath.

"Hey."

Panic shot through him and Agamemnon clapped a hand to his chest, making a fist with the other one as he whirled around to find his boss, Cole Bradenton, standing behind him. Bradenton raised both hands in surrender.

"Whoa, relax, man."

"What's wrong with you, Cole, sneaking up on me like that?" Agamemnon snapped. He sniffed, glancing at the sidewalk, embarrassed that he had been so easily spooked. "Made me jump out of my skin."

"I'm sorry. Really."

The sincerity in Bradenton's voice was unsettling. Agamemnon glanced up at his friend and employer and saw that Bradenton's face seemed even thinner than usual, and the Chinese dragon tattooed on the man's throat undulated as Bradenton swallowed several times in quick succession.

"What is it?" Agamemnon asked.

"Maybe you oughta come in now. We've got all the customers we're going to get tonight," Bradenton told him.

For a long moment Agamemnon glanced along the quiet street and the neon skyline above. Truth was, he would rather have stayed out here. As unnerving as the desolation was, it was better than having to look into the anxious faces of the club's patrons. But when Bradenton reached up to put a hand on his arm, the massive bouncer reached up to touch the scar on his face—for some reason it ached today—and turned to follow him back inside.

The regulars gathered within all had drinks in their hands or on the bar in front of them. Some of them—screw the ordinance—were smoking cigarettes as they pressed into the crowd clustered together so that they could see the television. Someone probably should have shut off the music—nobody was paying attention to it and they were all straining to hear the TV—but apparently they were so wrapped up in it, none of them had thought of it yet.

The television mounted above the bar showed a series of images that Agamemnon had trouble making sense of. Paris. The Eiffel Tower. File footage of people walking along the Seine on a warm, sunny day. And then images of armed soldiers and military vehicles lined in front of one of those huge walls that had blocked off the outside world from the cities and towns that had gone missing. *Slushwalls*, Agamemnon had named them, though he kept the word mainly to himself. They looked like the gray, filthy slush on the sidewalk after a New York snowstorm. But you could sort of see through them, like they were a veil or something, except it never seemed real, what you saw on the other side, because it looked like there was just nothing at all.

Nothing at all.

Like whatever had been there really was gone, the way the news anchors were all saying.

Agamemnon frowned as new images appeared on screen, video clips of other slushwalls and other cities. They showed the Kremlin in Moscow. A minute later, he saw the Eiffel Tower again. The reporters and analysts and U.N. spokespeople were yammering on about various efforts being made to figure out what was going on, but none of them seemed to really be talking about what the latest news was, what these images were.

A shiver went through him. Agamemnon hated contacts, hated glasses, and wasn't about to have some fucking doctor take lasers to his eyes. The net result of this was that he had to squint to read the words scrolling across the bottom of the screen on the news ticker. That's where he saw it.

Paris and Moscow latest cities to go missing.

Agamemnon took a step backward and ran his huge hand over the smoothness of his bald head. He felt warm, clammy, though it was cool outside.

How can that be? Paris and Moscow? His mind was reeling. Most of the other places that had been taken so far were pretty small potatoes. Salzburg, Austria, had been the biggest city to disappear, the others mainly out-of-the-way cities or small villages.

"Jesus," Agamemnon whispered. He glanced around for Bradenton and spotted the harsh-looking man with his arm around Maggie Gross, a fortyish barfly who spent most of her nights in the Lounge looking for love and only getting lost. Bradenton had Maggie pulled tight to his side and the woman leaned on him as though without him she would fall forever.

"Cole?" Agamemnon began.

Bradenton glanced over his shoulder.

"Did you try calling Octavian? I know what he said, but—"

"I left a couple of messages," Bradenton replied. "He's . . . there's no answer."

Agamemnon put his hand on the back of his neck as though that might cool him down. Every fiber of his being screamed for him to do something, to take some kind of action, but what the hell could he do that other people couldn't? It frustrated him, knowing he had to wait it out just like the whisky-and-beer-stinking patrons who were crowded around the bar.

He and Bradenton had seen crazy shit before. Octavian had helped them out of a couple of jams. Terrified the hell out of him, but now it looked like those incidents had been small potatoes.

A lull had come between songs on the sound system. He knew the rotation by heart at this point. The Robert Johnson song that had been playing would be followed in a couple of seconds by classic ZZ Top. It was that kind of bar. But this time, in the pause between tunes, in that breath-holding moment, Agamemnon heard the crack of wood behind him. He turned, frowning, looking toward the booths at the back of the bar. Nobody was back there. The place was empty.

For a moment his eyes lingered on the shadowed booths and he remembered the last time Peter Octavian had been in. Agamemnon and Bradenton hadn't had any idea that the Mister Nowhere freak was a demon, but they knew something freaky was going on. Octavian had saved some lives, killed the demon, made a hell of a mess of the floor. Not for the first time, Agamemnon wondered how that demon had managed to keep all those people inside of it. Now he realized that maybe they had not been inside it all along.

Maybe the demon's gullet had been a kind of door.

By killing the thing, Octavian had shut the door, but everything that was going on in the world made Agamemnon wonder now what was on the other side.

A chill went up his back and Agamemnon looked back at the front of the bar, where something moved past the windows in the dark. The door was closed, but unlocked. Without him standing guard, anybody could walk right in.

Suddenly overcome with alarm, a tremor of instinct in the back of his mind, Agamemnon went to the door and pushed it open. He stood for a long moment on the sidewalk. There was nothing at all out there, the city was still quiet, silent as the dead. But there was a kind of buzzing in the back of his head, a sense of peril that he had learned to trust over the years. This wasn't the first time Agamemnon had had an instinct about something. That demon, Mister Nowhere . . . he'd made the huge man's head buzz like this too.

Somewhere far off a dog began to bark. The night wind blew cool across Agamemnon's face, but now there was a stink on it, a stench that was not wafting up from the subway tunnels but coming across the city from somewhere else. More dogs began to bark, a whole chorus of them joining in with the first, and then it was like every dog in the city had gotten pissed off all at once.

Police sirens started to wail, assaulting the darkness. Close by there was a shattering of glass and a woman screamed, and then an alarm began to peal. A clang of metal came from off to Agamemnon's right and he looked over to see one of the iron gratings in the sidewalk jump in its frame as though it had been struck from below.

Back in The Voodoo Lounge, Cole Bradenton swore loudly and people started to mutter in fright. It took Agamemnon only a second to realize what had upset them. He could not hear the droning of the television news anchors anymore. The TV signal was dead.

The sirens came closer. The dogs barked louder. Across the street, Agamemnon was sure he saw things moving in the darkness.

Above, the sky had begun to turn orange.

All of his fear disappeared. Agamemnon rose up to his full height, muscles rippling in his arms and back. He withdrew into The Voodoo Lounge, shut and locked the door.

Then he waited. This was his job, after all.

Nobody and nothing got through this door unless it was through him.

Nobody and nothing.

———

IN the middle of the bullring in Ronda, Peter shouted a curse in Greek and stared upward. The moment of their arrival here there had still been a glimmer of pinprick stars, a layer of the real world beyond the filthy orange sky in this twisted dimension. Now that was gone and only the hideous, rotten light remained. The air tasted differently and there was a rank odor that he had not scented in Wickham. Whatever dimension the Tatterdemalion had dragged these cities to, it was becoming more hellish with each passing moment.

"Peter!" Allison snapped. "In the stands!"

Octavian spun, studying the shifting shadows of the seating galleries that circled the bullring. Almost as though sparked by his scrutiny, the hidden corners became suddenly alive with motion. Like swarming insects, Whispers began to scramble down over the seats to leap over the low walls and into the bullring. Many of them crouched on the walls, tendril-tongues jutting out from beneath their eerily featureless faces, their indigo carapaces gleaming a hideous bruise-purple in the deep orange light.

"Enough of this," Peter muttered to himself. He had had

his fill of these hard-shelled, vicious demons in Wickham.

Allison stood ready to fight. Keomany's eyelids fluttered as she reached out, trying to touch the spirit of the world from which they had just been removed.

"Buy us a minute!" he instructed Allison.

He raced to Keomany and put a hand on her shoulder. She hissed a breath in through her teeth and her lids opened, brown eyes the color of pennies in the tainted light.

"I can feel her," Keomany said.

Peter did not have to ask who she meant. Keomany was talking about Gaea, the goddess spirit of nature, whom the earthwitches worshipped. He nodded.

"Let's do this. Just like in Wickham."

Allison grunted, drawing his attention. Peter glanced over and saw that the Whispers had reached her. But then it was not Allison anymore. She had morphed in a single eyeblink into an enormous Bengal tiger. The tiger's huge paws lashed out and she began to tear the Whispers apart.

But she could not stop them all.

Magick like rage blossomed in Peter's left hand, a crackling sphere of green fire. It shot from his palm and enveloped five of the Whispers in a moment, incinerating them where they stood. The others hesitated, and Allison launched herself at them, ripping with claws and jagged teeth.

"Now," Keomany rasped.

Peter turned to find that she had thrown her head back, her hair flying out behind her as if blown by some unseen wind. The earthwitch was beautiful, stunning in her power. The ground beneath their feet trembled and fissures split the earth. Tree roots pushed from the soil, shooting upward to impale Whispers, twining in the air and reaching out to crush other demons in their grasp.

"Gaea!" Keomany cried, the word tearing from her throat as though she were speaking to a lover in the throes of passion.

Whispering words he had learned in Hell, Peter held out his hands to either side and a web of pure golden light burst into being between his palms, stretching from one to the other. The earth beneath Keomany's feet blossomed with greenery and bright flowers that had not been there a moment ago. Without breaking the circuit of magick between his hands, Peter reached down and touched a finger to the petals of a gentle lily.

The Whispers hissed loudly and all of them froze as that golden light shot straight into the sky from the open petals of that lily. Keomany and Peter stood on either side of the flower and both of them gazed upward, where a hole had been torn in the sky, revealing black night and starlit heavens beyond.

"Allison!" Peter shouted. "Come closer."

With a rumbling growl the tiger leaped nearer to the golden light, which began to spread, the dimension rip around them growing wider. The Whispers were not put off, however. It was perhaps four in the morning in Spain and dawn still a ways off. The demons danced around them, tendrils darting from beneath their face-shells. With a loud hiss they began to attack again.

Allison tore them apart. Peter was in awe of her fury and her bloodlust. The rage that burned in her was unlike anything he had ever seen, and he knew that she must have made the perfect predator for the U.N.

A spasm of pain wracked his body and he groaned. The magick that coursed through him began to falter.

"What is it?" Keomany asked, her legs now twined with vines that had grown up from the ground. "Are you hurt?"

Ebony talons clacking together, a Whisper leaped over lashing tree branches at her. Peter felt suddenly weak, barely able to keep the magick going that was ripping at the dimension tear, opening it wider, trying to drag Ronda back to the world where it belonged. He stretched out a hand and a spark of blue light leaped from his fingers ineffectually.

Keomany whipped toward the Whisper, screaming at it in defiance. From the broadening ring of earth-sky above came a bolt of lightning that struck the demon. It sizzled and charred, withering to little more than ash in an instant.

"Fuck off," Keomany snarled at it. Then she turned to Peter. "What's wrong? I can feel you faltering."

Octavian gritted his teeth, angry with himself and filled with hatred for the Tatterdemalion, the creature responsible for all of this. Allison continued to shatter the body shells of

Whispers, to snap them in half, to tear them apart. The bull-ring was strewn with their remains. Only a handful of the things remained alive, but Peter knew there would be many more where these had come from.

"Opening the portal that got us here cost me a lot," he reluctantly admitted, even as he reached deeper within himself, tapping into his darkest emotions. There was an undercurrent of cruelty in all of the magick he knew, which was what made it so unlike earthcraft. Now he touched it, and summoned it into his grasp in a way he had not done since his time in Hell. With a snarl that surprised him, Peter spat the words to a spell that he had learned, but never recited before.

Green light spilled out of his mouth and nostrils, filling him up so completely that he thought he would vomit magick. It emanated from his pores, causing his skin to glow green. His vision shifted and he could see the orange sky no longer—everything he saw now was a bright, vibrant green, and he knew that his eyes must be glowing with the dark sorcery he had woven into himself.

Keomany pointed across the bullring and vines shot from the earth to lash at a pair of Whispers that had foolishly thought to escape her. Now she turned, saw Peter, and her mouth gaped, her eyes widening.

"Peter . . . what . . ." She could not get the question out.

Nausea roiled in him. His skin felt as if it was on fire, his muscles taut as he began to rise off the ground. The few remaining Whispers let out a low, keening whistle he had not heard from the monsters before, and they turned and began to run. Peter let them go. The huge tiger did not bother to chase them either, turning now to stare at him even as Allison's body shifted and contorted until she wore her human face again.

"I needed more power," he said, his voice echoing strangely in his own ears. "Do you think sorcery comes from within the mage? Some does, I suppose, but not all. Not most." His eyes shifted toward Keomany. "Like your earth-craft, Keomany, my magick comes from elsewhere. I use it only for the best purposes, but I summon it from dark places. From the shadows."

The golden light that burned upward from the lily that had grown near Keomany remained untinged by the humming verdant power that now crackled around Peter, but the tear they had made in this dark dimension grew no larger. They had punctured it, returned a few square yards of this city back to the Spanish countryside it had been gouged from. No more.

"This thing . . . this Tatterdemalion, whatever power it is that wore those rags in Wickham . . . this place belongs to that entity. We can barely steal back this bullring, never mind an entire city . . . never mind all the cities it has stolen."

"We have to find another way," Keomany said. Her eyes had changed, the spirit of Gaea filling her so completely that they glowed pure white, with tiny golden pupils.

Allison noticed it a moment after Peter did, for she stared at Keomany now. "What's happened to *you*?"

Keomany smiled. "She's in me now. Not completely, not that. But not like before . . . I feel her pain, her hysteria, but it doesn't hurt anymore. I also feel her power. I'm her tool. Gaea has put me here. I understand that now. I'm like a virus in this place."

From where he hovered slightly above the ground in the bullring, Peter could see that Keomany was right. The vines and roots had begun to spread. Though the tear in reality was not growing larger, every new growth punctured the Tatterdemalion's realm again. The virus was spreading.

Allison reached inside her jacket and pulled out a nine-millimeter automatic pistol. She checked the cartridge of bullets, then jacked it back into the weapon. When she looked up at the other two again, the three of them in a strange triangle at the center of the bullring, she shook her head.

"I don't know what the fuck is going on with you two. Great. You're all hyped up with power now. Wonderful. So tell me, what does that mean? If you're right, Peter, and we can't shake these cities loose, if we can't return them to *our* world, what good is it being here at all? We're just going to get fucking killed."

Octavian took a deep breath. The magick that burned in him was nearly overwhelming. He could feel every nerve ending, every pore, every follicle of hair. It was extraordinary, but at the same time, he could feel the current of dark emotion that ran beneath it and vowed to himself that he would use this sorcery, and not let it use him.

"Maybe we will," he allowed, the sphere of energy dissipating around him as his feet once more touched the ground. When he turned his head to peer at Allison, sparks of green fire flew from his eyes. "Then again, maybe we won't."

Allison smiled at him.

"What?" Keomany asked. "What am I missing?"

"He has a plan," Allison said.

Peter glanced around at the shadows of the seating galleries, searching the dark for more Whispers. There were none to be found. All of them had been slain or fled out of the bullring, out into the city of Ronda, where he knew at this very moment Whispers were slipping into houses and slashing throats, slaughtering innocents, and destroying homes purely for the sake of havoc. Why? That was the question. Out of pure malice, or because it was what the Tatterdemalion desired, what it had instructed them to do.

"I don't have a plan," Octavian confessed. Then he smiled at the women. "I have a theory."

A rumble of thunder filled the air and the wind whipped down into the bullring, carrying the stench of Hell along with it. Keomany was not responsible for this wind. It came from here, and not from Gaea. When Peter turned toward the sound of thunder, he saw precisely what he had expected to see.

Due south, orange-black thunderheads filled the sky, hanging low and ominous. A storm was brewing in the distance, and it was coming this way.

"Oh, shit." Keomany stared at the raging storm, at the red lightning that lit up the thunderclouds.

"He's not in Ronda yet," Peter said. "But he's coming."

"It's just like you told me," Allison said. Despite her immortality, despite that she was nearly unkillable, she sounded terrified. "What the hell is that? How can it do that? Son of a bitch, Peter, how can we fight something on this level?"

"I told you," Peter replied without looking at her. "I've got a theory."

With the verdant, electric magick blazing up in him, Peter turned toward the huge double doors of the bullring. With a wave of his hand, a wave of sorcerous power arced across the ground, shearing the air and tearing up the dirt. The doors exploded outward, shattered.

He looked at Allison. "I need an aerial recon, Allie. Keep back from the storm, but give me everything you can. What other cities you see, if there's anyone else here fighting the demons."

The vampire shapeshifted instantly into a massive falcon. Allison flapped her broad wings and tilted her head, birdlike, to regard him. She flew off the ground, soaring above their heads, and circled once around the bullring.

"Where are you going?" the falcon cried, its words a shriek.

Peter smiled at Keomany. "We're going to meet the storm."

Together they began to walk toward the shattered gates. Tangled vines followed her, and where she walked, the golden light followed, gashing open the sky above so that tiny slices of Ronda began to spill back into the world.

———

NIKKI opened her eyes.

She lay on Peter's bed—the bed where, if not for the shitstorm the world was involved with, they would likely have been making love that very moment—and she blinked several times. A quick glance at the clock told her that she had been asleep less than half an hour. After looking around her lover's apartment to see what had changed in the time they had been apart, and to admire his latest paintings, she had lain down upon his bed with the radio on and her nose in a book, and promptly fallen asleep.

Her eyelids fluttered tiredly. The light was still on but she was completely unmotivated to get up and shut it off. She had fallen asleep early but it was late enough now that it didn't matter. There was a vague sensation teasing at her brain—something more than the dim urge to pee that accompanied it. No, this was something more.

Something had woken her, some sound that had been jar-

ring enough to reach down into her peaceful slumber and jolt
her awake. For several long moments she lay there and listened and then her eyes began to close once more, the radio
still playing low.

The song ended abruptly and a voice broke in. The volume was so low and Nikki nearly asleep and so the words
meant nothing to her, but the suddenness of the interruption
made her brows knit in consternation, even with her eyes
still closed.

Almost unwilling, she began to listen more closely, trying
to make out the words.

Then the radio died.

Nikki's eyes snapped open and she froze. She had not
gotten up to shut off the light, yet the room was dark. Dark,
and silent.

From upstairs there came a terrible, piercing scream.
Nikki was fully awake now and she sat up in bed, listening
intently. It had been a woman's voice. And now the scream
was punctuated by a thump of feet upon stairs.

"Suze!" a man's voice shouted, frenzied. "Suze!"

Barely able to catch her breath, Nikki rose from the bed
and slipped on her blue jeans. She pulled on a shirt as fast
as she could, but even as she did so, the noises from the
home of the Balents, Peter's landlords, continued. More
thumping of feet was nearly drowned out by a second
scream, this one cut off so sharply that there could be no
misinterpreting the reason for its cessation.

Oh, fuck, Nikki thought. *Oh, God, what am I doing here?*
A scowl crossed her face; she hated the sound of the little
voice in her head, hated the fear in it, hated its cowardice.
But she could not stop her heart from hammering in her
throat, or the pain in her chest, or the way she held her
breath.

Upstairs, Jarrod Balent began to shriek now in a voice
that should never have issued from the throat of a man. There
were words in there, cries to his God and a repetition of his
wife's name. Glass shattered and there were other thumps
that reverberated down into the basement apartment, the
sound of something crashing into the floor and the walls.

Not something, you know what it is, Nikki thought. It's
him. It's Peter's fucking landlord.

"Please, no," she whispered, and she held her hands to
her mouth so as not to scream. Nikki had no idea with whom
she was pleading, but regardless, no answer was forthcoming.

She had pulled her clothes on, thinking she might rush
upstairs, might do something to help them. But that was after
Suze Balent's initial scream. Nikki Wydra had faced horrors
before, had dealt with things that would have forced a lot of
people to curl up in a corner and whimper. In New Orleans,
in Wickham . . .

But now Nikki made a terrible discovery. Despite all that
she had done and experienced, despite the terrifying, amazing
things she had done, in the end, she was merely ordinary.

An ordinary woman.

Alone, in the dark.

Other sounds came now from the Balents' home upstairs.
Subtler, softer sounds, and yet in an old row house like this
not even a cat could move without causing the errant board
to squeak. Things were moving upstairs.

Nikki bit her lip. Slowly, as if she had to learn how to
control each muscle in her body all over again, she began to
move along the corridor into the front room of Peter's apartment.

How did it come to this? Nikki thought. Images flashed
through her mind, of the day she left Peter behind to move
to Los Angeles, of the day she found out she had a record
contract, of Keomany appearing in the audience the night of
her showcase performance, of the demons in Wickham, of
Allison insisting that she remain behind.

*Fucking Allison. Jesus, look what it's come to. You stupid
bitch, look what you've done to me.*

Something scraped at the door. Nikki froze as she entered
the front room, body rigid as she stared at the windows high
up on the wall that looked out at, ankle-level, at the street.
The light that shone through those windows was a dirty orange and it cast a sickening pall across the room.

A whimper escaped her lips and Nikki hated herself for
it. Somewhere in this apartment, she knew that Peter kept
his old sword, the one that he had wielded five and a half

centuries before as a warrior of Byzantium. Mentally she catalogued every crevice of the apartment, every place he might have stowed the blade. She would find it. She would—

With a splintering crack, something pierced the door. It was hideous, a sharp, writhing, wormlike thing protruding into the apartment. Nikki backed up two steps, hissing as though she had been burned, and then she recognized it, knew what it was. The spike that had punched through the door was the tongue or antenna or whatever it was of one of those demons, one of the Whispers.

It probed the air inside the apartment, and Nikki knew with grim certainty that it was *looking* for her.

CHAPTER 18

HENRI Lamontagne sat up and began to cry; a high, keening wail that was filled with anguish and lunacy. And yet somehow Kuromaku thought that if the boy could cry like that, he hadn't lost his mind at all. What other response would have been appropriate? The boy was not screaming; he sat up, rapt with attention as he stared out the car window at the Whispers as they scaled the outer walls of whitewashed buildings and tore the bars off windows. Some of the houses had glass-enclosed balconies and the faceless, armored demons crashed into those homes easily. Some of them scampered on rooftops.

On the side of the road the Whispers could be seen dragging people from their homes, some of them through windows still edged with jagged glass, and then ripping their heads off their bodies. Where there were lamp posts, the Whispers set the heads up for decoration.

Of course Henri was crying.

Of course he was.

The boy had been shaken from his catatonic state, and yet his mother Antoinette was the one who seemed mentally paralyzed.

"Stop it!" she screamed over and over. "Stop it, stop it, stop it!" And then her praying began again.

Kuromaku was now crouched on the roof of the car, clutching the door frame, his katana ready. The air was close and damp, the orange light tainting everything it touched. Even the wind that whipped Kuromaku's face smelled rank, diseased.

The vampire had noticed an odd thing. In Mont de Moreau there had been a great many demons other than these Whispers, some of them familiar to him. He had long since reasoned that incursions into his own reality, breaches like the one he and Sophie had witnessed in Paris only days ago, had been the punctures that had allowed the Whispers to slip in as well. The Whispers were from a Hell all their own, he surmised, and whatever intelligence was orchestrating them had sent them through to hold those breaches open, to allow it to drag those cities into this pocket Hell dimension.

Some of the familiar demons, the ignorant savages, that had paved the way for the Whispers, had been drawn into this collective Hell as well, but they were not welcome here. The Whispers were killing them, too.

Now, in Ronda, the other breeds of demons—the Nektum and the winged carrion beasts, the quilled monstrosities and the gelatinous giants floating across the sky—were all gone. Only the Whispers remained.

This was *their* realm.

The engine whined as Sophie guided the Volkswagen up the hill. The town was Spanish, Kuromaku could tell from the architecture, but he had no idea where they were. Not that it mattered. All that did matter at this point was getting through the town as fast as they could, getting to the other side, reaching the edges of the influence of whatever power was controlling all of this.

The wind carried Henri's cries away, but suddenly they grew louder. It took Kuromaku only a moment to realize that the boy was not the only child crying. He held on to the door frame more tightly, glanced around quickly, ears tracking, eyes searching.

Just ahead, where the road they were on was joined by two others as they merged into one wider avenue, still leading up the hill, Kuromaku saw a second-floor balcony, a frame of glass shards. Inside that frame a pair of Whispers slashed at one another, tugging at the limbs of a wailing toddler as they fought over the little boy.

Behind the wheel, Sophie must have seen it as well. She tapped the brakes, beginning to slow.

"Drive!" Kuromaku roared, slapping the roof of the car.

"It's . . . they have a child!" she shouted out the window, unaware that he had already seen the demons and their prize. "Hold on!"

Sophie hit the brakes. The Volkswagen shuddered to a halt. Kuromaku hissed a curse in Japanese and leaped down from the car. They were in the midst of the place where the three roads merged into one, out in the open. All of the activity around them, the Whispers shattering glass, slaughtering people . . . all of it stopped. Only the screams and cries of the wounded and terrified reached him now, and the barking of dogs. Henri Lamontagne stared out at him from the back seat of the car, having ceased his own crying. His mother lay curled into a fetal position against one of the doors as if she had been trying to push herself into that corner, make herself disappear.

Teeth gritted tightly together, Kuromaku threw open Sophie's door and slid in behind the wheel, roughly forcing her into the passenger's seat. Silently, he put the car in gear and hit the accelerator. The tires kicked up dust from the road. He did not have to look at Sophie to know that she was staring at him in horror.

"Do something," Sophie whispered, so low that her words were barely audible over the engine. There was a crack in her voice. But then she said the words again and her voice was louder, angrier.

"Do something, damn you! You can save them, Kuromaku. What good is it, being what you are, if you don't try to save them?"

He seethed, his nostrils flaring. Nausea churned in his gut and he forced himself not to look at either side of the road, not to bear witness to whatever atrocities they were leaving behind with every rotation of the tires.

"Kuromaku!" Sophie shouted in despair.

"Stop!" he snapped back, glancing momentarily at her before returning his attention to the road. Up ahead there were two buildings that had begun to burn.

"Think a moment," he instructed her. "This is a war, Sophie. I am sorry, *chérie*, but it is true. We are behind enemy lines. That's what this has all been about . . . getting back to our allies, our comrades, so that we can launch a counterattack."

"But *you* can—"

"Yes, yes, I'm a vampire. All the things I can do," he said, jerking the wheel to the right, ignoring the steeples of houses of worship higher on the hill to his left. They offered no sanctuary; he knew that now. They would be defiled just like the rest of this city.

"But I can't save anyone in this damned place and still protect you. I couldn't keep Henri's father from a savage death and it's only through luck that the boy and his mother are still alive."

Henri sobbed even louder in the back seat. Antoinette said nothing, but she reached out from her huddled terror and pulled her son closer to her, both of them swaying with the rocking of the car as Kuromaku weaved around a few vehicles that had been abandoned.

"The object is to get the three of you out of here alive, and then to return with enough force to wipe out the demons and destroy whatever evil is responsible for this. Every death we leave behind will haunt me, Sophie," he said, glancing at her, trying to make her understand the pain in his heart, "but how many more will die if this is not stopped? I cannot stop it alone. For now, the Whispers are ignoring us. They're caught up in their bloodlust, taking the easier targets. But—"

From the back seat came the voice of Antoinette Lamontagne; every word seemed as though it had been scarred into existence.

"They are not ignoring us anymore," the woman said. Then, in French, she added, "When Sophie stopped the car . . ."

No more words were necessary. Kuromaku shot a look over his shoulder just in time to see the sharp edges of a demon's carapace running from the sidewalk toward the car.

One of them landed on the roof and its tendril-tongue punched a whole through the metal, shattering the dome of the interior light. Kuromaku turned in silence, his foot pressing more heavily upon the accelerator. Through the windshield he saw Whispers coming out of buildings and two of them leaping off the roof of a three-story structure on the left.

"If we die now," Kuromaku told Sophie, without turning toward her, "it's for nothing."

Sophie whispered something to him in French, words of quiet endearment that seemed wildly inappropriate at that moment. And yet Kuromaku found that they gave him strength and determination and he hunched over the steering wheel further.

The Volkswagen crested the hill and started down. Through the mass of Whispers that now swarmed the car, he could see that the road curved slightly and then there was a broad gorge with a bridge across it.

They were not going to get there.

A Whisper leaped onto the hood of the car and its ebony talons slashed down and splintered the windshield. The glass spider-webbed but did not shatter.

"Take the wheel again!" Kuromaku shouted.

"Go!" Sophie snapped without hesitation.

The moment he saw that her hand was on the wheel, he transfigured himself, shifting his body mass to mist. He could feel the moisture of himself on her as she moved into the driver's seat and then he slipped out the window. As mist, Kuromaku enveloped the Whisper on the hood of the car, and then with a thought he transformed again, bursting into a cloud of fire that engulfed the Whisper completely.

Once more he took human form, katana in hand, and the blade began to sing, hacking at the demons that crowded in around the car. A crush of Whispers pushed in, some of them being driven down beneath the car, broken by its weight. But there were too many for Kuromaku to slaughter himself, and as the car careened wildly, others leaped onto it, punching talons through the metal to hang on, shattering windows and grabbing hold of the frames, trying to reach inside to tear at Antoinette and her boy.

Sophie cried out as her arm was slashed, but she kept both hands on the wheel as they thundered toward the bridge. From what Kuromaku had seen, there were many of them on this side, but none of the Whispers on the other side of the gorge.

Then, in the midst of hacking a Whisper in two, shattering its carapace with his blade, he glanced back the way they had come. In the distance, the Spanish town silhouetted against it, there hung a massive storm front, dark, orange-tinted clouds rolling in, a hurricane spawned in Hell itself. For just a single instant it seemed to him that there was a face in the storm, slitted red eyes and a gaping, grinning mouth.

The wind whipped up even harder—enough so that it tore several Whispers away from the car and nearly knocked Kuromaku off as well—and an acid rain began to fall that burned his flesh where it touched him.

Up ahead a road intersected with the one they were on.

On either side of that road, Kuromaku saw something that stunned him even more than the cruel hint of a face in the oncoming storm. To the left and right there were tanks, and trucks, and soldiers in body armor and helmets. Human soldiers.

The Whispers saw them as well and must have sensed them as a new threat, for many of the demons turned away from the Volkswagen and began a new onslaught against the military vehicles.

The soldiers opened fire.

━━━

ALLISON soared, wings outstretched, but this time there was no joy in flight. Peter had told her about the Tatterdemalion, about the dark power that lurked within the oncoming storm, and she felt a cold dread deep within her. This hellish place was unlike anything in her experience. Despite the monstrous thing that she was and the horrors that she had seen, the way the sky bent at the far horizons frightened her. They had been displaced, pulled into a twisted landscape, away from the world she knew. Allison Vigeant was afraid.

It pissed her off.

The oncoming storm whipped against her as though it hoped to keep the falcon back, but Allison stretched out her wings and kept her talons pulled up beneath her and she flew directly toward the tower of thunderclouds that was marching across Ronda from the south. It felt to her as though it was not merely the wind and the heaviness of the air bearing down on her, but the gaze of some ancient and terrible god.

Across the cleft of Ronda—on the other side of the bridge that connected the new city to the old—Allison saw something that made her lose a wingbeat. Tanks. And not merely tanks, but other military vehicles as well, some carrying British markings, others those of the United Nations.

No fucking way, she thought. *Task Force Victor.*

Most of the soldiers on the other side of the gorge had their faces covered and from this height and distance she could not make out the features of the few who did not, but she knew it was Task Force Victor. Allison had figured that without Octavian, they wouldn't have been able to get through the barrier into this demon world, but somehow they had managed. It made her wonder if there was more here than mere chance, if the creature responsible for all of this was simply playing with them all. Task Force Victor might just be more victims brought into this particular Hell to play the role of the damned.

For a moment, the tiniest sliver of guilt went through her. She had been sent to collect Peter, after all, to bring him back so that he could work with Task Force Victor. But Octavian wanted to take a more direct approach, and Allison preferred it as well. Henning and his lackeys could rot here, for all she cared. She wasn't here for them.

Welcome to the party, boys, she thought.

Her wings beat against the gale as the winds whipped even harder at her. The sky darkened, orange firmament charring black as though the embers of a fire hung above. The towering thunderclouds spread and seemed to breathe as they rolled on toward her and she dipped her beak and flew lower, over the cleft of Ronda, headed for a better look at the military forces arrayed on the ground below.

Gunfire ripped the sky. The soldiers were in the midst of combat. Whispers had moved in from all around them, slipping along the streets and emerging from the shattered doors and windows of once-beautiful buildings half a millennium old or more. Then, amidst the chaos, Allison saw a single figure spinning like a dervish—changing, misting, taking flesh once more—and she was stunned. A shadow, a vampire, warring against the Whispers with a gleaming sword. And she knew him, recognized him by his blade and the body language of his combat style.

Kuromaku.

It felt to her in that moment as though some greater power were at work here. Not merely the evil of the demon in the storm, but something beyond the storm, beyond this world entirely. Kuromaku would be an invaluable ally.

If he survived the next several minutes.

Allison knew that she had to go to his aid, but not without first alerting Peter to his old friend's presence. She also wanted a closer look at the Whispers. Where were they all coming from?

Rain had begun to fall from the sky, pelting the falcon. It beaded up on Allison's wings, thick and greasy, her feathers sticking together. The rain drove her down. She would have to land. To change. The bridge over the cleft was just below her.

And then she *saw* them. Below the ramparts, Whispers scuttled spiderlike up the cliff face, scaling the craggy wall of the gorge. Allison dipped her right wing and soared in a half-circle, coming back around even as her feathers became too heavy. Far, far below, at the base of the cleft, the Guadalevin River was dry now, having been cut off from its source. There on the riverbed, partially obscured by the trees that grew on either side of the cleft, she saw something else.

The beast was gigantic, a huge black, pulsing monstrosity. It was on its side, dozens of small legs beneath it, and curled up like some horrid insectoid fetus. If it had not been folded in upon itself in such a way, Allison estimated it would have been as long as fifty feet. And from that place at its middle, which it seemed to have twisted round to protect, Whispers crawled.

They slid wetly from the demon's midsection, climbed out of the pouch made by its position on the ground, and stood shakily. After a moment, each of the things would get its bearings and they would begin to scramble across the dry riverbed toward the cliff and to climb toward the top of the gorge.

Newborns, Allison thought.

It's their mother.

A moment later the greasy, heavy rain at last became too much for her and she tucked her wings against her falcon's body and swooped toward the bridge below. Peter and Keomany would be waiting for her on the north side. The storm was rushing in, the Tatterdemalion was coming, but Allison could not think about that at the moment, nor about Kuromaku's plight. Her mind was seared, branded with the image of that demonic matriarch giving birth to one monster after another, an endless supply.

Kuromaku was going to be overwhelmed. Task Force Victor and the other soldiers didn't have a prayer.

Those thoughts were followed immediately by the realization that unless she, Peter, and Keomany could destroy the beast down inside the cleft of Ronda, neither did they.

———

ONLY when Sophie tasted the copper tang of blood in her mouth did she realize that she had bitten her lip. She sucked on the wound, swallowed her blood, and blew out air in short breaths as though she could dispel her fear that way. Her hands gripped the steering wheel and unconsciously she began to brake.

"Stop!" Kuromaku shouted.

She could barely hear him over the howling wind and the sound of gunfire, but Sophie made the word out well enough to slow the car to a standstill. The engine rumbled. In the back seat, Henri Lamontagne began to sob loudly once again but Antoinette was silent save for the sound of her thumping her head over and over against the door. It was as though insanity was being carried to them on the storm or falling with the fat, hissing raindrops, and soon they would all be infected.

The Whispers had turned their attention to the soldiers now, and so the street around the car was clear when Kuromaku leaped down from the roof and bent to her window. His hair was slick with oily rain and the wind buffeted him. Silhouetted in the orange light he looked almost like a monster himself, save for those gentle eyes. He reached out to stroke the tips of his fingers across her cheeks and nodded once.

"Hurry!" he told her. "I don't know where they came from, but those soldiers are human. Take the boy and his mother. Drive straight through the demons if you have to."

Sophie hesitated, wanting very much to refuse, to stay with him, but she knew better. What could she do, after all, in the face of such evil? Yet without anyone to look after, to protect, Kuromaku could do a great deal. Though she understood, it pained her to know that he must be relieved to be free of her.

"I'll go," she said.

The ronin vampire gave her a curt, respectful bow. Sophie took a breath and looked out through the windshield again. The Volkswagen was pointed down a hill, a hundred and fifty yards from the bridge that crossed the gorge ahead. It had taken her a bit, but she had realized now what city they were in. It was Ronda, in Spain, a place she had not visited since her father had taken her there when she was no more than ten.

Whispers had spread across the road, blocking the bridge. As she watched, she saw more of them scrambling up over the edge of the gorge, climbing out of the cleft of Ronda to join the others. That's where they were coming from, then. Somewhere down inside the cleft.

Sophie turned to share this observation with Kuromaku, trying to block out the sobbing of Henri Lamontagne and the thump of his mother's skull on the door. But Kuromaku was no longer beside the car. She scanned ahead and saw that he had run in advance of the car. Striding swiftly, the undead warrior advanced upon the mass of demons that were even now attacking the foot soldiers who surrounded the military vehicles. Kuromaku seemed not to notice the weapons fire that cut down demons and tore into pavement around him.

Teeth gritted, Sophie accelerated. Her lip was still bleeding, a tiny drop sliding down her chin, but she ignored it.

The car rocked in the heavy gale and she kept her hands tight on the wheel. Her eyes stung and she didn't know if it was the wind or if she was crying. She did not want to know.

"Quiet!" a voice shouted. "Be quiet!"

It sounded like her own voice.

The Volkswagen raced down the hill. Soldiers on top of a tank were waving wildly, trying to turn her away. The gun turret was aimed almost directly at her but Sophie did not even slow down. Whispers were ripped apart by gunfire only feet ahead of the car and then several bullets punctured the hood of the Volkswagen. Her chest hurt and she could not breathe and she crouched down slightly behind the wheel, expecting to be shot at any moment.

But she could not stop now. The Whispers were after her again. She had gotten too close now and drawn their attention and Henri Lamontagne had at last stopped sobbing when one of them thumped down on the roof. Gunfire tore it off the car, chunks of its armored form tumbling onto the trunk lid as they raced onward. The windshield wipers were on but the rain was thick as mucous now and smeared across the glass.

Sophie aimed the car at a phalanx of soldiers ahead. Beyond them was a large truck that must have been their transport vehicle and she wondered if she and Antoinette and Henri would be safe inside that truck. Some of the soldiers were still trying to wave her off but others were now beckoning to her, hurrying her on.

Not that she needed the invitation.

Sophie hit the brakes, the tires sliding on the sticky-slick ground. The Volkswagen slewed to the left and for a terrible instant she thought that she would sideswipe the soldiers, imagined the car sliding over them, crushing them, and just continuing on until it tumbled into the cleft of Ronda.

The car shuddered to a halt and she bit her lip again, sending a jolt of pain through her, a fresh gush of blood into her throat and down her chin. Sophie popped the door open, staring wide-eyed at the soldiers in their helmets and dark face masks.

"Help us!" she called in English, and then in French.

A dozen weapons came to bear upon her and her heart

seemed to freeze as the mouths of those guns gaped darkly at her. She knew she was going to die.

From amid the soldiers came the strangest man, a thin, pale figure with close-shorn red hair and glasses. He wore the garb of a priest and he shoved two of the soldiers aside to force his way through.

"Get down!" the priest screamed at her.

Confused, fear still making her head spin, Sophie turned in time to see two Whispers reaching for her and a third with its hand shoved in through the rear window of the Volkswagen, dragging a weeping Antoinette out of the car by her hair. One of them lunged for her, grabbed her by the arms, its talons tearing her skin. Even with the viscous rain and the orange light she could see her reflection in that featureless shell that covered its head. The sharp tendril that jutted from beneath its face-shell darted toward her eyes.

Screaming, Sophie pulled backward, letting her legs fall out from under her, letting her weight carry her down. The Whisper lost its grip on her arm but it hissed, cocked its head to one side, and then descended upon her.

Weapons fire echoed across the cleft of Ronda and off the buildings and the demon was torn apart. One arm up to shield herself from the falling pieces of its body and shards of its carapace, she saw bullets shatter the other two as well. Broken glass scraping her back, Antoinette Lamontagne fell from the shattered car window to the street. After a moment in which everything seemed to freeze except for the storm, her little boy popped his face up from inside the car and peered out the window in terror.

Above the gunfire and the sound of soldiers shouting, she heard a voice close by, gentle tones asking if she was all right. Sophie glanced up and saw the red-headed priest above her, reaching down to help her up. She took his hand, glanced over his shoulder, and saw two other clergymen. They raised their hands as though about to praise her and the air around them shimmered slightly. The tiny hairs on her arms stood up, static electricity sheathing her.

"What . . . what are you doing?" she asked in French.

The priest glanced worriedly around. "Protecting you as best we can," he replied in English.

That same static seemed to flow from him, and Sophie glanced behind her to see that it surrounded Antoinette as well. The other two clergymen rushed out and retrieved Henri from the car and in moments all six of them were hustling back among the soldiers, behind the battle line. The feeling of static went away, that kind of electric hum on her skin, and Sophie found that she missed it.

They were behind the gunfire now, away from the bullets and the Whispers. Sophie's body was wracked with sudden spasms and she nearly fell to her knees. The priest supported her until she recovered her balance. It was all she could do not to break down, to scream out all the horror and terror she had been holding in since this had all begun.

"What's your name?" the priest asked, pulling her even farther away from the fighting, between a tank and the empty troop carrier.

With a crack of ear-splitting thunder, the tank fired into the street. Sophie glanced up and saw a building on the edge of the cleft—a building that must have been there five hundred years—begin to collapse in upon itself, sending up a cloud of dust.

"*Bonjour?* Hello?" the priest said. "Your name?"

"Sophie," she said, as though only just remembering. "Sophie Duvic."

He held out his hand, an odd bit of formality in the middle of chaos. "Father Jack Devlin."

Sophie took his hand, but already the priest had glanced away from her. His eyes were on the massive thunderheads that were rolling in from the south, the hideous storm that roiled and churned, lightning sparking from cloud to cloud.

"We should get cover," he said.

Kuromaku, Sophie thought. She tugged at the priest's hand. "I cannot. My friend is still back there."

"The woman and the boy," Father Jack said, gesturing past her. "The other priests have them."

Sophie turned and saw the two clergymen who had been with Father Jack helping Antoinette and her son into the back of the troop carrier. A medic was with them, already looking at Antoinette's wounds.

"Not them," Sophie said.

The priest put a hand on her arm but she pulled away. She glanced around for a vantage point that would allow her to see the melee without putting herself between the soldiers and the demons again, but the only point she could see was the tank in front of her. Without hesitation, Sophie started for it.

"Wait!" Father Jack called, grabbing at her. "You can't go up there!"

Sophie spun and glared at him. "I have to make sure he's all right. I . . . I need him here with me, safe. He wouldn't leave me behind. I won't leave him."

For a moment the pale man only gazed at her from behind his spectacles. Then he nodded. "All right, but not up there. Come this way."

He led her around behind the tank and on the other side of it was an open Jeep and a second tank, both vehicles surrounded by soldiers who were strafing the bridge and the rim of the cleft with gunfire to keep new Whispers from joining the others. The demons were swarming though, and some of them slipped through the hail of bullets. A chill ran through Sophie. There were buildings all around. The broad intersection was flanked on either side by military vehicles and soldiers, with Whispers in the middle of the street and on the bridge and coming up from the cleft, but she knew from seeing them before that these weren't the only ones. Her gaze ticked to the windows of the buildings around them.

There were other Whispers, she was sure. She wondered what they were waiting for.

The storm was coming on, the wind blowing so hard that her hair whipped at her face and her clothes flapped against her body and she had to work to keep her balance. Her hair was drenched with that viscous rain and she reached up to wipe it out of her eyes as Father Jack hurried her over to the Jeep. The soldiers ignored them, smearing the rain across their faceguards between firing off rounds of bullets. The staccato gunfire ripped the air and pounded her eardrums.

Sophie squinted through the storm and the chaos and in the orange-black light she saw two men standing in the back of the Jeep. One of them was a formidable-looking military man in commando garb but without the helmet and mask the others wore. The second man was a slim, elderly, white-haired priest. The old man's face was lit up as though he were in the midst of the rapture.

"Destroy them!" the priest was shouting, the words cutting through the rain and the report of weapons fire. "Kill the devils!"

Father Jack dragged Sophie up beside the Jeep and he reached up and tugged at the sleeve of the older priest. The man glanced down and a different kind of light gleamed in his eyes now, not the fervor of religion but the arrogance of superiority.

"Bishop Gagnon!" Father Jack shouted to be heard over the gunfire, spitting out some of the vile rain that had gotten into his mouth. "Michel, this woman needs help! Her friend is still out there! Tell the Commander that—"

"Her friend?" the Bishop cried, a kind of hysteria in his voice and his eyes now. "Her friend, you say?" And then a terrible, sneering rage transformed his features and the old man stepped down from the Jeep. In one swift motion he cracked the back of his bony hand against Father Jack's face, knocking off his glasses. The priest fell to his knees in shock and in pursuit of his spectacles.

Startled, Sophie took a step back and stared at the Bishop, whose name and accent were French.

"What is wrong with you?" she shouted through the storm in her native tongue, not caring at all that it was a clergyman she was talking to.

The old man turned on her. "Get out of here, girl!" he snapped. Then he, too, lapsed into French. "Let the soldiers protect you. All the souls in Hell should be so fortunate. Demons surround us, and your friend is only a demon with another face."

Sophie stared at him, her mind reeling. She had thought them unaware that Kuromaku was out there among the Whispers. Now she realized that wasn't the case at all. They had seen him, all right, and they knew what he was. In the midst of all the chaos they had seen him transforming as he did battle with the Whispers.

"No," she whispered. Then she shouted it. "No! He is not

like them! Not a monster! You cannot just leave him out there!"

The smile that spread across the Bishop's face then unnerved her more than staring straight into the cruelly blank countenance of a Whisper demon.

"Leave him? We're not going to leave him there. Trust me on that, my dear."

A phalanx of soldiers rushed around them, hurrying to provide support to their comrades. The eruption of gunfire seemed even closer and Sophie winced. Someone nearby screamed and she glanced over and saw that two Whispers had somehow made it past the soldiers and climbed atop the tank. They were ravaging one of the men who stood atop it, slashing at him as two other soldiers on top of the tank shouted in panic, trying to get a clean shot at the demons.

Talons slashed down and the soldier's left arm was severed, his throat was torn out, and then his head was ripped violently from his body, leaving only ragged flesh and muscle and a stump of the man's spine. Blood splashed toward Sophie and the Bishop and spattered Father Jack as he stood, at last having recovered his glasses.

Sophie screamed and seemed to sink into herself. Her entire body seemed to curl inward and she wanted nothing more than to disappear. She flinched away from every gunshot, and from the presence of the Bishop and Father Jack. Pressure built up inside of her until at last she screamed again, letting it out, letting it all go. Fresh tears streamed down her face, but for the first time, a terrible truth had lodged itself in her brain.

If she wanted to survive all of this, it was up to her. Not Kuromaku, and not any soldiers. Her.

When she glanced up, she saw several Whispers leaping out from the top of a building to land on the tank. But the soldiers were taking no more chances. Bullets strafed the air, ripped apart the demons, with little regard as to whether or not one of their own might get hit. On the street beyond the line of soldiers, however, she knew that other men must be dying. There were simply too many of the Whispers. Too many of them.

Sophie stared at the Bishop. It was her turn to smile. "Kuromaku's a vampire. You can't kill him. Almost nothing can kill him."

The Bishop's nostrils flared. Thick beads of greasy water slid down his face. "Yes. *Almost* nothing."

Sophie shook her head in abrupt denial. "You can't. You . . . what are you going to do?"

"Me? I'm a man of God, girl. I'm not going to do anything."

His meaning was clear. He might not be doing anything, but the man up in the Jeep—whom he had called "the Commander"—obviously was. Her gaze ticked upward and she saw the intense man raise a pair of high-tech field goggles to his eyes and scan the street to the east and the cleft to the south. It made no sense, none at all. The Whispers were everywhere. No matter how many of them the soldiers killed, there seemed to be more. And yet these men were intent upon killing Kuromaku.

Why? I don't understand, Sophie thought.

But before she could speak those words, Father Jack moved past her toward the Jeep. His face was no longer pale, but pink with anger. He reached for the door and began to climb up, glaring at the Commander, who did not notice Father Jack's approach.

"Where the hell are those V-rounds?" the Commander snapped, one hand clapped to his ear. Sophie realized the man was speaking into some sort of communications rig but couldn't see it.

"Commander!" Father Jack shouted, his words stripped away by the wind. "Commander Henning!"

The Bishop reached out and snagged him by the jacket. "Where are you going, Father Devlin?"

The priest tried to shake himself loose but his superior now had both hands on him and was attempting to pull him away from the Jeep. To Sophie's astonishment, Father Jack whirled around and punched the old man, connecting with a solid crack of knuckle on cheekbone. The Bishop staggered backward but Father Jack wasn't done. He followed after the old man and struck him again, and the Bishop went down onto the slick pavement.

Father Jack stood over him, fuming, eyes obscured behind

his rain-spattered glasses. "You are not a man of God!" he
spat, veins standing out on his neck. "You are a fucking
lunatic."

When the priest raised his hand to point at the Bishop,
his fingers glowed a dim, fiery blue.

"Stay there."

Father Jack reached for Sophie's hand and she took it.
Together they jumped up into the Jeep. A pair of soldiers
moved to stop them, one of them grabbing Sophie's leg, but
she shook him off and froze him in place with a furious glare.

"Back off!" she barked.

"Commander!" Jack called.

When at last Commander Henning turned toward them,
Sophie saw in his eyes that he had been completely aware
of what was transpiring around him. The conflict among
them had not escaped his notice, as she had assumed.

"Go away, Father Devlin," the Commander said, his eyes
slitted against the storm, his commando uniform plastered to
his body.

Another soldier in helmet and mask—just as eerily faceless as the demons, she thought now—ran up beside the Jeep
with an automatic rifle.

"Commander!" the soldier shouted. And when Henning
glanced down, the soldier passed the weapon up to him,
along with a pair of ammunition clips. Commander Henning
popped the clip out of the weapon and inserted one of the
new ones.

"Commander!" Father Jack shouted again.

The man ignored him. He climbed out onto the hood of
the Jeep. Sophie began to shake her head as she jumped onto
the rear seat of the vehicle. Past Father Jack and Commander
Henning, over the heads of the soldiers in the street, she
could see the anarchy in the midst of the intersection. Whispers capered, dodging gunfire, moving swiftly toward the
soldiers, their thin, armored forms elusive in the rain and the
driving storm. Bullets cracked their shells, and their corpses
littered the road. But there were so many. So many.

And among them, a thing unlike any Sophie had ever
seen. A lone figure, a dervish, shifting and changing. Swords-
man, tiger, mist, wolf, raven, samurai . . . Kuromaku. Stray

bullets struck him but wounded him not at all.

Commander Henning raised the automatic rifle and took aim.

"He's on our side!" Father Jack roared, and he lunged forward.

Henning cracked the butt of the weapon across the priest's face and Father Jack fell backward, out of the Jeep. He struck his head on the pavement and was still. It was insane. The Commander was diverting his attention from the creatures that threatened to overwhelm his men to focus on Kuromaku. He barely looked at Sophie as he raised the weapon again.

There was no thought in what she did next.

Sophie leaped down from the Jeep and raced toward the line of soldiers from behind. They were firing indiscriminately now, and as she approached them, it felt as though her eardrums would burst. Then she had reached them and she shoved through a narrow space between two dark-clad soldiers and ran past them.

Out into the street.

The Whispers were all hissing, their tendril-tongues darting in front of their blank skull-shells as bullets tore them apart. But not all of them were dying. Some of them were close by and they started for her instantly, sensing her, tendrils pointing toward her as though to a magnet.

They swarmed. Thick mucous rain pelted her. The wind buffeted her. Sophie raced toward the demons, peering through the storm and the Whispers for Kuromaku. In the midst of the intersection she stopped, threw back her head, and screamed.

"Kuromaku! They're going to kill you! Find cover!"

Much of the gunfire had silenced. Staccato bursts echoed across buildings off to her right and out over the gorge to her left. Behind her there were only short ripples of fire.

The Whispers closed in around her. They slowed, as if to savor her. She could hear the clack of their carapaces; there were so many of them around her that they blocked out that putrid orange light.

Then Kuromaku was there. His sword whickered through the air and he hacked two of the demons to pieces, spattering

her with ichor thick as the hellish rain. The others turned to
defend themselves and he lashed into them.

"No!" she cried. "Find cover! Find cover!"

But Kuromaku did not listen. She ought to have known
he would not. He had vowed to protect her and he was going
to do precisely that. In trying to save Kuromaku, she had
slowed him down, made him a better target.

Sophie spun and stared back at the Jeep, saw Commander
Henning take aim. Fresh gunfire ripped through the air, echoes dancing around the intersection. Bullets tore the ground.
Kuromaku was hit in the shoulder, blood splashing from the
wound, and he staggered.

She saw the confusion in his eyes even as he slashed the
katana out again, decapitating another Whisper. Sophie
shouted again for him to take cover, beckoning him toward
her. Blinking in surprise, shaking his head as if disoriented,
Kuromaku staggered toward her. Another bullet grazed his
left leg and he spun in toward her, spinning the blade, clearing a circle around them.

Sophie grabbed him and pulled herself close so that her
own body was a shield between Kuromaku and Commander
Henning's bullets. If the soldiers were willing to kill her to
get to him . . . *oh, Lord, please help us*, she thought.

"Those bullets," she said, "can they kill you? The Commander thinks they can."

Kuromaku's features were grim, his eyes narrow and
dark. "He's right."

"Get us out of here, then! Without Antoinette and her boy,
we can fly! Carry me. Please, Kuromaku, let's go!"

"I cannot," he replied as the wind howled around them.
"That is what the bullets do. The chemical in them, it takes
away my power to change."

Sophie stared at him, lips parted in horror. Fresh tears slid
down her face, and the Whispers began to close in.

CHAPTER 19

THE storm raged, churning the sky above the southern half of the city of Ronda. The wind was hot, and seeded with pure malice. Peter could feel the malevolence of the Tatterdemalion in the air as it whipped against him, but he would not let it slow him down. He needed more time—time to think and to plan, to study the Tatterdemalion and formulate a strategy—but he wasn't going to get it.

The time was now.

Despite the magick that blazed around his hands, crackling between his fingers, he had never felt so frail, so human.

After they had left the bullring behind, he and Keomany had seen very few of the Whispers, mostly lurking in the shadows inside the buildings they passed—restaurants and apartments and hotels. Peter tried not to think of the people inside those buildings, the human beings fighting for their lives with every passing second. Cries had issued from the upper floor of one building and Keomany had started off in that direction, but Peter had stopped her.

There was no time. The storm had arrived. Heavy, oily rain had begun to fall and it was as though the clouds were the eyes of the Tatterdemalion, and it was watching them. It was far too late for them to try to save a single life; such a delay might cost thousands, even millions more. It might cost the world.

Peter squinted his eyes against the wind and the rain. There was a terrible stench in the air and it assaulted his nostrils, causing his eyes to water. His clothes whipped against his body but he set himself against the gale and kept on. The distant report of gunfire thudded dully in the air, a nearly constant sound, as if the bullets were the grinding of some giant engine. Peter had at first thought that perhaps the people of Ronda were fighting back, but the sounds he heard weren't from the sort of weaponry people had in their homes. He would see soon enough, he supposed, where the shots were coming from.

Up ahead there was a broad plaza with a monument at its center and beyond that he could see part of the bridge Keomany had told him about, and the rest of the city rising up on the horizon beneath the terrible face of the storm.

Around the monument was a ring of demons, skeletal Whispers crouched at the base of the stone memorial like gargoyles. He cursed silently the momentary delay they would cost. It would have been so much easier to wait for the Tatterdemalion to come to him, for he was certain the sinister presence had noted him. But he remembered too well what had happened in Wickham and knew that it was possible that the Tatterdemalion might not attack him at all, might simply ignore him and go about its work. They had to bring it to them, force it to pay attention.

That was where Keomany came in.

Keomany, he thought, frowning. She had been beside him a moment ago. Now, when he turned around, he saw that she had fallen behind. She was strikingly beautiful, her black hair like curtains of silk around her face, and her eyes glowed a bright gold. Keomany Shaw walked in a cascade of warm, soft earth light that touched her as though Gaea herself had reached down into this hellish dimension and touched her servant with a finger, a shaft of her divine spirit.

It was the dawn. In Spain, the sun was coming up, and where Keomany walked, she was slitting open a narrow window to the world to which this city belonged. Lit up like that, it was as though Keomany had become a goddess. Behind her she had left a swath of that warm morning light. It was still dim, still early back in the world, but day was breaking. Where she walked, sprigs of green grass grew up from the pavement without any help from Peter's magick. He had helped Keomany to break through, to connect with the spirit of Gaea, but now that the two were entwined, the power coursing through Keomany had nothing to do with the kind of sorcery Peter wielded.

Where that filthy rain fell, the light of the other world's dawn evaporated it. Peter's clothes and hair were becoming sodden and the slick rain streaked his face, but Keomany was untouched by it. Ever since they had left the bullring, she had kept up with him, but now she had slowed and was staring at the street in front of her. After a moment, Keomany crouched and touched the pavement with outstretched fingers.

Peter glanced over at the blank face-shells of the Whispers around the monument at the center of the plaza. They were completely still as though they thought he might not notice them. Only the sharp tendrils that hung beneath their skull carapaces were in motion, sensing his presence, perhaps waiting to see what he would do. Or perhaps it was Keomany they were afraid of.

"What are you up to?" he whispered.

Beneath his feet the ground began to tremble. Startled, he spun back to look at Keomany, his hands crackling with magickal energy. Even as he turned, he saw the pavement beneath her fingers shatter and fall aside as branches and leaves thrust up from the ground. The sky above split open and light shone down in a widening circle as the tree grew and its branches spread wide.

An olive tree, fully grown, stood in the midst of the plaza in a pool of Spanish morning light. Keomany stood beneath its branches, so slim and petite in its shadow. She reached up and plucked an olive from its branches and then glanced over at Peter, smiling. Her eyes gleamed even more brightly as she laughed.

"I found a flaw," she said. "There are places where the walls between here and home are very thin."

With a flip of her silken hair she glanced southward at

the towering thunderheads, the roiling, unnatural storm clouds. "It isn't as all-powerful as it thinks it is."

Keomany walked up beside Peter and he could smell the fresh air of home swirling around her, could feel the golden glow of the natural light that bathed her. It felt right and it gave him hope. Despite his exhaustion from transporting them here, he felt stronger now.

"What do you say we kick some ass?" she asked.

Peter nodded once. The fingers of his left hand hooked downward, almost clawlike, and then he lashed out with a flick of his wrist and a scythe of green light sliced across the square. His attack cut three of the Whispers in half and threw the other two to the ground, ichor seeping from cracks in their armored forms. The stone monument shattered.

As if sensing the new strength in them, the power and resolve, the wind blew harder but they forged ahead through the storm. The bridge was ahead, the stones coated with a film of rain that puddled instead of running off the way it should have. An explosion echoed out across the bridge—across the gorge that spread out to either side, the gash that separated the halves of the city—and Peter peered through the filthy rain, wiping the viscous fluid from his eyes.

Amid the gunfire he had been hearing since they left the bullring, there had been occasional small explosions, like mortar shells. Now he saw the source. On the other side of the bridge, in the intersection at the bottom of the hill that led up into the heights of Ronda, there were military vehicles, including at least two tanks that he could see. More gunfire echoed across the gorge.

"Peter, look," Keomany said, pointing.

Above the bridge they saw her. Allison had become a falcon to search the city from the sky, but now she was falling, plummeting toward the ground and changing as she fell. From bird she became woman. End over end she tumbled, too fast. The only thing he could think of was that she must somehow have been knocked unconscious. He thrust out his hands, palm up, and began to mutter to himself. This was simple magick, but delicate. He had not had much use for gentleness of late and so it took him a fraction of a second, a single inhalation of breath, to steady himself.

Midway through a spin that would have ended with her head splitting on the stone bridge, Allison turned to mist. Keomany let out a cry of relief and ran ahead, stepping away from the tear she had created in this reality as though leaving the spotlight upon a stage. She had detached from her connection to Gaea, it appeared, at least for the moment. Peter followed her, racing toward the edge of the new city, where they could look down upon the wide gorge and the ancient, arched stone bridge.

Several feet away, Allison coalesced once more into flesh. Instantly the rain began to plaster her red hair to her skull. Her eyes were wild.

"You're all right," Peter said.

Allison only nodded, moving quickly to the edge of the bridge to stare down into the Cleft of Ronda.

"What did you see?" he asked, forced to shout over the storm, which began to roar even louder around them, screaming through the gorge below.

"Have a look," she called back, a grim cast to her features.

Peter pushed through the rain and laid his hands on the stone wall of the bridge. Keomany did the same and together the three of them looked down into the Cleft at the abomination that lay on the dry riverbed, its flesh pulsing. Octavian felt bile burn the back of his throat at the sight of the grotesque thing and the demons that emerged wetly from its abdomen.

"Brood mother," he told Keomany.

Her eyes had lost that golden glow when she had run to Allison's aid, but now the light gleamed once more in Keomany's gaze. The rain had beaded upon her face and hair, sliding down her cheeks like syrup tears. Above, a new shaft of daylight burned down through the orange-black sky and christened her anew.

All of this happened in an eyeblink. Then Allison tore herself away from the sight of the hideous giant in the gorge and turned to Peter again.

"Here's the deal. Task Force Victor's over there with a bunch of British soldiers."

"They're not our priority," Peter replied gravely. "The Tatterdemalion is. The storm is here, it's all around us, but the bastard hasn't come for us yet. Maybe it's not planning to. We've got to get its . . ." He paused and went to look down into the gorge again. And then Peter Octavian smiled. "Attention. We've got to get its attention."

"Agreed," Allison said. "But Kuromaku's over there too."

Peter blinked several times in surprise, trying to make sense of this new information. He frowned and pulled his gaze from the brood mother at the base of the cliffs and bridge and turned to stare at the tanks again.

Kuromaku. Where the hell did he come from?

Not that it mattered. Kuromaku was his brother, or as near as any man had ever been. He was also the finest warrior Peter had ever known. Allison was staring at Peter expectantly and he nodded to her.

"Go get him. Meet us down in the gorge."

Keomany's head snapped around, sparks slipping from her eyes and turning to golden mist. "Down there? What are we going down there for?"

Peter's nostrils flared with anger and distaste and he glared up into the storm, the wind howling and the rain pelting his face.

"The Tatterdemalion's an arrogant bastard. He thinks we can't hurt him. We're going to prove him wrong."

———

PAIN seared through Kuromaku's shoulder and leg where the bullets had struck. The viscous rain smeared his vision and all around him the Whispers moved in. He wiped at his eyes and could see that more and more of the demons were swarming up over the edge of the Cleft. There were too many of them; too many even for the soldiers. He could hear the screams of men and women tearing across the intersection as the Whispers began to slip through the crossfire. The staccato bursts of gunfire slowed. There were still stray bullets that tore the pavement nearby, but very few. The soldiers were too occupied with the swarm around them, or simply had not fallen so far that they would kill an innocent woman to take the life of a vampire.

Unlike those attacking the soldiers, the Whispers that surrounded Kuromaku and Sophie moved slowly, filled with dark purpose. The circle closed inexorably around them, stalking carefully, as though the demons sensed that Kuromaku had been wounded. They had no nostrils that he could see, but he suspected that somehow they smelled the blood.

Blood, Kuromaku thought. The irony was too much. *I'm bleeding.* He could no longer shapeshift, that ability had been taken from him by the chemical carried in the bullets that had struck him. Sophie had made it clear that the Commander of these military forces was trying to kill him. There was no sense to it, no logic, but he did not bother to question it. He was a vampire, and the United Nations had a special section of their military that hunted vampires.

The chemical stabilized his molecules, preventing him from changing. The cruelest irony was that it had been developed by a vampire, a creature named Hannibal, who had used it to slaughter those of his own kind who would not follow him. It had been the U.N. task force that had first put the chemical in ammunition.

Kuromaku's gaze ticked around the circle of Whispers that took a step closer, their tongues darting at him, tasting the air, perhaps even tasting his anxiety. They could tear him apart, if the bullets did not get him first.

But it was not for himself that he was anxious.

"Stay behind me," he told Sophie, not daring to sneak a glance at her porcelain features or those perfect blue eyes for fear they would distract him a second too long. She was holding on tightly to him and now he pulled her hands away from his body, ushering her back.

"I will be moving quickly. You must try to stay close but not interfere, not get in the way."

"They'll kill you," Sophie said, her voice little more than a rasp above the sound of the wind and rain.

"They'll kill us both," Kuromaku replied, wiping again at his eyes, letting his katana hang by his side as he studied the Whispers intently. "We need to get to cover."

"There isn't any!" she cried. "They're in all the buildings. They're . . . the bridge!"

Kuromaku frowned and glanced at her, then over at the bridge.

"I didn't see any demons on the other side," Sophie said. "Do you think we can—"

"Perhaps," he interrupted. "Perhaps." Slowly he glanced around the circle again and then at last he did meet her gaze, seeing desperation and fierce passion in her eyes. He nodded. "We're going to run. Stay with me."

Kuromaku raised his sword. The pointed tongues of every single Whisper in the circle darted out toward it. At this sign that their prey was going to fight, they hissed, the sound almost lost in the rain and wind, and then they lunged.

With his free hand, Kuromaku held on to Sophie's wrist. He slashed the katana out, decapitating one of the Whispers, and the demon fell into the path of two others. They tried to leap over their fallen brother and collided, only to be wounded, their carapaces cracked by Kuromaku's sword. The others were swarming in, but Kuromaku had opened a hole in the circle.

He spun, pulling Sophie behind him, keeping her out of the way of his blade. She paused, planted her left foot, and shot the right out in a sideways kick that knocked one of the demons backward into a tangle of scything limbs. Kuromaku swore and pulled her closer behind him. He admired her will to fight in order to survive but there were too many of them and he saw only one chance for them to make it through this.

A hissing Whisper leaped at him over the corpse of another Kuromaku had killed and he raised his blade. The demon impaled itself on the tip of the sword. Kuromaku stepped forward, thrust the katana deeper, and twisted it, coring out a hole in the Whisper's chest.

In his mind's eye, he saw the hole he had first made in the circle. They were moving in almost too fast for him to move, but he had to go. If they did not flee now, they would never escape. This time when he spun, he did not pull Sophie behind him. Instead, he turned around and reached out to clutch her tight against his chest.

The hole he had made in the circle was filled by a single Whisper that crouched atop the shattered and bleeding remains of the dead. It raised its talons, tensed to spring.

Kuromaku pressed forward, pushing Sophie toward the demon's razor talons ahead of him. She did not scream, only flinched in silence, turning her face away from the Whisper. Its tongue darted toward her, all of its focus on her.

The vampire ronin punched the tip of his katana through the demon's face-shell and it fell instantly limp, hanging by its skull on the blade. Kuromaku used the sword to toss the Whisper aside and withdrew his blade with a wet, sucking sound from the wound in its face. The way in front of them was open save the remains of dead Whispers.

"Run!" he screamed to Sophie, shoving her ahead of him. As she leaped over the demon corpses, he turned and defended her flight, cleaving the nearest Whisper in two with a swipe of his blade that scraped loudly on its armor.

Then Kuromaku turned and followed Sophie, leaping over the demon remains, nearly slipping in their filthy blood and the greasy rain. The wind pushed at him and the showers from the sky plastered his clothes to his body, making them stiff and heavy. In his heart he felt a loss unlike anything he had felt before, even when he had put his life and humanity behind him and become a vampire.

He could not fly. He could not mist. He could not change.

An ember of rage blazed up in his gut, a thirst for revenge . . . for blood. It had been days now since he had drunk and he thought that perhaps this time he would take what he required from the men who had tried to kill him.

Then he glanced ahead of him and saw Sophie running along the street toward the bridge that spanned the Cleft. She had already passed through the intersection. Along the side streets to the left and right the Whispers were overwhelming the soldiers. There seemed more of them than ever but they paid little attention to Sophie, all of their focus on the men and women with guns. Weapons fire still echoed off buildings but only in short bursts now. The tanks fired several times, but wildly, shattering walls and tumbling masonry into the streets.

It would not be long now before the Whispers overtook them completely. More of them were crawling out of the Cleft to the left of the bridge; no matter how many the soldiers killed, it wouldn't be enough.

Kuromaku ran after Sophie, beginning to catch up with her. Whispers crawling up from the Cleft ignored her, passing on the left within forty or fifty feet of her as they ran at the tanks and troop carriers. To the right loomed a massive structure, a centuries-old building that had once been a convent, if Kuromaku's memory served him.

On the roof of the convent he saw several dark figures capering in the rain—a handful of Whispers whose focus was not on the soldiers—and he knew that his vengeance would have to wait. The Whispers tracked her movement toward the bridge. First Kuromaku would have to get Sophie to safety. Only then could he indulge his fury at the loss he had suffered.

The bullet wound in his left shoulder pained him and he smelled the metallic scent of his own blood, but Kuromaku would not let it slow him down. He was grateful than the bullet that had struck his leg had only grazed him, otherwise the Whispers that gave chase would have dragged him down by now. He ignored the pain and pressed on, running faster than any human, catching up quickly to Sophie. Though the storm raged around them, it seemed almost as though they had entered the eye of a hurricane. The wind and rain continued, but the war had opened up a path for them.

Twenty feet from the bridge Sophie paused to glance back at him, to check on his progress. Kuromaku was nearly on top of her and was forced to pause as well. The Whispers were predators; he had observed them enough to guess their patterns. The moment they paused, Kuromaku turned to look up into the heavy, driving, mucous-rain. Shielding his eyes, he saw three figures darker than the storm leap out from the roof of the convent.

The Whispers were raining down upon them from the sky.

Kuromaku shoved Sophie away toward the bridge again. She needed no verbal instruction this time and set off running once more. The vampire ronin followed her just a few feet, then turned his back on the bridge and prepared himself to defend her retreat.

A mortar shell struck the wall of the convent and it exploded, killing one of the Whispers as it fell. Kuromaku scrambled backward out of the way of the crumbling masonry, but the other two Whispers were crushed beneath it. The soldiers were his enemies, but without knowing it, they had aided him. The irony sketched a dark grin across his features.

Another bullet struck him, this one entering low on his right side, chipping bone as it lodged in his ribcage.

The katana dropped from Kuromaku's hand. Clutching the wound, he fell to his knees. He swayed, narrowing his gaze as he glanced around him. He saw the Whispers he had believed he had left behind now moving more quickly to catch up with him, talons clacking on pavement. Bullets whined in the air around him. The lunatics were still shooting at him; in the midst of all this death, someone was still determined to kill him.

As Kuromaku struggled to get to his feet, he turned toward the bridge and his eyes widened in alarm. Sophie had turned back for him. He shouted her name as she raced at him but she ignored him, ice blue eyes unflinching.

"No!" he called. "Get out of here!"

Sophie sneered at him. "Shut up, you pompous ass. You wouldn't leave me behind, and I won't leave you." Then a stricken look crossed her eyes, burdened with heartache and desperation. "I can't."

In the moment Kuromaku forgot all about the feelings he had developed for her, about the taste of her lips on his or his desire for her. All he could think of, just then, was the giggling little girl who had hidden from him beneath the dining table in her father's home in Paris. It occurred to him that in his mind there were two Sophies, and that all along he had been doing everything in his power to save them both.

But the girl Sophie had been had disappeared years before. She picked the katana up from the pavement with a scrape of steel and turned toward the demons, prepared to defend him. To die for him.

To die *with* him.

———

FATHER Jack stared at Commander Henning in shock. The brawny military man clung to the side of the tank with one hand and fired wildly with the weapon in his right.

"Fall back, you motherfuckers! Fall back!" he screamed

into the comm unit built into his collar, eyes wild, face and balding pate smeared with greasy rain.

The priest had never seen anyone look quite so insane.

Soldiers pushed by him all around and Father Jack struggled with the collision of too many variant emotions. He feared for his life. There were too many Whispers and they were closing in too quickly. The rain could not wash away the stench of blood. The wind could not drown out the screams of men and women as they were disemboweled. The British and U.N. forces led by Commander Henning had been routed, and now they had to retreat or they would be decimated down to the last soldier.

"Father, come on!" a soldier snapped at him, the woman's voice muffled by the helmet that hid her face.

She grabbed his arm and tried to guide him away, toward a troop carrier whose engine was already roaring. Other soldiers stood in the back of the truck and fired short, sharp bursts from their weapons at Whispers that got too close. They were hunting now, the demons, being careful, knowing they had their prey on the run.

But along with his fear, Father Jack felt a surge of disgust that rose like bile in the back of his throat, not for the horrors they faced, but for the behavior of Commander Henning and of his own superior, His Eminence the Bishop, Michel Gagnon. Or *the bastard*, as Jack had come to think of him.

Henning was obsessed with vampires, which may have made him the right man to lead the U.N.'s Task Force Victor, but also had driven him over the edge during this battle. He should have seen much sooner the slaughter that was going on around him, should have retreated to avoid a further massacre. Instead, Henning had lingered, trying to get finish off the vampire he had wounded, the vampire who had been *on their side*.

Bishop Gagnon was partially to blame. There was the light of zealotry in his eyes, the spark of utter madness. He had been more than happy to let the French woman who had arrived with the vampire run out among the Whispers, risking her life to save her friend. The Bishop and Henning both were content to leave her to die.

Father Jack cursed his own cowardice. He ought to have

gone after the two of them himself. His magick was not strong enough to destroy so many demons, and even if it was, he had no doubt that Bishop Gagnon would have urged the Commander to shoot him in the back. In the chaos, no one would question such a thing, and the two men seemed to have found a kinship with one another. Henning wouldn't have flinched at the suggestion.

Guilt warred with fear and disgust in Jack Devlin's heart. Already several Jeeps had torn off down Calle Tenorio, pursued by Whispers. They would be all right, though. There were other demons in Ronda, but this seemed to be their nest. If he and the Bishop could create a passage out of this dimension, those that retreated from the nest would probably survive.

"Father, let's go!" the soldier shouted at him again, her words torn away by a wind so powerful that they had to bend into it to remain upright.

"You go!" he roared at her, and once again he pulled away.

The tank had begun to move, grinding pavement beneath its treads, slowly lumbering after the troop carriers and Jeeps as they also started to roll away from the intersection, away from the Cleft of Ronda.

But Henning was still on top of the tank with two of his men. The soldiers flanking him were shooting at the Whispers that tried to scrabble up the sides of the tank, but Henning concentrated his fire on the entrance to the bridge . . . on the place where the pretty, petite blond French woman raised a Japanese sword and tried to protect her wounded friend from the demons that surrounded them.

Henning's bullets struck some of the demons, but Father Jack knew it wasn't the Whispers the Commander was aiming for. Up on top of the tank he swore loudly, cursing the moving tank and his wild aim.

The last of the troop carriers was side by side with the tank now, and Jack was between them. Through the howling storm he heard a familiar voice calling out to him.

"Father Devlin! Let's go now, Father. Live to fight another day."

He turned around quickly and saw Bishop Gagnon low-

ering a hand down toward him from the back of the troop
carrier. The vehicle had rumbled to a halt in order to let
several soldiers and Father Jack climb aboard, but it was the
Bishop who was reaching out to him. A flash of doubt went
through Jack then. Was this man truly mad, or merely pious?
Despite all that had happened—though Jack had earlier
knocked him down—Michel was willing to set their differ-
ences aside in this desperate moment.

Father Jack reached up and took the Bishop's hand. With
the other he grabbed the side of the troop carrier and began
to haul himself up. Gunfire punctuated his efforts, far too
near. The tank turret exploded with another mortal shell.

Bishop Gagnon froze when Jack was halfway up the side
of the truck, trying to get his left leg inside. With a frown,
the priest looked up into his superior's eyes.

The Bishop grinned cruelly. "You were a great disappointment to me, Jack."

He let go. Father Jack tumbled back to the street, flailing
his arms, and when he struck the pavement, the breath was
knocked out of him. For a moment he could only lie there.
The soldiers were firing wildly, too busy with the job of
staying alive to notice what the Bishop had done. But Michel
Gagnon, he of the austere countenance and severe eyes and
snow white hair, he only smiled and raised a hand to wave
goodbye to Jack with two fingers, almost a salute, as the
troop carrier began to pull away.

The storm seemed almost to shove him down but Father
Jack struggled to climb once more to his feet, spitting out
the greasy raindrops that slithered into his mouth. A new
emotion filled him now. It was hatred. All gangly legs,
glasses smeared with rain, he regained his footing as the tank
fired again, the sound cracking the sky around him. The troop
carrier with Bishop Gagnon picked up speed, about to pass
the tank, when the Whispers fell upon it. They rained down
from the buildings along Calle Tenorio and lunged up from
the street, from beneath the tank, from the shadows of broken
windows in the House of Don Bosco on the northwest side
of the street.

Their numbers were too great. The Whispers disarmed
them, stripped them of their weapons, and tore off their

limbs. Through the driving rain, in that gray-orange light, Father Jack saw one of the demons punch its razor-talons through Bishop Gagnon's face. The old man's corpse fell out of the troop carrier and was crushed beneath its wheels, even as the vehicle, driverless now, crashed into the House of Don Bosco.

For a moment, Father Jack only stared. Then he realized that other than the tank—its engine roaring louder as it gained speed and began to pull away from him—he was alone with the Whispers.

"Oh, shit," he whispered.

Then he ran, racing toward the tank. On top of it he saw Commander Henning, still firing that assault rifle with its special ammunition, still trying to kill the vampire as they pulled away from the bridge. No way could Henning have killed him from this distance with that kind of gun. A rifle with a scope, maybe, but not with that. Not without incredible luck.

But still the man was trying, screaming to his men to retreat, cursing the demons and the vampire he so badly wanted dead.

Father Jack reached the tank, grabbed hold of a rung on its side and started hauling himself up. As he did so, a pair of Whispers appeared from behind the tank as though they had just materialized, though he suspected they had come from inside one of the buildings. They lunged for him. The priest held on to the rung with both hands, running alongside the moving vehicle, and prepared to kick the demons. His heart skipped a beat, his throat was dry.

Bullets tore the Whispers apart.

Jack looked up to see one of Henning's task force soldiers staring down at him. The man reached a hand down and the priest had a flashback to Bishop Gagnon's deceit, but he felt he had no choice. The tank was the last target for the Whispers that swarmed into the street now. He grabbed the man's hand and pulled himself up on top of the tank and they rumbled away down the street.

But Commander Henning was not through. He kept firing. Father Jack looked back the way they'd come and saw, in the distance, the French woman and her vampire companion.

The vampire had his sword back now and the two of them were leaning on one another, fending off Whispers as they inched closer to the bridge.

Henning's assault rifle dry-fired on an empty clip. The madman popped it out and reached into his jacket for a fresh one. Jack realized that the man would have run out of that special ammunition long ago, but that it did not matter. Normal bullets could kill the vampire now. If only Henning could hit him.

"Die, you motherfucker!" the Commander screamed. The other members of the task force on top of the tank ignored him as if his behavior were completely normal, but the two of them were keeping themselves, Henning, and now Father Jack alive.

Henning fired again.

A shriek filled the air, like that of a bird of prey. Father Jack glanced up and saw the broad wingspan of a giant falcon above him. Then it was gone and a thick mist surrounded him and the others for only a moment.

When the mist dissipated, there was a woman standing on top of the tank with them, her eyes severe, her dark red hair swept back away from her face. Father Jack had seen her picture hundreds of times, had seen her on television in years past, before she had become what she was now. He had a file on her in his office back in New York.

Allison Vigeant snarled as she reached out and grabbed Commander Henning by the throat. She shook him like a rag doll and his assault rifle at last fell from his hands, clattering off the side of the tank. The two soldiers turned their weapons on her instantly but Allison reached out and slapped one of them so hard he fell to his knees, barely able to stay on board the tank. She tore the gun from the other's grip and cracked him across the forehead with it. He fell to the street with a sickening thud as the tank rolled on through the rain, and then Allison hauled back and shot a hard kick at the soldier still trying to cling to the tank. He, too, fell.

Then she turned her attention to Henning again.

"You think I'm going to let you kill my friends? You stupid fuck! When was it going to be my turn?" Allison screamed at Henning. "Huh? I know you weren't going to rest until we were all dead. When was it going to be me?"

"Not . . . soon . . . enough . . ." Henning choked, her hand tightening on his throat.

"You can say that again," she snarled.

Allison hissed, baring needle fangs impossibly long, and she sank her teeth into his throat. Blood sprayed her face and clothes as she drank greedily, sloppily from him. Rain slithered down her hair, turning it darker red, almost black. After several seconds she held him, limp and dead, away from her again.

"Fucker!" she screamed. "You son of a bitch!"

She threw the corpse off the tank and rounded on Father Jack, her mouth and chin smeared with bright red blood that ran down her throat. He held his hands up to ward her off.

"You're Father Devlin?" she demanded.

Stunned, he nodded.

Allison grabbed him up in her arms as though he were nothing more than a child and leaped off the tank, landing easily on the street. She set him down even as the Whispers began to move in.

"Peter told me about you," she said. "Lucky you." There wasn't a trace of humor in her voice.

She pointed back the way they'd come, toward the bridge and the swarming Whispers, toward the other vampire and the blond French woman.

"Run for the bridge. I'll keep you alive."

"Is it safe on the other side?" he asked, hoping.

Bloody lips curled back from those red-stained fangs. "You're in Hell, father. Nowhere is safe."

CHAPTER 20

HIGH above the dry bed of the Guadelevin River, Peter Octavian held his arms wide, his head thrown back, and his breath catching in his throat. Magick flowed out of him and through him, a circuit that lit his eyes with a cobalt blue glow and caused his hair to stand on end. Blue electric sparks danced across his body, and tendrils of that magick leaped from his fingertips to touch the interior of the sphere of energy in which he held himself and Keomany Shaw aloft over the Cleft of Ronda.

The rocks and trees were far below, with only magick suspending the two of them. Peter felt it coursing through him, yet instead of draining him, this immersion in the sorcerous power that surged within him only seemed to invigorate him. For all the spells and enchantments he had learned, that was only ritual, the knowledge necessary to tap the dark energies that churned in the world around him, in the many parallel universes whose science was yet undiscovered. In addition to that knowledge, however, there must be the will, the innate power, to become a mage.

So it was that he felt stronger than ever. The sphere sizzled, burning the air at his extremities, and he willed it to descend into the gorge.

"It's amazing," Keomany whispered.

Inside that sphere, he could hear her perfectly. Peter glanced at her and saw that golden light gleaming in her eyes. A shaft of Spanish morning light fifteen feet wide enveloped them so that the blue sphere of magickal energy was bathed in sunshine. Inside that sphere, Peter could smell fresh air, the breath of his own world, spring in Europe.

It was a gift and he was grateful to Keomany for it.

"When this is done," he said as the sphere dropped more quickly past stone walls and outcroppings, past hidden battlements built centuries past to guard the city from attack. "If we survive, I want to spend more time outside . . . less time alone, in my apartment, with a paintbrush. I've spent far too much time trying to recreate the things I relished in my youth instead of appreciating the world as it is now. The scents on the air. The sound of the wind. I owe you that."

Keomany smiled at him and took a deep breath. Her eyes closed a moment. "Wind chimes. I want to hear the sound of wind chimes again."

But when her eyes opened, there was no wistfulness there, only dark purpose. She nodded at Peter and he in return. He glanced down at the sight that awaited him, the horror they had both been avoiding as they descended. The walls of the Cleft were steep until they reached a plateau on either side where trees and bushes grew. Below that, rock that had calved off the cliffsides over the ages was arranged in strange architecture on the banks of the dry river.

One hundred feet above the rocks.

Eighty.

Fifty.

Peter reached out to hold Keomany's hand. The sphere's integrity wavered only the tiniest bit. He felt it lurch beneath them, an airplane passing through momentary turbulence, an air pocket. The filthy, oily rain and the Tatterdemalion's storm could not be heard from within that protective shield.

"Now," Peter whispered.

Keomany stared downward again, at the enormous brood mother, the colossal insectoid demon that lay curled on its side in the dry riverbed as newborn Whispers slipped from a pouch in its belly. The demon spawn climbed to their feet, shaky as colts at first, and then quickly grew more stable and began to caper across the rocks toward the wall of the gorge, and to climb upward . . . to prey upon the people who still hid away in their homes in Ronda.

The Whispers had not been here long enough to slaughter the whole town. Ronda's tribulations had only just begun. Much of its population might still survive if they could stop this now.

The earthwitch shuddered with revulsion and Peter *felt* that emotion from her, shared it through the connection that was now theirs. Just as he felt the touch of Gaea, felt the pure spirit of the earth, the soul of nature, passing through him. He feared that he might taint it, that somehow the dark magicks he practiced and the horrid deeds he had once performed might stain the radiance of the power now sluicing through him, washing over him from Keomany's spirit into his own.

Then he realized how arrogant a thought that was, the idea that he could have such an impact on something so much greater than he was.

Peter was a conduit only. Like the eternal balance of chaos and order, like his fingers meeting Keomany's, his sorcery twined with the natural magicks that she had tapped. As one they reached downward, the light of the Spanish morning that burned down upon them through that tear between dimensions shone upon the riverbed.

The light of another world, of Gaea herself, touched the soil of this hellish dimension yet again, far more powerful than before. Peter allowed the sphere to sink even closer toward the ground, perhaps twenty feet above the rocks.

The tear between worlds widened. Above them the churning storm was driven back, the black-orange thunderheads ripped asunder, and the area of clear blue sky and golden sunlight widened.

The brood mother began to scream. Where it struck the exposed flesh of her belly, the skin began to blister. The enormous creature curled more tightly in upon itself to hide away from the sunshine, and unlike its offspring, its outer shell protected it.

But as the circle of light widened, the Whispers began to

burn. They ran blindly, hissing, tendril-tongues darting about. Some tried to slip back into their mother's dark embrace but the brood queen had closed herself off to them in order to survive. As they ran, a high keening wail beginning to issue from them like the whistle of a teapot, the Whispers burst into flame one by one.

Their carapaces charred, glowed like burning embers, and then began to disintegrate as the fire ate them. In seconds, those who had been unfortunate enough to be touched by the sun were nothing more than dust. Yet the brood mother remained.

The ground beneath the hideous, massive demon trembled and a fissure opened in the dry riverbed. Though the power flowed through Peter as well, though he tried to expand upon it, tried to paint the walls of the gorge with the light and vibrant life of another world, he had no idea what to expect. More pear trees, he thought.

But there were no trees, this time.

From that fissure in the floor of the river came a sudden torrent of water, a spray that fountained from the dry bed and began to flow over the rocks. The touch of the water made the massive brood mother twitch, but nothing more. It began to splash the demon, to flow around it, and Peter realized what he and Keomany had done with Gaea's power and his own magick.

They had brought the river back. Or at least a part of it.

The gap in the storm above, the calm blue sky, continued to expand slowly. The sunlight shone down and the river water glistened as it flowed. But there were still dozens, perhaps hundreds, of Whispers climbing the walls of the gorge and no telling how many more already up in the city. The slaughter would go on.

For now.

But the Whispers were not their target.

"Now what?" Keomany asked.

Peter frowned. "I'd hoped the sun would take out the mother as well. Looks like a more direct approach is necessary." He glanced at her. "You'll be all right?"

Keomany smiled beatifically. "More than all right."

He wondered what it would have been like to be so infused with the natural spirit, the soul of an entire planet. Likely Gaea had barely touched her, for no single being could contain all of that. He himself had only tasted the essence of that magick and he wanted to languish in it, to invite it in. But it was not to be. A taste was all Peter was ever destined to have.

He broke contact with Keomany. In that instant it was as though every brush with darkness he had ever experienced came rushing back into him. The first time he had slain an enemy in service to his father the emperor, and watched the Turk die on his sword. The night he had laid his throat bare to Karl Von Reinman and let his life drain out into the old vampire's mouth, given himself over to the hunger. All of the death he had wrought upon enemies, and upon those who were only prey, until he had realized that he had always been a warrior and never wanted to be a predator.

His time in Hell. Seemingly endless years of agony. The learning of sorcery, the mastering of magick ... opening himself up again to the ominous powers that ebbed and flowed like the tides across the universe.

When he let go of Keomany's fingers, Peter was reminded of all of that. Reminded of what he was. A bitterness surged up within him, yet it was a sort of melancholy that felt familiar to him. Those touches of darkness, despite his benevolent intentions ... they were what reminded him what it was to be human. They made him a better man.

Peter Octavian, born Nicephorus Dragases, bastard son of an emperor. Monster. Warrior. Mage. But in the end, still just a man. For a long time he had feared that frailty, that simplicity, and now he remembered that once upon a time it had been all he ever wanted. To be simply a man.

Eyes narrowed, he gritted his teeth and felt the magick flowing through him again. He glanced at Keomany and nodded once, and the sphere fell. It hurtled the last twenty feet and dissipated the moment it touched the rocks. Peter landed as though he had leaped from that height. Behind him, Keomany grunted as her feet struck ground, and she rolled, scrambling to get up again. The tear in the fabric of dimensions narrowed slightly above them, the hellstorm pushing at its edges, but Keomany's earth magick was enough.

Peter stood bathed in the sunlight, ten feet from the brood mother. From here it looked even more massive than it had from above, like some whale that had been dragged into the gorge. Its thin outer shell pulsed with life and that skin steamed with the touch of the sun, but did not burn. The stench of the thing, this close, was terrible. Half of the demon was in sunlight, washed in several inches of water where the river spurted up from a fissure in the ground. The other half still lay within the hellish orange light of this dimension, buffeted by the driving rain, dripping with liquid that ran like thickening blood down its side.

This was their only solution. He knew that. If this did not work, he was out of ideas. The Tatterdemalion was far more powerful than anything he had ever imagined. Even the demon lords that had tortured him in Hell were only physical creatures, terrible and cruel, but nothing like this thing, like this . . . Hellgod.

Peter purposefully walked out of the sunlight, into the awful darkness and the roiling storm. The wind bent him over with its strength, the greasy rain slicked his hair and soaked his clothing anew. He ran the back of his hand across the stubble on his chin and then he raised both hands above his hand.

"You think we're insignificant!" he screamed. "But you made a mistake. You never should have shown yourself to me. You never should have let me know we'd gotten your attention. The only reason you'd have done that—whatever the hell you are—is if we could hurt you."

Jaw clenched, Peter lowered his gaze, staring at the brood mother. "And now the time's come," he whispered, the storm stealing the words as they issued from his lips. "Time to hurt you."

The energy around his hands blazed more brightly. Once more he began to lift off the ground, barely even realizing it. The magick was in his control, but only just. Sorcerous power filled him, raised him, thrumming through his body. There in the hideous orange-black storm—only a few feet from the splash of sunlight from his homeworld—Peter Octavian raised his hands above his head and let the power wash through him. His teeth bled, and the backs of his eyes hurt, and his bones ached down deep.

The light that glowed around his upraised hands shifted from blue to a deep, bruise-dark purple. Slowly, the mage brought his palms together, whispering words in a language only the darkness knew. Sparks of gleaming ebony began to circle round one another in the midst of that energy contained between his palms—a galaxy at his fingertips.

Peter brought his hands together, grabbed hold of the magick that burned there as though he were Zeus snatching bolts of lightning from the air. The purple light solidified in his hands and sliced his skin, a hiltless sword whose blade was sharp as glass.

In silence he moved, leaping up through the rain, the sorcerous blade above his head, a beacon of magick whose light flickered up through the Cleft and off the bridge and the buildings far above.

The brood mother still lay half in, half out of the splash of sunlight Keomany had brought through, Gaea's light. But the gigantic demon must have sensed Peter, or understood his words. As he fell down upon her with that magickal blade, the monstrosity unfurled its body, moving far faster than could be expected of such a massive creature. It opened up, and muscles undulating beneath that hideous shell, it rolled onto its belly, onto the dozens of legs there. In a sliver of a moment he saw the wide wet slit of its pouch from which thousands of Whispers had been born. Even now Peter saw the limbs of one of the mother's children poking from that birth canal, hiding from the sunlight that might destroy it.

The brood mother whipped its head around toward him and he saw countless amber eyes glowing there. Its maw opened as if it might attack or spew some unknown effluent upon him, but despite its incredible speed, it was too late.

The mage brought down the keen edge of the blade formed from the most ancient of magicks and it split the brood mother's face in two, slashing eyes and flesh and black, twisted bone beneath. The sorcerous power of that sword burned the flesh like acid, eating away at its victim, spreading like fire as the brood mother screamed.

Its body thrashed but the damage was done. Its tail end

whipped around, hauling itself out of the earthlight, but Peter had already retreated. The brood mother howled, a sound like a thousand bats squealing out their radar cries.

Peter stumbled back toward Keomany, who stared in abject horror at the result of his magick. Under the light of her golden gaze and as he reentered the earthlight that spilled through the dimensional tear above her, he felt filthy and vulgar, his own sorcery a thing to be despised.

But the sword still burned in his hands. His palms still dripped blood where the blade had sliced them. The brood mother had been a monster, had given birth to uncountable demons, but he had no sense that it was any more than a breeder, a mindless beast, no better than an animal. Its spawn were evil, he had seen that in them, felt it. But killing this creature brought him no sense of victory. None at all.

Hundreds were likely already dead in Ronda, maybe thousands. Dozens of buildings were already destroyed. And it was only beginning. If Wickham was any indication, other cities had already suffered worse . . . the fires and the slaughter and the torture . . . and the Tatterdemalion was only going to spread his influence farther, dragging city after city into this tiny Hell dimension, this place the Hellgod might well have created solely for this purpose.

Peter did not know why the Tatterdemalion had not simply swarmed across the earth with his Whispers, following nightfall around the world, bringing this storm to each new time zone and blotting out the sun. Why take it piece by piece instead of taking it all?

Unless he couldn't take it all, Peter thought. His mind flooded all at once with a barrage of questions and suppositions, all of which revolved around the idea that the Tatterdemalion had to do things slowly because it was not as powerful as it appeared to be. *What if it's only a god in this little pocket universe?* he wondered.

With the storm screaming and the rain pouring down and the death and destruction the Hellgod had wrought, its power was all around him. Yet he had already reasoned that it had given up Wickham too easily, that they had *taken* it from him. And had the Tatterdemalion been unable or unwilling to cross into the portion of Wickham that Peter and Keomany had returned to its rightful place?

All of these thoughts churned in his mind. Peter knew the answer was here, knew that the key to stopping the Hellgod was not in snatching back sections of the earth that it had stolen, but somewhere in the morass of questions he had about its limitations.

In the midst of the chaos storm he and Keomany stood in the dimensional rip and Peter glanced over at her once more. The rocks around her feet had been pushed aside by new plant growth that erupted from the ground. Olive branches grew and twisted around her legs like vines.

"What now?" she asked, and her voice had changed. It seemed almost to ring in his ears.

Peter took a quick look around. There were still Whispers climbing the walls of the Cleft—the last that would ever be born of their mother, though he was not foolish enough to think it was impossible there was another brood mother somewhere. But killing the Whispers would avail them nothing at the moment.

Nothing.

He stared up into the storm in fury and frustration. His fingers clenched the magickal blade more tightly, and fresh blood flowed on his palms and dripped to the ground. He had expected some kind of reaction, thought that the death of the brood mother would draw the Tatterdemalion down where it might be more vulnerable.

"Damn you!" Peter screamed, stepping once more from the sweet-smelling shaft of earthlight that surrounded Keomany. "You're so damned all-powerful? What are you afraid of, then?"

Behind him, Peter heard Keomany gasp and call his name. He turned and saw that she was pointing up at the bridge, at the extraordinary architecture that had gone into constructing its arches.

Atop the bridge, four figures stood looking over the edge. Allison was one of them and he knew Kuromaku must be among the others, for that had been her goal, rescuing him. But he could not make out their faces from this distance and did not know who the other two were.

Peter glanced at Keomany again, about to suggest that they ascend the gorge and meet the others to determine how to proceed. But before he could speak, there was a sudden lull in the storm, a quiet, ironically, that silenced him. The wind died and the rain was falling straight down. The thunderheads had grown darker all across Ronda and they hung heavier, lower, as though the storm might fall upon the city and swallow it whole. It roiled and pulsed as though it was alive.

Which, of course, it was.

Looks like I got your attention after all, Peter thought.

Then green lightning began to arc up from the ground, piercing those pustulent clouds, and thunder like the world was exploding began to roll across the sky, so loud Peter felt it inside, thumping against his heart.

Lightning hit the bridge.

JACK Devlin had studied sorcery for most of his adult life. In his magickal arsenal were a handful of summoning spells, wards and bindings, exorcisms, and a total of three deadly attacks that were specific to some of the demon species he had dealt with in the past. Nowhere in his studies did it say anything about defense against lightning.

And he didn't have a fucking thing that would hold an eighteenth-century bridge together when it was dead set on falling apart.

As the first bolts of lightning struck the bridge, he was thrown to his knees. Sophie Duvic—the French woman who was companion to the vampire Kuromaku—screamed and swore loudly. For his part, Kuromaku said nothing. He was badly injured, barely able to stand on his own two feet but making a go of it. The grimly handsome Asian vampire would not die of his wounds—a vampire could not bleed to death—but there were other ways for him to die if he could not fight to stay alive.

Several bolts of lightning struck the bridge simultaneously. Enormous chunks of masonry blew out of the chest-high walls on either side, and in the center of the bridge a sinkhole appeared in the stone. It had begun to collapse.

Kuromaku staggered to the edge of the bridge and his head struck on the stone wall. He went down hard and Sophie was right behind him, crawling, shouting at him that now was not the time, that she was not going to let him die now after all they had been through. Father Jack could hear the hysteria creeping into her voice and was just amazed it had taken her this time.

The lightning came again, the thunder right on top of them now, and when it bellowed across the sky, Jack clapped his hands to his ears and cried out in pain. Beneath his feet the bridge began to sway.

Allison Vigeant ran past him, struggling to keep her feet, and went to Sophie and Kuromaku. He knew he ought to go to them, that as a man of God he should stay and help them get off the bridge. And he *was* praying to his God, that was for sure.

But Father Jack hesitated. He didn't know these people. *Get your ass off the bridge right now!* his mind screamed. But he couldn't do that. It would have made him no better than Bishop Gagnon, and Jack would not have been able to stomach that.

"Damn it," he muttered, and he ran toward the other three, knowing that he had made an irrevocable choice, that he had thrown his fate together with theirs. And then he realized how foolish a thought that was, that his fate had been entwined with theirs from the moment this hellish place had swallowed him.

With inhuman strength Allison hefted Kuromaku off the ground. Father Jack reached for one of his arms to help him walk but the vampire pulled away, indicating that he was all right. Sophie gave the priest a grateful look and they all started toward the north side of the bridge. The collapsed portion was ahead, but south would lead back to the Whispers and none of them wanted to risk that.

The wind buffeted them. Father Jack pressed himself together with the others, a wall of flesh—mortal and immortal—marching across the bridge as it trembled with each lightning strike, each rumble of thunder. The oily, mucous rain made their feet slide on the stone but they did not slow.

The storm fell upon them. A tornado finger dipped down

out of the clouds like the blood red hand of the devil himself and touched the bridge just in front of them. The winds tore the stone away in massive chunks, ripped a wound in the granite structure of the bridge, and it gave way, falling apart beneath their feet.

Once more Father Jack screamed to God for salvation. But there was no answer. Out of the corner of his eye he saw Allison transform into a falcon again, and out of reflex he began to formulate in his mind the spell that would allow him to levitate. But then a piece of masonry struck him in the chest, cracking ribs and knocking the air out of him, and Father Jack was falling. He slammed into Kuromaku and their limbs tangled as they fell. He heard Sophie calling out to God in her native tongue but her pleas garnered no more response than his own.

Amid the rubble of that massive bridge, they tumbled down into the Cleft of Ronda. As they fell, Father Jack felt a kind of peace envelop him that he had never known, a certainty of faith that he had always longed for but never found.

His time had come.

He did not flail as he fell, but gave himself up to God's will.

With the ground rushing up toward him, the bridge collapsing all around him, Father Jack closed his eyes.

And he stopped falling. The sensation of plummeting ceased and he felt his hair standing up with static electricity. His eyes snapped open again and everything around him was a bright, glowing green for he was seeing it through the magickal field of energy with which Peter Octavian had caught him and Kuromaku and Sophie.

"Oh, Jesus, thank you," Jack whispered, glancing up at the sky, where he saw the tear in the heavens where the light of the Spanish morning poured through, a hole in this Hell.

A moment later the descent began again, but more slowly this time. Peter brought them down to the rocky riverbank. The falcon flew down to join them and Allison took human form once more. Jack's chest ached where he had been struck and a sharp pain confirmed for him that he had cracked a couple of ribs, but he was alive.

Relief washed through him, but along with it came awe. He stared at Peter and Keomany and marveled at the changes in them. The slim, delicately beautiful Asian woman had become a kind of goddess in her own right, at least at first glance. Golden light spilled and misted from her eyes, and in the midst of the sunshine that burned through into this Hell from another world, her hair blew in a breeze that was not part of this storm. Keomany was rooted to the place she stood, branches wound around her legs, moving slowly with a lover's caress.

Then there was Peter. If Keomany had taken on the aspect of a goddess, Father Jack saw in Octavian another face, the grim visage of a dark god of war or some terrible archangel. Hair and clothing drenched, still he burned with a purplish glow that sent sparks snaking along his body, and in his hands he held a long, massive sword crafted from color and fire and light, from pure magick. Blood dripped from his hands.

"Jack," Peter said, his voice somehow carrying through the storm. He smiled, but there was something unsettling in the expression. "Good to see you again."

Then, holding his sorcerous blade in one hand, Peter stepped into the darkness, away from the gash Keomany had torn between worlds. The woman, Sophie, had been helping Kuromaku to stand but now the vampire stepped away from his human companion and despite his wounds he stood tall. Peter went to him and took Kuromaku into his arms and the two embraced as though they were brothers long apart.

"Peter," Allison said, gaze darting around, on guard as the thunder boomed and rolled across the sky. Lightning still danced above but the storm seemed to have calmed some. "Your plan isn't working. Can you get us out of here, back to our own world? Maybe from there we can—"

Octavian whirled on her, deep furrows in his brow. To Father Jack the mage looked somehow younger, his face thinner, his eyes brighter.

"Stop, Allison," Peter growled. "If we can't stop it here, there won't be a home to return to."

The vampire woman nodded. "All right. We stay and fight in Hell."

Peter shook his head. "This isn't Hell. Trust me."

Father Jack turned his back on them and stared up at the storm, at the hideous tower of orange-black thunderclouds, and he was certain he saw a face there, a terrible visage gazing down at them and silently laughing.

"You're right," the priest told him. "We make our own Hells. This is just another demon with a fucking attitude problem."

—————

PETER could no longer feel the slashes in his hands. His skin burned with the power that coursed through him. Every bone and muscle seemed to ache and yet he felt as though he could have leveled the city with the magick that was in him.

Fury and despair warred in his heart, but he would not give in to either. He glanced at the others—at courageous Jack Devlin and fiercely loyal Allison, at his brother Kuromaku, who was much missed and now had been crippled, and at the beautiful yet ordinary human woman who stood by him.

Peter turned his back on them and stared at Keomany. The earthwitch raised her chin, feeling his attention upon her. Gold light seeped from her eyes and danced in her black silken hair. She smiled at him.

"No time like the present, Peter," Keomany said. "You got its attention but it still isn't coming. It's *afraid* of you. I want to hurt the bastard. My parents' ghosts won't rest until I do."

Peter nodded. "Let's do it, then." He turned to the others but his focus was mainly on Allison and Kuromaku, undead warriors, trusted friends. "Be ready for anything."

He raised his hands and then opened them. Drops of blood hit the stones at his feet and a burst of light splashed from his palms; the sword he had conjured was gone. The mage stepped into the shaft of sunlight that still burned through the storm above, giving them a glimpse of the beautiful blue sky that ought to have hung above Ronda on this morning. He inhaled the scents of flowers carried on the breeze.

Keomany reached her hands out to him. The branches that

curled around her legs seemed to grow higher up her thighs, holding on to her more tightly. She smiled and in that moment Peter felt he was gazing into the face of Gaea herself.

He took her hands, felt sharp pain as the cuts in his hands brushed her palms, his blood smearing her skin. This time when he began to summon the magick within him, he did not feel the resistance he had felt before. His sorcery might have been woven from chaos, and her earthcraft tapping the natural soul of the world, the order of things, but chaos and order had met before. They danced eternally, knew each other intimately.

Peter whispered ancient words and Keomany glanced over at him and nodded as though she understood. He thought perhaps she had. Gaea, after all, was far older than the beings that had first wielded the sorcery Peter had at his disposal.

"Let's take the son of a bitch down," Keomany said.

The mage smiled at the incongruity of her coarse words coming from the lips of a goddess of purity. Then he nodded again.

"By all means."

Keomany bent toward him and kissed him gently on the lips. A spasm went through Peter and he threw his head back. Something had passed from her to him, a small piece of the spirit that filled her. He not only could taste and smell the air around him, but could feel what was beyond this small patch of sunlight, could sense the world. Through the connection they had made, he *felt* Gaea, felt the earth.

"What are you doing, my brother?" Kuromaku asked, his low voice soothing as always.

Peter glanced at him, there in the storm. "Taking it back," he replied.

His eyes fluttered closed. He could feel the branches that had wrapped around Keomany's legs and could hear the splash of water that had erupted out of the ground ten feet away, a kind of fountain that flowed down into the dry riverbed and off away out of the gorge. In his mind's eye he could see the exact size and shape of the tear Keomany had ripped between dimensions.

From the two of them, earthwitch and mage, power emanated. They reached out together with the power that raged through the circuit they created and they *pushed*.

Peter felt it give way even before he heard the astonished gasp of Kuromaku's friend and the appreciative mutterings of Father Jack and Allison. He opened his eyes and saw that they were all bathed in sunlight now, that shoots of green plant life had spurted up from between the rocks at their feet. Above, the swath of blue sky had opened wider, pushing the storm back.

Keomany's fingers tightened around his hands and the pain in the gashes in his palms barely registered. He gave her his magick, helped to connect her to Gaea, and he relished the way it felt to touch the earth spirit. Keomany laughed happily and golden mist poured from her eyes. Another wave of power pulsed from the two of them and the rocks and trees trembled. The entire Cleft of Ronda was returned to the world in which it belonged. The ruins of the bridge were painted with morning light, showing the way portions of the arches still stood, jagged remnants of brilliant architecture. The breach stretched to include the ramparts to the south of the gorge and the state-owned hotel that sat upon the north wall of the Cleft.

With a roar, the river flowed again. Allison and Father Jack had to move farther up the banks to avoid being washed away as the water raced down to fill the bed of the river, splashing and rolling and at last returning to the course it had followed forever.

"You're doing it!" Father Jack told them. "Thank the Lord, you're doing it!"

Peter had known it was an almost impossible feat; that it was not merely Ronda, but Derby and Hidalgo and who knew how many other cities that had been gathered here in this Hell, stacked one beside the other. But he allowed himself the tiniest spark of hope.

His heart soared.

Together, he and Keomany pushed farther.

But this time, something pushed back. A crack of thunder so loud it shook the walls of the gorge and resounded across the sky. Keomany cried out in anguish and Peter felt a spike of pain that raced up his spine and seemed to stab into his

brain. Blackness swam at the edges of his vision and he fell
to his knees. Even as his hopes were dashed, though, something tugged at the back of his mind, a niggling little bit of
observation that he could not avoid. When the Hellgod had
pushed back, he had felt something, a connection not unlike
the one Keomany had to Gaea, to her own world.

But this was a connection to somewhere else. The power
of the Tatterdemalion was not of this dimension. Peter had
suspected that the Hellgod was not of this tiny universe, but
now he *felt* it, and it made a new kind of sense to him. The
demon was a visitor here, just as they were.

We make our own Hells, Father Jack had said. And Peter
now felt certain that the Tatterdemalion had made this one,
created this pocket dimension in order to have a place to
torment his conquests, to drag the cities of Earth and per-
petrate his horrors upon its people.

Peter shook his head, clearing his vision, and realized that
he was no longer holding Keomany's hands.

"No, oh no please!" Sophie cried.

Peter saw Keomany, then. She had collapsed on the rocks
at the riverside. She was moving, alive, and her eyes still
glimmered with a faint golden glow. But all around them the
storm raged in again, the blue patch torn in the sky above
began to narrow and the sunlight to disappear, eaten by the
wind and the rain and the power of a Hellgod that had at last
deigned to pay attention to them.

The light contracted, the dimensional rip closed until all
that remained was a shaft of light perhaps six feet around,
just enough to outline Keomany there on the rocks. It was a
spotlight upon the earthwitch as she sat up, buried her face
in her hands, and began to weep.

"No," Peter whispered to himself as the wind struck him
again and the greasy rain struck his face, ran down his cheeks
like oily tears.

"Whispers!" Allison shouted.

The mage glanced around to see that she was right. The
southern wall of the gorge was dotted with the skeletal demons as they clambered down the sheer rock face. Whatever
their instructions had been before, the Tatterdemalion must
have changed his mind.

Father Jack came up beside Peter, standing tall, his hands held up, ready to cast a spell. "I guess you finally got its attention."

Then, amid the wailing of the wind, he heard another sound, a scream carried to him on the storm, just the hint of it reaching his ears before being whipped away again. Peter glanced around, wondering where it had come from. The others were all preparing to fight off the Whispers that came quickly down the gorge like a hundred giant spiders. But that scream . . . Peter heard it again. A voice, crying out in terror . . . crying his name.

He looked up at the ruins of the bridge, and there he saw her, hanging above the jagged remains of the arches that had supported the structure, no more than two hundred feet in the air. She was nude, her body streaked with gashes Peter presumed had been made by the talons of Whispers. The wind swirled around her and she hung there, dangling in the breeze like a rag doll.

Peter whispered her name. And then he shouted it.

"Nikki!"

CHAPTER 21

WITH a snarl Peter spread his arms wide and there was an audible pop as the air crackled with energy and a sphere of verdant light blossomed into existence around him. He felt the magick all through him now and his bones no longer hurt. It was as though his physical form had been transmuted into pure magick, as though the energy that swirled around him was just as much his flesh as the fingers that directed it.

An afterthought, he glanced at Allison. The vampire looked almost feral, crouched and ready for battle, her red hair slicked back on her scalp by the rain.

"Keep them safe," he told her.

Then he rose up off the ground, energy sphere lifting him upward with dizzying speed. He shot toward the ruins of the bridge, aware of his surroundings—of the Whispers clambering down the cliffs into the gorge and the lightning and the storm that was ripping at the city—but focused now only on the fragile, pale, nude body of his lover hanging there above the jagged ruins.

In his mind's eye he saw the face of Meaghan Gallagher, a woman he had loved who had sacrificed her life to save others. And he saw Allison, saw her as she had looked the first time they had met, and remembered the way she had

gazed at Cody with love before he had been killed and her
innocence had been ripped from her.

Not Nikki, he thought, teeth clenched so tightly his jaw
hurt. *Not Nikki.*

He would rush to her, envelop her in the protective circle
of his magick, and lower her gently to the ground. He would
cover her nudity with his shirt and investigate the slashes in
her skin, and he would hold her. Peter saw all of this in his
mind and he knew that it had to be.

Once upon a time he had been immortal . . . fate had al-
tered him, given him a second chance at humanity. At first
he had embraced the opportunity, relished the idea that time
would one day run out for him. But it had been centuries
since he had walked among his fellow humans as just an
ordinary man, since he had had to really *live* in the world.
And so he had retreated to old patterns, keeping mostly to
himself. He might have claimed immortality again at any
time—had Allison or Kuromaku bring him into the Shadows
once more—but instead he found himself trapped by his desire to be human, and his terror of what that meant.

No second chances. That was the truth of humanity. As
an immortal he could live as he pleased and watch the world
go by around him, years passing with the speed of a single
dawn to dusk. But mortality meant he only had one chance,
one journey. And this hard truth had wrought in him a fear
of living that left him very much alone.

All of this went through his mind in the seconds it took
for him to levitate himself to where Nikki hung naked and
bleeding above the ruins. But as adrenaline rushed through
him, he knew she would be all right, that she had to be, for
despite his power he was just a man now, mortal, and he
could not bear the thought of going on without her.

The wind raged around the sphere, battering against it,
slowing Peter down. He was perhaps twenty feet from her
when he saw the first rags whipping around in the storm.
Strips of cloth, dishrags, clean laundry plucked from a
clothesline somewhere.

Ice formed along his spine.

In the time it took him to travel ten feet, rags and laundry
flew together, layered upon one another, to create the shape

of a man. In an eyeblink the Tatterdemalion had arrived, his arms outlined beneath bath towels and a clutch of grease-stained mechanics' rags, burning eyes cloaked in a hood fashioned from a pretty, floral-patterned sundress.

The Tatterdemalion held Nikki from behind, the two of them borne aloft on the winds. Its fingers were made of women's panties, twisted into knots by the storm, and it clutched her throat.

"You were warned," the Tatterdemalion said, its voice the whisper of the storm in Peter's ears.

"Nikki," he called to her. Through that sphere and the roar of the wind he could not have expected her to hear him. It took him a moment to dredge up from within him a spell that would have let his voice carry to her as though he were right beside her. A flash of irony went through him that such simple magick should be a challenge to him when sorcery of a more brutal nature was simplicity itself, but he ignored the thought.

This was not a time for subtle magicks.

He had no doubt that the Tatterdemalion would hear his voice, regardless of the storm. After all, it *was* the storm.

"Give her to me," Peter demanded. Magickal flames licked up from his fingers and the sphere around him took on a reddish hue.

The wind blew the sundress-cloak across its face and Peter saw the outline of the Tatterdemalion's features, ridged and gruesome, with a protruding lower jaw and a mouth that stretched Jack-o'-lantern wide. With the cotton over its face, he could see it grin.

"You have become quite a nuisance. And I did warn you. Foolish mage. I am still adding more of your world to this one, but I don't have room for all of it. There will be cities left, entire nations, in fact. But someone will have to help rebuild; someone will have to hunt the demons that all of these breaches into your world have unleashed. Every hole I have made was torn through several other places as well . . . it will be years before you have catalogued all of the things that now run free in your world.

"They need you at home, Octavian.

"I give you a second opportunity. Take your friends," it

said, the voice of the wind now joined by a rumble of nearby
thunder. The wind whipped the cloak away from its face
again and there was only darkness beneath that hood now,
not even those glowing eyes. Cloth fingers raised Nikki's
unconscious face up so that Peter could see her clearly. Her
eyelids fluttered and she seemed about to wake.

*"Take your lover and return to your world. Pick up the
pieces. And be glad I don't have enough room for all of
Earth in here."*

The Tatterdemalion seemed to offer Nikki up to Peter,
and yet it proffered her only tentatively, prepared at any moment to destroy her. It had brought her here like it had
brought everything here. It had somehow captured her and
yet kept her alive.

Puzzle pieces clicked into place in his mind. Peter hesitated, let the Tatterdemalion assume that he was considering
its demands. He glanced back down into the gorge, where
Father Jack and Kuromaku fought with blade and spell
against the Whispers returning to the site of their mother's
murder. Keomany kept Sophie safe inside the single shaft of
sunlight that still streamed from the breach in the Tatterdemalion's world, that umbilical back to the Earth dimension.

"There will not be a third opportunity."

As Peter turned, lightning flashed, casting shadows of
Nikki's fragile nakedness, illuminating the face within the
cloak of the Tatterdemalion at last. Peter winced at the demon's visage, but not merely from its hideousness. The face
was constructed of gravel and dust and embers from a fire.
As he had always thought, there was nothing within those
rags to animate them. Nothing within.

Only power from outside. Only the storm.

He hesitated.

A dust devil swept up from the ruins of the bridge, a
slender finger of tornado that brought sharp-edged bits of
crumbled masonry swirling up toward them. Stone struck
Nikki's right leg and Peter heard the sickening crunch of
bone shattering, saw fresh blood spilling from the wound. A
sliver glanced off her arm and slashed her shoulder and her
left breast.

"But you won't just give her to me and let me leave."

Peter glared into the Tatterdemalion's nothing face, dread filling him just as surely as did the magick that coursed through him.

When he had looked down, Kuromaku had raised his sword in a gesture that the two had used many centuries before in another war on Spanish soil. The gesture translated into one word. *Stall.*

"Of course not," the Tatterdemalion said. *"You and the others depart. When you have gone, your lover will be returned to you there. Go now."*

Peter nodded. "All right. We'll go. But I want you to answer one question first."

Lightning flashed across the orange-black sky. The Tatterdemalion hesitated and Peter saw that it pulled Nikki closer against itself as though suspicious of his capitulation.

"Ask."

Peter narrowed his eyes and his nostrils flared. He asked the question, though he already knew the answer.

"What are you so afraid of?"

—————

KUROMAKU had seen his old comrade-in-arms, his friend and brother, only rarely since Peter had become human again. Never had he been so grateful for the presence of another. His honor as a warrior, his skill as a ronin, would not allow him to confess, even in his private thoughts, that there was no hope of victory. But it was clear to him that this had been the case only minutes before.

He was crippled.

It was not the gunshot wounds that had done this, but the effect of those first two bullets, the chemical they carried. Still he thirsted for blood, perhaps more now than at any time in the past sixty or seventy years—since the terrible events one night in Hong Kong—and still he was very difficult to kill. But he could not change his form, could not shapeshift at all. He had seen Allison fly, transform herself into a falcon and spread her wings, and already it broke his heart.

Kuromaku was hollow. Miraculously, through all of this,

the warrior still held his katana, but his truest weapon was gone.

Still, crippled and bleeding and hollow, he had been trained a samurai. If he died, it would be with honor. This Hellgod the others talked about, this Tatterdemalion, it would not have presented Nikki, would not be parleying with Peter right now, if it weren't afraid of him. That meant that Peter could hurt the demon. But Kuromaku knew the mage well enough to know he would not sacrifice Nikki to do that.

So Nikki had to be taken out of the equation.

The pain of his wounds was terrible. The thirst was upon him. He did not need the blood to survive, but every drop that seeped from the bullet holes in his flesh made him crave it all the more. There were no fangs in his mouth but his lips were pulled back in a rictus as though he might bare them.

The Whispers paid the price for his pain and thirst. Kuromaku had fought with injuries before, long ago when he was still human, still merely a samurai instead of a vampire ronin. Now the Whispers scrambled across the rocks, their scythe-like limbs clacking on the ground, and they waded across the water that remained in the Guadalevin, which was going dry once more now that the earthwitch had been stopped.

Kuromaku stood ankle deep in the water and met them as they came. He spun and hacked and thrust and that katana did not fail him, nor did his injured body. The trickling water seeped with filthy demon blood and became thick with the viscous rain. Demon corpses, shattered carapaces, severed limbs and heads began to build up around him and he had to step back.

To his left the priest, Jack, had barely managed to stay alive. There seemed only two magickal attacks he had mastered that were effective against the Whispers, one of which caused them to burst into flame from within and the other of which only seemed to paralyze them. The priest was a slender, bony man with cracked eyeglasses who prayed loudly to his God. And perhaps, Kuromaku thought, his God was with him, for somehow despite his pitiful magick and the exhaustion evident in the priest's features, he had managed to hold his own.

The priest had dignity and courage. Kuromaku was honored to fight beside him.

Like Peter, Allison had been a welcome sight upon her first appearance. According to the priest and Sophie, she had saved Kuromaku's life. He was grateful, but also simply pleased to be in her presence, despite his envy that she still had the ability to change herself and he did not. She was beautiful and yet full of despair, a tragic heart, but she was fierce. In the first few moments when the Whispers attacked, she had killed more than a dozen of them.

But now Kuromaku and Father Jack were on their own.

Back a ways from the bank of the river, Sophie hewed close to the earthwitch, Keomany. The witch was not powerful enough to defeat the Hellgod's sorcery, but she still retained a link to their world, to their dimension. Sunlight bathed the two women and prevented the Whispers from getting near to them, though fifteen or twenty of the demons stalked the perimeter of that shaft of sunlight as if searching for a way in. Sophie was safe, as long as Keomany was with her.

Several times Sophie called to Kuromaku to warn him of demons slipping stealthily up on his flank, and he managed to defend himself in time. Now when he glanced back at Sophie, he saw that Keomany had begun again. Her eyes glowed with golden light that cascaded like a river of tears down her face and her hair had begun to blow again in a wind that did not come from the storm. Fresh shoots erupted from the rocks around her, flowers blossomed on the ground.

The rift between dimensions widened once more, just slightly, and sunlight washed over the Whispers that had been stalking around Keomany and Sophie. The demons raised their darting tongues and hissed as their carapaces steamed and blistered, and then they disintegrated in a flash of embers.

Kuromaku glanced over at Father Jack. "Now!" he called.

The priest nodded, finishing a spell in Latin that knocked a trio of Whispers back away from him. The demons fell into the shallow water and twitched in pain from the impact, but they survived.

Then, side by side, Kuromaku and Jack Devlin ran along

the bank of the river toward the rubble and ruin of the devastated bridge. In the air above what remained of the arches that had been the foundation of the bridge, Kuromaku saw Peter levitating in a sphere of magickal energy that burned around him as it shifted from green to crimson. A wind tore down from the Tatterdemalion where the rag-creature hung, holding on to Nikki, and a twist of churning air brought debris up to batter her, the sharp rocks gashing fresh wounds in her bare flesh.

"We need a clear view of it," Father Jack called to Kuromaku as he stumbled, picking his way across the rubble.

Kuromaku glanced back at the Whispers giving chase but paid them no mind. They had seconds to spare in which to act out their plan. Still, he did not bother to tell the priest that a clear view was not going to help them.

Father Jack stopped and planted his feet. Kuromaku heard the clack of Whispers' talons on the rocks behind him. He raised his katana and the priest grabbed hold of the hilt as well, his own hands laid over Kuromaku's. Father Jack rattled off a brief stream of Latin—the same spell he had been using against the Whispers, the one that had caused them to immolate from within.

"Lord, deliver us," the priest said.

Kuromaku heard the words only because of a momentary lull in the storm. The wounded vampire felt the magick pass into his hands and into his sword. The hilt thrummed with sorcerous power and then, unseen, the spell was cast from the tip of the blade.

In the air, in the midst of confrontation with Peter, the Tatterdemalion burst into flames, rags and clothing igniting in an instant. Blazing with fire, it stretched an arm out toward them, cloth finger indicating its attackers with sinister portent.

With a crack of thunder, lightning flashed out of the sky and struck them both. Father Jack went rigid, screaming, and his eyes burst, his hair catching on fire. Kuromaku felt his own hair begin to burn, felt the lightning shooting through him, every muscle taut and shrieking with pain. He jittered where he stood for several seconds after the lightning had struck and receded, and then Kuromaku fell to the rocks be-

side the corpse of Father Jack Devlin, his nostrils filled with
the stench of charred flesh.

Peter had not known what Kuromaku had planned but he
had been certain of its intent—to get Nikki away from the
Tatterdemalion and provide him an opening to act. He had
risked driving the Hellgod over the edge of reason in order
to distract it, gambling that Kuromaku would make his move
in the meantime.

Kuromaku had come through.

And he had paid the price for his valor, struck by lightning, his body smoking even now where it lay on the rocks
beside the corpse of Father Jack Devlin. Kuromaku might
yet survive, but despite his dabbling in magick, Jack had
been only human. He was surely dead.

"Damn you!" Peter screamed at the Tatterdemalion.

But it wasn't listening. The rags and clothing that the
Hellgod had brought to life, a cotton homunculus, where
aflame. The viscous rain fell in a torrent now, dousing those
flames, but there were seconds to spare when the Hellgod
was distracted by the plight of the scarecrow face it had
offered up to them in effigy.

Nikki's eyes were fully open now. She was rigid, still
trapped in the tempest that coalesced to keep her dangling
there in the sky, but she met Peter's gaze. The flames on the
Tatterdemalion scorched her skin and she cried out in pain.

Something just past Nikki and the burning Tatterdemalion
caught Peter's eye and instantly he understood the rest of the
plan Kuromaku had laid. Battered by the tumultuous winds,
the falcon flew at the Tatterdemalion from behind.

Tendrils of magickal flame—his own lightning—snaked
from Peter's fingers, replenishing the crimson sphere of sorcery that held him aloft. Though it had been five years since
he had become human again, he bared his teeth as though
he were flashing needle fangs.

Just as it would have collided with the Tatterdemalion,
the falcon dispersed into a cloud of mist, swept around the
Hellgod even as the rains finally doused the last of the
flames, and then Allison Vigeant coalesced in human form
once more. Even as she took flesh, Allison reached out and
wrapped her arms around Nikki.

Allison tore Nikki—naked, bleeding, and terrified—away from the Tatterdemalion and the two of them fell.

The Hellgod screamed in fury. Thunder rolled across the sky and lightning tore through the state hotel on the edge of the Cleft of Ronda. Arcs of electricity from the sky shot down into the gorge. Peter thrust out his left hand and with the same sorcery he was using to hold himself aloft he snatched Allison and Nikki when they were less than fifty feet from the ground. He slowed their descent but did not stop it.

His attention could stay with them only a moment, and he was forced to let them drop the last eight or ten feet, but he counted on Allison to take the brunt of the fall.

"A terrible mistake, Octavian!" the Tatterdemalion screamed, the floral sundress pasted to its face again, its mouth wide as it roared its fury at him. *"This is my world!"*

Peter sneered through the scrim of scarlet magick that separated them. "Yes, your world. Your plaything. But not the dimension you come from. You said it yourself. You brought Nikki here, just like you brought everything else!"

The Tatterdemalion faltered slightly, and Peter knew that he was right about all of it. The mage opened his arms wide and the sphere of magick around him burst outward and enveloped the Tatterdemalion, trapping it inside with him.

"Father Jack said it, before you killed him. He said we make our own Hells. And that's what you did."

"Fool! You cannot destroy me! I am not even truly here, only my essence, only my influence."

The Tatterdemalion exploded in a burst of energy that singed Peter's face and clothes. The rags and clothing whipped at him, flying around inside the sphere, beating on the crimson prison Peter had trapped it in, lashing at their captor.

Peter Octavian smiled grimly. "I know that. I *felt* it, the world you really come from. This place isn't a parallel universe. It's just some toy you created, a pocket you sewed into your own reality. You found my home dimension and saw it was vulnerable, so you built a place where you could be a god.

"Well, now it's time for both of us to go home."

There was a roar inside the sphere with him. The rags whipped at him, bruising and scratching him. Lightning struck that magickal energy but it could not break through. Peter let the sphere drop from the air above the ruins, saw through a veil of red magick the Whispers on the banks of the river. The demons had stopped and stared up with their blank faces at the mage and his captive as the sphere lowered.

The power of the Tatterdemalion strained against Peter's magick and it felt to the mage as though he were being stretched on the rack, his bones and muscles tearing with the effort of keeping the monstrous Hellgod imprisoned.

Below him Peter saw Allison and Nikki, the latter draped in Allison's jacket, running toward the place where Keomany and Sophie stood amid the rift between worlds, that sanctuary of sunlight. Keomany held on to Sophie, preventing her from running to the place where lightning had struck Kuromaku and Father Jack down.

"I will be free!" a voice boomed within the sphere.

Peter felt his ears begin to bleed.

"Like hell," he muttered.

The sphere hovered inches above the ground. The others called to Peter. Allison began to run to him.

"Keep them alive!" he called to her.

Then he expanded the sphere again, feeling as though he were about to be swallowed by the darkness of the storm, as though his very spirit were unraveling. He caught Keomany up in tendrils of his magick and then she was there with him. Peter Octavian stared into those golden, glowing eyes and he felt refreshed by the sunlight that tore through the storm above, following her.

Yet there was doubt and fear on her face. She was the vessel of Gaea, and yet she was also just Keomany Shaw, a shopkeeper from Wickham, Vermont. This was the evil that had destroyed her town and slaughtered her parents, here with her in this magickal enclosure.

"What are you doing?" Keomany asked, her voice pleading. "Peter, what are we supposed to—"

He reached out and touched her face, feeling the smooth skin, smelling the scents of flowers and grass. "You're tied to Gaea now. You feel her and she feels you. Right?"

Keomany nodded, frightened, the golden light in her eyes
faltering.

"Hold on to that connection."

The remnants of the Tatterdemalion whipped at him.
Thunder shook all of Ronda. A building up above the gorge
burst into flames and a piece of the cliff wall calved off and
crashed down into the nearly dry riverbed. It had fallen silent,
however. The Hellgod was also afraid.

Already exhausted and in pain, Peter's body trembled as
he summoned all the sorcerous power he had accumulated
in his time in Hell and in all of his studies. With his right
hand he held on to Keomany and once more he could feel
the umbilical that led back to Gaea through her. More importantly, he could feel yet again the cord that tied the Tatterdemalion to its own reality. Focusing upon that, he reached
out his left hand, fingers splayed wide, and he spoke a single
syllable in the language of Hell.

He tore a hole in the air, a shimmering vertical pool of
mercury, a portal between dimensions. With Keomany beside
him, he stepped through.

All the strength went out of Peter, drained from him, and
he fell to his knees. His stomach lurched and he bent over,
vomiting on the floor, which was as smooth and perfect as
glass. Disoriented, he swayed, and then he felt Keomany's
hand on his shoulder. He reached for her, and when he
glanced up at her face and saw the golden light misting from
her eyes, the light bathed his face and he did not feel quite
so weak and lost.

On his knees the mage looked around.

They were in an enormous chamber, seemingly without
any exit. It was formed of a smooth, reflective surface the
blue of a robin's egg, and though he could not find its source,
there was light pulsing softly within that cavernous cell.

For cell it was.

"Is that it?" Keomany asked, voice low and tinged with
wonder.

Peter only nodded. On the other side of the massive chamber was a single creature, an abomination easily a dozen feet
high. Its body was armored with a carapace not unlike the

Whispers, an indigo shell. Its upper half reminded him of nothing so much as the four-armed, hideous goddess Kali, and its lower half was not unlike that of a scorpion, massive spiked tail wavering up in back of it.

The horror's eyes glowed a rotten orange that seemed all too familiar. It glared at them, took several cautious steps backward, and its massive stinger went rigid, aimed directly at Peter.

The mage had seen the face of the Hellgod only behind a cotton mask and outlined in ash and dust, but there was no mistaking it. The Tatterdemalion spoke then, its impossibly wide mouth opening, protruding lower jaw grinding against the upper. Its words were in a demon-tongue Peter could not even begin to decipher. But one word was familiar.

His own name. "Octavian."

It was horrible, this thing. But Peter was confused by its surroundings. What was this world, this doorless, windowless chamber? This was the Hellgod's home dimension, he was certain of it. But there had to be far more to this reality, more creatures, more demons, even Hellish cities . . . an entire universe. Yet the Tatterdemalion was confined here.

And then he understood.

"It's a prison," he said, the words echoing off the glassy walls.

"Yes," Keomany whispered in response. "In a world of dark magick and evil, it's so monstrous that they have to keep it caged here."

The Hellgod hissed, a hydraulic sound not unlike the voice of the Whispers, and it began to move slowly in at them, stinger twitching as it drew closer. This thing that had been unable to exert its power over its own reality, unable to torment this world with its magick, and so it had turned its attention elsewhere, explored other dimensions, and found one that it saw as easy prey.

"No," Peter said, the one word bouncing all around the cavern. "The fighting's over. You're done."

He felt drained already, as though he had burned up the magick within him like fuel. But it was still there, traces of it, echoes of it. The mage reached out one final time and grabbed Keomany's wrist. He held up his free hand and tendrils of magickal energy exploded from his fingers once more, weaving a new sphere, a new cage for the demon. The magick was blood red now and it felt to Peter as though it were his own blood, leeching out of him as he grabbed the Hellgod, paralyzed it there in that sphere. Its stinger was the only thing still moving, and it struck at its new, smaller prison again and again, and with each blow Peter winced in pain.

Scarlet light gleamed off the smooth glass cavern.

Peter closed his eyes. With Keomany to guide him he felt backward along the same umbilical they had used to arrive here. His sorcery twined with it, caressed the spirit of Gaea.

The mage stepped back into Ronda with Keomany at his side. The storm had begun to subside but the sky was still orange, the rain still thick and oily. He heard a voice call "Holy shit!" as he dragged the Hellgod through into the realm it had created.

But Peter did not stop there. The shaft of sunlight from their dimension, that Spanish morning light, bathed him and Keomany both. But that was not enough.

The next portal was easy to form. It was as though he slipped his fingers into a space between that sunlight and the darkness of the storm and opened up a door. He led Keomany through. He heard the rushing of the Guadalevin River. The earthwitch gasped and she shuddered as she moved into the full presence of her goddess again at last.

The slit in reality remained open behind them and Peter could smell the stink of that Hell blowing through it on the wind from another dimension. They stood at the bottom of the Cleft of Ronda. The river rushed nearby. Above them, however, there was no city. No bridge. And no sign that there had ever been a settlement on that plateau.

The mage glanced around and could see the shimmering barrier that surrounded Ronda and all of the other cities the Tatterdemalion had stolen, but this time they were on the *inside* of the dimensional rift. The Spanish morning light—probably verging on toward afternoon now—still shone above and the breeze still blew in from the mountains carrying the scent of the countryside upon it, but anyone outside the barrier would have seen it as a blank spot upon the world.

It was as though where the city ought to have been, reality was out of focus.

Peter had no idea how the Hellgod had accomplished it. It came from a dimension unknown to this world's sorcerers and its magick was a total mystery.

But the thing he thought of as the Tatterdemalion was *here*, now. The place it had wanted to destroy, and yet had wanted to avoid entering at all costs. If it had the power to take cities away upon a whim, it could have left its prison and come to Earth at any time. With its magicks and its ferociousness it might have conquered.

So why had it not?

There was only one reason that made any sense to Peter. That it could not. It could not wield the storm here, could not send its demon spawn Whispers out in the sun; its magicks had limited power here.

With a grunt of final effort, Peter dragged the blood-red sphere through the tear in reality and into that null field in the Cleft of Ronda, a geography that had been reconstructed in that alternate dimension by the magicks of the Hellgod.

Octavian fell to his knees, too weak to stand a moment longer. Barely able to kneel. The Hellgod was freed as the sphere dissipated, his magick exhausted.

Keomany looked radiant in the sunshine. Her silken hair blew across her face, her expression one of grief, of mourning for her lost parents, and yet of resolution as well.

The Hellgod hissed once more, its carapace steaming in the sunlight but not burning. It raised its stinger and charged at Peter, muttering in its demon-tongue.

A fresh wind kicked up across the rocks and the rushing river, and it seemed to emanate from Keomany herself. She raised her hands and the ground shook, knocking the Hellgod off its many feet. Before it could right itself, branches shot from among the rocks, impaling it.

At the top of the gorge, the ravaged city of Ronda began to fade back into reality. Peter and Keomany found themselves in the midst of another battle, as their friends materialized around them. Allison was protecting Sophie and Nikki from the Whispers, which were incinerated almost instantly by the warm sunshine of that spring day.

The Tatterdemalion thrashed and cried out as more and more shoots of green and wood punched through its carapace from below and then shot out through cracks in its armor above. It was a demon, a monster, but its fear of this place had always been that here its magicks could not protect it. Here, it was only flesh.

A small grove of olive trees grew up to maturity within the space of seconds, and tore the Hellgod apart.

It was the last thing Peter Octavian saw before surrendering at last to the shadows of unconsciousness.

EPILOGUE

"SO the priest, Devlin, he was dead, right?"

The late afternoon sunshine cast long shadows out across the North Platte River. It was the last day of May and the spring air still held a hint of the past winter, a bit of a chill that slipped across the Nebraska countryside when evening was coming on.

Allison Vigeant sat on the grassy bank of the river with her knees pulled up under her chin, remembering another river. She shivered, but it was not from the chill.

"Yeah," she agreed. "That part of the report was true, at least. I didn't . . . I mean, I only knew him for a little while, and it was in the middle of all that, the shit hitting the fan, everything. He had a lot of courage. Peter says he was a nice guy, as well. Quiet. Funny."

Carl Melnick sat beside her on the grass. He looked very out of place there, uncomfortable in his khaki pants and brown suede shoes and a button-down shirt. The aging newsman's salt-and-pepper hair seemed to have thinned somewhat in the weeks since she had last seen him. But she suspected that the whole world felt a little older these days. The official death toll was just shy of eight hundred thousand and it would have been much higher if they had not reclaimed the lost cities when they had. Paris and New York had been brought back only hours after they had disappeared. Another day and . . . Allison did not like to think about that. It was a catastrophe of previously unimaginable proportions.

She shook her head, a bitter chuckle issuing from her lips.

"What?" Carl asked.

"Nothing. Just sad, really. Seems like Devlin was a good guy. A hero, if you go in for the word. We could use a lot more like him. Dealing with what happened."

Melnick cleared his throat and narrowed his gaze, studying her though she averted her eyes. "Dealing with what else might happen. Bad enough when you told the world there really were such things as demons and vampires among us. Now they've gotta get used to the idea that there are things as powerful as this somewhere out there, on the other side of some black hole or something. Stephen fucking Hawking meets *The Exorcist*. Just what the world needed to know."

"At least this time I wasn't the one to have to tell them." Allison glanced up at Melnick and smiled before returning her attention to the gentle rush of the river. It soothed her. "The world will get by. Humans are a pretty resilient species. And I have it on good authority that the earth itself is healthier than ever."

Her old friend raised an eyebrow. "You said something like that before. What's that mean, exactly?"

She had not told him about Keomany Shaw. Now Allison just returned the upraised eyebrow. "Let's just say there's more than one kind of magick, Carl."

Melnick raised both his hands; the skin on them was wrinkled and dry. "All right. Be mysterious. Just don't expect me to trust you again. You promised me you'd give me the story."

Allison did not turn her focus away from the river. "I did. I told you what happened."

"You told me *part* of what happened."

With a long sigh she nodded and turned to him. "What more do you want to know?"

"Kuromaku. The other one like . . . the other vampire," Melnick said tentatively. "What happened to him. Reports from the site didn't say anything about you, but they didn't mention him either. It's like the U.N. wants to pretend vampires don't exist anymore."

"We still exist. We're just not public enemy number one anymore."

Melnick nodded in understanding.

Allison brushed the hair away from her face and went on. "Kuromaku should've died. Even a shadow can't sustain that kind of damage and survive. Without being able to heal himself . . ."

"Should've died. But he didn't. How did you save him? You said Henning shot him with the coagulant."

She flinched and shot him a dark look. "You know I hate that word. It doesn't do anything to the blood."

"Sorry. But it's not supposed to exist, so there's no name for it. The online vampire fanatics call it that."

Allison waved his apology away. "Never mind. You're right, though. Kuromaku'd been shot. He couldn't shift anymore." She pressed her lips together in hesitation and then at last forged on. "There's a cure. A way to reverse it. Pretty simple, actually. He was lying there on the rocks near the priest. Both of them were badly burned but Kuromaku isn't human. He was still alive but he wouldn't have lasted long."

Allison lifted up her left arm and glanced at the smooth, perfect flesh of her wrist. Not a trace of cut or scar. "I cut myself open and I bled onto him. Into his mouth and on the places where he was burned the worst."

The news producer hissed air in through his teeth. "That reversed it? Your blood? It started the process going again in him?"

Allison nodded. "The blood of another vampire. He healed himself after that."

For a long time the two of them just sat there. The shadows grew longer and the eastern sky began to darken. It would be dusk soon. All across the world, nightfall had abruptly taken on a menace far more profound than it had held in centuries.

"So where is he now?"

They had been talking about Kuromaku, but Allison knew that it was not the Japanese vampire that Carl was asking about. Most of the world believed the press—that the U.N.

and the Church of the Resurrection had joined together to combat the evil that had infected the globe, losing some of their best and brightest along the way, yet triumphing in the end. But though the truth could not be confirmed, word had spread of the actions of Peter Octavian, Kuromaku, and Allison herself. It was Peter whom Carl was inquiring about.

Allison gave him an apologetic shrug. "You know I can't tell you that."

"I know. But I have to ask. It's in my nature."

"And it's your job."

Carl's expression changed, a kind of cloud passing over his features. "I'm not going to run with any of this, you know," he told her. "You owed me the truth, Allison, but I can keep it to myself. I've done it plenty of times before, believe it or not. You might be surprised by the things I know."

She gazed at him a long moment before nodding. "I might. But then again, I might not."

Allison stood and brushed the grass from the seat of her blue jeans. "Go ahead and tell the story. As much as you want to. It isn't just your nature, Carl. It's in your blood. Don't forget, once upon a time it was in mine, too. Until something else got in there that I can't get out."

Huffing, out of shape, Carl also rose. Allison embraced him briefly and then stepped back, toward the river. Past him she could see the Range Rover he had rented at the airport. He had come all this way just to see her, had not even asked her what inspired her to meet with him in North Platte, Nebraska, what the hell she wanted to visit this place for at all. It occurred to her that he was a veteran newsman, and that he likely knew exactly what had drawn her here, knew not only that it had once been home to a man she loved, now long dead, but that this was the last place they had been happy.

The last place she had ever been happy.

"What will you do now?" he asked.

Allison slid her arms around herself and shivered, wondering if the onset of dusk was making it colder, or if it was just her.

"There's still work to do. There are so few vampires left

they barely seem worth tracking, but if Octavian's right, all the recent breaches into our world set loose things a lot worse than a couple of ancient vampires hiding out in a cave."

Carl cleared his throat again. When Allison glanced over, this time it was he who would not meet her gaze.

"What?" she asked.

Her old friend looked up. "While they were busy retreating, running for their lives, some of the guys from Task Force Victor saw you kill Commander Henning. They'll be hunting you."

Allison nodded. "It was only a matter of time. If it wasn't this, it would've been something else."

With that she *changed*. Red hair became brown, thick and curly. Hazel eyes turned truly green. Her nose was thinner and there was a splash of freckles across her cheeks.

"Oh, shit," Carl Melnick gasped, eyes wide. It was the only time Allison had ever seen him truly astonished. "I didn't know you could do that."

"Use your head," Allison chided him. "Haven't you ever wondered? We hang on to our old faces the way we hang on to everything else we cherish from the past. It helps us remember who we are. But that doesn't mean we can't let go when the time comes. We can be anything we want to be."

Carl was still staring as she changed once more, her body shifting shape completely, becoming the falcon, a form that had become almost more comfortable for her than her human one. Allison spread her wings and with a cry she flew away from the grassy bank, high above the water.

Flying.

It felt extraordinary to her still.

Allison flew toward the setting sun, chasing the day.

———

IT was early in the morning on the first of June when Keomany at last turned along Orchard Hill Road and started on the final leg of her journey. She had told Cat and Tori to expect her the night before, but had ended up spending the night in Montpelier instead. She had had some paperwork to clear up regarding her parents' estate, but she had put it behind her now.

As she drove up the hill among the corn stalks and at last came in sight of Summerfields Orchard, she was overwhelmed with emotion. Here, somehow, was the homecoming she had expected to feel in her brief return to the ravaged remains of Wickham, but had not. The moment she saw the apple trees and the big barn and the sign for Summerfields, a burden was lifted from her that she had not even realized she was still carrying.

Suddenly the music on the radio sounded sharper. The light coming through her windshield was brighter. When she breathed in the fresh air that streamed through her open window, she felt her eyes brimming with tears but could not discern within her own heart if they were born of grief or joy.

Keomany parked in the lot outside the barn. Summerfields was open for business, she was happy to see. There were five other cars in the lot—not a huge number, but far better than she had expected after the changes the world had undergone in the past weeks. Before she got out of the car, she wiped at the moist corners of her eyes and caught sight of her face in the rearview mirror. For just a moment she was certain that she saw a golden glint of light there, and then she blinked and it was gone.

The power that Gaea had lent her was gone, but Keomany still felt that connection to the goddess, to the earth. It was a connection that she knew Peter and the others wanted her to use to aid them in their work, and Keomany was willing, but not just yet.

Not yet.

First she needed to rest, to find herself in the embrace of friends, to share with people who loved her all that had happened, all she had felt. She had to know if there was a home for her, somewhere.

When she stepped out of the car, she heard a cry of joy. Keomany glanced up and saw Tori Osborne rushing down from the open door of the barn, the beads in her tightly braided hair clacking together. Behind her, more slowly but with the same grin spread across her face, came the Amazonian Cat Hein.

Keomany laughed. It felt extraordinary. It felt like a blessing.

It would be complicated for her to stay here, given what she had once felt for Tori and that the two women were a couple; married, even, thanks to Vermont law. But they had asked, and Keomany hadn't had the strength to say no. She was so happy now that she had not. And who knew? At the Bealtienne festival she'd spent a giddy, athletic night with No Last Name Zach. He was obviously a friend of theirs, another earthwitch. Maybe Keomany would meet him again; maybe this time she'd find out his last name.

Tori threw her arms around Keomany and spun her around. By the time Tori released her, Cat had joined them and she embraced Keomany as well, lifting her off the ground in her strong arms. She was a different woman from the one whose body had been ravaged by her bond with Gaea.

"Welcome back to the fold, little sister," Cat said. Then she kissed Keomany on the forehead. "Welcome home."

Keomany wanted to believe that so very badly. Other members of the coven had lived here in the past, off and on. There was certainly room. But still she was uncertain.

"Are you guys sure this is going to be all right?"

Tori gave her a dirty look. "Come with me," she demanded, and then she hurried off, pausing only to beckon to Keomany as she raced up toward the barn.

Keomany glanced at Cat.

"I'd do what she says if I were you. We all do, around here. It's just better that way."

The tall, blond woman smiled so sweetly that Keomany could do nothing save comply. Together they followed Tori back up to the barn. By the time they got there, Cat's wife had emerged once again, this time with a wooden board in her hands. With the way the light hit it, a moment went by before Keomany registered what the board was.

A sign.

It was a beautiful, engraved and hand-painted wooden sign upon which had been etched the words *Sweet Some-*

things in large letters, and then, printed neatly beneath them, *Confections by Keomany Shaw.*

"We've already cleared a corner in the shop for you. Danny's in there building new counter space and display cases," Cat said.

Keomany could not breathe. She bit her lip, gaze ticking back and forth between the two women. Shaking, she reached out and grabbed each of them by a hand.

Only when she tasted the salt of her tears did she realize she was crying.

———

"I thought I'd find you here."

Peter did not turn around as Nikki came up behind him, but he held his hand out and felt her fingers twine with his. When she moved next to him, he released her hand and slid an arm around her, holding her close. She lay her head against him and for several moments he simply relished the feel of her there, the light rise and fall of her shoulders as she breathed in the sweet, pungent air of Kuromaku's vineyard estate.

At last he pulled his gaze away from the spot in the midst of the vineyards where they had buried Jack Devlin's remains. He turned to Nikki, and when she glanced up at him, Peter kissed her, first on the nose, and then on her mouth, his lips just grazing hers, almost as though the kiss were an accident. He closed his eyes and rested his forehead against hers.

"What's the news from home?"

Nikki trembled slightly. "Weird. I can't think of L.A. as home."

"Where is home, then?"

She hesitated as though she were afraid of her own answer. Her gaze wavered but at length resolved itself and she stared into his eyes.

"That's up to you."

Peter took a deep breath and let it out, unable to hide the lopsided grin that teased the corners of his mouth. Where *was* home? He had lived so many places over the centuries. According to his agent, Carter Strom, his apartment in Manhattan had been destroyed, the Balents were dead . . . the only good news was that The Voodoo Lounge had escaped the horror unscathed, save for a few minor injuries the bouncer, Agamemnon, had sustained in its defense.

Home. Nikki was going to leave it to him to decide how to define the word. At length, he nodded. It was going to take some thought. "All right. So . . . what's the news from L.A.?"

Nikki nuzzled against him, there in the midst of the vineyards, perhaps fifty yards from the sprawling estate Kuromaku called home.

" 'Shock My World' went to number eleven. Not top ten, but . . . well, eleven doesn't suck. And with everything that's happened, the tour's on hold until fall, at least. But the label's willing to be patient. Things are still up in the air, but my manager says it looks like they want to launch all over again in October."

Peter brushed blond tresses away from her face. "That's amazing. That's wonderful, Nik. It gives me hope."

She frowned. "How's that?"

Peter smiled. "With all that's happened . . . somebody still believes there's going to be a working economy. That there'll be people willing to part with their money. Somebody still believes there's a place in this world for music."

"There's always a place for music."

He thought about that for a while, just holding her against him, feeling her heartbeat matching rhythm with his own.

"Sophie's going to stay," he said.

Nikki chuckled. "That's not really a surprise, is it? After what she's been through, nothing else will seem the same. I . . . I remember. What it's like the first time."

For several minutes they merely stood there in silence. Peter felt as though he never wanted to let her go. In his mind's eye were scarred the images of those last moments in Ronda, when he was certain that the Tatterdemalion would kill her. Nikki still had stitches on the worst of the wounds she had received, and the gashes on her face were going to require plastic surgery before she could perform in public again.

"So," Nikki began again, hesitant. "Sophie and Kuromaku

are staying here for now. I have to get back to L.A. soon. What . . . what are your plans?"

Peter was surprised at the question. He had not spelled out his feelings or his future plans to her, but he had felt certain she could read his heart in his eyes every time he looked at her. Perhaps she had, but did not want to trust her own intuition.

He released her and stepped back. For a moment he looked up at the house, at the breathtaking array of flowers that grew all around it. Keomany had had a hand in that. He knew that, inside, Kuromaku and Sophie were preparing an elaborate dinner. It was something they had found they loved to do together.

Peter returned his gaze to Nikki.

"Ever since my heart started to beat again, I've been trying to figure out what it means to be . . . human. To know that my days are numbered. It made me sink into myself in a way I never want to do again. I didn't want the magick that I have, didn't want to be a sorcerer at all. There's a weight that comes with it, a responsibility that I thought was too much for an ordinary man."

"You're far from ordinary," Nikki admonished him.

Peter nodded. There was no arrogance in it, merely truth. Though their defeat of the Tatterdemalion had drained him, exhausted much of the power in him, possibly forever, he still had enough skill with and knowledge of magick to make him far more than ordinary.

"But I *wanted* to be," he confessed. "I just wanted to live. I couldn't figure out how to do even that right, because when I realized how much I wanted to live, I realized something else, too. I didn't want to die. And I didn't want to watch any more of the people I love die either. I thought it might be better to be alone."

Peter shook his head at the foolishness of this notion. Nikki smiled and touched his face and she nodded as if to say she understood.

"I lost track of my friends. My family. That's what they are, really. My family. I'm grateful to have realized what a mistake that was. We've got a war to fight. Call it a crusade, even. It's going to be years before we figure out what the

Tatterdemalion let loose on Earth, whether by accident or design. Some of us are uniquely suited to doing something about it. And we will.

"*I* will. Even if it takes the rest of my life. Otherwise, what's the point of being here at all, of surviving? And if I can fight this war surrounded by the people I love . . . all the more reason to stay alive," he said quietly, the breeze rustling through the vineyards.

Nikki searched his eyes. "I'm part of this thing, you know," she said. "Don't count me out just because I won't be here."

Peter smiled. "We have to be vigilant, Nikki. But that doesn't mean there aren't other things in life. Music, for instance. We don't *all* have to move in with Kuromaku."

He reached out once again to caress her face.

"I never should have let you go without me the last time. That's another mistake I won't make again."

Nikki gazed at him for a long moment, an expression of surprise etched upon her features.

"You're coming to L.A.?"

"Just when you *have* to be there. We don't actually have to live in Los Angeles, do we? It's a short flight from San Francisco."

"San Francisco," she mused. "That could work."

Peter took her hand and the two of them turned to walk back through the vineyards, the rich smell of the earth all around them. He knew that out there in the world there lurked unknown horrors, things he had not yet imagined that waited in the shadows for the darkness to fall.

But today, at least, the sun still shone brightly above them and he had his chosen family around him. Nightfall would come soon, as it always did, but Peter would not concern himself with the dark until it arrived upon his doorstep.

Even then, he would face it with the knowledge that night was, ever and always, followed by morning.

CHRISTOPHER GOLDEN is the award-winning, *L.A. Times* bestselling author of such novels as *The Ferryman, Strangewood, The Gathering Dark, Of Saints and Shadows,* and the *Body of Evidence* series of teen thrillers. Along with Amber Benson he co-created the animated web serial *Ghosts of Albion.*

Golden has also written or co-written a great many books and comic books related to the TV series *Buffy the Vampire Slayer* and *Angel,* as well as the script for both *Buffy the Vampire Slayer* video games, which he co-wrote with frequent collaborator Tom Sniegoski. His other comic book work includes stories featuring such characters as Batman, Spider-Man, Hellboy, and the miniseries *Doctor Fate: The Curse.*

Golden was born and raised in Massachusetts, where he still lives with his family. He graduated from Tufts University. At present he is at work on *The Boys Are Back in Town,* a new novel for Bantam Books, and—with Tom Sniegoski—a new series for Ace entitled *The Menagerie.* Please visit him at www.christophergolden. com.